THE VINTAGE BRADBURY

THE
VINTAGE
BRADBURY

Ray Bradbury's

own selection

of his best stories

With an introduction by

GILBERT HIGHET

VINTAGE BOOKS

A DIVISION OF RANDOM HOUSE, INC.   NEW YORK

Vintage Books Edition, July 1990

Copyright © 1965 by Ray Bradbury

All rights reserved under International and Pan-American Copyright Conventions. Published in the United States by Vintage Books, a division of Random House, Inc., New York, and simultaneously in Canada by Random House of Canada Limited, Toronto. Originally published by Vintage Books, a division of Random House, Inc., in 1965.

Library of Congress Cataloging-in-Publication Data
Bradbury, Ray, 1920–
    The Vintage Bradbury : Ray Bradbury's own selection of his best stories / with an introduction by Gilbert Highet.
        p.   cm.
    ISBN 0-679-72946-1
    1. Science fiction, American.   I. Title.
PS3503.R167A6   1990
813'.54—dc20   90-33217
                                                               CIP

Manufactured in the United States of America
10 9 8 7 6 5 4 3 2 1

Introduction

One of the most difficult things to achieve in writing fiction is individuality. Hundreds of novels, thousands of short stories are produced every year. Most of them differ from one another only in the locality of their settings, the credibility of their plots, and the atrocity of their sexual and sadistic episodes. Few indeed are those authors whose style and intelligence and interpretation of life are so intense, so distinguished, that their work can be instantly recognized by any sensitive reader, and once recognized can never be forgotten. The fact has been described in a fine antithesis by Truman Capote, himself a highly original author: he is reported to have said of some current novel, "That's not writing, that's typewriting."

Ray Bradbury is one of the most original living American authors: all his work is stamped with the inimitable mark of individuality. No one else could possibly have written his stories. He himself would be utterly incapable of turning out those huge masses of literary meatballs and fictional frankfurters which pour from the publishing kitchens to glut even the most avid reader.

Take his style. A curious mixture of poetry and colloquialism, it is so brisk and economical that it never becomes cloying, so full of unexpected quirks that it is never boring. Occasionally I find it a little too intense and breathless. Ray himself sometimes looks and talks like an enthusiastic teen-ager who has just discovered his own strength, pulled the Sword from the Stone, and believes that he can cope with the world. But there is not a shadow of doubt that it is his own creation, and that it communicates his own clear vision both of the real and of the unreal.

Next, take his subjects. Whatever they are, they are not realistic. But they are human. Real life presses in upon us all the time—usually in the form of crowds or machines. Most of the bad fiction written today, as novels, short stories, and TV and motion-picture plays, is painfully realistic, in that it shows men and women more as objects than as subjects, conditioned and dominated by machines and crowds rather than living genuine lives of their own. With this kind of realism Ray Bradbury has nothing to do. His stories take place in the world of the spirit. He would have written stories equally disconcerting and equally distinguished if he had been born, not in 1920, but in 1820, or 1520, or 20 A.D. Whatever the qualities may be for which future generations will admire him—and they will—we can be sure that he will not be studied as a mirror of external American life in the mid-twentieth century.

What does he write about? Magic. Ghosts. Dreams turning out true, truth dissolving into dreams. The world, which seems dully solid to grownups, transformed into exciting and sometimes appalling fantasy in the minds of children. The future—which we are trying to mold, but which (he knows) will prove to be startlingly different from our plans and our dreams, even our fears. Aristotle said that in making a story it was better to have it impossible and probable, than unconvincing and possible. Most of Ray's stories are impossible—so far; but they are certainly convincing.

He has been misunderstood. He has been underestimated. He will gain a wider and more thoughtful public than he had at first; and his work will last. But he has been misinterpreted. He has often been described as a writer of "science fiction." This is a mistake. He knows little about science; he cares even less. He is a visionary. Technology he scarcely admires and scarcely uses. If it occupies his mind at all, it is not as a convenience or a source of extra muscle-power, but as a possible extension of the abilities of the human spirit. The idea that he can pick up a small machine in California and talk to someone in New York does not excite him. But he once told me that he would be truly enthralled by the invention of a machine which could recover the sounds of the distant past. If we can detect those impossibly distant objects called quasars, why cannot we recapture the sounds of Gettysburg, the words of the first performance of *Hamlet*, the speeches at the trial of Socrates?

Ray Bradbury is not a science-fiction writer. He is an author of tales of fantasy. His American predecessor is Edgar Allan Poe. His French predecessor is Villiers de l'Isle-Adam. His German predecessor is the author of the Tales of Hoffmann. His English predecessors are (in part, though not wholly) Wells and Kipling. His Greek predecessors are Lucian, and (before him) the creator of Cloud-Cuckoo-Land, Aristophanes.

Fantasy detached from machinery is rare nowadays. Fantasy which enlarges rather than degrades human life has been rare at all times. Franz Kafka was a fantast like Ray Bradbury; but he was a bitter and hopeless pessimist, in whose world everyone struggled and was defeated and did not even glimpse a glory in the mind. Ray Bradbury is both a pessimist and an optimist. The man who is freed from his own hateful skeleton to become as flat and fluid as a mollusc; the explorer of space who, while being burnt to death, becomes a shooting star; the playroom where, out of the imaginations of two quiet bored children, are born horrific monsters; the automated house which survives the death of its occupants and the end of the world —these and other conceptions of Ray Bradbury's are horrors. They are not so foul, not so bestial as the horrors which fill our hospitals and prisons; but they are horrors.

Beside them, he puts puzzles. Peter Pan, the boy who would not grow up—is he a hero, or a horror? J. M. Barrie made him a lovable fairy, usually acted by mature women so slender that they can (with the help of complex mechanisms) fly. Ray Bradbury makes him a real boy, who cannot grow up, but cannot fly: one who suffers both the torments of youth and the tortures of age. And beside both horrors and puzzles, he puts beautiful and moving fantasies of a future world where we may be as happy as we all wish to be, and memories of a boyhood universe where even the worst monsters can be overcome by energy and confidence—the same sort of energy and confidence which have transformed him from an eager self-taught tale-spinner into a distinguished American author.

Gilbert Highet

Contents

THE VINTAGE BRADBURY

The Watchful Poker Chip of H. Matisse

When first we meet George Garvey he is nothing at all. Later he'll wear a white poker-chip monocle, with a blue eye painted on it by Matisse himself. Later, a golden bird cage might trill within George Garvey's false leg, and his good left hand might possibly be fashioned of shimmering copper and jade.

But at the beginning—gaze upon a terrifyingly ordinary man.

"Financial section, dear?"

The newspapers rattle in his evening apartment.

"Weather man says 'rain tomorrow.'"

The tiny black hairs in his nostrils breathe in, breathe out, softly, softly, hour after hour.

"Time for bed."

By his look, quite obviously born of several 1907 wax window dummies. And with the trick, much admired by magicians, of sitting in a green velour chair and—vanishing! Turn your head and you forgot his face. Vanilla pudding.

Yet the merest accident made him the nucleus for the wildest avant-garde literary movement in history!

Garvey and his wife had lived enormously alone for twenty years. She was a lovely carnation, but the hazard of meeting *him* pretty well kept visitors off. Neither husband nor wife suspected Garvey's talent for mummifying people instantaneously. Both claimed they were satisfied sitting alone nights after a brisk day at the office. Both worked at anonymous jobs. And sometimes even they could not recall the name of the colorless company which used them like white paint on white paint.

Enter the avant-garde! Enter the Cellar Septet!

These odd souls had flourished in Parisian basements listening to a rather sluggish variety of jazz, preserved a highly volatile relationship six months or more, and, returning to the United States on the point of clamorous disintegration, stumbled into Mr. George Garvey.

"My God!" cried Alexander Pape, erstwhile potentate of the clique. "I met the most astounding bore. You simply must see him! At Bill Timmins' apartment house last night, a note said he'd return in an hour. In the hall this Garvey chap asked if I'd like to wait in his apartment. There we sat, Garvey, his wife, myself! Incredible! He's a monstrous Ennui, produced by our materialistic society. He knows a billion ways to paralyze you! Absolutely rococo with the talent to induce stupor, deep slumber, or stoppage of the heart. What a case study. Let's *all* go visit!"

They swarmed like vultures! Life flowed to Garvey's door, life sat in his parlor. The Cellar Septet perched on his fringed sofa, eying their prey.

Garvey fidgeted.

"Anyone wants to smoke——" He smiled faintly. "Why —go right ahead—*smoke*."

Silence.

The instructions were: "Mum's the word. Put him on the spot. That's the only way to see what a colossal *norm* he is. American culture at absolute zero!"

After three minutes of unblinking quiet, Mr. Garvey leaned forward. "Eh," he said, "what's *your* business, Mr. . . . ?"

"Crabtree. The poet."

Garvey mused over this.

"How's," he said, "business?"

Not a sound.

Here lay a typical Garvey silence. Here sat the largest manufacturer and deliverer of silences in the world; name one, he could provide it packaged and tied with throat-clearings and whispers. Embarrassed, pained, calm, serene, indifferent, blessed, golden or nervous silences; Garvey was *in* there.

Well, the Cellar Septet simply wallowed in this particular evening's silence. Later, in their cold-water flat, over a bottle of "adequate little red wine" (they were experiencing a phase which led them to contact *real* reality) they tore this silence to bits and worried it.

"Did you *see* how he fingered his collar! Ho!"

"By God, though, I must admit he's almost 'cool.' Mention Muggsy Spanier and Bix Beiderbecke. Notice his expression. *Very* cool. I wish *I* could look so uncaring, so unemotional."

Ready for bed, George Garvey, reflecting upon this extraordinary evening, realized that when situations got out of hand, when strange books or music were discussed, he panicked, he froze.

This hadn't seemed to cause undue concern among his rather oblique guests. In fact, on the way out, they had shaken his hand vigorously, thanked him for a splendid time!

"What a really expert A-number-1 bore!" cried Alexander Pape, across town.

"Perhaps he's secretly laughing at us," said Smith, the minor poet, who never agreed with Pape if he was awake.

"Let's fetch Minnie and Tom; they'd love Garvey. A rare night. We'll talk of it for months!"

"Did you notice?" asked Smith, the minor poet, eyes

closed smugly. "When you turn the taps in their bathroom?" He paused dramatically. "*Hot* water."

Everyone stared irritably at Smith.

They hadn't thought to *try*.

The clique, an incredible yeast, soon burst doors and
windows, growing.

"You haven't met the Garveys? My God! Lie back down
in your coffin! Garvey *must* rehearse. No one's *that* boorish
without Stanislavsky!" Here the speaker, Alexander Pape,
who depressed the entire group because he did perfect
imitations, now aped Garvey's slow, self-conscious delivery:

" '*Ulysses*? Wasn't that the book about the Greek, the
ship, and the one-eyed monster! Beg pardon?' " A pause.
" 'Oh.' " Another pause. " 'I see.' " A sitting back.
" '*Ulysses* was written by *James Joyce*? Odd. I could *swear*
I remember, years ago, in school . . .' "

In spite of everyone *hating* Alexander Pape for his brilliant imitations, they roared as he went on:

" 'Tennessee Williams? Is he the man who wrote that
hillbilly "Waltz?" ' "

"Quick! What's Garvey's home address?" everyone
cried.

"My," observed Mr. Garvey to his wife, "life is fun these
days."

"It's you," replied his wife. "Notice, they hang on your
every word."

"Their attention is rapt," said Mr. Garvey, "to the point
of hysteria. The least thing I say absolutely explodes them.
Odd. My jokes at the office always met a stony wall. Tonight, for instance, I wasn't trying to be funny at all. I
suppose it's an unconscious little stream of wit that flows
quietly under everything I do or say. Nice to know I have
it in reserve. Ah, there's the bell. Here we go!"

"He's especially rare if you get him out of bed at four

A.M.," said Alexander Pape. "The combination of exhaustion and *fin de siècle* morality is a regular salad!"

Everyone was pretty miffed at Pape for being first to think of seeing Garvey at dawn. Nevertheless, interest ran high after midnight in late October.

Mr. Garvey's subconscious told him in utmost secrecy that he was the opener of a theatrical season, his success dependent upon the staying power of the ennui he inspired in others. Enjoying himself, he nevertheless guessed why these lemmings thronged to his private sea. Underneath, Garvey was a surprisingly brilliant man, but his unimaginative parents had crushed him in the Terribly Strange Bed of their environment. From there he had been thrown to a larger lemon-squeezer: his Office, his Factory, his Wife. The result: a man whose potentialities were a time bomb in his own parlor. Garvey's repressed subconscious half recognized that the avant-gardists had never met anyone like him, or rather had met millions like him but had never considered studying one before.

So here he was, the first of autumn's celebrities. Next month it might be some abstractionist from Allentown who worked on a twelve-foot ladder shooting house-paint, in two colors only, blue and cloud-gray, from cake-decorators and insecticide-sprayers on canvas covered with layers of mucilage and coffee grounds, who simply needed appreciation to grow! or a Chicago tin-cutter of mobiles, aged fifteen, already ancient with knowledge. Mr. Garvey's shrewd subconscious grew even more suspicious when he made the terrible mistake of reading the avant-garde's favorite magazine, *Nucleus*.

"This article on Dante, now," said Garvey. "Fascinating. Especially where it discusses the spatial metaphors conveyed in the foothills of the *Antipurgatorio* and the *Paradiso Terrestre* on top of the Mountain. The bit about Cantos XV-XVIII, the so-called 'doctrinal cantos,' is brilliant!"

How did the Cellar Septet react?

Stunned, all of them!

There was a noticeable chill.

They departéd in short order when instead of being a delightfully mass-minded, keep-up-with-the-Joneses, machine-dominated chap leading a wishy-washy life of quiet desperation, Garvey enraged them with opinions on *Does Existentialism Still Exist*, or *Is Kraft-Ebbing?* They didn't want opinions on alchemy and symbolism given in a piccolo voice, Garvey's subconscious warned him. They only wanted Garvey's good old-fashioned plain white bread and churned country butter, to be chewed on later at a dim bar, exclaiming how priceless!

Garvey retreated.

Next night he was his old precious self. Dale Carnegie? Splendid religious leader! Hart Schaffner & Marx? Better than Bond Street! Member of the After-Shave Club? That was Garvey! Latest Book-of-the-Month? Here on the table! Had they ever tried Elinor Glyn?

The Cellar Septet was horrified, delighted. They let themselves be bludgeoned into watching Milton Berle. Garvey laughed at everything Berle said. It was arranged for neighbors to tape-record various daytime soap operas which Garvey replayed evenings with religious awe, while the Cellar Septet analyzed his face and his complete devotion to *Ma Perkins* and *John's Other Wife*.

Oh, Garvey was getting sly. His inner self observed: You're on top. Stay there! Please your public! Tomorrow, play the Two Black Crows records! Mind your step! Bonnie Baker, now . . . that's it! They'll shudder, incredulous that you really like her singing. What about Guy Lombardo? That's the tickct!

The mob-mind, said his subconscious. You're symbolic of the crowd. They came to study the dreadful vulgarity of this imaginary Mass Man they pretend to hate. But they're fascinated with the snake-pit.

Guessing his thought, his wife objected. "They *like* you."

"In a frightening sort of way," he said. "I've lain awake figuring why they should come see me! Always hated and bored myself. Stupid, tattletale-gray man. Not an original

thought in my mind. All I know now is: I love company.
I've always wanted to be gregarious, never had the chance.
It's been a ball these last months! But their interest is
dying. I want company forever! What shall I do?"
His subconscious provided shopping lists.
Beer. It's unimaginative.
Pretzels. Delightfully "passé."
Stop by Mother's. Pick up Maxfield Parrish painting,
the flyspecked, sunburnt one. Lecture on same tonight.

By December Mr. Garvey was really frightened.

The Cellar Septet was now quite accustomed to Milton
Berle and Guy Lombardo. In fact, they had rationalized
themselves into a position where they acclaimed Berle as
really too *rare* for the American public, and Lombardo was
twenty years ahead of his time; the nastiest people liked
him for the commonest reasons.

Garvey's empire trembled.

Suddenly he was just another person, no longer di-
verting the tastes of friends, but frantically pursuing them
as they seized at Nora Bayes, the 1917 Knickerbocker
Quartette, Al Jolson singing "Where Did Robinson Crusoe
Go With Friday on Saturday Night," and Shep Fields and
his Rippling Rhythm. Maxfield Parrish's rediscovery left
Mr. Garvey in the north pasture. Overnight, everyone
agreed, "Beer's intellectual. What a shame so many idiots
drink it."

In short, his friends vanished. Alexander Pape, it was
rumored, for a lark, was even considering hot water for his
cold-water flat. This ugly canard was quashed, but not
before Alexander Pape suffered a comedown among the
cognoscenti.

Garvey sweated to anticipate the shifting taste! He in-
creased the free food output, foresaw the swing back to
the Roaring Twenties by wearing hairy knickers and dis-
playing his wife in a tube dress and boyish bob long before anyone else.

But, the vultures came, ate, and ran. Now that this
frightful Giant, TV, strode the world, they were busily re-

embracing radio. Bootlegged 1935 transcriptions of *Vic and Sade* and *Pepper Young's Family* were fought over at intellectual galas.

At long last, Garvey was forced to turn to a series of miraculous tours de force, conceived and carried out by his panic-stricken inner self.

The first accident was a slammed car door.

Mr. Garvey's little fingertip was neatly cut off!

In the resultant chaos, hopping about, Garvey stepped on, then kicked the fingertip into a street drain. By the time they fished it out, no doctor would bother sewing it back on.

A happy accident! Next day, strolling by an oriental shop, Garvey spied a beautiful *objet d'art*. His peppy old subconscious, considering his steadily declining box office and his poor audience-rating among the avant-garde, forced him into the shop and dragged out his wallet.

"Have you seen Garvey lately!" screamed Alexander Pape on the phone. "My God, go see!"

"What's *that?*"

Everyone stared.

"Mandarin's finger-guard." Garvey waved his hand casually. "Oriental antique. Mandarins used them to protect the five-inch nails they cultivated." He drank his beer, the gold-thimbled little finger cocked. "Everyone hates cripples, the sight of things missing. It was sad losing my finger. But I'm happier with this gold thing-amajig."

"It's a much nicer finger now than any of us can *ever* have." His wife dished them all a little green salad. "And George has the *right* to use it."

Garvey was shocked and charmed as his dwindling popularity returned. Ah, art! Ah, life! The pendulum swinging back and forth, from complex to simple, again to complex. From romantic to realistic, back to romantic. The clever man could sense intellectual perihelions, and prepare for the violent new orbits. Garvey's subconscious brilliance sat up, began to eat a bit, and some days dared to walk about, trying its unused limbs. It caught fire!

"How unimaginative the world is," his long-neglected

other self said, using his tongue. "If somehow my leg were severed accidentally I wouldn't wear a wooden leg, no! I'd have a gold leg crusted with precious stones made, and part of the leg would be a golden cage in which a bluebird would sing as I walked or sat talking to friends. And if my arm were cut off I'd have a new arm made of copper and jade, all hollow inside, a section for dry ice in it. And five other compartments, one for each finger. 'Drink, anyone?' I'd cry. Sherry? Brandy? Dubonnet? Then I'd twist each finger calmly over the glasses. From five fingers, five cool streams, five liqueurs or wines. I'd tap the golden faucets shut. 'Bottoms up!' I'd cry.

"But, most of all, one almost wishes that one's eye would offend one. Pluck it out, the Bible says. It *was* the Bible, wasn't it? If that happened to me, I'd use no grisly glass eyes, by God. None of those black pirate's patches. Know what I'd do? I'd mail a poker chip to your friend in France, *what*'s his name? *Matisse!* I'd say, 'Enclosed find poker chip, and personal check. Please paint on this chip one beautiful blue human eye. Yrs., sincerely, G. Garvey!' "

Well, Garvey had always abhorred his body, found his eyes pale, weak, lacking character. So he was not surprised a month later (when his Gallup ran low again) to see his right eye water, fester, and then pull a complete blank!

Garvey was absolutely bombed!

But—equally—secretly pleased.

With the Cellar Septet smiling like a jury of gargoyles at his elbow, he airmailed the poker chip to France with a check for fifty dollars.

The check returned, uncashed, a week later.

In the next mail came the poker chip.

H. Matisse had painted a rare, beautiful blue eye on it, delicately lashed and browed. H. Matisse had tucked this chip in a green-plush jeweler's box, quite obviously as delighted as was Garvey with the entire enterprise.

Harper's Bazaar published a picture of Garvey, wearing the Matisse poker-chip eye, and yet another of Matisse, himself, painting the monocle after considerable experimentation with three dozen chips!

H. Matisse had had the uncommon good sense to summon a photographer to Leica the affair for posterity. He was quoted. "After I had thrown away twenty-seven eyes, I finally got the very one I wanted. It flies posthaste to Monsieur Garvey!"

Reproduced in six colors, the eye rested balefully in its green-plush box. Duplicates were struck off for sales by the Museum of Modern Art. The Friends of the Cellar Septet played poker, using red chips with blue eyes, white chips with red eyes, and blue chips with white eyes.

But there was only *one* man in New York who wore the original Matisse monocle and that was Mr. Garvey.

"I'm *still* a nerve-racking bore," he told his wife, "but now they'll never know what a dreadful ox I am underneath the monocle and the mandarin's finger. And if their interest should happen to dwindle again, one can always arrange to lose an arm or leg. No doubt of it. I've thrown up a wondrous façade; no one will ever find the ancient boor again."

And as his wife put it only the other afternoon: "I hardly think of him as the old George Garvey any more. He's changed his name. Giulio, he wants to be called. Sometimes, at night, I look over at him and call, 'George,' but there's no answer. There he is, that mandarin's thimble on his little finger, the white and blue Matisse poker-chip monocle in his eye. I wake up and look at him often. And do you know? Sometimes that incredible Matisse poker chip seems to give out with a *monstrous* wink."

The Veldt

"George, I wish you'd look at the nursery."

"What's wrong with it?"

"I don't know."

"Well, then."

"I just want you to look at it, is all, or call a psychologist in to look at it."

"What would a psychologist want with a nursery?"

"You know very well what he'd want." His wife paused in the middle of the kitchen and watched the stove busy humming to itself, making supper for four.

"It's just that the nursery is different now than it was."

"All right, let's have a look."

They walked down the hall of their soundproofed Happylife Home, which had cost them thirty thousand dollars installed, this house which clothed and fed and rocked them to sleep and played and sang and was good to them. Their approach sensitized a switch somewhere and the nursery light flicked on when they came within ten feet of it. Similarly, behind them, in the halls, lights went on and off as they left them behind, with a soft automaticity.

"Well," said George Hadley.

They stood on the thatched floor of the nursery. It was forty feet across by forty feet long and thirty feet high; it had cost half again as much as the rest of the house. "But nothing's too good for our children," George had said.

The nursery was silent. It was empty as a jungle glade at hot high noon. The walls were blank and two dimensional. Now, as George and Lydia Hadley stood in the center of the room, the walls began to purr and recede into crystalline distance, it seemed, and presently an African veldt appeared, in three dimensions, on all sides, in color, reproduced to the final pebble and bit of straw. The ceiling above them became a deep sky with a hot yellow sun.

George Hadley felt the perspiration start on his brow.

"Let's get out of this sun," he said. "This is a little too real. But I don't see anything wrong."

"Wait a moment, you'll see," said his wife.

Now the hidden odorophonics were beginning to blow a wind of odor at the two people in the middle of the baked veldtland. The hot straw smell of lion grass, the cool green smell of the hidden water hole, the great rusty smell of animals, the smell of dust like a red paprika in the hot air. And now the sounds: the thump of distant antelope feet on grassy sod, the papery rustling of vultures. A shadow passed through the sky. The shadow flickered on George Hadley's upturned, sweating face.

"Filthy creatures," he heard his wife say.

"The vultures."

"You see, there are the lions, far over, that way. Now they're on their way to the water hole. They've just been eating," said Lydia. "I don't know what."

"Some animal." George Hadley put his hand up to shield off the burning light from his squinted eyes. "A zebra or a baby giraffe, maybe."

"Are you sure?" His wife sounded peculiarly tense.

"No, it's a little late to be sure," he said, amused. "Nothing over there I can see but cleaned bone, and the vultures dropping for what's left."

"Did you hear that scream?" she asked.

"No."

"About a minute ago?"

"Sorry, no."

The lions were coming. And again George Hadley was filled with admiration for the mechanical genius who had conceived this room. A miracle of efficiency selling for an absurdly low price. Every home should have one. Oh, occasionally they frightened you with their clinical accuracy, they startled you, gave you a twinge, but most of the time what fun for everyone, not only your own son and daughter, but for yourself when you felt like a quick jaunt to a foreign land, a quick change of scenery. Well, here it was!

And here were the lions now, fifteen feet away, so real, so feverishly and startlingly real that you could feel the prickling fur on your hand, and your mouth was stuffed with the dusty upholstery smell of their heated pelts, and the yellow of them was in your eyes like the yellow of an exquisite French tapestry, the yellows of lions and summer grass, and the sound of the matted lion lungs exhaling on the silent noontide, and the smell of meat from the panting, dripping mouths.

The lions stood looking at George and Lydia Hadley with terrible green-yellow eyes.

"Watch out!" screamed Lydia.

The lions came running at them.

Lydia bolted and ran. Instinctively, George sprang after her. Outside, in the hall, with the door slammed, he was laughing and she was crying, and they both stood appalled at the other's reaction.

"George!"

"Lydia! Oh, my dear poor sweet Lydia!"

"They almost got us!"

"Walls, Lydia, remember; crystal walls, that's all they are. Oh, they look real, I must admit—Africa in your parlor—but it's all dimensional, superreactionary, supersensitive color film and mental tape film behind glass screens. It's all odorophonics and sonics, Lydia. Here's my handkerchief."

"I'm afraid." She came to him and put her body against him and cried steadily. "Did you see? Did you *feel?* It's too real."

"Now, Lydia . . ."

"You've got to tell Wendy and Peter not to read any more on Africa."

"Of course—of course." He patted her.

"Promise?"

"Sure."

"And lock the nursery for a few days until I get my nerves settled."

"You know how difficult Peter is about that. When I punished him a month ago by locking the nursery for even a few hours—the tantrum he threw! And Wendy too. They *live* for the nursery."

"It's got to be locked, that's all there is to it."

"All right." Reluctantly he locked the huge door. "You've been working too hard. You need a rest."

"I don't know—I don't know," she said, blowing her nose, sitting down in a chair that immediately began to rock and comfort her. "Maybe I don't have enough to do. Maybe I have time to think too much. Why don't we shut the whole house off for a few days and take a vacation?"

"You mean you want to fry my eggs for me?"

"Yes." She nodded.

"And darn my socks?"

"Yes." A frantic, watery-eyed nodding.

"And sweep the house?"

"Yes, yes—oh, yes!"

"But I thought that's why we bought this house, so we wouldn't have to do anything?"

"That's just it. I feel like I don't belong here. The house is wife and mother now, and nursemaid. Can I compete with an African veldt? Can I give a bath and scrub the children as efficiently or quickly as the automatic scrub bath can? I cannot. And it isn't just me. It's you. You've been awfully nervous lately."

"I suppose I have been smoking too much."

"You look as if you didn't know what to do with yourself

in this house, either. You smoke a little more every morning and drink a little more every afternoon and need a little more sedative every night. You're beginning to feel unnecessary too."

"Am I?" He paused and tried to feel into himself to see what was really there.

"Oh, George!" She looked beyond him, at the nursery door. "Those lions can't get out of there, can they?"

He looked at the door and saw it tremble as if something had jumped against it from the other side.

"Of course not," he said.

At dinner they ate alone, for Wendy and Peter were at a special plastic carnival across town and had televised home to say they'd be late, to go ahead eating. So George Hadley, bemused, sat watching the dining-room table produce warm dishes of food from its mechanical interior.

"We forgot the ketchup," he said.

"Sorry," said a small voice within the table, and ketchup appeared.

As for the nursery, thought George Hadley, it won't hurt for the children to be locked out of it awhile. Too much of anything isn't good for anyone. And it was clearly indicated that the children had been spending a little too much time on Africa. That *sun.* He could feel it on his neck, still, like a hot paw. And the *lions.* And the smell of blood. Remarkable how the nursery caught the telepathic emanations of the children's minds and created life to fill their every desire. The children thought lions, and there were lions. The children thought zebras, and there were zebras. Sun—sun. Giraffes—giraffes. Death and death.

That *last.* He chewed tastelessly on the meat that the table had cut for him. Death thoughts. They were awfully young, Wendy and Peter, for death thoughts. Or, no, you were never too young, really. Long before you knew what death was you were wishing it on someone else. When you were two years old you were shooting people with cap pistols.

But this—the long, hot African veldt—the awful death in the jaws of a lion. And repeated again and again.

"Where are you going?"

He didn't answer Lydia. Preoccupied, he let the lights glow softly on ahead of him, extinguish behind him as he padded to the nursery door. He listened against it. Far away, a lion roared.

He unlocked the door and opened it. Just before he stepped inside, he heard a faraway scream. And then another roar from the lions, which subsided quickly.

He stepped into Africa. How many times in the last year had he opened this door and found Wonderland, Alice, the Mock Turtle, or Aladdin and his Magical Lamp, or Jack Pumpkinhead of Oz, or Dr. Doolittle, or the cow jumping over a very real-appearing moon—all the delightful contraptions of a make-believe world. How often had he seen Pegasus flying in the sky ceiling, or seen fountains of red fireworks, or heard angel voices singing. But now, this yellow hot Africa, this bake oven with murder in the heat. Perhaps Lydia was right. Perhaps they needed a little vacation from the fantasy which was growing a bit too real for ten-year-old children. It was all right to exercise one's mind with gymnastic fantasies, but when the lively child mind settled on *one* pattern . . . ? It seemed that, at a distance, for the past month, he had heard lions roaring, and smelled their strong odor seeping as far away as his study door. But, being busy, he had paid it no attention.

George Hadley stood on the African grassland alone. The lions looked up from their feeding, watching him. The only flaw to the illusion was the open door through which he could see his wife, far down the dark hall, like a framed picture, eating her dinner abstractedly.

"Go away," he said to the lions.

They did not go.

He knew the principle of the room exactly. You sent out your thoughts. Whatever you thought would appear.

"Let's have Aladdin and his lamp," he snapped.

The veldtland remained; the lions remained.

"Come on, room! I demand Aladin!" he said.

Nothing happened. The lions mumbled in their baked pelts.

"Aladin!"

He went back to dinner. "The fool room's out of order," he said. "It won't respond."

"Or——"

"Or what?"

"Or it *can't* respond," said Lydia, "because the children have thought about Africa and lions and killing so many days that the room's in a rut."

"Could be."

"Or Peter's set it to remain that way."

"Set it?"

"He may have got into the machinery and fixed something."

"Peter doesn't know machinery."

"He's a wise one for ten. That I.Q. of his——"

"Nevertheless——"

"Hello, Mom. Hello, Dad."

The Hadleys turned. Wendy and Peter were coming in the front door, cheeks like peppermint candy, eyes like bright blue agate marbles, a smell of ozone on their jumpers from their trip in the helicopter.

"You're just in time for supper," said both parents.

"We're full of strawberry ice cream and hot dogs," said the children, holding hands. "But we'll sit and watch."

"Yes, come tell us about the nursery," said George Hadley.

The brother and sister blinked at him and then at each other. "Nursery?"

"All about Africa and everything," said the father with false joviality.

"I don't understand," said Peter.

"Your mother and I were just traveling through Africa with rod and reel; Tom Swift and his Electric Lion," said George Hadley.

"There's no Africa in the nursery," said Peter simply.

"Oh, come now, Peter. We know better."

"I don't remember any Africa," said Peter to Wendy "Do you?"

"No."

"Run see and come tell."

She obeyed.

"Wendy, come back here!" said George Hadley, but she was gone. The house lights followed her like a flock of fireflies. Too late, he realized he had forgotten to lock the nursery door after his last inspection.

"Wendy'll look and come tell us," said Peter.

"She doesn't have to tell *me*. I've seen it."

"I'm sure you're mistaken, Father."

"I'm not, Peter. Come along now."

But Wendy was back. "It's not Africa," she said breathlessly.

"We'll see about this," said George Hadley, and they all walked down the hall together and opened the nursery door.

There was a green, lovely forest, a lovely river, a purple mountain, high voices singing, and Rima, lovely and mysterious, lurking in the trees with colorful flights of butterflies, like animated bouquets, lingering in her long hair. The African veldtland was gone. The lions were gone. Only Rima was here now, singing a song so beautiful that it brought tears to your eyes.

George Hadley looked in at the changed scene. "Go to bed," he said to the children.

They opened their mouths.

"You heard me," he said.

They went off to the air closet, where a wind sucked them like brown leaves up the flue to their slumber rooms.

George Hadley walked through the singing glade and picked up something that lay in the corner near where the lions had been. He walked slowly back to his wife.

"What is that?" she asked.

"An old wallet of mine," he said.

He showed it to her. The smell of hot grass was on it

and the smell of a lion. There were drops of saliva on it, it had been chewed, and there were blood smears on both sides.

He closed the nursery door and locked it, tight.

In the middle of the night he was still awake and he knew his wife was awake. "Do you think Wendy changed it?" she said at last, in the dark room.

"Of course."

"Made it from a veldt into a forest and put Rima there instead of lions?"

"Yes."

"Why?"

"I don't know. But it's staying locked until I find out."

"How did your wallet get there?"

"I don't know anything," he said, "except that I'm beginning to be sorry we bought that room for the children. If children are neurotic at all, a room like that———"

"It's supposed to help them work off their neuroses in a healthful way."

"I'm starting to wonder." He stared at the ceiling.

"We've given the children everything they ever wanted. Is this our reward—secrecy, disobedience?"

"Who was it said, 'Children are carpets, they should be stepped on occasionally'? We've never lifted a hand. They're insufferable—let's admit it. They come and go when they like; they treat us as if we were offspring. They're spoiled and we're spoiled."

"They've been acting funny ever since you forbade them to take the rocket to New York a few months ago."

"They're not old enough to do that alone, I explained."

"Nevertheless, I've noticed they've been decidedly cool toward us since."

"I think I'll have David McClean come tomorrow morning to have a look at Africa."

"But it's not Africa now, it's *Green Mansions* country and Rima."

"I have a feeling it'll be Africa again before then."

A moment later they heard the screams.

Two screams. Two people screaming from downstairs. And then a roar of lions.

"Wendy and Peter aren't in their rooms," said his wife.

He lay in his bed with his beating heart. "No," he said. "They've broken into the nursery."

"Those screams—they sound familiar."

"Do they?"

"Yes, awfully."

And although their beds tried very hard, the two adults couldn't be rocked to sleep for another hour. A smell of cats was in the night air.

"Father?" said Peter.

"Yes."

Peter looked at his shoes. He never looked at his father any more, nor at his mother. "You aren't going to lock up the nursey for good, are you?"

"That all depends."

"On what?" snapped Peter.

"On you and your sister. If you intersperse this Africa with a little variety—oh, Sweden perhaps, or Denmark or China——"

"I thought we were free to play as we wished."

"You are, within reasonable bounds."

"What's wrong with Africa, Father?"

"Oh, so now you admit you have been conjuring up Africa, do you?"

"I wouldn't want the nursery locked up," said Peter coldly. "Ever."

"Matter of fact, we're thinking of turning the whole house off for about a month. Live sort of a carefree one-for-all existence."

"That sounds dreadful! Would I have to tie my own shoes instead of letting the shoe tier do it? And brush my own teeth and comb my hair and give myself a bath?"

"It would be fun for a change, don't you think?"

"No, it would be horrid. I didn't like it when you took out the picture painter last month."

"That's because I wanted you to learn to paint all by yourself, son."

"I don't want to do anything but look and listen and smell; what else *is* there to do?"

"All right, go play in Africa."

"Will you shut off the house sometime soon?"

"We're considering it."

"I don't think you'd better consider it any more, Father."

"I won't have any threats from my son!"

"Very well." And Peter strolled off to the nursery.

"Am I on time?" said David McClean.

"Breakfast?" asked George Hadley.

"Thanks, had some. What's the trouble?"

"David, you're a psychologist."

"I should hope so."

"Well, then, have a look at our nursery. You saw it a year ago when you dropped by; did you notice anything peculiar about it then?"

"Can't say I did; the usual violences, a tendency toward a slight paranoia here or there, usual in children because they feel persecuted by parents constantly, but, oh, really nothing."

They walked down the hall. "I locked the nursery up," explained the father, "and the children broke back into it during the night. I let them stay so they could form the patterns for you to see."

There was a terrible screaming from the nursery.

"There it is," said George Hadley. "See what you make of it."

They walked in on the children without rapping.

The screams had faded. The lions were feeding.

"Run outside a moment, children," said George Hadley. "No, don't change the mental combination. Leave the walls as they are. Get!"

With the children gone, the two men stood studying the lions clustered at a distance, eating with great relish whatever it was they had caught.

"I wish I knew what it was," said George Hadley. "Sometimes I can almost see. Do you think if I brought high-powered binoculars here and——"

David McClean laughed dryly. "Hardly." He turned to study all four walls. "How long has this been going on?"

"A little over a month."

"It certainly doesn't *feel* good."

"I want facts, not feelings."

"My dear George, a psychologist never saw a fact in his life. He only hears about feelings; vague things. This doesn't feel good, I tell you. Trust my hunches and my instincts. I have a nose for something bad. This is very bad. My advice to you is to have the whole damn room torn down and your children brought to me every day during the next year for treatment."

"Is it that bad?"

"I'm afraid so. One of the original uses of these nurseries was so that we could study the patterns left on the walls by the child's mind, study at our leisure, and help the child. In this case, however, the room has become a channel toward—destructive thoughts, instead of a release away from them."

"Didn't you sense this before?"

"I sensed only that you had spoiled your children more than most. And now you're letting them down in some way. What way?"

"I wouldn't let them go to New York."

"What else?"

"I've taken a few machines from the house and threatened them, a month ago, with closing up the nursery unless they did their homework. I did close it for a few days to show I meant business."

"Ah, ha!"

"Does that mean anything?"

"Everything. Where before they had a Santa Claus now they have a Scrooge. Children prefer Santas. You've let this room and this house replace you and your wife in your children's affections. This room is their mother and father, far more important in their lives than their real parents.

And now you come along and want to shut it off. No wonder there's hatred here. You can feel it coming out of the sky. Feel that sun. George, you'll have to change your life. Like too many others, you've built it around creature comforts. Why, you'd starve tomorrow if something went wrong in your kitchen. You wouldn't know how to tap an egg. Nevertheless, turn everything off. Start new. It'll take time. But we'll make good children out of bad in a year, wait and see."

"But won't the shock be too much for the children, shutting the room up abruptly, for good?"

"I don't want them going any deeper into this, that's all."

The lions were finished with their red feast.

The lions were standing on the edge of the clearing watching the two men.

"Now *I'm* feeling persecuted," said McClean. "Let's get out of here. I never have cared for these damned rooms. Make me nervous."

"The lions look real, don't they?" said George Hadley. "I don't suppose there's any way——"

"What?"

"—that they could *become* real?"

"Not that I know."

"Some flaw in the machinery, a tampering or something?"

"No."

They went to the door.

"I don't imagine the room will like being turned off," said the father.

"Nothing ever likes to die—even a room."

"I wonder if it hates me for wanting to switch it off?"

"Paranoia is thick around here today," said David McClean. "You can follow it like a spoor. Hello." He bent and picked up a bloody scarf. "This yours?"

"No." George Hadley's face was rigid. "It belongs to Lydia."

They went to the fuse box together and threw the switch that killed the nursery.

• • •

The two children were in hysterics. They screamed and pranced and threw things. They yelled and sobbed and swore and jumped at the furniture.

"You can't do that to the nursery, you can't!"

"Now, children."

The children flung themselves onto a couch, weeping.

"George," said Lydia Hadley, "turn on the nursery, just for a few moments. You can't be so abrupt."

"No."

"You can't be so cruel."

"Lydia, it's off, and it stays off. And the whole damn house dies as of here and now. The more I see of the mess we've put ourselves in, the more it sickens me. We've been contemplating our mechanical, electronic navels for too long. My God, how we need a breath of honest air!"

And he marched about the house turning off the voice clocks, the stoves, the heaters, the shoe shiners, the shoe lacers, the body scrubbers and swabbers and massagers, and every other machine he could put his hand to.

The house was full of dead bodies, it seemed. It felt like a mechanical cemetery. So silent. None of the humming hidden energy of machines waiting to function at the tap of a button.

"Don't let them do it!" wailed Peter at the ceiling, as if he was talking to the house, the nursery. "Don't let Father kill everything." He turned to his father. "Oh, I hate you!"

"Insults won't get you anywhere."

"I wish you were dead!"

"We were, for a long while. Now we're going to really start living. Instead of being handled and massaged, we're going to *live*."

Wendy was still crying and Peter joined her again. "Just a moment, just one moment, just another moment of nursery," they wailed.

"Oh, George," said the wife, "it can't hurt."

"All right—all right, if they'll just shut up. One minute, mind you, and then off forever."

"Daddy, Daddy, Daddy!" sang the children, smiling with wet faces.

"And then we're going on a vacation. David McClean is coming back in half an hour to help us move out and get to the airport. I'm going to dress. You turn the nursery on for a minute, Lydia, just a minute, mind you."

And the three of them went babbling off while he let himself be vacuumed upstairs through the air flue and set about dressing himself. A minute later Lydia appeared.

"I'll be glad when we get away," she sighed.

"Did you leave them in the nursery?"

"I wanted to dress too. Oh, that horrid Africa. What can they see in it?"

"Well, in five minutes we'll be on our way to Iowa. Lord, how did we ever get in this house? What prompted us to buy a nightmare?"

"Pride, money, foolishness."

"I think we'd better get downstairs before those kids get engrossed with those damned beasts again."

Just then they heard the children calling, "Daddy, Mommy, come quick—quick!"

They went downstairs in the air flue and ran down the hall. The children were nowhere in sight. "Wendy? Peter!"

They ran into the nursery. The veldtland was empty save for the lions waiting, looking at them. "Peter, Wendy?"

The door slammed.

"Wendy, Peter!"

George Hadley and his wife whirled and ran back to the door.

"Open the door!" cried George Hadley, trying the knob. "Why, they've locked it from the outside! Peter!" He beat at the door. "Open up!"

He heard Peter's voice outside, against the door.

"Don't let them switch off the nursery and the house," he was saying.

Mr. and Mrs. George Hadley beat at the door. "Now, don't be ridiculous, children. It's time to go. Mr. McClean'll be here in a minute and . . ."

And then they heard the sounds.

The lions on three sides of them, in the yellow veldt grass, padding through the dry straw, rumbling and roaring in their throats.

The lions.

Mr. Hadley looked at his wife and they turned and looked back at the beasts edging slowly forward, crouching, tails stiff.

Mr. and Mrs. Hadley screamed.

And suddenly they realized why those other screams had sounded familiar.

"Well, here I am," said David McClean in the nursery doorway. "Oh, hello." He stared at the two children seated in the center of the open glade eating a little picnic lunch. Beyond them was the water hole and the yellow veldtland; above was the hot sun. He began to perspire. "Where are your father and mother?"

The children looked up and smiled. "Oh, they'll be here directly."

"Good, we must get going." At a distance Mr. McClean saw the lions fighting and clawing and then quieting down to feed in silence under the shady trees.

He squinted at the lions with his hand up to his eyes.

Now the lions were done feeding. They moved to the water hole to drink.

A shadow flickered over Mr. McClean's hot face. Many shadows flickered. The vultures were dropping down the blazing sky.

"A cup of tea?" asked Wendy in the silence.

Hail and Farewell

But of course he was going away, there was nothing else to do, the time was up, the clock had run out, and he was going very far away indeed. His suitcase was packed, his shoes were shined, his hair was brushed, he had expressly washed behind his ears, and it remained only for him to go down the stairs, out the front door, and up the street to the small-town station where the train would make a stop for him alone. Then Fox Hill, Illinois, would be left far off in his past. And he would go on, perhaps to Iowa, perhaps to Kansas, perhaps even to California; a small boy twelve years old with a birth certificate in his valise to show he had been born forty-three years ago.

"Willie!" called a voice downstairs.

"Yes!" He hoisted his suitcase. In his bureau mirror he saw a face made of June dandelions and July apples and warm summer-morning milk. There, as always, was his look of the angel and the innocent, which might never, in the years of his life, change.

"Almost time," called the woman's voice.

"All right!" And he went down the stairs, grunting and smiling. In the living room sat Anna and Steve, their clothes painfully neat.

"Here I am!" cried Willie in the parlor door.

Anna looked like she was going to cry. "Oh, good Lord, you can't really be leaving us, can you, Willie?"

"People are beginning to talk," said Willie quietly. "I've been here three years now. But when people begin to talk, I know it's time to put on my shoes and buy a railway ticket."

"It's all so strange. I don't understand. It's so sudden," Anna said. "Willie, we'll miss you."

"I'll write you every Christmas, so help me. Don't you write me."

"It's been a great pleasure and satisfaction," said Steve, sitting there, his words the wrong size in his mouth. "It's a shame it had to stop. It's a shame you had to tell us about yourself. It's an awful shame you can't stay on."

"You're the nicest folks I ever had," said Willie, four feet high, in no need of a shave, the sunlight on his face.

And then Anna *did* cry. "Willie, Willie." And she sat down and looked as if she wanted to hold him but was afraid to hold him now; she looked at him with shock and amazement and her hands empty, not knowing what to do with him now.

"It's not easy to go," said Willie. "You get used to things. You want to stay. But it doesn't work. I tried to stay on once after people began to suspect. 'How horrible!' people said. 'All these years, playing with our innocent children,' they said, 'and us not guessing! Awful!' they said. And finally I had to just leave town one night. It's not easy. You know darned well how much I love both of you. Thanks for three swell years."

They all went to the front door. "Willie, where're you going?"

"I don't know. I just start traveling. When I see a town that looks green and nice, I settle in."

"Will you ever come back?"

"Yes," he said earnestly with his high voice. "In about

twenty years it should begin to show in my face. When it does, I'm going to make a grand tour of all the mothers and fathers I've ever had."

They stood on the cool summer porch, reluctant to say the last words. Steve was looking steadily at an elm tree. "How many other folks've you stayed with, Willie? How many adoptions?"

Willie figured it, pleasantly enough. "I guess it's about five towns and five couples and over twenty years gone by since I started my tour."

"Well, we can't holler," said Steve. "Better to've had a son thirty-six months than none whatever."

"Well," said Willie, and kissed Anna quickly, seized at his luggage, and was gone up the street in the green noon light, under the trees, a very young boy indeed, not looking back, running steadily.

The boys were playing on the green park diamond when he came by. He stood a little while among the oak-tree shadows, watching them hurl the white, snowy baseball into the warm summer air, saw the baseball shadow fly like a dark bird over the grass, saw their hands open in mouths to catch this swift piece of summer that now seemed most especially important to hold on to. The boys' voices yelled. The ball lit on the grass near Willie.

Carrying the ball forward from under the shade trees, he thought of the last three years now spent to the penny, and the five years before that, and so on down the line to the year when he was really eleven and twelve and fourteen and the voices saying: "What's wrong with Willie, missus?" "Mrs. B., is Willie late a-growin'?" "Willie, you smokin' cigars lately?" The echoes died in summer light and color. His mother's voice: "Willie's twenty-one today!" And a thousand voices saying: "Come back, son, when you're fifteen; *then* maybe we'll give you a job."

He stared at the baseball in his trembling hand, as if it were his life, an interminable ball of years strung around and around and around, but always leading back to his twelfth birthday. He heard the kids walking toward him;

he felt them blot out the sun, and they were older, standing around him.

"Willie! Where you goin'?" They kicked his suitcase.

How tall they stood in the sun. In the last few months it seemed the sun had passed a hand above their heads, beckoned, and they were warm metal drawn melting upward; they were golden taffy pulled by an immense gravity to the sky, thirteen, fourteen years old, looking down upon Willie, smiling, but already beginning to neglect him. It had started four months ago:

"Choose up sides! Who wants Willie?"

"Aw, Willie's too little; we don't play with 'kids.' "

And they raced ahead of him, drawn by the moon and the sun and the turning seasons of leaf and wind, and he was twelve years old and not of them any more. And the other voices beginning again on the old, the dreadfully familiar, the cool refrain: "Better feed that boy vitamins, Steve." "Anna, does shortness *run* in your family?" And the cold fist knocking at your heart again and knowing that the roots would have to be pulled up again after so many good years with the "folks."

"Willie, where you goin'?"

He jerked his head. He was back among the towering, shadowing boys who milled around him like giants at a drinking fountain bending down.

"Goin' a few days visitin' a cousin of mine."

"Oh." There was a day, a year ago, when they would have cared very much indeed. But now there was only curiosity for his luggage, their enchantment with trains and trips and far places.

"How about a coupla fast ones?" said Willie.

They looked doubtful, but, considering the circumstances, nodded. He dropped his bag and ran out; the white baseball was up in the sun, away to their burning white figures in the far meadow, up in the sun again, rushing, life coming and going in a pattern. Here, *there!* Mr. and Mrs. Robert Hanlon, Creek Bend, Wisconsin, 1932, the first couple, the first year! Here, *there!* Henry and Alice Boltz, Limeville, Iowa, 1935! The baseball flying. The Smiths, the Eatons, the Robinsons! 1939! 1945! Husband and wife, husband and wife, husband and wife, no children, no children! A knock on this door, a knock on that.

"Pardon me. My name is William. I wonder if——"

"A sandwich? Come in, sit down. Where you *from*, son?"

The sandwich, a tall glass of cold milk, the smiling, the nodding, the comfortable, leisurely talking.

"Son, you look like you been traveling. You run *off* from somewhere?"

"No."

"Boy, are you an orphan?"

Another glass of milk.

"We always wanted kids. It never worked out. Never knew why. One of those things. Well, well. It's getting late, son. Don't you think you better hit for home?"

"Got no home."

"A boy like you? Not dry behind the ears? Your mother'll be worried."

"Got no home and no folks anywhere in the world. I wonder if—I wonder—could I sleep here tonight?"

"Well, now, son, I don't just know. We never considered taking in——" said the husband.

"We got chicken for supper tonight," said the wife, "enough for extras, enough for company. . . ."

And the years turning and flying away, the voices, and the faces, and the people, and always the same first conversations. The voice of Emily Robinson, in her rocking chair, in summer-night darkness, the last night he stayed with her, the night she discovered his secret, her voice saying:

"I look at all the little children's faces going by. And I sometimes think, What a shame, what a shame, that all these flowers have to be cut, all these bright fires have to be put out. What a shame these, all of these you see in schools or running by, have to get tall and unsightly and wrinkle and turn gray or get bald, and finally, all bone and wheeze, be dead and buried off away. When I hear them

laugh I can't believe they'll ever go the road I'm going.
Yet here they *come!* I still remember Wordsworth's poem:
'When all at once I saw a crowd, A host of golden
daffodils; Beside the lake, beneath the trees, Fluttering
and dancing in the breeze.' That's how I think of children,
cruel as they sometimes are, mean as I know they can be,
but not yet showing the meanness around their eyes or *in*
their eyes, not yet full of tiredness. They're so eager for
everything! I guess that's what I miss most in older folks,
the eagerness gone nine times out of ten, the freshness
gone, so much of the drive and life down the drain. I like
to watch school let out each day. It's like someone threw a
bunch of flowers out the school front doors. How does it
feel, Willie? How does it feel to be young forever? To look
like a silver dime new from the mint? Are you happy? Are
you as fine as you *seem?*"

The baseball whizzed from the blue sky, stung his hand
like a great pale insect. Nursing it, he hears his memory
say:
"I worked with what I had. After my folks died, after I
found I couldn't get man's work anywhere, I tried carni-
vals, but they only laughed. 'Son,' they said, 'you're not a
midget, and even if you are, you look like a *boy!* We want
midgets with midgets' *faces!* Sorry, son, sorry.' So I left
home, started out, thinking: What *was* I? A boy. I looked
like a boy, sounded like a boy, so I might as well go on
being a boy. No use fighting it. No use screaming. So what
could I do? What job was handy? And then one day I saw
this man in a restaurant looking at another man's pictures
of his children. 'Sure wish I had kids,' he said. 'Sure wish I
had kids.' He kept shaking his head. And me sitting a few
seats away from him, a hamburger in my hands. I sat
there, *frozen!* At that very instant I knew what my job
would be for all the rest of my life. There *was* work for
me, after all. Making lonely people happy. Keeping myself
busy. Playing forever. I knew I had to play forever. Deliver a few papers, run a few errands, mow a few lawns,
maybe. But *hard* work? No. All I had to do was be a

mother's son and a father's pride. I turned to the man down the counter from me. 'I beg your pardon,' I said. I *smiled* at him. . . ."

"But, Willie," said Mrs. Emily long ago, "didn't you ever get lonely? Didn't you ever want—*things*—that grown-ups wanted?"

"I fought that out alone," said Willie. "I'm a boy, I told myself, I'll have to live in a boy's world, read boys' books, play boys' games, cut myself off from everything else. I can't be both. I got to be only one thing—young. And so I played that way. Oh, it wasn't easy. There were times ——" He lapsed into silence.

"And the family you lived with, they never knew?"

"No. Telling them would have spoiled everything. I told them I was a runaway; I let them check through official channels, police. Then, when there was no record, let them put in to adopt me. That was best of all; as long as they never guessed. But then, after three years, or five years, they guessed, or a traveling man came through, or a carnival man saw me, and it was over. It always had to end."

"And you're very happy and it's nice being a child for over forty years?"

"It's a living, as they say. And when you make other people happy, then you're almost happy too. I got my job to do and I do it. And anyway, in a few years now I'll be in my second childhood. All the fevers will be out of me and all the unfulfilled things and most of the dreams. Then I can relax, maybe, and play the role all the way."

He threw the baseball one last time and broke the reverie. Then he was running to seize his luggage. Tom, Bill, Jamie, Bob, Sam—their names moved on his lips. They were embarrassed at his shaking hands.

"After all, Willie, it ain't as if you're going to China or Timbuktu."

"That's right, isn't it?" Willie did not move.

"So long, Willie. See you next week!"

"So long, so long!"

And he was walking off with his suitcase again, looking at the trees, going away from the boys and the street where he had lived, and as he turned the corner a train whistle screamed, and he began to run.

The last thing he saw and heard was a white ball tossed at a high roof, back and forth, back and forth, and two voices crying out as the ball pitched now up, down, and back through the sky, "Annie, annie, over! Annie, annie, over!" like the crying of birds flying off to the far south.

In the early morning, with the smell of the mist and the cold metal, with the iron smell of the train around him and a full night of traveling shaking his bones and his body, and a smell of the sun beyond the horizon, he awoke and looked out upon a small town just arising from sleep. Lights were coming on, soft voices muttered, a red signal bobbed back and forth, back and forth in the cold air. There was that sleeping hush in which echoes are dignified by clarity, in which echoes stand nakedly alone and sharp. A porter moved by, a shadow in shadows.

"Sir," said Willie.

The porter stopped.

"What town's this?" whispered the boy in the dark.

"Valleyville."

"How many people?"

"Ten thousand. Why? This your stop?"

"It looks green." Willie gazed out at the cold morning town for a long time. "It looks nice and quiet," said Willie.

"Son," said the porter, "you know where you *going*?"

"Here," said Willie, and got up quietly in the still, cool, iron-smelling morning, in the train dark, with a rustling and stir.

"I hope you know what you're doing, boy," said the porter.

"Yes, sir," said Willie. "I know what I'm doing." And he was down the dark aisle, luggage lifted after him by the porter, and out in the smoking, steaming-cold, beginning-to-lighten morning. He stood looking up at the porter and the black metal train against the few remaining stars. The train gave a great wailing blast of whistle, the porters cried out all along the line, the cars jolted, and his special porter waved and smiled down at the boy there, the small boy there with the big luggage who shouted up to him, even as the whistle screamed again.

"What?" shouted the porter, hand cupped to ear.

"Wish me luck!" cried Willie.

"Best of luck, son," called the porter, waving, smiling. "Best of luck, boy!"

"Thanks," said Willie, in the great sound of the train, in the steam and roar.

He watched the black train until it was completely gone away and out of sight. He did not move all the time it was going. He stood quietly, a small boy twelve years old, on the worn wooden platform, and only after three entire minutes did he turn at last to face the empty streets below.

Then, as the sun was rising, he began to walk very fast, so as to keep warm, down into the new town.

A Medicine for Melancholy

(or: The Sovereign Remedy Revealed!)

"Send for some leeches; bleed her," said Doctor Gimp.

"She has no blood left!" cried Mrs. Wilkes. "Oh, Doctor, what ails our Camillia?"

"She's not right."

"Yes, yes?"

"She's poorly." The good doctor scowled.

"Go on, go on!"

"She's a fluttering candle flame, no doubt."

"Ah, Doctor Gimp," protested Mr. Wilkes. "You but tell us as you go out what we told you when you came in!"

"No, more! Give her these pills at dawn, high noon, and sunset. A sovereign remedy!"

"Damn, she's *stuffed* with sovereign remedies now!"

"Tut-tut! That's a shilling as I pass downstairs, sir."

"Go down and send the Devil up!" Mr. Wilkes shoved a coin in the good doctor's hand.

Whereupon the physician, wheezing, taking snuff,

sneezing, stamped down into the swarming streets of London on a sloppy morn in the spring of 1762.

Mr. and Mrs. Wilkes turned to the bed where their sweet Camillia lay, pale, thin, yes, but far from unlovely, with large wet lilac eyes, her hair a creek of gold upon her pillow.

"Oh," she almost wept. "What's to become of me? Since the start of spring, three weeks, I've been a ghost in my mirror; I frighten me. To think I'll die without seeing my twentieth birthday."

"Child," said the mother. "Where do you hurt?"

"My arms. My legs. My bosom. My head. How many doctors—six?—have turned me like a beef on a spit. No more. Please, let me pass away untouched."

"What a ghastly, what a mysterious illness," said the mother. "Oh, do something, Mr. Wilkes!"

"What?" asked Mr. Wilkes angrily. "She won't have the physician, the apothecary, or the priest!—and Amen to that!—they've wrung me dry! Shall I run in the street then and bring the Dustman up?"

"Yes," said a voice.

"What!" All three turned to stare.

They had quite forgotten her younger brother, Jamie, who stood picking his teeth at a far window, gazing serenely down into the drizzle and the loud rumbling of the town.

"Four hundred years ago," he said serenely, "it was tried, it worked. Don't bring the Dustman up, no, no. But let us hoist Camillia, cot and all, maneuver her downstairs, and set her up outside our door."

"Why? What for?"

"In a single hour"—Jamie's eyes jumped, counting—"a thousand folk rush by our gate. In one day, twenty thousand people run, hobble, or ride by. Each might eye my swooning sister, each count her teeth, pull her ear lobes, and all, all, mind you, would have a sovereign remedy to offer! One of them would just have to be right!"

"Ah," said Mr. Wilkes, stunned.

"Father!" said Jamie breathlessly. "Have you ever

known one single man who didn't think he personally
wrote *Materia Medica?* This green ointment for sour
throat, that ox-salve for miasma or bloat? Right now, ten
thousand self-appointed apothecaries sneak off down there,
their wisdom lost to us!"

"Jamie boy, you're incredible!"

"Cease!" said Mrs. Wilkes. "No daughter of mine will be
put on display in this or any street——"

"Fie, woman!" said Mr. Wilkes. "Camillia melts like
snow and you hesitate to move her from this hot room?
Come, Jamie, lift the bed!"

"Camillia?" Mrs. Wilkes turned to her daughter.

"I may as well die in the open," said Camillia, "where a
cool breeze might stir my locks as I . . ."

"Bosh!" said the father. "You'll not die. Jamie, heave!
Ha! There! Out of the way, wife! Up, boy, *higher!*"

"Oh," cried Camillia faintly. "I fly, I *fly* . . . !"

Quite suddenly a blue sky opened over London. The
population, surprised by the weather, hurried out into the
streets, panicking for something to see, to do, to buy. Blind
men sang, dogs jigged, clowns shuffled and tumbled, children chalked games and threw balls as if it were carnival
time.

Down into all this, tottering, their veins bursting from
their brows, Jamie and Mr. Wilkes carried Camillia like a
lady Pope sailing high in her sedan-chair cot, eyes
clenched shut, praying.

"Careful!" screamed Mrs. Wilkes. "Ah, she's dead! No.
There. Put her down. Easy . . ."

And at last the bed was tilted against the house front so
that the River of Humanity surging by could see Camillia,
a large pale Bartolemy Doll put out like a prize in the sun.

"Fetch a quill, ink, paper, lad," said the father. "I'll
make notes as to symptoms spoken of and remedies offered
this day. Tonight we'll average them out. Now——"

But already a man in the passing crowd had fixed Camillia with a sharp eye.

"She's sick!" he said.

"Ah," said Mr. Wilkes, gleefully. "It begins. The quill, boy. There. Go on, sir!"

"She's not well." The man scowled. "She does poorly."

"Does poorly——" Mr. Wilkes wrote, then froze. "Sir?" He looked up suspiciously. "Are you a physician?"

"I am, sir."

"I *thought* I knew the words! Jamie, take my cane, drive him off! Go, sir, be gone!"

But the man hastened off, cursing, mightily exasperated.

"She's not well, she does poorly . . . pah!" mimicked Mr. Wilkes, but stopped. For now a woman, tall and gaunt as a specter fresh risen from the tomb, was pointing a finger at Camillia Wilkes.

"Vapors," she intoned.

"Vapors," wrote Mr. Wilkes, pleased.

"Lung-flux," chanted the woman.

"Lung-flux!" Mr. Wilkes wrote, beaming. "Now, that's more *like* it!"

"A medicine for melancholy is needed," said the woman palely. "Be there mummy ground to medicine in your house? The best mummies are: Egyptian, Arabian, Hiras-phatos, Libyan, all of great use in magnetic disorders. Ask for me, the Gypsy, at the Flodden Road. I sell stone parsley, male frankincense——"

"Flodden Road, stone parsley—slower, woman!"

"Opobalsam, pontic valerian——"

"Wait, woman! Opobalsam, yes! Jamie, stop her!"

But the woman, naming medicines, glided on.

A girl, no more than seventeen, walked up now and stared at Camillia Wilkes.

"She——"

"One moment!" Mr. Wilkes scribbled feverishly. "—— magnetic disorders—pontic valerian—drat! Well, young girl, now. What do you see in my daughter's face? You fix her with your gaze, you hardly breathe. So?"

"She——" The strange girl searched deep into Camillia's eyes, flushed, and stammered. "She suffers from . . . from . . ."

"Spit it out!"

"She . . . she . . . oh!"

And the girl, with a last look of deepest sympathy, darted off through the crowd.

"Silly girl!"

"No, Papa," murmured Camillia, eyes wide. "Not silly. She *saw*. She *knew*. Oh, Jamie, run fetch her, make her tell!"

"No, she offered nothing! Whereas, the Gypsy, see her list!"

"I know it, Papa." Camillia, paler, shut her eyes.

Someone cleared his throat.

A butcher, his apron a scarlet battleground, stood bristling his fierce mustaches there.

"I have seen cows with this look," he said. "I have saved them with brandy and three new eggs. In winter I have saved myself with the same elixir——"

"My daughter is no cow, sir!" Mr. Wilkes threw down his quill. "Nor is she a butcher, nor is it January! Step back, sir, others wait!"

And indeed, now a vast crowd clamored, drawn by the others, aching to advise their favorite swig, recommend some country site where it rained less and shone more sun than in all England or your South of France. Old men and women, especial doctors as all the aged are, clashed by each other in bristles of canes, in phalanxes of crutches and hobble sticks.

"Back!" cried Mrs. Wilkes, alarmed. "They'll crush my daughter like a spring berry!"

"Stand off!" Jamie seized canes and crutches and threw them over the mob, which turned on itself to go seek their missing members.

"Father, I fail, I fail," gasped Camillia.

"Father!" cried Jamie. "There's but one way to stop this riot! Charge them! Make them pay to give us their mind on this ailment!"

"Jamie, you are my son! Quick, boy, paint a sign! Listen, people! Tuppence! Queue up please, a line! Tuppence to speak your piece! Get your money out, yes! That's it.

You, sir. You, madame. And you, sir. Now, my quill! Begin!"

The mob boiled in like a dark sea.

Camillia opened one eye and swooned again.

Sundown, the streets almost empty, only a few strollers now. Camillia moth-fluttered her eyelids at a familiar clinking jingle.

"Three hundred and ninety-nine, four hundred pennies!" Mr. Wilkes counted the last money into a bag held by his grinning son. "There!"

"It will buy me a fine black funeral coach," said the pale girl.

"Hush! Did you imagine, family, so many people, two hundred, would pay to give us their opinion?"

"Yes," said Mrs. Wilkes. "Wives, husbands, children are deaf to each other. So people gladly pay to have someone listen. Poor things, each today thought he and he alone knew quinsy, dropsy, glanders, could tell the slaver from the hives. So tonight we are rich and two hundred people are happy, having unloaded their full medical kit at our door."

"Gods, instead of quelling the riot, we had to drive them off snapping like pups."

"Read us the list, Father," said Jamie, "of two hundred remedies. Which one is true?"

"I care not," whispered Camillia, sighing. "It grows dark. My stomach is queasy from listening to the names! May I be taken upstairs?"

"Yes, dear. Jamie, lift!"

"Please," said a voice.

Half-bent, the men looked up.

There stood a Dustman of no particular size or shape, his face masked with soot from which shone water-blue eyes and a white slot of an ivory smile. Dust sifted from his sleeves and his pants as he moved, as he talked quietly, nodding.

"I couldn't get through the mob earlier," he said,

holding his dirty cap in his hands. "Now, going home, here I am. Must I pay?"

"No, Dustman, you need not," said Camillia gently.

"Hold on——" protested Mr. Wilkes.

But Camillia gave him a soft look and he grew silent.

"Thank you, ma'am." The Dustman's smile flashed like warm sunlight in the growing dusk. "I have but one advice."

He gazed at Camillia. She gazed at him.

"Be this Saint Bosco's Eve, sir, ma'am?"

"Who knows? Not *me*, sir!" said Mr. Wilkes.

"I think it *is* Saint Bosco's Eve, sir. Also, it is the night of the Full Moon. So," said the Dustman humbly, unable to take his eyes from the lovely haunted girl, "you must leave your daughter out in the light of that rising moon."

"Out under the moon!" said Mrs. Wilkes.

"Doesn't that make the lunatic?" asked Jamie.

"Beg pardon, sir." The Dustman bowed. "But the Full Moon soothes all sick animals, be they human or plain field beast. There is a serenity of color, a quietude of touch, a sweet sculpturing of mind and body in full moonlight."

"It may rain——" said the mother uneasily.

"I swear," said the Dustman quickly. "My sister suffered this same swooning paleness. We set her like a potted lily out one spring night with the moon. She lives today in Sussex, the soul of reconstituted health!"

"Reconstituted! Moonlight! And will cost us not one penny of the four hundred we collected this day, Mother, Jamie, Camillia."

"No!" said Mrs. Wilkes. "I won't have it!"

"Mother," said Camillia.

She looked earnestly at the Dustman.

From his grimed face the Dustman gazed back, his smile like a little scimitar in the dark.

"Mother," said Camillia. "I feel it. The moon will cure me, it will, it will. . . ."

The mother sighed. "This is not my day, nor night. Let me kiss you for the last time, then. There."

And the mother went upstairs.

Now the Dustman backed off, bowing courteously to all.
"All night, now, remember, beneath the moon, not the
slightest disturbance until dawn. Sleep well, young lady.
Dream, and dream the best. Good night."

Soot was lost in soot; the man was gone.

Mr. Wilkes and Jamie kissed Camillia's brow.

"Father, Jamie," she said. "Don't worry."

And she was left alone to stare off where at a great
distance she thought she saw a smile hung by itself in the
dark blink off and on, then go round a corner, vanishing.

She waited for the rising of the moon.

Night in London, the voices growing drowsier in the
inns, the slamming of doors, drunken farewells, clocks
chiming. Camillia saw a cat like a woman stroll by in her
furs, saw a woman like a cat stroll by, both wise, both
Egyptian, both smelling of spice. Every quarter hour or so
a voice drifted down from above:

"You all right, child?"

"Yes, Father."

"Camillia?"

"Mother, Jamie, I'm fine."

And at last. "Good night."

"Good night."

The last lights out. London asleep.

The moon rose.

And the higher the moon, the larger grew Camillia's
eyes as she watched the alleys, the courts, the streets, until
at last, at midnight, the moon moved over her to show her
like a marble figure atop an ancient tomb.

A motion in darkness.

Camillia pricked her ears.

A faint melody sprang out on the air.

A man stood in the shadows of the court.

Camillia gasped.

The man stepped forth into moonlight, carrying a lute
which he strummed softly. He was a man well-dressed,
whose face was handsome and, now anyway, solemn.

"A troubadour," said Camillia aloud.

The man, his finger on his lips, moved slowly forward and soon stood by her cot.

"What are you doing out so late?" asked the girl, unafraid but not knowing why.

"A friend sent me to make you well." He touched the lute strings. They hummed sweetly. He was indeed handsome there in the silver light.

"That cannot be," she said, "for it was told me, the *moon* is my cure."

"And so it will be, maiden."

"What songs do you sing?"

"Songs of spring nights, aches and ailments without name. Shall I name your fever, maiden?"

"If you know it, yes."

"First, the symptoms: raging temperatures, sudden cold, heart fast then slow, storms of temper, then sweet calms, drunkenness from having sipped only well water, dizziness from being touched only *thus*——"

He touched her wrist, saw her melt toward delicious oblivion, drew back.

"Depressions, elations," he went on. "Dreams——"

"Stop!" she cried, enthralled. "You know me to the letter. Now, name my ailment!"

"I will." He pressed his lips to the palm of her hand so she quaked suddenly. "The name of the ailment is Camillia Wilkes."

"How strange." She shivered, her eyes glinting lilac fires. "Am I then my own affliction? How sick I make myself! Even now, feel my heart!"

"I feel it, so."

"My limbs, they burn with summer heat!"

"Yes. They scorch my fingers."

"But now, the night wind, see how I shudder, cold! I die, I swear it, I die!"

"I will not let you," he said quietly.

"Are you a doctor, then?"

"No, just your plain, your ordinary physician, like another who guessed your trouble this day. The girl who would have named it but ran off in the crowd."

"Yes, I saw in her eyes she knew what had seized me. But, now, my teeth chatter. And no extra blanket!"

"Give room, please. There. Let me see: two arms, two legs, head and body. I'm all here!"

"What, sir!"

"To warm you from the night, of course."

"How like a hearth! Oh, sir, sir, do I *know* you? Your name?"

Swiftly above her, his head shadowed hers. From it his merry clear-water eyes glowed as did his white ivory slot of a smile.

"Why, Bosco, of course," he said.

"Is there not a saint by that name?"

"Given an hour, you will call me so, yes."

His head bent closer. Thus sooted in shadow, she cried with joyous recognition to welcome her Dustman back.

"The world spins! I pass away! The cure, sweet Doctor, or all is lost!"

"The cure," he said. "And the cure is *this* . . ."

Somewhere, cats sang. A shoe, shot from a window, tipped them off a fence. Then all was silence and the moon . . .

"Shh . . ."

Dawn. Tiptoeing downstairs, Mr. and Mrs. Wilkes peered into their courtyard.

"Frozen stone dead from the terrible night, I *know* it!"

"No, wife, look! Alive! Roses in her cheeks! No, more! Peaches, persimmons! She glows all rosy-milky! Sweet Camillia, alive and well, made whole again!"

They bent by the slumbering girl.

"She smiles, she dreams; what's that she says?"

"The sovereign," sighed the girl, "remedy."

"What, what?"

The girl smiled again, a white smile, in her sleep.

"A medicine," she murmured, "for melancholy."

She opened her eyes.

"Oh, Mother, Father!"

"Daughter! Child! Come upstairs!"

"No." She took their hands, tenderly. "Mother? Father?"

"Yes?"

"No one will see. The sun but rises. Please. Dance with me."

They did not want to dance.

But, celebrating they knew not what, they did.

The Fruit at the Bottom of the Bowl

William Acton rose to his feet. The clock on the
mantel ticked midnight.

He looked at his fingers and he looked at the large room
around him and he looked at the man lying on the floor.
William Acton, whose fingers had stroked typewriter keys
and made love and fried ham and eggs for early breakfasts, had now accomplished a murder with those same ten
whorled fingers.

He had never thought of himself as a sculptor and yet,
in this moment, looking down between his hands at the
body upon the polished hardwood floor, he realized that
by some sculptural clenching and remodeling and twisting
of human clay he had taken hold of this man named Don-
ald Huxley and changed his physiognomy, the very frame
of his body.

With a twist of his fingers he had wiped away the ex-
acting glitter of Huxley's gray eyes; replaced it with a
blind dullness of eye cold in socket. The lips, always pink

and sensuous, were gaped to show the equine teeth, the yellow incisors, the nicotined canines, the gold-inlaid molars. The nose, pink also, was now mottled, pale, discolored, as were the ears. Huxley's hands, upon the floor, were open, pleading for the first time in their lives, instead of demanding.

Yes, it was an artistic conception. On the whole, the change had done Huxley a share of good. Death made him a handsomer man to deal with. You could talk to him now and he'd have to listen.

William Acton looked at his own fingers.

It was done. He could not change it back. Had anyone heard? He listened. Outside, the normal late sounds of street traffic continued. There was no banging of the house door, no shoulder wrecking the portal into kindling, no voices demanding entrance. The murder, the sculpturing of clay from warmth to coldness was done, and nobody knew.

Now what? The clock ticked midnight. His every impulse exploded him in a hysteria toward the door. Rush, get away, run, never come back, board a train, hail a taxi, get, go, run, walk, saunter, but get the blazes *out* of here!

His hands hovered before his eyes, floating, turning.

He twisted them in slow deliberation; they felt airy and feather-light. Why was he staring at them this way? he inquired of himself. Was there something in them of immense interest that he should pause now, after a successful throttling, and examine them whorl by whorl?

They were ordinary hands. Not thick, not thin, not long, not short, not hairy, not naked, not manicured and yet not dirty, not soft and yet not callused, not wrinkled and yet not smooth; not murdering hands at all—and yet not innocent. He seemed to find them miracles to look upon.

It was not the hands as hands he was interested in, nor the fingers as fingers. In the numb timelessness after an accomplished violence he found interest only in the *tips* of his fingers.

The clock ticked upon the mantel.

He knelt by Huxley's body, took a handkerchief from

Huxley's pocket, and began methodically to swab Huxley's throat with it. He brushed and massaged the throat and wiped the face and the back of the neck with fierce energy. Then he stood up.

He looked at the throat. He looked at the polished floor. He bent slowly and gave the floor a few dabs with the handkerchief, then he scowled and swabbed the floor; first, near the head of the corpse; secondly, near the arms. Then he polished the floor all around the body. He polished the floor one yard from the body on all sides. Then he polished the floor two yards from the body on all sides. Then he polished the floor three yards from the body in all directions. Then he——

He stopped.

There was a moment when he saw the entire house, the mirrored halls, the carved doors, the splendid furniture; and, as clearly as if it were being repeated word for word, he heard Huxley talking and himself just the way they had talked only an hour ago.

Finger on Huxley's doorbell. Huxley's door opening.

"Oh!" Huxley shocked. "It's *you*, Acton."

"Where's my wife, Huxley?"

"Do you think I'd tell you, really? Don't stand out there, you idiot. If you want to talk business, come in. Through that door. There. Into the library."

Acton had *touched* the library door.

"Drink?"

"I need one. I can't believe Lily is gone, that she——"

"There's a bottle of burgundy, Acton. Mind fetching it from that cabinet?"

Yes, fetch it. *Handle* it. *Touch* it. He did.

"Some interesting first editions there, Acton. Feel this binding. *Feel* of it."

"I didn't come to see books, I——"

He had *touched* the books and the library table and *touched* the burgundy bottle and burgundy glasses.

Now, squatting on the floor beside Huxley's cold body with the polishing handkerchief in his fingers, motionless, he stared at the house, the walls, the furniture about him, his eyes widening, his mouth dropping, stunned by what he realized and what he saw. He shut his eyes, dropped his head, crushed the handkerchief between his hands, wadding it, biting his lips with his teeth, pulling in on himself.

The fingerprints were everywhere, *everywhere!*

"Mind getting the burgundy, Acton, eh? The burgundy bottle, eh? With your fingers, eh? I'm terribly tired. You understand?"

A pair of gloves.

Before he did one more thing, before he polished another area, he must have a pair of gloves, or he might unintentionally, after cleaning a surface, redistribute his identity.

He put his hands in his pockets. He walked through the house to the hall umbrella stand, the hat rack. Huxley's overcoat. He pulled out the overcoat pockets.

No gloves.

His hands in his pockets again, he walked upstairs, moving with a controlled swiftness, allowing himself nothing frantic, nothing wild. He had made the initial error of not wearing gloves (but, after all, he hadn't *planned* a murder, and his subconscious, which may have known of the crime before its commitment, had not even hinted he might need gloves before the night was finished), so now he had to sweat for his sin of omission. Somewhere in the house there must be at least one pair of gloves. He would have to hurry; there was every chance that someone might visit Huxley, even at this hour. Rich friends drinking themselves in and out the door, laughing, shouting, coming and going without so much as hello-good-by. He would have until six in the morning, at the outside, when Huxley's friends were to pick Huxley up for the trip to the airport and Mexico City. . . .

Acton hurried about upstairs opening drawers, using the handkerchief as blotter. He untidied seventy or eighty drawers in six rooms, left them with their tongues, so to speak, hanging out, ran on to new ones. He felt naked, unable to do anything until he found gloves. He might scour the entire house with the handkerchief, buffing every possible surface where fingerprints might lie, then accidentally bump a wall here or there, thus sealing his own fate with one microscopic, whorling symbol! It would be putting his stamp of approval on the murder, that's what it would be! Like those waxen seals in the old days when they rattled papyrus, flourished ink, dusted all with sand to dry the ink, and pressed their signet rings in hot crimson tallow at the bottom. So it would be if he left one, mind you, *one* fingerprint upon the scene! His approval of the murder did not extend as far as affixing said seal.

More drawers! Be quiet, be curious, be careful, he told himself.

At the bottom of the eighty-fifth drawer he found gloves.

"Oh, my Lord, my Lord!" He slumped against the bureau, sighing. He tried the gloves on, held them up, proudly flexed them, buttoned them. They were soft, gray, thick, impregnable. He could do all sorts of tricks with hands now and leave no trace. He thumbed his nose in the bedroom mirror, sucking his teeth.

"NO!" cried Huxley.

What a wicked plan it had been.

Huxley had fallen to the floor, *purposely!* Oh, what a wickedly clever man! Down onto the hardwood floor had dropped Huxley, with Acton after him. They had rolled and tussled and clawed at the floor, printing and printing it with their frantic fingertips! Huxley had slipped away a few feet, Acton crawling after to lay hands on his neck and squeeze until the life came out like paste from a tube!

Gloved, William Acton returned to the room and knelt down upon the floor and laboriously began the task of swabbing every wildly infested inch of it. Inch by inch, inch by inch, he polished and polished until he could almost see his intent, sweating face in it. Then he came to a table and polished the leg of it, on up its solid body and along the knobs and over the top. He came to a bowl of wax fruit, burnished the filigree silver, plucked out the wax fruit and wiped them clean, leaving the fruit at the bottom unpolished.

"I'm certain I didn't touch *that*," he said.

After rubbing the table he came to a picture frame hung over it.

"I'm certain I didn't touch *that*," he said.

He stood looking at it.

He glanced at all the doors in the room. Which doors had he used tonight? He couldn't remember. Polish all of them, then. He started on the doorknobs, shined them all up, and then he curried the doors from head to foot, taking no chances. Then he went to all the furniture in the room and wiped the chair arms.

"That chair you're sitting in, Acton, is an old Louis XIV piece. *Feel* that material," said Huxley.

"I didn't come to talk furniture, Huxley! I came about Lily."

"Oh, come off it, you're not that serious about her. She doesn't love you, you know. She's told me she'll go with me to Mexico City tomorrow."

"You and your money and your damned furniture!"

"It's nice furniture. Acton; be a good guest and feel of it."

Fingerprints can be found on fabric.

"Huxley!" William Acton stared at the body. "Did you guess I was going to kill you? Did your subconscious suspect, just as my subconscious suspected? And did your subconscious tell you to make me run about the house handling, touching, *fondling* books, dishes, doors, chairs? Were you *that* clever and *that* mean?"

He washed the chairs dryly with the clenched handkerchief. Then he remembered the body—he hadn't dry-washed *it*. He went to it and turned it now this way, now that, and burnished every surface of it. He even shined the shoes, charging nothing.

While shining the shoes his face took on a little tremor of worry, and after a moment he got up and walked over to that table.

He took out and polished the wax fruit at the bottom of the bowl.

"Better," he whispered, and went back to the body.

But as he crouched over the body his eyelids twitched and his jaw moved from side to side and he debated, then he got up and walked once more to the table.

He polished the picture frame.

While polishing the picture frame he discovered——

The wall.

"That," he said, "is *silly*."

"Oh!" cried Huxley, fending him off. He gave Acton a shove as they struggled. Acton fell, got up, *touching* the wall, and ran toward Huxley again. He strangled Huxley. Huxley died.

Acton turned steadfastly from the wall, with equilibrium and decision. The harsh words and the action faded in his mind; he hid them away. He glanced at the four walls.

"Ridiculous!" he said.

From the corners of his eyes he saw something on one wall.

"I refuse to pay attention," he said to distract himself. "The next room, now! I'll be methodical. Let's see—altogether we were in the hall, the library, *this* room, and the dining room and the kitchen."

There was a spot on the wall behind him.

Well, *wasn't* there?

He turned angrily. "All right, all right, just to be *sure*," and he went over and couldn't find any spot. Oh, a *little* one, yes, right—*there*. He dabbed it. It wasn't a fingerprint anyhow. He finished with it, and his gloved hand leaned against the wall and he looked at the wall and the way it went over to his right and over to his left and how it went down to his feet and up over his head and he said softly, "No." He looked up and down and over and across and he said quietly, "That would be too much." How many square feet? "I don't give a good damn," he said. But unknown to his eyes, his gloved fingers moved in a little rubbing rhythm on the wall.

He peered at his hand and the wallpaper. He looked

over his shoulder at the other room. "I must go in there and polish the essentials," he told himself, but his hand remained, as if to hold the wall, or himself, up. His face hardened.

Without a word he began to scrub the wall, up and down, back and forth, up and down, as high as he could stretch and as low as he could bend.

"Ridiculous, oh my Lord, ridiculous!"

But you must be certain, his thought said to him.

"Yes, one *must* be certain," he replied.

He got one wall finished, and then . . .

He came to another wall.

"What time *is* it?"

He looked at the mantel clock. An hour gone. It was five after one.

The doorbell rang.

Acton froze, staring at the door, the clock, the door, the clock.

Someone rapped loudly.

A long moment passed. Acton did not breathe. Without new air in his body he began to fail away, to sway; his head roared a silence of cold waves thundering onto heavy rocks.

"Hey, in there!" cried a drunken voice. "I know you're in there, Huxley! Open up, damn it! This is Billy-boy, drunk as an owl, Huxley, old pal, drunker than *two* owls."

"Go away," whispered Acton soundlessly, crushed against the wall.

"Huxley, you're in there, I hear you *breathing!*" cried the drunken voice.

"Yes, I'm in here," whispered Acton, feeling long and sprawled and clumsy on the floor, clumsy and cold and silent. "Yes."

"Hell!" said the voice, fading away into mist. The footsteps shuffled off. "Hell . . ."

Acton stood a long time feeling the red heart beat inside his shut eyes, within his head. When at last he opened his eyes he looked at the new fresh wall straight ahead of him and finally got courage to speak. "Silly," he said. "This wall's flawless. I won't touch it. Got to hurry. Got to hurry. Time, time. Only a few hours before those damn-fool friends blunder in!" He turned away.

From the corners of his eyes he saw the little webs. When his back was turned the little spiders came out of the woodwork and delicately spun their fragile little half-invisible webs. Not upon the wall at his left, which was already washed fresh, but upon the three walls as yet untouched. Each time he stared directly at them the spiders dropped back into the woodwork, only to spindle out as he retreated. "Those walls are all right," he insisted in a half shout. "I won't *touch* them!"

He went to a writing desk at which Huxley had been seated earlier. He opened a drawer and took out what he was looking for. A little magnifying glass Huxley sometimes used for reading. He took the magnifier and approached the wall uneasily.

Fingerprints.

"But those aren't mine!" He laughed unsteadily. "I *didn't* put them there! I'm *sure* I didn't! A servant, a butler, or a maid perhaps!"

The wall was full of them.

"Look at this one here," he said. "Long and tapered, a woman's, I'd bet money on it."

"Would you?"

"I would!"

"Are you certain?"

"Yes!"

"Positive?"

"Well—yes."

"Absolutely?"

"Yes, damn it, yes!"

"Wipe it out, anyway, why don't you?"

"There, by God!"

"Out damned spot, eh, Acton?"

"And this one, over here," scoffed Acton. "That's the print of a fat man."

"Are you sure?"

"Don't start *that* again!" he snapped, and rubbed it out

He pulled off a glove and held his hand up, trembling, in the glary light.

"Look at it, you idiot! See how the whorls go? See?"

"That proves nothing!"

"Oh, all right!" Raging, he swept the wall up and down, back and forth, with gloved hands, sweating, grunting, swearing, bending, rising, and getting redder of face.

He took off his coat, put it on a chair.

"Two o'clock," he said, finishing the wall, glaring at the clock.

He walked over to the bowl and took out the wax fruit and polished the ones at the bottom and put them back, and polished the picture frame.

He gazed up at the chandelier.

His fingers twitched at his sides.

His mouth slipped open and the tongue moved along his lips and he looked at the chandelier and looked away and looked back at the chandelier and looked at Huxley's body and then at the crystal chandelier with its long pearls of rainbow glass.

He got a chair and brought it over under the chandelier and put one foot up on it and took it down and threw the chair violently, laughing, into a corner. Then he ran out of the room, leaving one wall as yet unwashed.

In the dining room he came to a table.

"I want to show you my Gregorian cutlery, Acton," Huxley had said. Oh, that casual, that *hypnotic* voice!

"I haven't time," Acton said. "I've got to see Lily——"

"Nonsense, look at this silver, this exquisite craftsmanship."

Acton paused over the table where the boxes of cutlery were laid out, hearing once more Huxley's voice, remembering all the touchings and gesturings.

Now Acton wiped the forks and spoons and took down all the plaques and special ceramic dishes from the wall itself. . . .

"Here's a lovely bit of ceramics by Gertrude and Otto Natzler, Acton. Are you familiar with their work?"

"It *is* lovely."

"Pick it up. Turn it over. See the fine thinness of the bowl, hand-thrown on a turntable, thin as eggshell, incredible. And the amazing volcanic glaze. Handle it, *go* ahead. I don't mind."

HANDLE IT. GO AHEAD. PICK IT UP!

Acton sobbed unevenly. He hurled the pottery against the wall. It shattered and spread, flaking wildly, upon the floor.

An instant later he was on his knees. Every piece, every shard of it, must be found. Fool, fool, fool! he cried to himself, shaking his head and shutting and opening his eyes and bending under the table. Find every piece, idiot, not one fragment of it must be left behind. Fool, fool! He gathered them. Are they all here? He looked at them on the table before him. He looked under the table again and under the chairs and the service bureaus and found one more piece by match light and started to polish each little fragment as if it were a precious stone. He laid them all out neatly upon the shining polished table.

"A lovely bit of ceramics, Acton. Go ahead—*handle* it."

He took out the linen and wiped it and wiped the chairs and tables and doorknobs and windowpanes and ledges and drapes and wiped the floor and found the kitchen, panting, breathing violently, and took off his vest and adjusted his gloves and wiped the glittering chromium. . . . "I want to show you my house, Acton," said Huxley. "Come along. . . ." And he wiped all the utensils and the silver faucets and the mixing bowls, for now he had forgotten what he had touched and what he had not. Huxley and he had lingered here, in the kitchen, Huxley prideful of its array, covering his nervousness at the presence of a potential killer, perhaps wanting to be near the knives if they were needed. They had idled, touched this, that, something else—there was no remembering what or how much or how many—and he finished the kitchen and came through the hall into the room where Huxley lay.

He cried out.

He had forgotten to wash the fourth wall of the room! And while he was gone the little spiders had popped from the fourth unwashed wall and swarmed over the already clean walls, dirtying them again! On the ceilings, from the chandelier, in the corners, on the floor, a million little whorled webs hung billowing at his scream! Tiny, tiny little webs, no bigger than, ironically, your—finger!"

As he watched, the webs were woven over the picture frame, the fruit bowl, the body, the floor. Prints wielded the paper knife, pulled out drawers, touched the table top, touched, touched, touched everything everywhere.

He polished the floor wildly, wildly. He rolled the body over and cried on it while he washed it, and got up and walked over and polished the fruit at the bottom of the bowl. Then he put a chair under the chandelier and got up and polished each little hanging fire of it, shaking it like a crystal tambourine until it tilted bellwise in the air. Then he leaped off the chair and gripped the doorknobs and got up on other chairs and swabbed the walls higher and higher and ran to the kitchen and got a broom and wiped the webs down from the ceiling and polished the bottom fruit of the bowl and washed the body and doorknobs and silverware and found the hall banister and followed the banister upstairs.

Three o'clock! Everywhere, with a fierce, mechanical intensity, clocks ticked! There were twelve rooms downstairs and eight above. He figured the yards and yards of space and time needed. One hundred chairs, six sofas, twenty-seven tables, six radios. And under and on top and behind. He yanked furniture out away from walls and, sobbing, wiped them clean of years-old dust, and staggered and followed the banister up, up the stairs, handling, erasing, rubbing, polishing, because if he left one little print it would reproduce and make a million more!—and the job would have to be done all over again and now it was four o'clock!—and his arms ached and his eyes were swollen and staring and he moved sluggishly about, on strange legs, his head down, his arms moving, swabbing and rubbing, bedroom by bedroom, closet by closet. . . .

They found him at six-thirty that morning.

In the attic.

The entire house was polished to a brilliance. Vases shone like glass stars. Chairs were burnished. Bronzes, brasses, and coppers were all aglint. Floors sparkled. Banisters gleamed.

Everything glittered. Everything shone, everything was bright!

They found him in the attic, polishing the old trunks and the old frames and the old chairs and the old carriages and toys and music boxes and vases and cutlery and rocking horses and dusty Civil War coins. He was half through the attic when the police officer walked up behind him with a gun.

"Done!"

On the way out of the house Acton polished the front doorknob with his handkerchief and slammed it in triumph!

Ylla

They had a house of crystal pillars on the planet Mars by the edge of an empty sea, and every morning you could see Mrs. K eating the golden fruits that grew from the crystal walls, or cleaning the house with handfuls of magnetic dust which, taking all dirt with it, blew away on the hot wind. Afternoons, when the fossil sea was warm and motionless, and the wine trees stood stiff in the yard, and the little distant Martian bone town was all enclosed, and no one drifted out their doors, you could see Mr. K himself in his room, reading from a metal book with raised hieroglyphs over which he brushed his hand, as one might play a harp. And from the book, as his fingers stroked, a voice sang, a soft ancient voice, which told tales of when the sea was red steam on the shore and ancient men had carried clouds of metal insects and electric spiders into battle.

Mr. and Mrs. K had lived by the dead sea for twenty years, and their ancestors had lived in the same house, which had turned and followed the sun, flower-like, for ten centuries.

Mr. and Mrs. K were not old. They had the fair, brownish skin of the true Martian, the yellow coin eyes, the soft musical voices. Once they had liked painting pictures with chemical fire, swimming in the canals in the seasons when the wine trees filled them with green liquors, and talking into the dawn together by the blue phosphorous portraits in the speaking room.

They were not happy now.

This morning Mrs. K stood between the pillars, listening to the desert sands heat, melt into yellow wax, and seemingly run on the horizon.

Something was going to happen.

She waited.

She watched the blue sky of Mars as if it might at any moment grip in on itself, contract, and expel a shining miracle down upon the sand.

Nothing happened.

Tired of waiting, she walked through the misting pillars. A gentle rain sprang from the fluted pillar tops, cooling the scorched air, falling gently on her. On hot days it was like walking in a creek. The floors of the house glittered with cool streams. In the distance she heard her husband playing his book steadily, his fingers never tired of the old songs. Quietly she wished he might one day again spend as much time holding and touching her like a little harp as he did his incredible books.

But no. She shook her head, an imperceptible, forgiving shrug. Her eyelids closed softly down upon her golden eyes. Marriage made people old and familiar, while still young.

She lay back in a chair that moved to take her shape even as she moved. She closed her eyes tightly and nervously.

The dream occurred.

Her brown fingers trembled, came up, grasped at the air. A moment later she sat up, startled, gasping.

She glanced about swiftly, as if expecting someone there before her. She seemed disappointed; the space between the pillars was empty.

Her husband appeared in a triangular door. "Did you call?" he asked irritably.

"No!" she cried.

"I thought I heard you cry out."

"Did I? I was almost asleep and had a dream!"

"In the daytime? You don't often do that."

She sat as if struck in the face by the dream. "How strange, how very strange," she murmured. "The dream."

"Oh?" He evidently wished to return to his book.

"I dreamed about a man."

"A man?"

"A tall man, six feet one inch tall."

"How absurd; a giant, a misshapen giant."

"Somehow"—she tried the words—"he looked all right. In spite of being tall. And he had—oh, I know you'll think it silly—he had *blue* eyes!"

"Blue eyes! Gods!" cried Mr. K. "What'll you dream next? I suppose he had *black* hair?"

"How did you *guess?*" She was excited.

"I picked the most unlikely color," he replied coldly.

"Well, black it was!" she cried. "And he had a very white skin; oh, he was *most* unusual! He was dressed in a strange uniform and he came down out of the sky and spoke pleasantly to me." She smiled.

"Out of the sky; what nonsense!"

"He came in a metal thing that glittered in the sun," she remembered. She closed her eyes to shape it again. "I dreamed there was the sky and something sparkled like a coin thrown into the air, and suddenly it grew large and fell down softly to land, a long silver craft, round and alien. And a door opened in the side of the silver object and this tall man stepped out."

"If you worked harder you wouldn't have these silly dreams."

"I rather enjoyed it," she replied, lying back. "I never suspected myself of such an imagination. Black hair, blue eyes, and white skin! What a strange man, and yet—quite handsome."

"Wishful thinking."

"You're unkind. I didn't think him up on purpose; he just came in my mind while I drowsed. It wasn't like a dream. It was so unexpected and different. He looked at me and he said, 'I've come from the third planet in my ship. My name is Nathaniel York——' "

"A stupid name; it's no name at all," objected the husband.

"Of course it's stupid, because it's a dream," she explained softly. "And he said, 'This is the first trip across space. There are only two of us in our ship, myself and my friend Bert.' "

"*Another* stupid name."

"And he said, 'We're from a city on *Earth;* that's the name of our planet,' " continued Mrs. K. "That's what he said. 'Earth' was the name he spoke. And he used another language. Somehow I understood him. With my mind. Telepathy, I suppose."

Mr. K turned away. She stopped him with a word. "Yll?" she called quietly. "Do you ever wonder if—well, if there *are* people living on the third planet?"

"The third planet is incapable of supporting life," stated the husband patiently. "Our scientists have said there's far too much oxygen in its atmosphere."

"But wouldn't it be fascinating if there *were* people? And they traveled through space in some sort of ship?"

"Really, Ylla, you know how I hate this emotional wailing. Let's get on with our work."

It was late in the day when she began singing the song as she moved among the whispering pillars of rain. She sang it over and over again.

"What's that song?" snapped her husband at last, walking in to sit at the fire table.

"I don't know." She looked up, surprised at herself. She put her hand to her mouth, unbelieving. The sun was setting. The house was closing itself in, like a giant flower, with the passing of light. A wind blew among the pillars; the fire table bubbled its fierce pool of silver lava. The wind stirred her russet hair, crooning softly in her ears. She stood silently looking out into the great sallow distances of sea bottom, as if recalling something, her yellow eyes soft and moist. " 'Drink to me only with thine eyes, and I will pledge with mine,' " she sang, softly, quietly, slowly. " 'Or leave a kiss within the cup, and I'll not ask for wine.' " She hummed now, moving her hands in the wind ever so lightly, her eyes shut. She finished the song.

It was very beautiful.

"Never heard that song before. Did you compose it?" he inquired, his eyes sharp.

"No. Yes. No, I don't know, really!" She hesitated wildly. "I don't even know what the words are; they're another language!"

"What language?"

She dropped portions of meat numbly into the simmering lava. "I don't know." She drew the meat forth a moment later, cooked, served on a plate for him. "It's just a crazy thing I made up, I guess. I don't know why."

He said nothing. He watched her drown meats in the hissing fire pool. The sun was gone. Slowly, slowly the night came in to fill the room, swallowing the pillars and both of them, like a dark wine poured to the ceiling. Only the silver lava's glow lit their faces.

She hummed the strange song again.

Instantly he leaped from his chair and stalked angrily from the room.

Later, in isolation, he finished supper.

When he arose he stretched, glanced at her, and suggested, yawning, "Let's take the flame birds to town tonight to see an entertainment."

"You don't *mean* it?" she said. "Are you feeling well?"

"What's so strange about that?"

"But we haven't gone for an entertainment in six months!"

'I think it's a good idea."

"Suddenly you're so solicitous," she said.

'Don't talk that way," he replied peevishly. "Do you or do you not want to go?"

She looked out at the pale desert. The twin white moons were rising. Cool water ran softly about her toes. She began to tremble just the least bit. She wanted very much to sit quietly here, soundless, not moving until this thing occurred, this thing expected all day, this thing that could not occur but might. A drift of song brushed through her mind.

"I——"

"Do you good," he urged. "Come along now."

"I'm tired," she said. "Some other night."

"Here's your scarf." He handed her a phial. "We haven't gone anywhere in months."

"Except you, twice a week to XI City." She wouldn't look at him.

"Business," he said.

"Oh?" She whispered to herself.

From the phial a liquid poured, turned to blue mist, settled about her neck, quivering.

The flame birds waited, like a bed of coals, glowing on the cool smooth sands. The white canopy ballooned on the night wind, flapping softly, tied by a thousand green ribbons to the birds.

Ylla laid herself back in the canopy and, at a word from her husband, the birds leaped, burning, toward the dark sky. The ribbons tautened, the canopy lifted. The sand slid whining under; the blue hills drifted by, drifted by, leaving their home behind, the raining pillars, the caged flowers, the singing books, the whispering floor creeks. She did not look at her husband. She heard him crying out to the birds as they rose higher, like ten thousand hot sparkles, so many red-yellow fireworks in the heavens, tugging the canopy like a flower petal, burning through the wind.

She didn't watch the dead, ancient bone-chess cities slide under, or the old canals filled with emptiness and dreams. Past dry rivers and dry lakes they flew, like the shadows of the moons, like a torch burning.

She watched only the sky.

The husband spoke.

She watched the sky.

"Did you hear what I said?"

"What?"

He exhaled. "You might pay attention."

"I was thinking."

"I never thought you were a nature lover, but you're certainly interested in the sky tonight," he said.

"It's very beautiful."

"I was figuring," said the husband slowly. "I thought I'd call Hulle tonight. I'd like to talk to him about us spending some time, oh, only a week or so, in the Blue Mountains. It's just an idea——"

"The Blue Mountains!" She held to the canopy rim with one hand, turning swiftly toward him.

"Oh, it's just a suggestion."

"When do you want to go?" she asked, trembling.

"I thought we might leave tomorrow morning. You know, an early start and all that," he said very casually.

"But we *never* go this early in the year!"

"Just this once, I thought——" He smiled. "Do us good to get away. Some peace and quiet. You know. You haven't anything *else* planned? We'll go, won't we?"

She took a breath, waited, and then replied, "No."

"What?" His cry startled the birds. The canopy jerked.

"No," she said firmly. "It's settled. I won't go."

He looked at her. They did not speak after that. She turned away.

The birds flew on, ten thousand firebrands down the wind.

In the dawn the sun, through the crystal pillars, melted the fog that supported Ylla as she slept. All night she had hung above the floor, buoyed by the soft carpeting of mist that poured from the walls when she lay down to rest. All night she had slept on this silent river, like a boat upon a soundless tide. Now the fog burned away, the mist level lowered until she was deposited upon the shore of wakening.

She opened her eyes.

Her husband stood over her. He looked as if he had stood there for hours, watching. She did not know why, but she could not look him in the face.

"You've been dreaming again!" he said. "You spoke out and kept me awake. I *really* think you should see a doctor."

"I'll be all right."

"You talked a lot in your sleep!"

"Did I?" She started up.

Dawn was cold in the room. A gray light filled her as she lay there.

"What was your dream?"

She had to think a moment to remember. "The ship. It came from the sky again, landed, and the tall man stepped out and talked with me, telling me little jokes, laughing, and it was pleasant."

Mr. K touched a pillar. Founts of warm water leaped up, steaming; the chill vanished from the room. Mr. K's face was impassive.

"And then," she said, "this man, who said his strange name was Nathaniel York, told me I was beautiful and— and kissed me."

"Ha!" cried the husband, turning violently away, his jaw working.

"It's only a dream." She was amused.

"Keep your silly, feminine dreams to yourself!"

"You're acting like a child." She lapsed back upon the few remaining remnants of chemical mist. After a moment she laughed softly. "I thought of some *more* of the dream," she confessed.

"Well, what is it, what *is* it?" he shouted.

"Yll, you're so bad-tempered."

"Tell me!" he demanded. "You can't keep secrets from me!" His face was dark and rigid as he stood over her.

"I've never seen you this way," she replied, half shocked, half entertained. "All that happened was this Nathaniel York person told me—well, he told me that he'd take me away into his ship, into the sky with him, and take me back to his planet with him. It's eally quite ridiculous."

"Ridiculous, is it!" he almost screamed. "You should have heard yourself, fawning on him, talking to him, singing with him, oh gods, all night; you should have *heard* yourself!"

"Yll!"

"When's he landing? Where's he coming down with his damned ship?"

"Yll, lower your voice."

"Voice be damned!" He bent stiffly over her. "And *in* this dream"—he seized her wrist—"didn't the ship land over in Green Valley, *didn't* it? Answer me!"

"Why, yes——"

"And it landed this afternoon, didn't it?" he kept at her.

"Yes, yes, I think so, yes, but only in a dream!"

"Well"—he flung her hand away stiffly—"it's good you're truthful! I heard every word you said in your sleep. You mentioned the valley and the time." Breathing hard, he walked between the pillars like a man blinded by a lighting bolt. Slowly his breath returned. She watched him as if he were quite insane. She arose finally and went to him. "Yll," she whispered.

"I'm all right."

"You're sick."

"No." He forced a tired smile. "Just childish. Forgive me, darling." He gave her a rough pat. "Too much work lately. I'm sorry. I think I'll lie down awhile——"

"You were so excited."

"I'm all right now. Fine." He exhaled. "Let's forget it. Say, I heard a joke about Uel yesterday, I meant to tell you. What do you say you fix breakfast, I'll tell the joke, and let's not talk about all this."

"It was only a dream."

"Of course." He kissed her cheek mechanically. "Only a dream."

At noon the sun was high and hot and the hills shimmered in the light.

"Aren't you going to town?" asked Ylla.

"Town?" He raised his brows faintly.

"This is the day you *always* go." She adjusted a flower cage on its pedestal. The flowers stirred, opening their hungry yellow mouths.

He closed his book. "No. It's too hot, and it's late."

"Oh." She finished her task and moved toward the door. "Well, I'll be back soon."

"Wait a minute! Where are you going?"

She was in the door swiftly. "Over to Pao's. She invited me!"

"Today?"

"I haven't seen her in a long time. It's only a little way."

"Over in Green Valley, isn't it?"

"Yes, just a walk, not far, I thought I'd——" She hurried.

"I'm sorry, really sorry," he said, running to fetch her back, looking very concerned about his forgetfulness. "It slipped my mind. I invited Dr. Nlle out this afternoon."

"Dr. Nlle!" She edged toward the door.

He caught her elbow and drew her steadily in. "Yes."

"But Pao——"

"Pao can wait, Ylla. We must entertain Nlle."

"Just for a few minutes——"

"No, Ylla."

"No?"

He shook his head. "No. Besides, it's a terribly long walk to Pao's. All the way over through Green Valley and then past the big canal and down, isn't it? And it'll be very, very hot, and Dr. Nlle would be delighted to see you. Well?"

She did not answer. She wanted to break and run. She wanted to cry out. But she only sat in the chair, turning her fingers over slowly, staring at them expressionlessly, trapped.

"Ylla?" he murmured. "You *will* be here, won't you?"

"Yes," she said after a long time. "I'll be here."

"All afternoon?"

Her voice was dull. "All afternoon."

. . .

Late in the day Dr. Nlle had not put in an appearance.
Ylla's husband did not seem overly surprised. When it was
quite late he murmured something, went to a closet, and
drew forth an evil weapon, a long yellowish tube ending in
a bellows and a trigger. He turned, and upon his face was
a mask, hammered from silver metal, expressionless, the
mask that he always wore when he wished to hide his
feelings, the mask which curved and hollowed so exquisitely to his thin cheeks and chin and brow. The mask
glinted, and he held the evil weapon in his hands, considering it. It hummed constantly, an insect hum. From it
hordes of golden bees could be flung out with a high
shriek. Golden, horrid bees that stung, poisoned, and fell
lifeless, like seeds on the sand.

"Where are you going?" she asked.

"What?" He listened to the bellows, to the evil hum. "If
Dr. Nlle is late, I'll be damned if I'll wait. I'm going out to
hunt a bit. I'll be back. You be sure to stay right here now,
won't you?" The silver mask glimmered.

"Yes."

"And tell Dr. Nlle I'll return. Just hunting."

The triangular door closed. His footsteps faded down
the hill.

She watched him walking through the sunlight until he
was gone. Then she resumed her tasks with the magnetic
dusts and the new fruits to be plucked from the crystal
walls. She worked with energy and dispatch, but on occasion a numbness took hold of her and she caught herself
singing that odd and memorable song and looking out
beyond the crystal pillars at the sky.

She held her breath and stood very still, waiting.

It was coming nearer.

At any moment it might happen.

It was like those days when you heard a thunderstorm
coming and there was the waiting silence and then the
faintest pressure of the atmosphere as the climate blew
over the land in shifts and shadows and vapors. And the
change pressed at your ears and you were suspended in

the waiting time of the coming storm. You began to tremble. The sky was stained and colored; the clouds were thickened; the mountains took on an iron taint. The caged flowers blew with faint sighs of warning. You felt your hair stir softly. Somewhere in the house the voice-clock sang, "Time, time, time, time . . ." ever so gently, no more than water tapping on velvet.

And then the storm. The electric illumination, the engulfments of dark wash and sounding black fell down, shutting in, forever.

That's how it was now. A storm gathered, yet the sky was clear. Lightning was expected, yet there was no cloud.

Ylla moved through the breathless summer house. Lightning would strike from the sky any instant; there would be a thunderclap, a boll of smoke, a silence, footsteps on the path, a rap on the crystalline door, and her *running* to answer. . . .

Crazy Ylla! she scoffed. Why think these wild things with your idle mind?

And then it happened.

There was a warmth as of a great fire passing in the air. A whirling, rushing sound. A gleam in the sky, of metal.

Ylla cried out.

Running through the pillars, she flung wide a door. She faced the hills. But by this time there was nothing.

She was about to race down the hill when she stopped herself. She was supposed to stay here, go nowhere. The doctor was coming to visit, and her husband would be angry if she ran off.

She waited in the door, breathing rapidly, her hand out.

She strained to see over toward Green Valley, but saw nothing.

Silly woman. She went inside. You and your imagination, she thought. That was nothing but a bird, a leaf, the wind, or a fish in the canal. Sit down. Rest.

She sat down.

A shot sounded.

Very clearly, sharply, the sound of the evil insect weapon.

Her body jerked with it.

It came from a long way off. One shot. The swift humming distant bees. One shot. And then a second shot, precise and cold, and far away.

Her body winced again and for some reason she started up, screaming, and screaming, and never wanting to stop screaming. She ran violently through the house and once more threw wide the door.

The echoes were dying away, away.

Gone.

She waited in the yard, her face pale, for five minutes.

Finally, with slow steps, her head down, she wandered about the pillared rooms, laying her hand to things, her lips quivering, until finally she sat alone in the darkening wine room, waiting. She began to wipe an amber glass with the hem of her scarf.

And then, from far off, the sound of footsteps crunching on the thin, small rocks.

She rose up to stand in the center of the quiet room. The glass fell from her fingers, smashing to bits.

The footsteps hesitated outside the door.

Should she speak? Should she cry out, "Come in, oh, come in"?

She went forward a few paces.

The footsteps walked up the ramp. A hand twisted the door latch.

She smiled at the door.

The door opened. She stopped smiling.

It was her husband. His silver mask glowed dully.

He entered the room and looked at her for only a moment. Then he snapped the weapon bellows open, cracked out two dead bees, heard them spat on the floor as they fell, stepped on them, and placed the empty bellows gun in the corner of the room as Ylla bent down and tried, over and over, with no success, to pick up the pieces of the shattered glass. "What were you doing?" she asked.

"Nothing," he said with his back turned. He removed the mask.

"But the gun—I heard you fire it. Twice."

"Just hunting. Once in a while you like to hunt. Did Dr. Nlle arrive?"

"No."

"Wait a minute." He snapped his fingers disgustedly. "Why, I remember *now*. He was supposed to visit us *tomorrow* afternoon. How stupid of me."

They sat down to eat. She looked at her food and did not move her hands. "What's wrong?" he asked, not looking up from dipping his meat in the bubbling lava.

"I don't know. I'm not hungry," she said.

"Why not?"

"I don't know; I'm just not."

The wind was rising across the sky; the sun was going down. The room was small and suddenly cold.

"I've been trying to remember," she said in the silent room, across from her cold, erect, golden-eyed husband.

"Remember what?" He sipped his wine.

"That song. That fine and beautiful song." She closed her eyes and hummed, but it was not the song. "I've forgotten it. And, somehow, I don't want to forget it. It's something I want always to remember." She moved her hands as if the rhythm might help her to remember all of it. Then she lay back in her chair. "I can't remember." She began to cry.

"Why are you crying?" he asked.

"I don't know, I don't know, but I can't help it. I'm sad and I don't know why, I cry and I don't know why, but I'm crying."

Her head was in her hands; her shoulders moved again and again.

"You'll be all right tomorrow," he said.

She did not look up at him; she looked only at the empty desert and the very bright stars coming out now on the black sky, and far away there was a sound of wind rising and canal waters stirring cold in the long canals. She shut her eyes, trembling.

"Yes," she said. "I'll be all right tomorrow."

The Little Mice

"They're very odd," I said. "The little Mexican couple."

"How do you mean?" asked my wife.

"Never a sound," I said. "Listen."

Ours was a house deep back in among tenements, to which another half house had been added. When my wife and I purchased the house, we rented the additional quarters which lay walled up against one side of our parlor. Now, listening at this particular wall, we heard our hearts beat.

"I know they're home," I whispered. "But in the three years they've lived here I've never heard a dropped pan, a spoken word, or the sound of a light switch. Good God, what are they *doing* in there?"

"I'd never thought," said my wife. "It *is* peculiar."

"Only one light on, that same dim little blue twenty-five-watt bulb they burn in their parlor. If you walk by and peer in their front door, there *he* is, sitting in his armchair, not saying a word, his hands in his lap. There she is, sitting in the other armchair, looking at him, saying nothing. They don't move."

"At first glance I always think they're not home," said my wife. "Their parlor's so dark. But if you stare long enough, your eyes get used to it and you can make them out, sitting there."

"Someday," I said, "I'm going to run in, turn on their lights, and yell! My God, if *I* can't stand their silence, how can they? They can talk, can't they?"

"When he pays the rent each month, he says hello."

"What else?"

"Good-by."

I shook my head. "When we meet in the alley he smiles and runs."

My wife and I sat down for an evening of reading, the radio, and talk. "Do they have a radio?"

"No radio, television, telephone. Not a book, magazine, or paper in their house."

"Ridiculous!"

"Don't get so excited."

"I know, but you can't sit in a dark room two or three years and not speak, not listen to a radio, not read or even eat, can you? I've never smelled a steak or an egg frying. Damn it, I don't believe I've ever heard them go to bed!"

"They're doing it to mystify us, dear."

"They're succeeding!"

I went for a walk around the block. It was a nice summer evening. Returning, I glanced idly in their front door. The dark silence was there, and the heavy shapes, sitting, and the little blue light burning. I stood a long time, finishing my cigarette. It was only in turning to go that I saw him in the doorway, looking out with his bland, plump face. He didn't move. He just stood there, watching me.

"Evening," I said.

Silence. After a moment, he turned, moving away into the dark room.

In the morning, the little Mexican left the house at seven o'clock, alone, hurrying down the alley, observing the same silence he kept in his rooms. She followed at eight o'clock, walking carefully, all lumpy under her dark coat, a black hat balanced on her frizzy beauty-parlor hair. They had gone to work this way, remote and silent, for years.

"Where do they work?" I asked at breakfast.

"He's a blast-furnace man at U.S. Steel here. She sews in a dress loft somewhere."

"That's hard work."

I typed a few pages of my novel, read, idled, typed some more. At five in the afternoon I saw the little Mexican woman come home, unlock her door, hurry inside, hook the screen, and lock the door tight.

He arrived at six sharp in a rush. Once on their back porch, however, he became infinitely patient. Quietly, raking his hand over the screen, lightly, like a fat mouse scrabbling, he waited. At last she let him in. I did not see their mouths move.

Not a sound during suppertime. No frying. No rattle of dishes. Nothing.

I saw the small blue lamp go on.

"That's how he is," said my wife, "when he pays the rent. Raps so quietly I don't hear. I just happen to glance out the window and there he is. God knows how long he's waited, standing, sort of 'nibbling' at the door."

Two nights later, on a beautiful July evening, the little Mexican man came out on the back porch and looked at me, working in the garden and said, "You're crazy!" He turned to my wife. "You're crazy too!" He waved his plump hand quietly. "I don't like you. Too much *noise*. I don't like you. You're crazy."

He went back into his little house.

August, September, October, November. The "mice," as we now referred to them, lay quietly in their dark nest. Once my wife gave him some old magazines with his rent receipt. He accepted these politely, with a smile and a bow, but no word. An hour later she saw him put the magazines in the yard incinerator and strike a match.

The next day he paid the rent three months in advance,

no doubt figuring that he would only have to see us up close once every twelve weeks. When I saw him on the street he crossed quickly to the other side to greet an imaginary friend. She, similarly, ran by me, smiling wildly, bewildered, nodding. I never got nearer than twenty yards to her. If there was plumbing to be fixed in their house, they went silently forth on their own, not telling us, and brought back a plumber who worked, it seemed, with a flashlight.

"God damnedest thing," he told me when I saw him in the alley. "Damn fool place there hasn't got any light bulbs in the sockets. When I asked where they all were, damn it, they just *smiled* at me!"

I lay at night thinking about the little mice. Where were they from? Mexico, yes. What part? A farm, a small village, somewhere by a river? Certainly no city or town. But a place where there were stars and the normal lights and darknesses, the goings and comings of the moon and the sun they had known the better part of their lives. Yet here they were, far, far away from home, in an impossible city, he sweating out the hell of blast furnaces all day, she bent to jittering needles in a sewing loft. They came home then to this block, through a loud city, avoided clanging streetcars and saloons that screamed like red parrots along their way. Through a million shriekings they ran back to their parlor, their blue light, their comfortable chairs, and their silence. I often thought of this. Late at night I felt if I put out my hand, in the dark of my own bedroom, I might feel adobe and hear a cricket and a river running by under the moon and someone singing softly to a faint guitar.

Late one December evening the next-door tenement burned. Flames roared at the sky, bricks fell in avalanches, and sparks littered the roof where the quiet mice lived.

I pounded their door.

"Fire!" I cried. "Fire!"

They sat motionless in their blue-lighted room.

I pounded violently. "You *hear?* Fire!"

The fire engines arrived. They gushed water into the

tenement. More bricks fell. Four of them smashed holes in the little house. I climbed to the roof, extinguished the small fires there, and scrambled down, my face dirty and my hands cut. The door to the little house opened. The quiet little Mexican and his wife stood in the doorway, solid and unmoved.

"Let me in!" I cried. "There's a hole in your roof; some sparks may have fallen in your bedroom!"

I pulled the door wide, pushed past them.

"No!" the little man grunted.

"Ah!" The little woman ran in a circle like a broken toy.

I was inside with a flashlight. The little man seized my arm.

I smelled his breath.

And then my flashlight shot through the rooms of their house. Light sparkled on a hundred wine bottles standing in the hall, two hundred bottles shelved in the kitchen, six dozen along the parlor wallboards, more of the same on bedroom bureaus and in closets. I do not know if I was more impressed with the hole in the bedroom ceiling or the endless glitter of so many bottles. I lost count. It was like an invasion of gigantic shining beetles, struck dead, deposited, and left by some ancient disease.

In the bedroom I felt the little man and woman behind me in the doorway. I heard their loud breathing and I could feel their eyes. I raised the beam of my flashlight away from the glittering bottles, I focused it carefully, and for the rest of my visit, on the hole in the yellow ceiling.

The little woman began to cry. She cried softly. Nobody moved.

The next morning they left.

Before we even knew they were going, they were half down the alley at 6 A.M., carrying their luggage, which was light enough to be entirely empty. I tried to stop them. I talked to them. They were old friends, I said. Nothing had changed, I said. They had nothing to do with the fire, I said, or the roof. They were innocent bystanders, I *insisted!* I would fix the roof myself, no charge, no charge to them! But they did not look at me. They looked at the house and at the open end of the alley ahead of them while I talked. Then, when I stopped they nodded to the alley as if agreeing that it was time to go, and walked off, and then began to run, it seemed, away from me, toward the street where there were streetcars and buses and automobiles and many loud avenues stretching in a maze. They hurried proudly, though, heads up, not looking back.

It was only by accident I ever met them again. At Christmas time, one evening, I saw the little man running quietly along the twilight street ahead of me. On a personal whim I followed. When he turned, I turned. At last, five blocks away from our old neighborhood, he scratched quietly at the door of a little white house. I saw the door open, shut, and lock him in. As night settled over the tenement city, a small light burned like blue mist in the tiny living room as I passed. I thought I saw, but probably imagined, two silhouettes there, he on his side of the room in his own particular chair, and she on her side of the room, sitting, sitting in the dark, and one or two bottles beginning to collect on the floor behind the chairs, and not a sound, not a sound between them. Only the silence.

I did not go up and knock. I strolled by. I walked on along the avenue, listening to the parrot cafés scream. I bought a newspaper, a magazine, and a quarter-edition book. Then I went home to where all the lights were lit and there was warm food upon the table.

The Small Assassin

Just when the idea occurred to her that she was being murdered she could not tell. There had been little subtle signs, little suspicions for the past month; things as deep as sea tides in her, like looking at a perfectly calm stretch of tropic water, wanting to bathe in it and finding, just as the tide takes your body, that monsters dwell just under the surface, things unseen, bloated, many-armed sharp-finned, malignant and inescapable.

A room floated around her in an effluvium of hysteria. Sharp instruments hovered and there were voices, and people in sterile white masks.

My name, she thought, what is it?

Alice Leiber. It came to her. David Leiber's wife. But it gave her no comfort. She was alone with these silent, whispering white people and there was great pain and nausea and death-fear in her.

I am being murdered before their eyes. These doctors, these nurses don't realize what hidden thing has happened to me. David doesn't know. Nobody knows except me and —the killer, the little murderer, the small assassin.

I am dying and I can't tell them now. They'd laugh and call me one in delirium. They'll see the murderer and hold him and never think him responsible for my death. But here I am, in front of God and man, dying, no one to believe my story, everyone to doubt me, comfort me with lies, bury me in ignorance, mourn me and salvage my destroyer.

Where is David? she wondered. In the waiting room, smoking one cigarette after another, listening to the long tickings of the very slow clock?

Sweat exploded from all of her body at once, and with it an agonized cry. Now. Now! Try and kill me, she screamed. Try, try, but I won't die! I won't!

There was a hollowness. A vacuum. Suddenly the pain fell away. Exhaustion, and dusk came around. It was over. Oh, God! She plummeted down and struck a black nothingness which gave way to nothingness and nothingness and another and still another. . . .

Footsteps. Gentle, approaching footsteps.

Far away, a voice said, "She's asleep. Don't disturb her."

An odor of tweeds, a pipe, a certain shaving lotion. David was standing over her. And beyond him the immaculate smell of Dr. Jeffers.

She did not open her eyes. "I'm awake," she said, quietly. It was a surprise, a relief to be able to speak, to not be dead.

"Alice," someone said, and it was David beyond her closed eyes, holding her tired hands.

Would you like to meet the murderer, David? she thought. I hear your voice asking to see him, so there's nothing but for me to point him out to you.

David stood over her. She opened her eyes. The room came into focus. Moving a weak hand, she pulled aside a coverlet.

The murderer looked up at David Leiber with a small, red-faced, blue-eyed calm. Its eyes were deep and sparkling.

"Why!" cried David Leiber, smiling. "He's a *fine* baby!"

. . .

Dr. Jeffers was waiting for David Leiber the day he came to take his wife and new child home. He motioned Leiber to a chair in his office, gave him a cigar, lit one for himself, sat on the edge of his desk, puffing solemnly for a long moment. Then he cleared his throat, looked David Leiber straight on and said, "Your wife doesn't like her child, Dave."

"What!"

"It's been a hard thing for her. She'll need a lot of love this next year. I didn't say much at the time, but she was hysterical in the delivery room. The strange things she said —I won't repeat them. All I'll say is that she feels alien to the child. Now, this may simply be a thing we can clear up with one or two questions." He sucked on his cigar another moment, then said, "Is this child a 'wanted' child, Dave?"

"Why do you ask?"

"It's vital."

"Yes. Yes, it is a 'wanted' child. We planned it together. Alice was so happy, a year ago, when——"

"Mmmm—— That makes it more difficult. Because if the child was unplanned, it would be a simple case of a woman hating the idea of motherhood. That doesn't fit Alice." Dr. Jeffers took his cigar from his lips, rubbed his hand across his jaw. "It must be something else, then. Perhaps something buried in her childhood that's coming out now. Or it might be the simple temporary doubt and distrust of any mother who's gone through the unusual pain and near-death that Alice has. If so, then a little time should heal that. I thought I'd tell you, though, Dave. It'll help you be easy and tolerant with her if she says anything about—well—about wishing the child had been born dead. And if things don't go well, the three of you drop in on me. I'm always glad to see old friends, eh? Here, take another cigar along for—ah—for the baby."

It was a bright spring afternoon. Their car hummed along wide, tree-lined boulevards. Blue sky, flowers, a warm wind. Dave talked a lot, lit his cigar, talked some more. Alice answered directly, softly, relaxing a bit more as the trip progressed. But she held the baby not tightly or warmly or motherly enough to satisfy the queer ache in Dave's mind. She seemed to be merely carrying a porcelain figurine.

"Well," he said, at last. smiling. "What'll we name him?"

Alice Leiber watched green trees slide by. "Let's not decide yet. I'd rather wait until we get an exceptional name for him. Don't blow smoke in his face." Her sentences ran together with no change of tone. The last statement held no motherly reproof, no interest, no irritation. She just mouthed it and it was said.

The husband, disquieted, dropped the cigar from the window. "Sorry," he said.

The baby rested in the crook of his mother's arm, shadows of sun and tree changing his face. His blue eyes opened like fresh blue spring flowers. Moist noises came from the tiny, pink, elastic mouth.

Alice gave her baby a quick glance. Her husband felt her shiver against him.

"Cold?" he asked.

"A chill. Better raise the window, David."

It was more than a chill. He rolled the window slowly up.

Suppertime.

Dave had brought the child from the nursery, propped him at a tiny, bewildered angle, supported by many pillows, in a newly purchased high chair.

Alice watched her knife and fork move. "He's not high-chair size," she said.

"Fun having him here, anyway," said Dave, feeling fine. "Everything's fun. At the office, too. Orders up to my nose. If I don't watch myself I'll make another fifteen thousand this year. Hey, look at Junior, will you? Drooling all down his chin!" He reached over to wipe the baby's mouth with his napkin. From the corner of his eye he realized that Alice wasn't even watching. He finished the job.

"I guess it wasn't very interesting," he said, back again at his food. "But one would think a mother'd take some interest in her own child!"

Alice jerked her chin up. "Don't speak that way! Not in front of him! Later, if you must."

"Later?" he cried. "In front of, in back of, what's the difference?" He quieted suddenly, swallowed, was sorry. "All right. Okay. I know how it is."

After dinner she let him carry the baby upstairs. She didn't tell him to; she *let* him.

Coming down, he found her standing by the radio, listening to music she didn't hear. Her eyes were closed, her whole attitude one of wondering, self-questioning. She started when he appeared.

Suddenly, she was at him, against him, soft, quick; the same. Her lips found him, kept him. He was stunned. Now that the baby was gone, upstairs, out of the room, she began to breathe again, live again. She was free. She was whispering, rapidly, endlessly.

"Thank you, thank you, darling. For being yourself, always. Dependable, so very dependable!"

He had to laugh. "My father told me, 'Son, provide for your family!' "

Wearily, she rested her dark, shining hair against his neck. "You've overdone it. Sometimes I wish we were just the way we were when we were first married. No responsibilities, nothing but ourselves. No—no babies."

She crushed his hand in hers, a supernatural whiteness in her face.

"Oh, Dave, once it was just you and me. We protected each other, and now we protect the baby, but get no protection from it. Do you understand? Lying in the hospital I had time to think a lot of things. The world is evil—"

"Is it?"

"Yes. It is. But laws protect us from it. And when there aren't laws, then love does the protecting. You're protected from my hurting you, by my love. You're vulnerable to me, of all people, but love shields you. I feel no fear of you, because love cushions all your irritations, unnatural instincts, hatreds, and immaturities. But—what about the baby? It's too young to know love, or a law of love, or anything, until we teach it. And in the meantime we're vulnerable to it."

"Vulnerable to a baby?" He held her away and laughed gently.

"Does the baby know the difference between right and wrong?" she asked.

"No. But it'll learn."

"But a baby is so new, so amoral, so conscience-free." She stopped. Her arms dropped from him and she turned swiftly. "That noise? What was it?"

Leiber looked around the room. "I didn't hear——"

She stared at the library door. "In there," she said, slowly.

Leiber crossed the room, opened the door and switched the library lights on and off. "Not a thing." He came back to her. "You're worn out. To bed with you—right now."

Turning out the lights together, they walked slowly up the soundless hall stairs, not speaking. At the top she apologized. "My wild talk, darling. Forgive me. I'm exhausted."

He understood, and said so.

She paused, undecided, by the nursery door. Then she fingered the brass knob sharply, walked in. He watched her approach the crib much too carefully, look down, and stiffen as if she'd been struck in the face. "David!"

Leiber stepped forward, reached the crib.

The baby's face was bright red and very moist; his small pink mouth opened and shut, opened and shut; his eyes were a fiery blue. His hands leapt about on the air.

"Oh," said Dave, "he's just been crying."

"Has he?" Alice Leiber seized the crib-railing to balance herself. "I didn't hear him."

"The door was closed."

"Is that why he breathes so hard, why his face is red?"

"Sure. Poor little guy. Crying all alone in the dark. He can sleep in our room tonight, just in case he cries."

"You'll spoil him," his wife said.

Leiber felt her eyes follow as he rolled the crib into their bedroom. He undressed silently, sat on the edge of the bed. Suddenly he lifted his head, swore under his breath, snapped his fingers. "Damn it! Forgot to tell you. I must fly to Chicago Friday."

"Oh, David." Her voice was lost in the room.

"I've put this trip off for two months, and now it's so critical I just *have* to go."

"I'm afraid to be alone."

"We'll have the new cook by Friday. She'll be here all the time. I'll only be gone a few days."

"I'm afraid. I don't know of what. You wouldn't believe me if I told you. I guess I'm crazy."

He was in bed now. She darkened the room; he heard her walk around the bed, throw back the cover, slide in. He smelled the warm woman-smell of her next to him. He said, "If you want me to wait a few days, perhaps I could——"

"No," she said, unconvinced. "You go. I know it's important. It's just that I keep thinking about what I told you. Laws and love and protection. Love protects you from me. But, the baby——" She took a breath. "What protects you from him, David?"

Before he could answer, before he could tell her how silly it was, speaking of infants, she switched on the bed light, abruptly.

"Look," she said, pointing.

The baby lay wide-awake in its crib, staring straight at him, with deep, sharp blue eyes.

The lights went out again. She trembled against him.

"It's not nice being afraid of the thing you birthed." Her whisper lowered, became harsh, fierce, swift. "He tried to kill me! He lies there, listens to us talking, waiting for you to go away so he can try to kill me again! I swear it!" Sobs broke from her.

"Please," he kept saying, soothing her. "Stop it, stop it. Please."

She cried in the dark for a long time. Very late she relaxed, shakingly, against him. Her breathing came soft, warm, regular, her body twitched its worn reflexes and she slept.

He drowsed.

And just before his eyes lidded wearily down, sinking him into deeper and yet deeper tides, he heard a strange little sound of awareness and awakeness in the room.

The sound of small, moist, pinkly elastic lips.

The baby.

And then—sleep.

In the morning, the sun blazed. Alice smiled.

David Leiber dangled his watch over the crib. "See, baby? Something bright. Something pretty. Sure. Sure. Something bright. Something pretty."

Alice smiled. She told him to go ahead, fly to Chicago, she'd be very brave, no need to worry. She'd take care of the baby. Oh, yes, she'd take care of him, all right.

The airplane went east. There was a lot of sky, a lot of sun and clouds and Chicago running over the horizon. Dave was dropped into the rush of ordering, planning, banqueting, telephoning, arguing in conference. But he wrote letters each day and sent telegrams to Alice and the baby.

On the evening of his sixth day away from home he received the long-distance phone call. Los Angeles.

"Alice?"

"No, Dave. This is Jeffers speaking."

"Doctor!"

"Hold on to yourself, son. Alice is sick. You'd better get the next plane home. It's pneumonia. I'll do everything I can, boy. If only it wasn't so soon after the baby. She needs strength."

Leiber dropped the phone into its cradle. He got up, with no feet under him, and no hands and no body. The hotel room blurred and fell apart.

"Alice," he said, blindly starting for the door.

The propellers spun about, whirled, fluttered, stopped; time and space were put behind. Under his hand, David felt the doorknob turn; under his feet the floor assumed reality, around him flowed the walls of a bedroom, and in the late-afternoon sunlight Dr. Jeffers stood, turning from a window, as Alice lay waiting in her bed, something carved from a fall of winter snow. Then Dr. Jeffers was talking, talking continuously, gently, the sound rising and falling through the lamplight, a soft flutter, a white murmur of voice.

"Your wife's too good a mother, Dave. She worried more about the baby than herself. . . ."

Somewhere in the paleness of Alice's face, there was a sudden constriction which smoothed itself out before it was realized. Then, slowly, half-smiling, she began to talk and she talked as a mother should about this, that and the other thing, the telling detail, the minute-by-minute and hour-by-hour report of a mother concerned with a doll-house world and the miniature life of that world. But she could not stop; the spring was wound tight, and her voice rushed on to anger, fear and the faintest touch of revulsion, which did not change Dr. Jeffers' expression, but caused Dave's heart to match the rhythm of this talk that quickened and could not stop:

"The baby wouldn't sleep. I thought he was sick. He just lay, staring, in his crib, and late at night he'd cry. So loud he'd cry, and he'd cry all night and all night. I couldn't quiet him, and I couldn't rest."

Dr. Jeffers' head nodded slowly, slowly. "Tired herself right into pneumonia. But she's full of sulfa now and on the safe side of the whole damn thing."

David felt ill. "The baby, what about the baby?"

"Fit as a fiddle; cock of the walk!"

"Thanks, Doctor."

The doctor walked off away and down the stairs, opened the front door faintly, and was gone.

"David!"

He turned to her frightened whisper.

"It was the baby again." She clutched his hand. "I try to lie to myself and say that I'm a fool, but the baby knew I was weak from the hospital, so he cried all night every night, and when he wasn't crying he'd be much too quiet.

I knew if I switched on the light he'd be there, staring up at me."

David felt his body close in on itself like a fist. He remembered seeing the baby, feeling the baby, awake in the dark, awake very late at night when babies should be asleep. Awake and lying there, silent as thought, not crying, but watching from its crib. He thrust the thought aside. It was insane.

Alice went on. "I was going to kill the baby. Yes, I was. When you'd been gone only a day on your trip I went to his room and put my hands about his neck; and I stood there, for a long time, thinking, afraid. Then I put the covers up over his face and turned him over on his face and pressed him down and left him that way and ran out of the room."

He tried to stop her.

"No, let me finish," she said, hoarsely, looking at the wall. "When I left his room I thought, It's simple. Babies smother every day. No one'll ever know. But when I came back to see him dead, David, he was alive! Yes, alive, turned over on his back, alive and smiling and breathing. And I couldn't touch him again after that. I left him there and I didn't come back, not to feed him or look at him or do anything. Perhaps the cook tended to him. I don't know. All I know is that his crying kept me awake, and I thought all through the night, and walked around the rooms and now I'm sick." She was almost finished now. "The baby lies there and thinks of ways to kill me. Simple ways. Because he knows I know so much about him. I have no love for him; there is no protection between us; there never will be."

She was through. She collapsed inward on herself and finally slept. David Leiber stood for a long time over her, not able to move. His blood was frozen in his body, not a cell stirred anywhere, anywhere at all.

The next morning there was only one thing to do. He did it. He walked into Dr. Jeffers' office and told him the whole thing, and listened to Jeffers' tolerant replies:

"Let's take this thing slowly, son. It's quite natural for mothers to hate their children, sometimes. We have a label for it—ambivalence. The ability to hate, while loving. Lovers hate each other, frequently. Children detest their mothers——"

Leiber interrupted. "I never hated my mother."

"You won't admit it, naturally. People don't enjoy admitting hatred for their loved ones."

"So Alice hates her baby."

"Better say she has an obsession. She's gone a step further than plain, ordinary ambivalence. A Caesarean operation brought the child into the world and almost took Alice out of it. She blames the child for her near-death and her pneumonia. She's projecting her troubles, blaming them on the handiest object she can use as a source of blame. We *all* do it. We stumble into a chair and curse the furniture, not our own clumsiness. We miss a golf-stroke and damn the turf or our club, or the make of ball. If our business fails we blame the gods, the weather, our luck. All I can tell you is what I told you before. Love her. Finest medicine in the world. Find little ways of showing your affection, give her security. Find ways of showing her how harmless and innocent the child is. Make her feel that the baby was worth the risk. After a while, she'll settle down, forget about death, and begin to love the child. If she doesn't come around in the next month or so, ask me. I'll recommend a good psychiatrist. Go on along now, and take that look off your face."

When summer came, things seemed to settle, become easier. Dave worked, immersed himself in office detail, but found much time for his wife. She, in turn, took long walks, gained strength, played an occasional light game of badminton. She rarely burst out any more. She seemed to have rid herself of her fears.

Except on one certain midnight when a sudden summer wind swept around the house, warm and swift, shaking the trees like so many shining tambourines. Alice wakened, trembling, and slid over into her husband's arms, and let him console her, and ask her what was wrong.

She said, "Something's here in the room, watching us."

He switched on the light. "Dreaming again," he said. "You're better, though. Haven't been troubled for a long time."

She sighed as he clicked off the light again, and suddenly she slept. He held her, considering what a sweet, weird creature she was, for about half an hour.

He heard the bedroom door sway open a few inches.

There was nobody at the door. No reason for it to come open. The wind had died.

He waited. It seemed like an hour he lay silently, in the dark.

Then, far away, wailing like some small meteor dying in the vast inky gulf of space, the baby began to cry in his nursery.

It was a small, lonely sound in the middle of the stars and the dark and the breathing of this woman in his arms and the wind beginning to sweep through the trees again.

Leiber counted to one hundred, slowly. The crying continued.

Carefully disengaging Alice's arm he slipped from bed, put on his slippers, robe, and moved quietly from the room.

He'd go downstairs, he thought, fix some warm milk, bring it up, and——

The blackness dropped out from under him. His foot slipped and plunged. Slipped on something soft. Plunged into nothingness.

He thrust his hands out, caught frantically at the railing. His body stopped falling. He held. He cursed.

The "something soft" that had caused his feet to slip rustled and thumped down a few steps. His head rang. His heart hammered at the base of his throat, thick and shot with pain.

Why do careless people leave things strewn about a house? He groped carefully with his fingers for the object that had almost spilled him headlong down the stairs.

His hand froze, startled. His breath went in. His heart held one or two beats.

The thing he held in his hand was a toy. A large, cumbersome, patchwork doll he had bought as a joke, for——
For the baby.

Alice drove him to work the next day.

She slowed the car halfway downtown, pulled to the curb and stopped it. Then she turned on the seat and looked at her husband.

"I want to go away on a vacation. I don't know if you can make it now, darling, but if not, please let me go alone. We can get someone to take care of the baby, I'm sure. But I just have to get away. I thought I was growing out of this—this *feeling*. But I haven't. I can't stand being in the room with him. He looks up at me as if he hates me, too. I can't put my finger on it; all I know is I want to get away before something happens."

He got out on his side of the car, came around, motioned to her to move over, got in. "The only thing you're going to do is see a good psychiatrist. And if he suggests a vacation, well, okay. But this can't go on; my stomach's in knots all the time." He started the car. "I'll drive the rest of the way."

Her head was down; she was trying to keep back tears. She looked up when they reached his office building. "All right. Make the appointment. I'll go talk to anyone you want, David."

He kissed her. "Now, you're talking sense, lady. Think you can drive home okay?"

"Of course, silly."

"See you at supper, then. Drive carefully."

"Don't I always? 'Bye."

He stood on the curb, watching her drive off, the wind taking hold of her long, dark, shining hair. Upstairs, a minute later, he phoned Jeffers and arranged an appointment with a reliable neuropsychiatrist.

The day's work went uneasily. Things fogged over; and

in the fog he kept seeing Alice lost and calling his name. So much of her fear had come over to him. She actually had him convinced that the child was in some ways not quite natural.

He dictated long, uninspired letters. He checked some shipments downstairs. Assistants had to be questioned, and kept going. At the end of the day he was exhausted, his head throbbed, and he was very glad to go home.

On the way down in the elevator he wondered, What if I told Alice about the toy—that patchwork doll I slipped on, on the stairs last night? Lord, wouldn't *that* back her off? No, I won't ever tell her. Accidents are, after all, accidents.

Daylight lingered in the sky as he drove home in a taxi. In front of the house he paid the driver and walked slowly up the cement walk, enjoying the light that was still in the sky and the trees. The white colonial front of the house looked unnaturally silent and uninhabited, and then, quietly, he remembered this was Thursday, and the hired help they were able to obtain from time to time were all gone for the day.

He took a deep breath of air. A bird sang behind the house. Traffic moved on the boulevard a block away. He twisted the key in the door. The knob turned under his fingers, oiled, silent.

The door opened. He stepped in, put his hat on the chair with his briefcase, started to shrug out of his coat, when he looked up.

Late sunlight streamed down the stairwell from the window near the top of the hall. Where the sunlight touched, it took on the bright color of the patchwork doll sprawled at the bottom of the stairs.

But he paid no attention to the toy.

He could only look, and not move, and look again at Alice.

Alice lay in a broken, grotesque, pallid gesturing and angling of her thin body, at the bottom of the stairs, like a crumpled doll that doesn't want to play any more, ever.

Alice was dead.

The house remained quiet, except for the sound of his heart.

She was dead.

He held her head in his hands, he felt her fingers. He held her body. But she wouldn't live. She wouldn't even try to live. He said her name, out loud, many times, and he tried, once again, by holding her to him, to give her back some of the warmth she had lost, but that didn't help.

He stood up. He must have made a phone call. He didn't remember. He found himself, suddenly, upstairs. He opened the nursery door and walked inside and stared blankly at the crib. His stomach was sick. He couldn't see very well.

The baby's eyes were closed, but his face was red, moist with perspiration, as if he'd been crying long and hard.

"She's dead," said Leiber to the baby. "She's dead."

Then he started laughing low and soft and continuously for a long time until Dr. Jeffers walked in out of the night and slapped him again and again across his face.

"Snap out of it! Pull yourself together!"

"She fell down the stairs, Doctor. She tripped on a patchwork doll and fell. I almost slipped on it the other night, myself. And now——"

The doctor shook him.

"Doc, Doc, Doc," said Dave, hazily. "Funny thing. Funny. I—I finally thought of a name for the baby."

The doctor said nothing.

Leiber put his head back in his trembling hands and spoke the words. "I'm going to have him christened next Sunday. Know what name I'm giving him? I'm going to call him Lucifer."

It was eleven at night. A lot of strange people had come and gone through the house, taking the essential flame with them—Alice.

David Leiber sat across from the doctor in the library.

"Alice wasn't crazy," he said, slowly. "She had good reason to fear the baby."

Jeffers exhaled. "Don't follow after her! She blamed the child for her sickness, now you blame it for her death. She stumbled on a toy, remember that. You can't blame the child."

"You mean Lucifer?"

"Stop calling him that!"

Leiber shook his head. "Alice heard things at night, moving in the halls. You want to know what made those noises, Doctor? They were made by the baby. Four months old, moving in the dark, listening to us talk. Listening to every word!" He held to the sides of the chair. "And if I turned the lights on, a baby is so small. It can hide behind furniture, a door, against a wall—below eye-level."

"I want you to stop this!" said Jeffers.

"Let me say what I think or I'll go crazy. When I went to Chicago, who was it kept Alice awake, tiring her into pneumonia? The baby! And when Alice didn't die, then he tried killing me. It was simple; leave a toy on the stairs, cry in the night until your father goes downstairs to fetch your milk, and stumbles. A crude trick, but effective. It didn't get me. But it killed Alice dead."

David Leiber stopped long enough to light a cigarette. "I should have caught on. I'd turn on the lights in the middle of the night, many nights, and the baby'd be lying there, eyes wide. Most babies sleep all the time. Not this one. He stayed awake, thinking."

"Babies don't think."

"He stayed awake doing whatever he *could* do with his brain, then. What in hell do we know about a baby's mind? He had every reason to hate Alice; she suspected him for what he was—certainly not a normal child. Something—different. What do you know of babies, Doctor? The general run, yes. You know, of course, how babies kill their mothers at birth. Why? Could it be resentment at being forced into a lousy world like this one?"

Leiber leaned toward the doctor, tiredly. "It all ties up. Suppose that a few babies out of all the millions born are instantaneously able to move, see, hear, think, like many animals and insects can. Insects are born self-sufficient. In a few weeks most mammals and birds adjust. But children take years to speak and learn to stumble around on their weak legs.

"But suppose one child in a billion is—strange? Born perfectly aware, able to think, instinctively. Wouldn't it be a perfect setup, a perfect blind for anything the baby might want to do? He could pretend to be ordinary, weak, crying, ignorant. With just a *little* expenditure of energy he could crawl about a darkened house, listening. And how easy to place obstacles at the top of stairs. How easy to cry all night and tire a mother into pneumonia. How easy, right at birth, to be so close to the mother that *a few deft maneuvers might cause peritonitis!*"

"For God's sake!" Jeffers was on his feet. "That's a repulsive thing to say!"

"It's a repulsive thing I'm speaking of. How many mothers have died at the birth of their children? How many have suckled strange little improbabilities who cause death one way or another? Strange, red little creatures with brains that work in a bloody darkness we can't even guess at. Elemental little brains, aswarm with racial memory, hatred, and raw cruelty, with no more thought than self-preservation. And self-preservation in this case consisted of eliminating a mother who realized what a horror she had birthed. I ask you, Doctor, what is there in the world more selfish than a baby? Nothing!"

Jeffers scowled and shook his head, helplessly.

Leiber dropped his cigarette down. "I'm not claiming any great strength for the child. Just enough to crawl around a little, a few months ahead of schedule. Just enough to listen all the time. Just enough to cry late at night. That's enough, more than enough."

Jeffers tried ridicule. "Call it murder, then. But murder must be motivated. What motive had the child?"

Leiber was ready with the answer. "What is more at

peace, more dreamfully content, at ease, at rest, fed, comforted, unbothered, than an unborn child? Nothing. It floats in a sleepy, timeless wonder of nourishment and silence. Then, suddenly, it is asked to give up its berth, is forced to vacate, rushed out into a noisy, uncaring, selfish world where it is asked to shift for itself, to hunt, to feed from the hunting, to seek after a vanishing love that once was its unquestionable right, to meet confusion instead of inner silence and conservative slumber! And the child *resents* it! Resents the cold air, the huge spaces, the sudden departure from familiar things. And in the tiny filament of brain the only thing the child knows is selfishness and hatred because the spell has been rudely shattered. Who is responsible for this disenchantment, this rude breaking of the spell? The mother. So here the new child has someone to hate with all its unreasoning mind. The mother has cast it out, rejected it. And the father is no better, kill him, too! He's responsible in *his* way!"

Jeffers interrupted. "If what you say is true, then every woman in the world would have to look on her baby as something to dread, something to wonder about."

"And why not? Hasn't the child a perfect alibi? A thousand years of accepted medical belief protects him. By all natural accounts he is helpless, not responsible. The child is born hating. And things grow worse, instead of better. At first the baby gets a certain amount of attention and mothering. But then as time passes, things change. When very new, a baby has the power to make parents do silly things when it cries or sneezes, jump when it makes a noise. As the years pass, the baby feels even that small power slip rapidly, forever away, never to return. Why shouldn't it grasp all the power it can have? Why shouldn't it jockey for position while it has all the advantages? In later years it would be too late to express its hatred. *Now* would be the time to strike."

Leiber's voice was very soft, very low.

"My little boy baby, lying in his crib nights, his face moist and red and out of breath. From crying? No. From climbing slowly out of his crib, from crawling long distances through darkened hallways. My little boy baby. I want to kill him."

The doctor handed him a water glass and some pills. "You're not killing anyone. You're going to sleep for twenty-four hours. Sleep'll change your mind. Take this."

Leiber drank down the pills and let himself be led upstairs to his bedroom, crying, and felt himself being put to bed. The doctor waited until he was moving deep into sleep, then left the house.

Leiber, alone, drifted down, down.

He heard a noise. "What's—what's *that?*" he demanded, feebly.

Something moved in the hall.

David Leiber slept.

Very early the next morning, Dr. Jeffers drove up to the house. It was a good morning, and he was here to drive Leiber to the country for a rest. Leiber would still be asleep upstairs. Jeffers had given him enough sedative to knock him out for at least fifteen hours.

He rang the doorbell. No answer. The servants were probably not up. Jeffers tried the front door, found it open, stepped in. He put his medical kit on the nearest chair.

Something white moved out of sight at the top of the stairs. Just a suggestion of a movement. Jeffers hardly noticed it.

The smell of gas was in the house.

Jeffers ran upstairs, crashed into Leiber's bedroom.

Leiber lay motionless on the bed, and the room billowed with gas, which hissed from a released jet at the base of the wall near the door. Jeffers twisted it off, then forced up all the windows and ran back to Leiber's body.

The body was cold. It had been dead quite a few hours.

Coughing violently, the doctor hurried from the room, eyes watering. Leiber hadn't turned on the gas himself. He *couldn't* have. Those sedatives had knocked him out, he wouldn't have wakened until noon. It wasn't suicide. Or was there the faintest possibility?

Jeffers stood in the hall for five minutes. Then he

walked to the door of the nursery. It was shut. He opened it. He walked inside and to the crib.

The crib was empty.

He stood swaying by the crib for half a minute, then he said something to nobody in particular.

"The nursery door blew shut. You couldn't get back into your crib where it was safe. You didn't plan on the door blowing shut. A little thing like a slammed door can ruin the best of plans. I'll find you somewhere in the house, hiding, pretending to be something you are not."

The doctor looked dazed. He put his hand to his head and smiled palely. "Now I'm talking like Alice and David talked. But, I can't take any chances. I'm not sure of anything, but I can't take any chances."

He walked downstairs, opened his medical bag on the chair, took something out of it and held it in his hands.

Something rustled down the hall. Something very small and very quiet. Jeffers turned rapidly.

I had to operate to bring you into this world, he thought. Now I guess I can operate to take you out of it. . . .

He took half-a-dozen slow, sure steps forward into the hall. He raised his hand into the sunlight.

"See, baby! Something bright—something pretty!"

A scalpel.

The Anthem
Sprinters

"Do you doubt——? the Connemara Runners are best!"

"No! The Galway Cinema Ramblers!"

"The Waterford Shoes!"

These words, sprung out on the smoky air in a great commotion of tongues, ricocheted off the bar mirrors, passed undiminished through hiss of spigot, clink of glass and a great fish-scaling of coins, to reach me at the far rim of the crowd.

Alert, I turned my ear.

"When it comes to that, the Dear Patriots are the men——"

"The Queen's Own Evaders! No finer team e'er took the incline. Their reflex: uncanny. Of course, here in Dublin, our grandest man is Doone."

"Doone, hell! Hoolihan!"

The argument raged above the tenor's singing, the concertinas dying hard in the Four Provinces saloon at the top of Grafton Street in the heart of Dublin. The argument was all the more violent because it was getting on late at night. With the clock nearing 10, there was the sure threat of everything going shut at once, meaning ale taps, accordions, piano lids, soloists, trios, quartets, pubs, sweetshops and cinemas. In a great heave like the Day of Judgment, half Dublin's population would be thrown out into raw lamplight, there to find themselves wanting in gum-machine mirrors. Stunned, their moral and physical sustenance plucked from them, the souls would wander like battered moths for a moment, then wheel about for home. All the more reason, then, for fiery arguments to warm the blood against the cold.

"Doone!"

"Doone, my hat! Hoolihan!"

At which point the smallest, loudest man, turning, saw the curiosity enshrined in my all-too-open face and shouted:

"You're American, of course! And wondering what we're up to? Would you bet on a mysterious sporting event of great local consequence? Nod once, and come here!"

I nodded, smiled and strolled my Guinness through the uproar and jostle as one violinist gave up destroying a tune, and an old man took his hands out of the piano's mouth and hurried over.

"Name's Timulty!" The little man gripped my hand.

"Douglas," I said. "I write for motion pictures."

"Fillums!" gasped everyone.

"Films," I admitted, modestly.

"It staggers belief!" Timulty seized me tighter. "You'll be the best judge in history. In sports now, do you know the cross-country, 440 and such man-on-foot excursions?"

"I have personally witnessed two complete Olympic Games."

"Not just fillums, but the world competition." Timulty grabbed his friends for support. "Then, good grief, surely you've heard of the special all-Irish decathlon event which has to do with picture theaters?"

"I've heard only what I take to be the names of teams, tonight."

"Hear more, then! Hoolihan!"

An even littler fellow, pocketing his wet harmonica, leapt forward, beaming. "Hoolihan. That's me. The best anthem sprinter in all Ireland!"

"*What* sprinter?" I asked.

"A-n-t-" spelled Hoolihan, much too carefully, "-h-e-m. Anthem. Sprinter. The fastest."

"Have you been to the Dublin cinemas?" asked Timulty.

"Last night," I said. "I saw a Clark Gable film. Night before, an old Charles Laughton. Night before *that*——"

"Enough! You're fanatic, as are all the Irish. If it weren't for cinemas and pubs to keep the poor and workless off the street or in their cups, we'd have pulled the cork and let the isle sink long ago. Well!" He clapped his hands. "When the picture ends each night, have you observed a peculiarity of the breed?"

"End of the picture?" I mused. "Hold on. You can't mean the national anthem, can you?"

"*Can* we, boys?" cried Timulty.

"We can!" cried all.

"Any night, every night, for tens of dreadful years, at the end of each damn fillum, as if you'd never heard the baleful tune before," grieved Timulty, "the orchestra strikes up for Ireland. And what happens *then?*"

"Why," said I, falling in with it, "if you're any man at all, you try to get out of the theater in those few precious moments between THE END of the film and the start of the anthem."

"Buy the Yank a drink!"

"After all," I said, "I'm in Dublin four months now. The anthem has begun to pale. No disrespect meant."

"And none taken!" said Timulty. "But, breathing the same air 10,000 times makes the senses reel. So, as you've noted, in that God-sent three- or four-second interval, any audience in its right mind beats it the hell out. And the best of the crowd is——"

"Doone," I said. "Or Hoolihan. Your anthem sprinters!"

They smiled at me. I smiled at them.

We were all so proud of my intuition, that I bought them a round of Guinness.

"Here's to"—I lifted my glass—"the Connemara Runners——?"

"Right!"

"The Galway Cinema Ramblers? The Waterford Shoes?"

"Don't forget the Dear Patriots, and the finest out-of-the-country team of them all, the Queen's Own Evaders," said Timulty.

"Let me guess," said I. "With a name like that, the Evaders must be Irish living in London, who run extra fast so as not to be in the theater when 'God Save the Queen' is played!"

Licking the suds from our lips, we regarded each other with benevolence.

"Now," said Timulty, his voice husky with emotion, his eyes squinted off at the scene, "at this very moment, 100 yards down the hill in the dark of the Grafton Street theater, seated in the fourth row center is——"

"Doone," said I.

"The man's eerie." Hoolihan tipped his cap to me.

"Doone's there all right, seeing the Deanna Durbin fillum brought back by the asking. And in just 10 minutes the cinema will be letting the customers out. Now, if we should send Hoolihan here in for a speed and agility test, Doone would be quick to the challenge."

"He's not at the show just for the anthem sprint, is he?"

"Good grief, no. It's the Deanna Durbin songs. Doone plays piano here, for sustenance. But, casually noting the entrance of his competitor Hoolihan, who will be conspicuous by his late arrival just across the aisle, well, Doone would know what was up. Saluting each other, they would listen to the dear music until FINIS hove in sight."

"Sure—" Hoolihan danced lightly on his toes, flexing his elbows. "Let me at him, let me *at* him!"

Timulty peered close at me. "Sir, I observe your bewildered disbelief. How is it, you ask, full-grown men have time for such as this? Well, time is the one thing the Irish have in oversupply. With no jobs at hand, what's minor in your country must be made to look major in ours. We have never seen the elephant, but we've learned a bug under a microscope is the greatest beast on earth. So, while it hasn't left the Isles, the anthem sprint's a high-blooded sport. Now, introductions are in order. Here's Fogarty, exit-watcher supreme!"

Fogarty jumped forward, dark eyes piercing left and right.

"Nolan and Clannery, aisle-superintendent judges!"

The two men, called, linked arms and bowed.

"Clancy, timekeeper. And general spectators: O'Neill, Bannion and the Kelly boys, count 'em! Come on!"

I felt as if a vast street-cleaning machine, one of those brambled monsters all mustache and scouring brush, had seized me and now floated me out down the hill toward the multiplicity of little blinking lights where the cinema lured us on.

"Now listen to the rules!" shouted Timulty, hustling beside me. "The essential thing is theaters, of course!"

"Of course!" I yelled back.

"There be the liberal, free-thinking theaters with grand aisles, grand lobbies, exists, and even grander, more spacious latrines. Some with so much porcelain the echoes alone put you in shock. Then there's the parsimonious mousetrap cinemas with aisles that squeeze the breath from you, seats that knock your knees, and doors best sidled out of on your way to the GENTS' in the sweetshop across the alley. Each theater is carefully assessed before, during and after a sprint, so a man is judged by whether the carpets are worn and trip him, and if there's men and women en masse, or mostly men or mostly women to fight his way through. The worst, of course, is children at the flypaper matinées. The temptation with kids is to lay into them as you'd harvest hay, tossing them like windrows to left and right. So we've stopped that. Now mostly it's nights, here at the Grafton!"

The mob stopped. The twinkling marquee lights sparkled in our eyes and flushed our cheeks rosy.

"The ideal cinema," sighed Fogarty.

"Because . . ." explained Clannery, "its aisles are not too wide nor too narrow, its exits well-placed, the door hinges oiled; the crowds a proper mixture of sporting-bloods and folk who mind to leap aside should a sprinter, squandering his energy, come vaulting up the aisle."

I had a sudden thought. "Do you—handicap your runners?"

"Strange you'd speak of that. Sometimes by shifting exits, when the old are too well known. Or seat one chap in the sixth, another in the third row. And if a man turns terrible feverish swift, we add the greatest known handicap of all——"

"Drink . . . ?" I wondered.

"What else? Doone, being fleet, is a two-handicap man. Nolan!" Timulty flourished a bottle. "Run this in. Make Doone take two swigs. *Big* ones."

Nolan ran.

Timulty pointed. "While Hoolihan here, having already wandered through all Four Provinces of the pub this night, is amply weighted. Even all!"

"Go now, Hoolihan," said Fogarty. "'Let our money be a light burden on you. Burst out that exit, five minutes from now, victorious and first!"

"Synchronize watches!" said Clancy.

"Synchronize my back-behind," said Timulty. "Which of us has more than dirty wrists to stare at? You alone, Clancy, have the time. Hoolihan, inside!"

Hoolihan shook hands with all, as if leaving to tour the world. Waving, he vanished in cinema dark.

Nolan came running back out with an empty bottle.

"Doone's handicapped."

"Good! Now, Clannery, Nolan, check and be sure the sprinters sit opposite each other in the fourth row, caps on, coats half buttoned, scarves furled."

Nolan and Clannery ducked in.

"Two minutes!" announced Clancy. "In two minutes it's——"

"Post time," I said.

"You're a dear lad," admitted Timulty.

Nolan and Clannery hotfooted out.

"All set! Right seats, everything!"

" 'Tis almost over! You can tell. Toward the end of any fillum," confided Clannery, "the music has a way of getting out of hand."

"It's loud," agreed Nolan. "Full orchestra and chorus behind the singing maid. I must come for the entirety tomorrow. Lovely."

"Is it?" said everyone. "What's the tune?"

"Ah, off with the tune!" shouted Timulty. "One minute to go and you ask the tune? Lay the bets. Who's for Doone, who Hoolihan?"

In the multitudinous jabbering and passing about of paper and shillings, I held out four bob.

"Doone," I said.

"Without having *seen* him?"

"A dark horse," I whispered.

"Well said! Clannery, Nolan, inside, watch sharp there's no jumping the FINIS."

In went Clannery and Nolan, happy as boy-dogs.

"Make an aisle; Yank, you over here, with me!"

The men rushed to form a rough aisle on each side of the two closed main-exit doors.

"Fogarty, lay your ear to the door!"

Fogarty did; his eyes widened.

"The damn music's *extra* loud!"

One of the Kelly boys nudged his brother. "It will be over soon. Whoever's to die is dying this moment. Whoever's to live is bending over him."

"Louder still!" Fogarty, eyes shut, head pressed to the panel, twitched his hands as if to adjust a radio. "There! The grand ta-ta that comes just as FINIS or THE END jumps on screen!"

"They're off!" I murmured.

"Stand back!" cried Timulty.

We all stared at the door.

"There's the anthem! Tenshun!"

We all stood erect, still staring.

"I hear feet running!" gasped Fogarty.

"Whoever it is had a good start before the anthem——"

The door burst wide.

Hoolihan plunged into view, smiling such a smile as only breathless victors know.

"Hoolihan!" cried the winners.

"Doone!" groaned the losers. "Where's Doone?"

For, while Hoolihan was first, his competitor was nowhere in the soon dispersed and vanished crowd.

"The idiot didn't come out the wrong door——?"

Timulty ventured into the empty lobby.

"Doone?"

No answer.

Someone flung the GENTS'-room door wide.

"Doone?"

Not an echo.

"Babe in the manger," hissed Timulty. "Can it be he's broken a leg and is fallen in there somewhere with the mortal agonies?"

"That's *it!*"

The island of men changed gravities and heaved now toward and through the inner door, down the aisle, I jumping in the air twice to see over the mob's head. It was dim in the vast theater.

"Doone!"

At last we were bunched together near the fourth row on the aisle, exclaiming at what we saw.

Doone, still seated, his hands folded, his eyes shut.

Dead?

None of that.

A tear, large, luminous and beautiful, fell on his cheek. His chin was wet. It was sure he had been crying for some minutes.

The men peered into his face, circling, leaning.

"Doone, are ya sick? What?"

"Ah, God," cried Doone. He shook himself to find the strength, somewhere, to speak.

"Ah, God," he said at last, "she has the voice of an angel."

"Angel!!!?"

"That one up there." He nodded.

We all turned to stare at the empty silver screen.

"Is it Deanna Durbin . . . ?"

Doone sobbed. "The dear dead voice of me grandmother——"

"Your grandma's underside!" exclaimed Timulty. "She'd no such voice as that!"

"You mean to say," I interrupted, "it was just the Durbin girl kept you from the sprint?"

"Just!" Doone blew his nose and dabbed his eyes. "Just! Why, it would be sacrilege to bound from a cinema after such a recital. You might as well jump across the altar at a wedding or waltz about at a funeral!"

"You could've at least warned us it was no contest," said Timulty.

"How could I? It just crept over me in a divine sickness. That last bit she sang, 'The Lovely Isle of Innisfree,' was it not, Clannery?"

"What else did she sing?" asked Fogarty.

"What *else* did she sing?" cried Timulty. "He's just lost half of our day's wages and you ask what else she sang! Get off!"

"Sure, it's money runs the world," Doone agreed, seated there, closing up his eyes, "but it is music holds down the friction."

"What's going on below!?" cried someone, above.

A man leaned from the balcony, puffing a cigarette. "What's all the rouse?"

"The projectionist," whispered Timulty. Aloud: "Hello, Phil, darling! It's only the team. We've a bit of a problem here, Phil, in ethics, not to say aesthetics. We wonder if, well, could you run the anthem over?"

"Run it over?!"

The winners milled about, rumbling.

"A lovely idea." Doone smiled at himself.

"It is," said Timulty, all guile. "An act of God incapacitated Doone——"

"A 10th-run flicker from the olden days caught him by the short hairs is all," said one of the Kellys.

"All!" protested Doone.

"I think I handicapped him too much," said Nolan, thinking back.

"So the fair thing is——" Timulty, unperturbed, looked to heaven. "Phil, dear boy, also is the last reel of the Deanna Durbin fillum still there?"

"It ain't in the LADIES'," said Phil, smoking steadily.

"What a wit the boy has! Now, Phil, could you just thread it back through the machine and give us the FINIS again, too?"

"Is that what you *all* want?" asked Phil.

The thought of another contest was too good to be passed. Slowly, everyone nodded.

"All right!" Phil shouted. "A shilling on Hoolihan!"

The winners laughed and hooted; they looked to win again. The losers turned on their man: "Do you hear the insult, Doone? Stay awake, man! When the girl sings, damn it, go deaf!"

"There's no audience!" said Timulty, glancing about, "and without them there's no obstacles, no real contest!"

"Why," Fogarty blinked around, "let's *all* of us be the audience."

"Fine!" Beaming, everyone threw himself into a seat.

"Pardon," I said. "There's no one outside, to judge."

Everyone stiffened, turned to look at me in surprise.

"Ah?" said Timulty. "Well. Nolan, outside!"

Nolan, cursing, trudged up the aisle.

Phil stuck his head from the projection booth above.

"Are ya clods down there ready?"

"If the girl is and the anthem is!"

The lights went out.

I found myself seated next in from Doone, who whispered fervently, "Poke me, lad, keep me alert to practicalities instead of ornamentation, eh?"

"Shut up!" hissed someone. "There's the mystery."

And there indeed it was, the mystery of song and art and life, if you will, the young girl singing on the time-haunted screen.

"Ah, look, ain't she lovely?" Doone smiled ahead. "Do you hear?"

"The bet, Doone," I whispered. "We *lean* on you. Ready?"

"All right," he groused. "Let me stir my bones. Jesus save me!"

"What?"

"I never thought to test. My right leg. It's dead it is!"

"Asleep, you mean?" I asked, appalled.

"Dead or asleep, I'm sunk! Lad, lad, you must run *for* me! Here's my cap and scarf!"

"Your cap——?"

"When victory is yours, show them, and we'll tell how you ran to replace this fool leg of mine!"

He clapped the cap on, tied the scarf.

"But wait!" I protested.

"You'll do brave. Just remember, it's FINIS and no sooner! Her song's almost up. Are you tensed?"

"God, *am* I!" I said.

"Blind passions, they win, boy. Plunge straight. If you step on someone, don't look back. There! The song's done! He's kissing her——"

"The FINIS!" I cried. I leapt into the aisle.

I ran up the aisle! I'm first, I thought. I'm ahead!

I hit the door as the anthem began.

I slammed through into the lobby—safe!

I've won! I thought, incredulous, with Doone's cap and scarf the victory laurels upon and about me! Won! Won for the team!

I turned to greet the loser, hand out.

But the door had swung and remained shut.

Only then did I hear the shouts and yells inside.

Good Lord! I thought, six men, pretending to be the exiting crowd, have somehow tripped, fallen across Hoolihan's way. Otherwise, why am I the first and only? There's a fierce combat in there this second, winners and losers locked in mortal wrestling attitudes, above and below the seats.

I've won! I wanted to yell, throwing wide the doors. Break it up!

I stared into an abyss where nothing stirred.

Nolan came to peer over my shoulder.

"That's the Irish for you," he nodded. "Even more than the race, it's the Muse they like."

For what were the voices yelling in the dark?

"Run it over! Again! The last song! Phil!"

Whistles. Foot-stomps. Applause.

"Don't no one move. I'm in heaven. Doone, how right you were!"

Nolan passed me, going in to sit.

I stood for a long moment looking down along all the rows where the teams of anthem sprinters sat, none having stirred, wiping their eyes.

"Phil, darling . . . ?" called Timulty, somewhere up front.

"And this time," added Timulty, "*without* the anthem."

Applause.

The dim lights flashed off. The screen glowed like a great warm hearth.

I looked back out at the bright sane world of Grafton Street, the Four Provinces pub, the hotels, shops and night-wandering folk. I hesitated.

Then, to the tune of 'The Isle Somewhere of Innisfree,' I took off cap and scarf, hid these laurels under a seat, and slowly, luxuriously, with all the time in the world, sat myself down . . .

And the Rock Cried Out

The raw carcasses, hung in the sunlight, rushed at them, vibrated with heat and red color in the green jungle air, and were gone. The stench of rotting flesh gushed through the car windows, and Leonora Webb quickly pressed the button that whispered her door window up.

"Good Lord," she said, "those open-air butcher shops."

The smell was still in the car, a smell of war and horror.

"Did you see the flies?" she asked.

"When you buy any kind of meat in those markets," John Webb said, "you slap the beef with your hand. The flies lift from the meat so you can get a look at it."

He turned the car around a lush bend in the green rain-jungle road.

"Do you think they'll let us into Juatala when we get there?"

"I don't know."

"Watch out!"

He saw the bright things in the road too late, tried to

swerve, but hit them. There was a terrible sighing from the right front tire, the car heaved about and sank to a stop. He opened his side of the car and stepped out. The jungle was hot and silent and the highway empty, very empty and quiet at noon.

He walked to the front of the car and bent, all the while checking his revolver in its underarm holster.

Leonora's window gleamed down. "Is the tire hurt much?"

"Ruined, utterly ruined!" He picked up the bright thing that had stabbed and slashed the tire.

"Pieces of a broken machete," he said, "placed in adobe holders pointing toward our car wheels. We're lucky it didn't get *all* our tires."

"But *why?*"

"You know as well as I." He nodded to the newspaper beside her, at the date, the headlines:

**OCTOBER 4TH, 1963: UNITED STATES,
EUROPE SILENT!**

The radios of the U.S.A. and Europe are dead. There is a great silence. The War has spent itself.

It is believed that most of the population of the United States is dead. It is believed that most of Europe, Russia, and Siberia is equally decimated. The day of the white people of the earth is over and finished.

"It all came so fast," said Webb. "One week we're on another tour, a grand vacation from home. The next week —this."

They both looked away from the black headlines to the jungle.

The jungle looked back at them with a vastness, a breathing moss-and-leaf silence, with a billion diamond and emerald insect eyes.

"Be careful, Jack."

He pressed two buttons. An automatic lift under the front wheels hissed and hung the car in the air. He jammed a key nervously into the right wheel plate. The tire, frame and all, with a sucking pop, bounced from the wheel. It was a matter of seconds to lock the spare in place and roll the shattered tire back to the luggage compartment. He had his gun out while he did all this.

"Don't stand in the open, please, Jack."

"So it's starting already." He felt his hair burning hot on his skull. "News travels fast."

"For God's sake," said Leonora. "They can *hear* you!"

He stared at the jungle.

"I know you're in there!"

"Jack!"

He aimed at the silent jungle. "I see you!" He fired four, five times, quickly, wildly.

The jungle ate the bullets with hardly a quiver, a brief slit sound like torn silk where the bullets bored and vanished into a million acres of green leaves, trees, silence, and moist earth. The brief echo of the shots died. Only the car muttered its exhaust behind Webb. He walked around the car, got in, and shut the door and locked it.

He reloaded the gun, sitting in the front seat. Then they drove away from the place.

They drove steadily.

"Did you see anyone?"

"No. You?"

She shook her head.

"You're going too fast."

He slowed only in time. As they rounded a curve another clump of the bright flashing objects filled the right side of the road. He swerved to the left and passed.

"Sons-of-bitches!"

"They're not sons-of-bitches, they're just people who never had a car like this or anything at all."

Something ticked across the windowpane.

There was a streak of colorless liquid on the glass.

Leonora glanced up. "Is it going to rain?"

"No, an insect hit the plane."

Another tick.

"Are you sure that was an insect?"

Tick, tick, tick.

"Shut the window!" he said, speeding up.

Something fell in her lap.

She looked down at it. He reached over to touch the thing. "Quick!"

She pressed the button. The window snapped up.

Then she examined her lap again.

The tiny blowgun dart glistened there.

"Don't get any of the liquid on you," he said. "Wrap it in your handkerchief—we'll throw it away later."

He had the car up to sixty miles an hour.

"If we hit another road block, we're done."

"This is a local thing," he said. "We'll drive out of it."

The panes were ticking all the time. A shower of things blew at the window and fell away in their speed.

"Why," said Leonora Webb, "they don't even *know* us!"

"I only wish they did." He gripped the wheel. "It's hard to kill people you know. But not hard to kill strangers."

"I don't want to die," she said simply, sitting there.

He put his hand inside his coat. "If anything happens to me, my gun is here. Use it, for God's sake, and don't waste time."

She moved over close to him and they drove seventy-five miles an hour down a straight stretch in the jungle road, saying nothing.

With the windows up, the heat was oven-thick in the car.

"It's so silly," she said, at last. "Putting the knives in the road. Trying to hit us with the blowguns. How could they know that the next car along would be driven by white people?"

"Don't ask them to be that logical," he said. "A car is a car. It's big, it's rich. The money in one car would last them a lifetime. And anyway, if you road-block a car, chances are you'll get either an American tourist or a rich Spaniard, comparatively speaking, whose ancestors should have behaved better. And if you happen to road-block another Indian, hell, all you do is go out and help him change tires."

"What time is it?" she asked.

For the thousandth time he glanced at his empty wrist. Without expression or surprise, he fished in his coat pocket for the glistening gold watch with the silent sweep hand. A year ago he had seen a native stare at this watch and stare at it and stare at it with almost a hunger. Then the native had examined him, not scowling, not hating, not sad or happy; nothing except puzzled.

He had taken the watch off that day and never worn it since.

"Noon," he said.

Noon.

The border lay ahead. They saw it and both cried out at once. They pulled up, smiling, not knowing they smiled. . . .

John Webb leaned out the window, started gesturing to the guard at the border station, caught himself, and got out of his car. He walked ahead to the station where three young men, very short, in lumpy uniforms, stood talking. They did not look up at Webb, who stopped before them. They continued conversing in Spanish, ignoring him.

"I beg your pardon," said John Webb at last. "Can we pass over the border into Juatala?"

One of the men turned for a moment. "Sorry, *señor*."

The three men talked again.

"You don't understand," said Webb, touching the first man's elbow. "We've *got* to get through."

The man shook his head. "Passports are no longer good. Why should you want to leave our country, anyway?"

"It was announced on the radio. All Americans to leave the country, immediately."

"Ah, *sí, sí*." All three soldiers nodded and leered at each other with shining eyes.

"Or be fined or imprisoned, or both," said Webb.

"We could let you over the border, but Juatala would give you twenty-four hours to leave, also. If you don't believe me, listen!" The guard turned and called across the border, "Aye, there! Aye!"

In the hot sun, forty yards distant, a pacing man turned, his rifle in his arms.

"Aye there, Paco, you want these two people?"

"No, *gracias—gracias*, no," replied the man, smiling.

"You see?" said the guard, turning to John Webb.

All of the soldiers laughed together.

"I have money," said Webb.

The men stopped laughing.

The first guard stepped up to John Webb and his face was now not relaxed or easy; it was like brown stone.

"Yes," he said. "They always have money. I know. They come here and they think money will do everything. But what is money? It is only a promise, *señor*. This I know from books. And when somebody no longer likes your promise, what then?"

"I will give you anything you ask."

"Will you?" The guard turned to his friends. "He will give me *anything* I ask." To Webb: "It was a joke. *We* were always a joke to you, weren't we?"

"No."

"*Mañana*, you laughed at us; *mañana*, you laughed at our siestas and our *mañanas*, didn't you?"

"Not me. Someone else."

"Yes, you."

"I've never been to this particular station before."

"I know you, anyway. Run here, do this, do that. Oh, here's a peso, buy yourself a house. Run over there, do this, do that."

"It wasn't me."

"He looked like you, anyway."

They stood in the sun with their shadows dark under them, and the perspiration coloring their armpits. The soldier moved closer to John Webb. "I don't have to do anything for you any more."

"You never had to before. I never asked it."

"You're trembling, *señor*."

"I'm all right. It's the sun."

"How much money have you got?" asked the guard.

"A thousand pesos to let us through, and a thousand for the other man over there."

The guard turned again. "Will a thousand pesos be enough?"

"No," said the other guard. "Tell him to report us!"

"Yes," said the guard, back to Webb again. "Report me. Get me fired. I was fired once, years ago, by you."

"It was someone else."

"Take my name. It is Carlos Rodriguez Ysotl. Go on now."

"I see."

"No, you don't see," said Carlos Rodriguez Ysotl. "Now give me two thousand pesos."

John Webb took out his wallet and handed over the money. Carlos Rodriguez Ysotl licked his thumb and counted the money slowly under the blue glazed sky of his country as noon deepened and sweat arose from hidden sources and people breathed and panted above their shadows.

"Two thousand pesos." He folded it and put it in his pocket quietly. "Now turn your car around and head for another border."

"Hold on now, damn it!"

The guard looked at him. "Turn your car."

They stood a long time that way, with the sun blazing on the rifle in the guard's hands, not speaking. And then John Webb turned and walked slowly, one hand to his face, back to the car and slid into the front seat.

"What're we going to do?" said Leonora.

"Rot. Or try to reach Porto Bello."

"But we need gas and our spare fixed. And going back over those highways . . . This time they might drop logs, and——"

"I know, I know." He rubbed his eyes and sat for a moment with his head in his hands. "We're alone, my God, we're alone. Remember how safe we used to feel? How safe? We registered in all the big towns with the American Consuls. Remember how the joke went? 'Everywhere you go you can hear the rustle of the eagle's wings!' Or was it the sound of paper money? I forget. Jesus, Jesus, the world got empty awfully quick. Who do I call on now?"

She waited a moment and then said, "I guess just me. That's not much."

He put his arm around her. "You've been swell. No hysterics, nothing."

"Tonight maybe I'll be screaming, when we're in bed, if we ever find a bed again. It's been a million miles since breakfast."

He kissed her, twice, on her dry mouth. Then he sat slowly back. "First thing is to try to find gas. If we can get that, we're ready to head for Porto Bello."

The three soldiers were talking and joking as they drove away.

After they had been driving a minute, he began to laugh quietly.

"What were you thinking?" asked his wife.

"I remember an old spiritual. It goes like this:

> " *'I went to the Rock to hide my face*
> *And the Rock cried out, "No Hiding Place,*
> *There's no Hiding Place down here."* ' "

"I remember that," she said.

"It's an appropriate song right now," he said. "I'd sing the whole thing for you if I could remember it all. And if I felt like singing."

He put his foot harder to the accelerator.

They stopped at a gas station and after a minute, when the attendant did not appear, John Webb honked the horn. Then, appalled, he snapped his hand away from the horn-ring, looking at it as if it were the hand of a leper.

"I shouldn't have done that."

The attendant appeared in the shadowy doorway of the gas station. Two other men appeared behind him.

The three men came out and walked around the car, looking at it, touching it, feeling it.

Their faces were like burnt copper in the daylight. They touched the resilient tires, they sniffed the rich new smell of the metal and upholstery.

"*Señor*," said the gas attendant at last.

"We'd like to buy some gas, please."

"We are all out of gas, *señor*."

"But your tank reads full. I see the gas in the glass container up there."

"We are all out of gas," said the man.

"I'll give you ten pesos a gallon!"

"*Gracias*, no."

"We haven't enough gas to get anywhere from here." Webb checked the gauge. "Not even a quarter gallon left. We'd better leave the car here and go into town and see what we can do there."

"I'll watch the car for you, *señor*," said the station attendant. "If you leave the keys."

"We can't do that!" said Leonora. "Can we?"

"I don't see what choice we have. We can stall it on the road and leave it to anyone who comes along, or leave it with this man."

"That's better," said the man.

They climbed out of the car and stood looking at it.

"It was a beautiful car," said John Webb.

"Very beautiful," said the man, his hand out for the keys. "I will take good care of it, *señor*."

"But, Jack——"

She opened the back door and started to take out the luggage. Over her shoulder, he saw the bright travel stickers, the storm of color that had descended upon and covered the worn leather now after years of travel, after years of the best hotels in two dozen countries.

She tugged at the valises, perspiring, and he stopped her hands and they stood gasping there for a moment, in the open door of the car, looking at these fine rich suitcases, inside which were the beautiful tweeds and woolens and silks of their lives and living, the forty-dollar-an-ounce perfumes and the cool dark furs and the silvery golf shafts. Twenty years were packed into each of the cases; twenty years and four dozen parts they had played in Rio, in Paris, in Rome and Shanghai, but the part they played most frequently and best of all was the rich and buoyant, amazingly happy Webbs, the smiling people, the ones who could make that rarely balanced martini known as the Sahara.

"We can't carry it all into town," he said. "We'll come back for it later. Later."

"But . . ."

He silenced her by turning her away and starting her off down the road.

"But we can't leave it there, we can't leave all our luggage and we can't leave our car! Oh look here now, I'll roll up the windows and lock myself in the car, while you go for the gas, why not?" she said.

He stopped and glanced back at the three men standing by the car, which blazed in the yellow sun. Their eyes were shining and looking at the woman.

"There's your answer," he said. "Come on."

"But you just *don't* walk off and leave a four-thousand-dollar automobile!" she cried.

He moved her along, holding her elbow firmly and with quiet decision. "A car is to travel in. When it's not traveling, it's useless. Right now, we've got to travel; that's everything. The car isn't worth a dime without gas in it. A pair of good strong legs is worth a hundred cars, if you use the legs. We've just begun to toss things overboard. We'll keep dropping ballast until there's nothing left to heave but our hides."

He let her go. She was walking steadily now, and she fell into step with him. "It's so strange. So strange. I haven't walked like this in years." She watched the motion of her feet beneath her, she watched the road pass by, she watched the jungle moving to either side, she watched her husband striding quickly along, until she seemed hypnotized by the steady rhythm. "But I guess you can learn anything over again," she said, at last.

The sun moved in the sky and they moved for a long while on the hot road. When he was quite ready, the husband began to think aloud. "You know, in a way, I think it's good to be down to essentials. Now instead of worrying over a dozen damned things, it's just two items— you and me."

"Watch it, here comes a car—we'd better . . ."

They half turned, yelled, and jumped. They fell away from the highway and lay watching the automobile hurtle past at seventy miles an hour. Voices sang, men laughed, men shouted, waving. The car sped away into the dust and vanished around a curve, blaring its double horns again and again.

He helped her up and they stood in the quiet road.

"Did you see it?"

They watched the dust settle slowly.

"I hope they remember to change the oil and check the battery, at least. I hope they think to put water in the radiator," she said, and paused. "They were singing, weren't they?"

He nodded. They stood blinking at the great dust cloud filtering down like yellow pollen upon their heads and arms. He saw a few bright splashes flick from her eyelids when she blinked.

"Don't," he said. "After all, it was only a machine."

"I loved it."

"We're always loving everything too much."

Walking, they passed a shattered wine bottle which steamed freshly as they stepped over it.

They were not far from the town, walking single file, the wife ahead, the husband following, looking at their feet as they walked, when a sound of tin and steam and bubbling water made them turn and look at the road behind them. An old man in a 1929 Ford drove along the road at a moderate speed. The car's fenders were gone, and the sun had flaked and burnt the paint badly, but he rode in the seat with a great deal of quiet dignity, his face a thoughtful darkness under a dirty Panama hat, and when he saw the two people he drew the car up, steaming, the engine joggling under the hood, and opened the squealing door as he said, "This is no day for walking."

"Thank you," they said.

"It is nothing." The old man wore an ancient yellowed white summer suit, with a rather greasy tie knotted loosely at his wrinkled throat. He helped the lady into the rear seat with a gracious bow of his head. "Let us men sit up front," he suggested, and the husband sat up front and the car moved off in trembling vapors.

"Well. My name is Garcia."

There were introductions and noddings.

"Your car broke down? You are on your way for help?" said *Señor* Garcia.

"Yes."

"Then let me drive you and a mechanic back out," offered the old man.

They thanked him and kindly turned the offer aside and he made it once again, but upon finding that his interest and concern caused them embarrassment, he very politely turned to another subject.

He touched a small stack of folded newspapers on his lap.

"Do you read the papers? Of course, you do. But do you read them as I read them? I rather doubt that you have come upon my system. No, it was not exactly myself that came upon it; the system was forced upon me. But now I know what a clever thing it has turned out to be. I always get the newspapers a week late. All of us, those who are interested, get the papers a week late, from the Capital. And this circumstance makes for a man being a clear-thinking man. You are very careful with your thinking when you pick up a week-old paper."

The husband and wife asked him to continue.

"Well," said the old man, "I remember once, when I lived in the Capital for a month and bought the paper fresh each day, I went wild with love, anger, irritation, frustration; all of the passions boiled in me. I was young. I exploded at everything I saw. But then I saw what I was doing: I was believing what I read. Have you noticed? You believe a paper printed on the very day you buy it? This has happened but only an hour ago, you think! It must be true." He shook his head. "So I learned to stand back away and let the paper age and mellow. Back here, in Colonia, I saw the headlines diminish to nothing. The week-old paper—why, you can spit on it if you wish. It is like a woman you once loved, but you now see, a few days later, she is not quite what you thought. She has rather a plain face. She is no deeper than a cup of water."

He steered the car gently, his hands upon the wheel as upon the heads of his good children, with care and affection. "So here I am, returning to my home to read my weekly papers, to peek sideways at them, to toy with them." He spread one on his knee, glancing down to it on occasion as he drove. "How white this paper is, like the mind of a child that is an idiot, poor thing, all blank. You can put anything into an empty place like that. Here, do you see? This paper speaks and says that the light-skinned people of the world are dead. Now that is a very silly thing to say. At this very moment, there are probably millions upon millions of white men and women eating their noon meals or their suppers. The earth trembles, a town collapses, people run from the town, screaming, *All is lost!* In the next village, the population wonders what all of the shouting is about, since *they* have had a most splendid night's repose. Ah, ah, what a sly world it is. People do not see how sly it is. It is either night or day to them. Rumor flies. This very afternoon all of the little villages upon this highway, behind us and ahead of us, are in carnival. The white man is dead, the rumors say, and yet here I come into the town with two very lively ones. I hope you don't mind my speaking in this way? If I do not talk to you I would then be talking to this engine up in the front, which makes a great noise speaking back."

They were at the edge of town.

"Please," said John Webb, "it wouldn't be wise for you to be seen with us today. We'll get out here."

The old man stopped his car reluctantly and said, "You are most kind and thoughtful of me." He turned to look at the lovely wife.

"When I was a young man I was very full of wildness

and ideas. I read all of the books from France by a man named Jules Verne. I see you know his name. But at night I many times thought I must be an inventor. That is all gone by; I never did what I thought I might do. But I remember clearly that one of the machines I wished to put together was a machine that would help every man, for an hour, to be like any other man. The machine was full of colors and smells and it had film in it, like a theater, and the machine was like a coffin. You lay in it. And you touched a button. And for an hour you could be one of those Eskimos in the cold wind up there, or you could be an Arab gentleman on a horse. Everything a New York man felt, you could feel. Everything a man from Sweden smelled, you could smell. Everything a man from China tasted, your tongue knew. The machine was like another man—do you see what I was after? And by touching many of the buttons, each time you got into my machine, you could be a white man or a yellow man or a Negrito. You could be a child or a woman, even, if you wished to be very funny."

The husband and wife climbed from the car.

"Did you ever try to invent that machine?"

"It was so very long ago. I had forgotten until today. And today I was thinking, we could make use of it, we are in need of it. What a shame I never tried to put it all together. Someday some other man will do it."

"Some day," said John Webb.

"It has been a pleasure talking with you," said the old man. "God go with you."

"*Adiós, Señor* Garcia," they said.

The car drove slowly away, steaming. They stood watching it go, for a full minute. Then, without speaking, the husband reached over and took his wife's hand.

They entered the small town of Colonia on foot. They walked past the little shops—the butcher shop, the photographer's. People stopped and looked at them as they went by and did not stop looking at them as long as they were in sight. Every few seconds, as he walked, Webb put up his hand to touch the holster hidden under his coat, secretly, tentatively, like someone feeling for a tiny boil that is growing and growing every hour and every hour . . .

The patio of the Hotel Esposa was cool as a grotto under a blue waterfall. In it caged birds sang, and footsteps echoed like small rifle shots, clear and smooth.

"Remember? We stopped here years ago," said Webb, helping his wife up the steps. They stood in the cool grotto, glad of the blue shade.

"*Señor* Esposa," said John Webb, when a fat man came forward from the desk, squinting at them. "Do you remember me—John Webb? Five years ago—we played cards one night."

"Of course, of course." *Señor* Esposa bowed to the wife and shook hands briefly. There was an uncomfortable silence.

Webb cleared his throat. "We've had a bit of trouble, *señor*. Could we have a room for tonight only?"

"Your money is always good here."

"You mean you'll actually give us a room? We'll be glad to pay in advance. Lord, we need the rest. But, more than that, we need gas."

Leonora picked at her husband's arm. "Remember? We haven't a car any more."

"Oh. Yes." He fell silent for a moment and then sighed. "Well. Never mind the gas. Is there a bus out of here for the Capital soon?"

"All will be attended to, in time," said the manager nervously. "This way."

As they were climbing the stairs they heard a noise. Looking out they saw their car riding around and around the plaza, eight times, loaded with men who were shouting and singing and hanging on to the front fenders, laughing. Children and dogs ran after the car.

"I would like to own a car like that," said *Señor* Esposa.

He poured a little cool wine for the three of them, standing in the room on the third floor of the Esposa Hotel.

"'To 'change,'" said *Señor* Esposa.

"I'll drink to that."

They drank. *Señor* Esposa licked his lips and wiped them on his coat sleeve. "We are always surprised and saddened to see the world change. It is insane, they have run out on us, you say. It is unbelievable. And now, well— you are safe for the night. Shower and have a good supper. I won't be able to keep you more than one night, to repay you for your kindness to me five years ago."

"And tomorrow?"

"Tomorrow? Do not take any bus to the Capital, please. There are riots in the streets there. A few people from the North have been killed. It is nothing. It will pass in a few days. But you must be careful until those few days pass and the blood cools. There are many wicked people taking advantage of this day, *señor*. For forty-eight hours anyway, under the guise of a great resurgence of nationalism, these people will try to gain power. Selfishness and patriotism, *señor*; today I cannot tell one from the other. So—you must hide. That is a problem. The town will know you are here in another few hours. This might be dangerous to my hotel. I cannot say."

"We understand. It's good of you to help *this* much."

"If you need anything, call me." *Señor* Esposa drank the rest of the wine in his glass. "Finish the bottle," he said.

The fireworks began at nine that evening. First one sky-rocket then another soared into the dark sky and burst out upon the winds, building architectures of flame. Each sky-rocket, at the top of its ride, cracked open and let out a formation of streamers in red and white flame that made something like the dome of a beautiful cathedral.

Leonora and John Webb stood by the open window in their unlit room, watching and listening. As the hour lat-ened, more people streamed into town from every road and path and began to roam, arm in arm, around the plaza, singing, barking like dogs, crowing like roosters, and then falling down on the tile sidewalks, sitting there, laughing, their heads thrown back, while the skyrockets burst explosive colors on the tilted faces. A brass band began to thump and wheeze.

"So here we are," said John Webb, "after a few hundred years of living high. So this is what's left of our white supremacy—you and I in a dark room in a hotel three hundred miles inside a celebrating country."

"You've got to see their side of it."

"Oh, I've seen it ever since I was that high. In a way, I'm glad they're happy. God knows they've waited long enough to be. But I wonder how long that happiness will last. Now that the scapegoat is gone, who will they blame for oppression, who will be as handy and as obvious and as guilty as you and I and the man who lived in this room before us?"

"I don't know."

"We were so convenient. The man who rented this room last month, he was convenient, he stood out. He made loud jokes about the natives' siestas. He refused to learn even a smattering of Spanish. Let them learn English, by God, and speak like men, he said. And he drank too much and whored too much with this country's women." He broke off and moved back from the window. He stared at the room.

The furniture, he thought. Where *he* put his dirty shoes upon the sofa, where *he* burnt holes in the carpet with cigarettes; the wet spot on the wall near the bed, God knows what or how he did *that*. The chairs scarred and kicked. It wasn't his hotel or his room; it was borrowed, it meant nothing. So this son-of-a-bitch went around the country for the past one hundred years, a traveling commercial, a Chamber of Commerce, and now here *we* are, enough like him to be his brother and sister, and there *they* are down there on the night of the Butlers' Ball. They don't know, or if they know they won't think of it, that tomorrow they'll be just as poor, just as oppressed as ever, that the whole machine will only have shifted into another gear.

Now the band had stopped playing below; a man had

leaped up, shouting, on the bandstand. There was a flash of machetes in the air and the brown gleam of half-naked bodies.

The man on the bandstand faced the hotel and looked up at the dark room where John and Leonora Webb now stood back out of the intermittent flares.

The man shouted.

"What does he say?" asked Leonora.

John Webb translated: " 'It is now a free world,' he says."

The man yelled.

John Webb translated again. "He says, 'We are *free!*' "

The man lifted himself on his toes and made a motion of breaking manacles. "He says, 'No one owns us, no one in all the world.' "

The crowd roared and the band began to play, and while it was playing, the man on the grandstand stood glaring up at the room window, with all of the hatred of the universe in his eyes.

During the night there were fights and pummelings and voices lifted, arguments and shots fired. John Webb lay awake and heard the voice of *Señor* Esposa below, reasoning, talking quietly, firmly. And then the fading away of the tumult, the last rockets in the sky, the last breakings of bottles on the cobbles.

At five in the morning the air was warming into a new day. There was the softest of taps on the bedroom door.

"It is me, it is Esposa," said a voice.

John Webb hesitated, half-dressed, numbed on his feet from lack of sleep, then opened the door.

"What a night, what a night!" said *Señor* Esposa, coming in, shaking his head, laughing gently. "Did you hear that noise? Yes? They tried to come up here to your room. I prevented this."

"Thank you" said Leonora, still in bed, turned to the wall.

"They were all old friends. I made an agreement with them, anyway. They were drunk enough and happy enough so they agreed to wait. I am to make a proposition to you two." Suddenly he seemed embarrassed. He moved to the window. "Everyone is sleeping late. A few are up. A few men. See them there on the far side of the plaza?"

John Webb looked out at the plaza. He saw the brown men talking quietly there about the weather, the world, the sun, this town, and perhaps the wine.

"*Señor*, have you ever been hungry in your life?"

"For a day, once."

"Only for a day. Have you always had a house to live in and a car to drive?"

"Until yesterday."

"Were you ever without a job?"

"Never."

"Did all of your brothers and sisters live to be twenty-one years old?"

"All of them."

"Even I," said *Señor* Esposa, "even *I* hate you a little bit now. For *I* have been without a home. *I* have been hungry. *I* have three brothers and one sister buried in that graveyard on the hill beyond the town, all dead of tuberculosis before they were nine years old."

Señor Esposa glanced at the men in the plaza. "Now, I am no longer hungry or poor, I have a car, I am alive. But I am one in a thousand. What can *you* say to them out there today?"

"I'll try to think of something."

"Long ago I stopped trying. *Señor*, we have *always* been a minority, we white people. I am Spanish, but I was born here. They tolerate me."

"We have never let ourselves think about our being a minority," said Webb, "and now it's hard to get used to the fact."

"You have behaved beautifully."

"Is that a virtue?"

"In the bull ring, yes; in war, yes; in anything like this, most assuredly yes. You do not complain, you do not make excuses. You do not run and make a spectacle of yourself. I think you are both very brave."

The hotel manager sat down, slowly, helplessly.

"I've come to offer you the chance to settle down," he said.

"We wanted to move on, if possible."

The manager shrugged. "Your car is stolen, I can do nothing to get it back. You cannot leave town. Remain then and accept my offer of a position in my hotel."

"You don't think there is any way for us to travel?"

"It might be twenty days, *señor*, or twenty years. You cannot exist without money, food, lodging. Consider my hotel and the work I can give you."

The manager arose and walked unhappily to the door and stood by the chair, touching Webb's coat, which was draped over it.

"What's the job?" asked Webb.

"In the kitchen," said the manager, and looked away.

John Webb sat on the bed and said nothing. His wife did not move.

Señor Esposa said, "It is the best I can do. What more can you ask of me? Last night, those others down in the plaza wanted both of you. Did you see the máchetes? I bargained with them. You were lucky. I told them you would be employed in my hotel for the next twenty years, that you were my employees and deserve my protection!"

"You said *that!*"

"*Señor, señor,* be thankful! Consider! Where will you go? The jungle? You will be dead in two hours from the snakes. Then can you walk five hundred miles to a capital which will not welcome you? No—you must face the reality." *Señor* Esposa opened the door. "I offer you an honest job and you will be paid the standard wages of two pesos a day, plus meals. Would you rather be with me, or out in the plaza at noon with our friends? Consider."

The door was shut. *Señor* Esposa was gone.

Webb stood looking at the door for a long while.

Then he walked to the chair and fumbled with the holster under the draped white shirt. The holster was empty. He held it in his hands and blinked at its emptiness and looked again at the door through which *Señor* Esposa had just passed. He went over and sat down on the bed beside his wife. He stretched out beside her and took her in his arms and kissed her, and they lay there, watching the room get brighter with the new day.

At eleven o'clock in the morning, with the great doors on the windows of their room flung back, they began to dress. There were soap, towels, shaving equipment, even perfume in the bathroom, provided by Mr. Esposa.

John Webb shaved and dressed carefully.

At eleven-thirty he turned on the small radio near their bed. You could usually get New York or Cleveland or Houston on such a radio. But the air was silent. John Webb turned the radio off.

"There's nothing to go back to—nothing to go back for —nothing."

His wife sat on a chair near the door, looking at the wall.

"We could stay here and work," he said.

She stirred at last. "No. We couldn't do that, not really. Could we?"

"No, I guess not."

"There's no way we could do that. We're being consistent, anyway; spoiled, but consistent."

He thought a moment. "We could make for the jungle."

"I don't think we can move from the hotel without being seen. We don't want to try to escape and be caught. It would be far worse that way."

He nodded.

They both sat a moment.

"It might not be too bad, working here," he said.

"What would we be living for? Everyone's dead—your father, mine, your mother, mine, your brothers, mine, all our friends, everything gone, everything we understood."

He nodded.

"Or if we took the job, one day soon one of the men would touch me and you'd go after him, you know you would. Or someone would do something to you, and *I'd* do something."

He nodded again.

They sat for fifteen minutes, talking quietly. Then, at last, he picked up the telephone and ticked the cradle with his finger.

"*Bueno*," said a voice on the other end.

"*Señor* Esposa?"

"*Sí.*"

"*Señor* Esposa," he paused and licked his lips, "tell your friends we will be leaving the hotel at noon."

The phone did not immediately reply. Then with a sigh *Señor* Esposa said, "As you wish. You are sure——?"

The phone was silent for a full minute. Then it was picked up again and the manager said quietly, "My friends say they will be waiting for you on the far side of the plaza."

"We will meet them there," said John Webb.

"And *señor*——"

"Yes."

"Do not hate me, do not hate us."

"I don't hate anybody."

"It is a bad world, *señor*. None of us know how we got here or what we are doing. These men don't know what they are mad at, except they are mad. Forgive them and do not hate them."

"I don't hate them or you."

"Thank you, thank you." Perhaps the man on the far end of the telephone wire was crying. There was no way to tell. There were great lapses in his talking, in his breathing. After a while he said, "We don't know why we do anything. Men hit each other for no reason except they are unhappy. Remember that. I am your friend. I would help you if I could. But I cannot. It would be me against the town. Good-by, *señor*." He hung up.

John Webb sat in the chair with his hand on the silent phone. It was a moment before he glanced up. It was a moment before his eyes focused on an object immediately before him. When he saw it clearly, he still did not move, but sat regarding it, until a look of immensely tired irony appeared on his mouth. "Look here," he said at last.

Leonora followed his motion, his pointing.

They both sat looking at his cigarette which, neglected on the rim of the table while he telephoned, had burnt down so that now it had charred a black hole in the clean surface of the wood.

It was noon, with the sun directly over them, pinning their shadows under them as they started down the steps of the Hotel Esposa. Behind them, the birds fluted in their bamboo cages, and water ran in a little fountain bath. They were as neat as they could get, their faces and hands washed, their nails clean, their shoes polished.

Across the plaza two hundred yards away stood a small group of men, in the shade of a store-front overhang. Some of the men were natives from the jungle area, with machetes gleaming at their sides. They were all facing the plaza.

John Webb looked at them for a long while. That isn't everyone, he thought, that isn't the whole country. That's only the surface. That's only the thin skin over the flesh. It's not the body at all. Just the shell of an egg. Remember the crowds back home, the mobs, the riots? Always the same, there or here. A few mad faces up front, and the quiet ones far back, not taking part, letting things go, not wanting to be in it. The majority not moving. And so the few, the handful, take over and move for them.

His eyes did not blink. If we could break through that shell—God knows it's thin! he thought. If we could talk our way through that mob and get to the quiet people beyond . . . Can I do it? Can I say the right things? Can I keep my voice down?

He fumbled in his pockets and brought out a rumpled cigarette package and some matches.

I can try, he thought. How would the old man in the Ford have done it? I'll try to do it his way. When we get across the plaza, I'll start talking, I'll whisper if necessary. And if we move slowly through the mob, we might just possibly find our way to the other people and we'll be on high ground and we'll be safe.

Leonora moved beside him. She was so fresh, so well groomed in spite of everything, so new in all this oldness, so startling, that his mind flinched and jerked. He found himself staring at her as if she'd betrayed him by her salt-whiteness, her wonderfully brushed hair and her cleanly manicured nails and her bright-red mouth.

Standing on the bottom step, Webb lit a cigarette, took two or three long drags on it, tossed it down, stepped on it, kicked the flattened butt into the street, and said, "Here we go."

They stepped down and started around the far side of the plaza, past the few shops that were still open. They walked quietly.

"Perhaps they'll be decent to us."

"We can hope so."

They passed a photographic shop.

"It's another day. Anything can happen. I believe that. No—I don't really believe it. I'm only talking. I've got to talk or I wouldn't be able to walk," she said.

They passed a candy shop.

"Keep talking, then."

"I'm afraid," she said. "This can't be happening to us! Are we the last ones in the world?"

"Maybe next to the last."

They approached an open air *carneceria*.

God! he thought. How the horizons narrowed, how they came in. A year ago there weren't four directions, there were a million for us. Yesterday they got down to four; we could go to Juatala, Porto Bello, San Juan Clementas, or Brioconbria. We were satisfied to have our car. Then when we couldn't get gas, we were satisfied to have our clothes, then when they took our clothes, we were satisfied to have a place to sleep. Each pleasure they took away left us with one other creature comfort to hold on to. Did you see how we let go of one thing and clutched another so quickly? I guess that's human. So they took away everything. There's nothing left. Except us. It all boils down to just you and me walking along here, and thinking too goddamn much for my own good. And what counts in the end is whether they can take you away from me or me away from you, Lee, and I don't think they can do that. They've got every-thing else and I don't blame them. But they can't really do anything else to us now. When you strip all the clothes away and the doodads, you have two human beings who were either happy or unhappy together, and we have no complaints."

"Walk slowly," said John Webb.

"I am."

"Not too slowly, to look reluctant. Not too fast, to look as if you want to get it over with. Don't give them the satisfaction, Lee, don't give them a damn bit."

"I won't."

They walked. "Don't even touch me," he said, quietly. "Don't even hold my hand."

"Oh, please!"

"No, not even that."

He moved away a few inches and kept walking steadily. His eyes were straight ahead and their pace was regular.

"I'm beginning to cry, Jack."

"Goddamn it!" he said, measuredly, between his teeth, not looking aside. "Stop it! Do you want me to run? Is that what you want—do you want me to take you and run into the jungle, and let them hunt us, is that what you want, goddamn it, do you want me to fall down in the street here and grovel and scream, shut up, let's do this right, don't give them *anything!*"

"All right," she said, hands tight, her head coming up. "I'm not crying now. I won't cry."

"Good, damn it, that's good."

And still, strangely, they were not past the *carnecería*. The vision of red horror was on their left as they paced steadily forward on the hot tile sidewalk. The things that hung from hooks looked like brutalities and sins, like bad consciences, evil dreams, like gored flags and slaughtered promises. The redness, oh, the hanging, evil-smelling wet-ness and redness, the hooked and hung-high carcasses, unfamiliar, unfamiliar.

As he passed the shop, something made John Webb

strike out a hand. He slapped it smartly against a strung-up side of beef. A mantle of blue buzzing flies lifted angrily and swirled in a bright cone over the meat.

Leonora said, looking ahead, walking, "They're all strangers! I don't know any of them. I wish I knew even *one* of them. I wish even *one* of them knew me!"

They walked on past the *carneceria*. The side of beef, red and irritable-looking, swung in the hot sunlight after they passed.

The flies came down in a feeding cloak to cover the meat, once it had stopped swinging.

Invisible Boy

She took the great iron spoon and the mummified frog and gave it a bash and made dust of it, and talked to the dust while she ground it in her stony fists quickly. Her beady gray bird-eyes flickered at the cabin. Each time she looked, a head in the small thin window ducked as if she'd fired off a shotgun.

"Charlie!" cried Old Lady. "You come outa there! I'm fixing a lizard magic to unlock that rusty door! You come out now and I won't make the earth shake or the trees go up in fire or the sun set at high noon!"

The only sound was the warm mountain light on the high turpentine trees, a tufted squirrel chittering around and around on a green-furred log, the ants moving in a fine brown line at Old Lady's bare, blue-veined feet.

"You been starving in there two days, darn you!" she panted, chiming the spoon against a flat rock, causing the plump gray miracle bag to swing at her waist. Sweating sour, she rose and marched at the cabin, bearing the pulverized flesh. "Come out, now!" She flicked a pinch of powder inside the lock. "All right, I'll come get you!" she wheezed.

She spun the knob with one walnut-colored hand, first one way, then the other. "O Lord," she intoned, "fling this door wide!"

When nothing flung, she added yet another philter and held her breath. Her long blue untidy skirt rustled as she peered into her bag of darkness to see if she had any scaly monsters there, any charm finer than the frog she'd killed months ago for such a crisis as this.

She heard Charlie breathing against the door. His folks had pranced off into some Ozark town early this week, leaving him, and he'd run almost six miles to Old Lady for company—she was by way of being an aunt or cousin or some such, and he didn't mind her fashions.

But then, two days ago, Old Lady, having gotten used to the boy around, decided to keep him for convenient company. She pricked her thin shoulder bone, drew out three blood pearls, spat wet over her right elbow, tromped on a crunch-cricket, and at the same instant clawed her left hand at Charlie, crying, "My son you are, you are my son, for all eternity!"

Charlie, bounding like a startled hare, had crashed off into the bush, heading for home.

But Old Lady, skittering quick as a gingham lizard, cornered him in a dead end, and Charlie holed up in this old hermit's cabin and wouldn't come out, no matter how she whammed door, window, or knothole with amber-colored fist or trounced her ritual fires, explaining to him that he was certainly her son *now*, all right.

"Charlie, you *there?*" she asked, cutting holes in the door planks with her bright little slippery eyes.

"I'm all of me here," he replied finally, very tired.

Maybe he would fall out on the ground any moment. She wrestled the knob hopefully. Perhaps a pinch too much frog powder had grated the lock wrong. She always overdid or underdid her miracles, she mused angrily, never doing them just *exact*, Devil take it!

"Charlie, I only wants someone to night-prattle to, someone to warm hands with at the fire. Someone to fetch kindling for me mornings, and fight off the spunks that come creeping of early fogs! I ain't got no fetchings on you for myself, son, just for your company." She smacked her lips. "Tell you what, Charles, you come out and I *teach* you things!"

"What things?" he suspicioned.

"Teach you how to buy cheap, sell high. Catch a snow weasel, cut off his head, carry it warm in your hind pocket. There!"

"Aw," said Charlie.

She made haste. "Teach you to make yourself shotproof. So if anyone bangs at you with a gun, nothing happens."

When Charlie stayed silent, she gave him the secret in a high fluttering whisper. "Dig and stitch mouse-ear roots on Friday during full moon, and wear 'em around your neck in a white silk."

"You're *crazy*," Charlie said.

"Teach you how to stop blood or make animals stand frozen or make blind horses see, all them things I'll teach you! Teach you to cure a swelled-up cow and unbewitch a goat. Show you how to make yourself invisible!"

"Oh," said Charlie.

Old Lady's heart beat like a Salvation tambourine.

The knob turned from the other side.

"You," said Charlie, "are funning me."

"No, I'm not," exclaimed Old Lady. "Oh, Charlie, why, I'll make you like a window, see right through you. Why, child, you'll be surprised!"

"Real invisible?"

"Real invisible!"

"You won't fetch onto me if I walk out?"

"Won't touch a bristle of you, son."

"Well," he drawled reluctantly, "all right."

The door opened. Charlie stood in his bare feet, head down, chin against chest. "Make me invisible," he said.

"First we got to catch us a bat," said Old Lady. "Start lookin'!"

She gave him some jerky beef for his hunger and watched him climb a tree. He went high up and high up and it was nice seeing him there and it was nice having

him here and all about after so many years alone with nothing to say good morning to but bird-droppings and silvery
snail tracks.

Pretty soon a bat with a broken wing fluttered down out
of the tree. Old Lady snatched it up, beating warm and
shrieking between its porcelain white teeth, and Charlie
dropped down after it, hand upon clenched hand, yelling.

That night, with the moon nibbling at the spiced pine
cones, Old Lady extracted a long silver needle from under
her wide blue dress. Gumming her excitement and secret
anticipation, she sighted up the dead bat and held the cold
needle steady-steady.

She had long ago realized that her miracles, despite all
perspirations and salts and sulphurs, failed. But she had
always dreamt that one day the miracles might start functioning, might spring up in crimson flowers and silver stars
to prove that God had forgiven her for her pink body and
her pink thoughts and her warm body and her warm
thoughts as a young miss. But so far God had made no
sign and said no word, but nobody knew this except Old
Lady.

"Ready?" she asked Charlie, who crouched cross-kneed,
wrapping his pretty legs in long goose-pimpled arms, his
mouth open, making teeth. "Ready," he whispered, shivering.

"There!" She plunged the needle deep in the bat's right
eye. "So!"

"Oh!" screamed Charlie, wadding up his face.

"Now I wrap it in gingham, and here, put it in your
pocket, keep it there, bat and all. Go on!"

He pocketed the charm.

"Charlie!" she shrieked fearfully. "Charlie, where *are*
you? I can't *see* you, child!"

"Here!" He jumped so the light ran in red streaks up his
body. "I'm here, Old Lady!" He stared wildly at his arms,
legs, chest, and toes. "I'm here!"

Her eyes looked as if they were watching a thousand
fireflies crisscrossing each other in the wild night air.

"Charlie, oh, you went *fast!* Quick as a humming-bird! Oh, Charlie, come *back* to me!"

"But I'm *here!*" he wailed.

"Where?"

"By the fire, the fire! And—and I can see myself. I'm not invisible at all!"

Old Lady rocked on her lean flanks. "Course *you* can see *you!* Every invisible person knows himself. Otherwise, how could you eat, walk, or get around places? Charlie, touch me. Touch me so I *know* you."

Uneasily he put out a hand.

She pretended to jerk, startled, at his touch. "*Ah!*"

"You mean to say you can't *find* me?" he asked. "Truly?"

"Not the least half rump of you!"

She found a tree to stare at, and stared at it with shining eyes, careful not to glance at him. "Why, I sure *did* a trick *that* time!" She sighed with wonder. "Whooeee. Quickest invisible I *ever* made! Charlie. Charlie, how you *feel?*"

"Like creek water—all stirred."

"You'll settle."

Then after a pause she added, "Well, what you going to do now, Charlie, since you're invisible?"

All sorts of things shot through his brain, she could tell. Adventures stood up and danced like hell-fire in his eyes, and his mouth, just hanging, told what it meant to be a boy who imagined himself like the mountain winds. In a cold dream he said, "I'll run across wheat fields, climb snow mountains, steal white chickens off'n farms. I'll kick pink pigs when they ain't looking. I'll pinch pretty girls' legs when they sleep, snap their garters in schoolrooms." Charlie looked at Old Lady, and from the shiny tips of her eyes she saw something wicked shape his face. "And other things I'll do, I'll do, I will," he said.

"Don't try nothing on me," warned Old Lady. "I'm brittle as spring ice and I don't take handling." Then: "What about your folks?"

"My folks?"

"You can't fetch yourself home looking like that. Scare

the inside ribbons out of them. Your mother'd faint straight back like timber falling. Think they want you about the house to stumble over and your ma have to call you every three minutes, even though you're in the room next her elbow?"

Charlie had not considered it. He sort of simmered down and whispered out a little "Gosh" and felt of his long bones carefully.

"You'll be mighty lonesome. People looking through you like a water glass, people knocking you aside because they didn't reckon you to be underfoot. And women, Charlie, *women*——"

He swallowed. "What about women?"

"No woman will be giving you a second stare. And no woman wants to be kissed by a boy's mouth they can't even *find!*"

Charlie dug his bare toe in the soil contemplatively. He pouted. "Well, I'll stay invisible, anyway, for a spell. I'll have me some fun. I'll just be pretty careful, is all. I'll stay out from in front of wagons and horses and Pa. Pa shoots at the nariest sound." Charlie blinked. "Why, with me invisible, someday Pa might just up and fill me with buckshot, thinkin' I was a hill squirrel in the dooryard. Oh . . ."

Old Lady nodded at a tree. "That's likely."

"Well," he decided slowly, "I'll stay invisible for tonight, and tomorrow you can fix me back all whole again, Old Lady."

"Now if that ain't just like a critter, always wanting to be what he can't be," remarked Old Lady to a beetle on a log.

"What you mean?" said Charlie.

"Why," she explained, "it was real hard work, fixing you up. It'll take a little *time* for it to wear off. Like a coat of paint wears off, boy."

"You!" he cried. "You did this to me! Now you make me back, you make me seeable!"

"Hush," she said. "It'll wear off, a hand or a foot at a time."

"How'll it look, me around the hills with just one hand showing!"

"Like a five-winged bird hopping on the stones and bramble."

"Or a foot showing!"

"Like a small pink rabbit jumping thicket."

"Or my head floating!"

"Like a hairy balloon at the carnival!"

"How long before I'm *whole?*" he asked.

She deliberated that it might pretty well be an entire year.

He groaned. He began to sob and bite his lips and make fists. "You magicked me, you did this, you did this thing to me. Now I won't be able to run home!"

She winked. "But you *can* stay here, child, stay on with me real comfort-like, and I'll keep you fat and saucy."

He flung it out: "You did this on purpose! You mean old hag, you want to keep me here!"

He ran off through the shrubs on the instant.

"Charlie, come back!"

No answer but the pattern of his feet on the soft dark turf, and his wet choking cry which passed swiftly off and away.

She waited and then kindled herself a fire. "He'll be back," she whispered. And thinking inward on herself, she said, "And now I'll have me my company through spring and into late summer. Then, when I'm tired of him and want a silence, I'll send him home."

Charlie returned noiselessly with the first gray of dawn, gliding over the rimed turf to where Old Lady sprawled like a bleached stick before the scattered ashes.

He sat on some creek pebbles and stared at her.

She didn't dare look at him or beyond. He had made no sound, so how could she know he was anywhere about? She couldn't.

He sat there, tear marks on his cheeks.

Pretending to be just waking—but she had found no sleep from one end of the night to the other—Old Lady stood up, grunting and yawning, and turned in a circle to the dawn.

"Charlie?"

Her eyes passed from pines to soil, to sky, to the far hills. She called out his name, over and over again, and she felt like staring plumb straight at him, but she stopped herself. "Charlie? Oh, Charles!" she called, and heard the echoes say the very same.

He sat suddenly, beginning to grin a bit, knowing he was close to her, yet she must feel alone. Perhaps he felt the growing of a secret power, perhaps he felt secure from the world, certainly he was *pleased* with his invisibility.

She said aloud, "Now where *can* that boy be? If he only made a noise so I could tell just where he is, maybe I'd fry him a breakfast."

She prepared the morning victuals, irritated at his continuous quiet. She sizzled bacon on a hickory stick. "The smell of it will draw his nose," she muttered.

While her back was turned he swiped all the frying bacon and devoured it hastily.

She whirled, crying out, "Lord!"

She eyed the clearing suspiciously. "Charlie, that *you?*"

Charlie wiped his mouth clean on his wrists.

She trotted about the clearing, making like she was trying to locate him. Finally, with a clever thought, acting blind, she headed straight for him, groping. "Charlie, where *are* you?"

A lightning streak, he evaded her, bobbing, ducking.

It took all her will power not to give chase; but you can't chase invisible boys, so she sat down, scowling, sputtering, and tried to fry more bacon. But every fresh strip she cut he would steal bubbling off the fire and run away far. Finally, cheeks burning, she cried, "I know where you are! Right *there!* I hear you run!" She pointed to one side of him, not too accurate. He ran again. "Now you're there!" she shouted. "There, and there!" pointing to all the places he was in the next five minutes. "I hear you press a grass blade, knock a flower, snap a twig. I got fine shell ears, delicate as roses. They can hear the stars moving!"

Silently he galloped off among the pines, his voice trailing back, "Can't hear me when I'm set on a rock. I'll just *set!*"

All day he sat on an observatory rock in the clear wind, motionless and sucking his tongue.

Old Lady gathered wood in the deep forest, feeling his eyes weaseling on her spine. She wanted to babble: "Oh, I see you, I see you! I was only fooling about invisible boys! You're right there!" But she swallowed her gall and gummed it tight.

The following morning he did the spiteful thing. He began leaping from behind trees. He made toad-faces, frog-faces, spider-faces at her, clenching down his lips with his fingers, popping his raw eyes, pushing up his nostrils so you could peer in and see his brain thinking.

Once she dropped her kindling. She pretended it was a blue jay startled her.

He made a motion as if to strangle her.

She trembled a little.

He made another move as if to bang her shins and spit on her cheek.

These motions she bore without a lid-flicker or a mouth-twitch.

He stuck out his tongue, making strange bad noises. He wiggled his loose ears so she wanted to laugh, and finally she did laugh and explained it away quickly by saying, "Sat on a salamander! Whew, how it poked!"

By high noon the whole madness boiled to a terrible peak.

For it was at that exact hour that Charlie came racing down the valley stark boy-naked!

Old Lady nearly fell flat with shock!

"Charlie!" she almost cried.

Charlie raced naked up one side of a hill and naked down the other—naked as day, naked as the moon, raw as the sun and a newborn chick, his feet shimmering and rushing like the wings of a low-skimming hummingbird.

Old Lady's tongue locked in her mouth. What could she say? Charlie, go dress? For *shame? Stop* that? *Could* she?

Oh, Charlie, Charlie, God! Could she say that now? *Well?*

Up on the big rock, she witnessed him dancing up and down, naked as the day of his birth, stomping bare feet, smacking his hands on his knees and sucking in and out his white stomach like blowing and deflating a circus balloon.

She shut her eyes tight and prayed.

After three hours of this she pleaded, "Charlie, Charlie, come here! I got something to *tell* you!"

Like a fallen leaf he came, dressed again, praise the Lord.

"Charlie," she said, looking at the pine trees, "I see your right toe. *There* it is."

"You do?" he said.

"Yes," she said very sadly. "There it is like a horny toad on the grass. And there, up there's your left ear hanging on the air like a pink butterfly."

Charlie danced. "I'm forming in, I'm forming in!"

Old Lady nodded. "Here comes your ankle!"

"Gimme *both* my feet!" ordered Charlie.

"You got 'em."

"How about my hands?"

"I see one crawling on your knee like a daddy-longlegs."

"How about the other one?"

"It's crawling too."

"I got a body?"

"Shaping up fine."

"I'll need my head to go home, Old Lady."

To go home, she thought wearily. "No!" she said, stubborn and angry. "No, you ain't got no head. No head at all," she cried. She'd leave that to the very last. "No head, no head," she insisted.

"No head?" he wailed.

"Yes, oh my God, yes, yes, you got your blamed head!" she snapped giving up. "Now fetch me back my bat with the needle in his eye!"

He flung it at her. "Haaaa-yoooo!" His yelling went all up the valley, and long after he had run toward home she heard his echoes, racing.

Then she plucked up her kindling with a great dry weariness and started back toward her shack, sighing, talking. And Charlie followed her all the way, *really* invisible now, so she couldn't see him, just hear him, like a pine cone dropping or a deep underground stream trickling, or a squirrel clambering a bough; and over the fire at twilight she and Charlie sat, him so invisible, and her feeding him bacon he wouldn't take, so she ate it herself, and then she fixed some magic and fell asleep with Charlie, made out of sticks and rags and pebbles, but still warm and her very own son, slumbering and nice in her shaking mother arms . . . and they talked about golden things in drowsy voices until dawn made the fire slowly, slowly wither out. . . .

Night Meeting

Before going on up into the blue hills, Tomás Gomez stopped for gasoline at the lonely station.

"Kind of alone out here, aren't you, Pop?" said Tomás.

The old man wiped off the windshield of the small truck. "Not bad."

"How do you like Mars, Pop?"

"Fine. Always something new. I made up my mind when I came here last year I wouldn't expect nothing, nor ask nothing, nor be surprised at nothing. We've got to forget Earth and how things were. We've got to look at what we're in here, and how *different* it is. I get a hell of a lot of fun out of just the weather here. It's *Martian* weather. Hot as hell daytimes, cold as hell nights. I get a big kick out of the different flowers and different rain. I came to Mars to retire and I wanted to retire in a place where everything is different. An old man needs to have things different. Young people don't want to talk to him, other old people bore hell out of him. So I thought the best thing for me is a place so different that all you got to do is open your eyes and you're entertained. I got this gas

station. If business picks up too much, I'll move on back to
some other old highway that's not so busy, where I can
earn just enough to live on and still have time to feel the
different things here."

"You got the right idea, Pop," said Tomás, his brown
hands idly on the wheel. He was feeling good. He had
been working in one of the new colonies for ten days
straight and now he had two days off and was on his way
to a party.

"I'm not surprised at anything any more," said the old
man. "I'm just looking. I'm just experiencing. If you can't
take Mars for what she is, you might as well go back to
Earth. Everything's crazy up here, the soil, the air, the
canals, the natives (I never saw any yet, but I hear they're
around), the clocks. Even my clock acts funny. Even *time*
is crazy up here. Sometimes I feel I'm here all by myself,
no one else on the whole damn planet. I'd take bets on it.
Sometimes I feel about eight years old, my body squeezed
up and everything else tall. Jesus, it's just the place for an
old man. Keeps me alert and keeps me happy. You know
what Mars is? It's like a thing I got for Christmas seventy
years ago—don't know if you ever had one—they called
them kaleidoscopes, bits of crystal and cloth and beads
and pretty junk. You held it up to the sunlight and looked
in through at it, and it took your breath away. All the
patterns! Well, that's Mars. Enjoy it. Don't ask it to be
nothing else but what it is. Jesus, you know that highway
right there, built by the Martians, is over sixteen centuries
old and still in good condition? That's one dollar and fifty
cents, thanks and good night."

Tomás drove off down the ancient highway, laughing
quietly.

It was a long road going into darkness and hills and he
held to the wheel, now and again reaching into his lunch
bucket and taking out a piece of candy. He had been
driving steadily for an hour, with no other car on the road,
no light, just the road going under, the hum, the roar, and
Mars out there, so quiet. Mars was always quiet, but

quieter tonight than any other. The deserts and empty seas swung by him, and the mountains against the stars.

There was a smell of Time in the air tonight. He smiled and turned the fancy in his mind. There was a thought. What did Time smell like? Like dust and clocks and people. And if you wondered what Time sounded like it sounded like water running in a dark cave and voices crying and dirt dropping down upon hollow box lids, and rain. And, going further, what did Time *look* like? Time looked like snow dropping silently into a black room or it looked like a silent film in an ancient theater, one hundred billion faces falling like those New Year balloons, down and down into nothing. That was how Time smelled and looked and sounded. And tonight—Tomás shoved a hand into the wind outside the truck—tonight you could almost *touch* Time.

He drove the truck between hills of Time. His neck prickled and he sat up, watching ahead.

He pulled into a little dead Martian town, stopped the engine, and let the silence come in around him. He sat, not breathing, looking out at the white buildings in the moonlight. Uninhabited for centuries. Perfect, faultless, in ruins, yes, but perfect, nevertheless.

He started the engine and drove on another mile or more before stopping again, climbing out, carrying his lunch bucket, and walking to a little promontory where he could look back at that dusty city. He opened his thermos and poured himself a cup of coffee. A night bird flew by. He felt very good, very much at peace.

Perhaps five minutes later there was a sound. Off in the hills, where the ancient highway curved, there was a motion, a dim light, and then a murmur.

Tomás turned slowly with the coffee cup in his hand.

And out of the hills came a strange thing.

It was a machine like a jade-green insect, a praying mantis, delicately rushing through the cold air, indistinct, countless green diamonds winking over its body, and red jewels that glittered with multifaceted eyes. Its six legs fell upon the ancient highway with the sounds of a sparse rain which dwindled away, and from the back of the machine a Martian with melted gold for eyes looked down at Tomás as if he were looking into a well.

Tomás raised his hand and thought Hello! automatically but did not move his lips, for this *was* a Martian. But Tomás had swum in blue rivers on Earth, with strangers passing on the road, and eaten in strange houses with strange people, and his weapon had always been his smile. He did not carry a gun. And he did not feel the need of one now, even with the little fear that gathered about his heart at this moment.

The Martian's hands were empty too. For a moment they looked across the cool air at each other.

It was Tomás who moved first.

"Hello!" he called.

"Hello!" called the Martian in his own language.

They did not understand each other.

"Did you say hello?" they both asked.

"What did you say?" they said, each in a different tongue.

They scowled.

"Who are you?" said Tomás in English.

"What are you doing here?" In Martian; the stranger's lips moved.

"Where are you going?" they said, and looked bewildered.

"I'm Tomás Gomez."

"I'm Muhe Ca."

Neither understood, but they tapped their chests with the words and then it became clear.

And then the Martian laughed. "Wait!" Tomás felt his head touched, but no hand had touched him. "There!" said the Martian in English. "That is better!"

"You learned my language, so quick!"

"Nothing at all!"

They looked, embarrassed with a new silence, at the steaming coffee he had in one hand.

"Something different?" said the Martian, eying him and the coffee, referring to them both, perhaps.

"May I offer you a drink?" said Tomás.

"Please."

The Martian slid down from his machine.

A second cup was produced and filled, steaming. Tomás held it out.

Their hands met and—like mist—fell through each other.

"Jesus Christ!" cried Tomás, and dropped the cup.

"Name of the Gods!" said the Martian in his own tongue.

"Did you see what happened?" they both whispered.

They were very cold and terrified.

The Martian bent to touch the cup but could not touch it.

"Jesus!" said Tomás.

"Indeed." The Martian tried again and again to get hold of the cup, but could not. He stood up and thought for a moment, then took a knife from his belt. "Hey!" cried Tomás. "You misunderstand. Catch!" said the Martian, and tossed it. Tomás cupped his hands. The knife fell through his flesh. It hit the ground. Tomás bent to pick it up but could not touch it, and he recoiled, shivering.

Now he looked at the Martian against the sky.

"The stars!" he said.

"The stars!" said the Martian, looking, in turn, at Tomás.

The stars were white and sharp beyond the flesh of the Martian, and they were sewn into his flesh like scintillas swallowed into the thin, phosphorescent membrane of a gelatinous sea fish. You could see stars flickering like violet eyes in the Martian's stomach and chest, and through his wrists, like jewelry.

"I can see through you!" said Tomás.

"And I through you!" said the Martian, stepping back.

Tomás felt of his own body and, feeling the warmth, was reassured. *I* am real, he thought.

The Martian touched his own nose and lips. "*I* have flesh," he said, half aloud. "*I* am alive."

Tomás stared at the stranger. "And if *I* am real, then *you* must be dead."

"No, you!"

"A ghost!"

"A phantom!"

They pointed at each other, with starlight burning in their limbs like daggers and icicles and fireflies, and then fell to judging their limbs again, each finding himself intact, hot, excited, stunned, awed, and the other, ah yes, that other over there, unreal, a ghostly prism flashing the accumulated light of distant worlds.

I'm drunk, thought Tomás. I won't tell anyone of this tomorrow, no, no.

They stood there on the ancient highway, neither of them moving.

"Where are you from?" asked the Martian at last.

"Earth."

"What is that?"

"There." Tomás nodded to the sky.

"When?"

"We landed over a year ago, remember?"

"No."

"And all of you were dead, all but a few. You're rare, don't you *know* that?"

"That's not true."

"Yes, dead. I saw the bodies. Black, in the rooms, in the houses, dead. Thousands of them."

"That's ridiculous. We're *alive!*"

"Mister, you're invaded, only you don't know it. You must have escaped."

"I haven't escaped; there was nothing to escape. What do you mean? I'm on my way to a festival now at the canal, near the Eniall Mountains. I was there last night. Don't you see the city there?" The Martian pointed.

Tomás looked and saw the ruins. "Why, that city's been dead thousands of years."

The Martian laughed. "Dead? I slept there yesterday!"

"And I was in it a week ago and the week before that,

and I just drove through it now, and it's a heap. See the broken pillars?"

"Broken? Why, I see them perfectly. The moonlight helps. And the pillars are upright."

"There's dust in the streets," said Tomás.

"The streets are clean!"

"The canals are empty right there."

"The canals are full of lavender wine!"

"It's dead."

"It's alive!" protested the Martian, laughing more now. "Oh, you're quite wrong. See all the carnival lights? There are beautiful boats as slim as women, beautiful women as slim as boats, women the color of sand, women with fire flowers in their hands. I can see them, small, running in the streets there. That's where I'm going now, to the festival; we'll float on the waters all night long; we'll sing, we'll drink, we'll make love. Can't you see it?"

"Mister, that city is dead as a dried lizard. Ask any of our party. Me, I'm on my way to Green City tonight; that's the new colony we just raised over near Illinois Highway. You're mixed up. We brought in a million board feet of Oregon lumber and a couple dozen tons of good steel nails and hammered together two of the nicest little villages you ever saw. Tonight we're warming one of them. A couple rockets are coming in from Earth, bringing our wives and girl friends. There'll be barn dances and whiskey——"

The Martian was now disquieted. "You say it is over *that* way?"

"There are the rockets." Tomás walked him to the edge of the hill and pointed down. "See?"

"No."

"Damn it, there they *are!* Those long silver things."

"No."

Now Tomás laughed. "You're blind!"

"I see very well. You are the one who does not see."

"But you see the new *town*, don't you?"

"I see nothing but an ocean, and water at low tide."

"Mister, that water's been evaporated for forty centuries."

"Ah, now, now, that *is* enough."

"It's true, I tell you."

The Martian grew very serious. "Tell me again. You do not see the city the way I describe it? The pillars very white, the boats very slender, the festival lights—oh, I see them *clearly!* And listen! I can hear them singing. It's no space away at all."

Tomás listened and shook his head. "No."

"And I, on the other hand," said the Martian, "cannot see what you describe. Well."

Again they were cold. An ice was in their flesh.

"Can it be . . . ?"

"What?"

"You say 'from the sky'?"

"Earth."

"Earth, a name, nothing," said the Martian. "*But* . . . as I came up the pass an hour ago . . ." He touched the back of his neck. "I felt . . ."

"Cold?"

"Yes."

"And now?"

"Cold again. Oddly. There was a thing to the light, to the hills, the road," said the Martian. "I felt the strangeness, the road, the light, and for a moment I felt as if I were the last man alive on this world. . . ."

"So did I!" said Tomás, and it was like talking to an old and dear friend, confiding, growing warm with the topic.

The Martian closed his eyes and opened them again. "This can only mean one thing. It has to do with Time. Yes. You are a figment of the Past!"

"No, you are from the Past," said the Earth Man, having had time to think of it now.

"You are so *certain.* How can you prove who is from the Past, who from the Future? What year is it?"

"Two thousand and one!"

"What does that mean to *me?*"

Tomás considered and shrugged. "Nothing."

"It is as if I told you that it is the year 4462853 s.e.c. It is nothing and more than nothing! Where is the clock to show us how the stars stand?"

"But the ruins prove it! They prove that *I* am the Future, *I* am alive, *you* are dead!"

"Everything in me denies this. My heart beats, my stomach hungers, my mouth thirsts. No, no, not dead, not alive, either of us. More alive than anything else. Caught between is more like it. Two strangers passing in the night, that is it. Two strangers passing. Ruins, you say?"

"Yes. You're afraid?"

"Who wants to see the Future, who *ever* does? A man can face the Past, but to think—the pillars *crumbled,* you say? And the sea empty, and the canals dry, and the maidens dead, and the flowers withered?" The Martian was silent, but then he looked on ahead. "But there they *are.* I *see* them. Isn't that enough for me? They wait for me now, no matter *what* you say."

And for Tomás the rockets, far away, waiting for *him,* and the town and the women from Earth. "We can never agree," he said.

"Let us agree to disagree," said the Martian. "What does it matter who is Past or Future, if we are both alive, for what follows will follow, tomorrow or in ten thousand years. How do you know that those temples are not the temples of your own civilization one hundred centuries from now, tumbled and broken? You do not know. Then don't ask. But the night is very short. There go the festival fires in the sky, and the birds."

Tomás put out his hand. The Martian did likewise in imitation.

Their hands did not touch; they melted through each other.

"Will we meet again?"

"Who knows? Perhaps some other night."

"I'd like to go with you to that festival."

"And I wish I might come to your new town, to see this ship you speak of, to see these men, to hear all that has happened."

"Good-by," said Tomás.

"Good night."

The Martian rode his green metal vehicle quietly away into the hills. The Earth Man turned his truck and drove it silently in the opposite direction.

"Good lord, what a dream that was," sighed Tomás, his hands on the wheel, thinking of the rockets, the women, the raw whiskey, the Virginia reels, the party.

How strange a vision was that, thought the Martian, rushing on, thinking of the festival, the canals, the boats, the women with golden eyes, and the songs.

The night was dark. The moons had gone down. Starlight twinkled on the empty highway where now there was not a sound, no car, no person, nothing. And it remained that way all the rest of the cool dark night.

The Fox
and the Forest

There were fireworks the very first night, things
that you should be afraid of perhaps, for they might remind you of other more horrible things, but these were
beautiful, rockets that ascended into the ancient soft air of
Mexico and shook the stars apart in blue and white fragments. Everything was good and sweet, the air was that
blend of the dead and the living, of the rains and the
dusts, of the incense from the church and the brass smell
of the tubas on the bandstand which pulsed out vast
rhythms of "La Paloma." The church doors were thrown
wide and it seemed as if a giant yellow constellation had
fallen from the October sky and lay breathing fire upon
the church walls; a million candles sent their color and
fumes about. Newer and better fireworks scurried like
tightrope-walking comets across the cool-tiled square,
banged against adobe café walls, then rushed on hot wires
to bash the high church tower, in which boys' naked feet
alone could be seen kicking and re-kicking, clanging and

tilting and re-tilting the monster bells into monstrous music. A flaming bull blundered about the plaza chasing laughing men and screaming children.

"The year is 1938," said William Travis, standing by his wife on the edge of the yelling crowd, smiling. "A good year."

The bull rushed upon them. Ducking, the couple ran, with fire balls pelting them, past the music and riot, the church, the band, under the stars, clutching each other, laughing. The bull passed, carried lightly on the shoulders of a charging Mexican, a framework of bamboo and sulphurous gunpowder.

"I've never enjoyed myself so much in my life." Susan Travis had stopped for her breath.

"It's amazing," said William.

"It will go on, won't it?"

"All night."

"No, I mean our trip."

He frowned and patted his breast pocket. "I've enough traveler's checks for a lifetime. Enjoy yourself. Forget it. They'll never find us."

"Never?"

"Never."

Now someone was setting off giant crackers, hurling them from the great bell-tolling tower of the church in a sputter of smoke, while the crowd below fell back under the threat and the crackers exploded in wonderful concussions among their dancing feet and flailing bodies. A wondrous smell of frying tortillas hung all about, and in the cafés men sat at tables looking out, mugs of beer in their brown hands.

The bull was dead. The fire was out of the bamboo tubes and he was expended. The laborer lifted the framework from his shoulders. Little boys clustered to touch the magnificent papier-mâché head, the real horns.

"Let's examine the bull," said William.

As they walked past the café entrance Susan saw the man looking out at them, a white man in a salt-white suit, with a blue tie and blue shirt, and a thin, sunburned face.

His hair was blond and straight and his eyes were blue, and he watched them as they walked.

She would never have noticed him if it had not been for the bottles at his immaculate elbow; a fat bottle of crème de menthe, a clear bottle of vermouth, a flagon of cognac, and seven other bottles of assorted liqueurs, and, at his fingertips, ten small half-filled glasses from which, without taking his eyes off the street, he sipped, occasionally squinting, pressing his thin mouth shut upon the savor. In his free hand a thin Havana cigar smoked, and on a chair stood twenty cartons of Turkish cigarettes, six boxes of cigars, and some packaged colognes.

"Bill——" whispered Susan.

"Take it easy," he said. "He's nobody."

"I saw him in the plaza this morning."

"Don't look back, keep walking. Examine the papier-mâché bull here. That's it, ask questions."

"Do you think he's from the Searchers?"

"They couldn't follow us!"

"They might!"

"What a nice bull," said William to the man who owned it.

"He couldn't have followed us back through two hundred years, could he?"

"Watch yourself, for God's sake," said William.

She swayed. He crushed her elbow tightly, steering her away.

"Don't faint." He smiled, to make it look good. "You'll be all right. Let's go right in that café, drink in front of him, so if he *is* what we think he is, he won't suspect."

"No, I couldn't."

"We've *got* to. Come on now. And so I said to David, that's ridiculous!" This last in a loud voice as they went up the café steps.

We are here, thought Susan. Who are we? Where are we going? What do we fear? Start at the beginning, she told herself, holding to her sanity, as she felt the adobe floor underfoot.

My name is Ann Kristen; my husband's name is Roger.

We were born in the year 2155 A.D. And we lived in a world that was evil. A world that was like a great black ship pulling away from the shore of sanity and civilization, roaring its black horn in the night, taking two billion people with it, whether they wanted to go or not, to death, to fall over the edge of the earth and the sea into radioactive flame and madness.

They walked into the café. The man was staring at them.

A phone rang.

The phone startled Susan. She remembered a phone ringing two hundred years in the future, on that blue April morning in 2155, and herself answering it:

"Ann, this is Rene! Have you heard? I mean about Travel in Time, Incorporated? Trips to Rome in 21 B.C., trips to Napoleon's Waterloo—any time, any place!"

"Rene, you're joking."

"No. Clinton Smith left this morning for Philadelphia in 1776. Travel in Time, Inc., arranges everything. Costs money. But, *think*—to actually see the burning of Rome, Kubla Khan, Moses and the Red Sea! You've probably got an ad in your tube mail now."

She had opened the suction mail tube and there was the metal foil advertisement:

ROME AND THE BORGIAS!
THE WRIGHT BROTHERS AT KITTY HAWK!

Travel in Time, Inc., can costume you, put you in a crowd during the assassination of Lincoln or Caesar! We guarantee to teach you any language you need to move freely in any civilization, in any year, without friction. Latin, Greek, ancient American colloquial. Take your vacation in *Time* as well as Place!

Rene's voice was buzzing on the phone. "Tom and I leave for 1492 tomorrow. They're arranging for Tom to sail with Columbus. Isn't it amazing!"

"Yes," murmured Ann, stunned. "What does the Government say about this Time Machine company?"

"Oh, the police have an eye on it. Afraid people might

evade the draft, run off and hide in the Past. Everyone has to leave a security bond behind, his house and belongings, to guarantee return. After all, the war's on."

"Yes, the war," murmured Ann. "The war."

Standing there, holding the phone, she had thought, Here is the chance my husband and I have talked and prayed over for so many years. We don't like this world of 2155. We want to run away from his work at the bomb factory, I from my position with disease-culture units. Perhaps there is a chance for us to escape, to run for centuries into a wild country of years where they will never find and bring us back to burn our books, censor our thoughts, scald our minds with fear, march us, scream at us with radios . . .

They were in Mexico in the year 1938.

She looked at the stained café wall.

Good workers for the Future State were allowed vacations into the Past to escape fatigue. And so she and her husband had moved back into 1938, a room in New York City, and enjoyed the theaters and the Statue of Liberty which still stood green in the harbor. And on the third day they had changed their clothes, their names, and had flown off to hide in Mexico!

"It *must* be him," whispered Susan, looking at the stranger seated at the table. "Those cigarettes, the cigars, the liquor. They give him away. Remember *our* first night in the Past?"

A month ago, their first night in New York, before their flight, drinking all the strange drinks, savoring and buying odd foods, perfumes, cigarettes of ten dozen rare brands, for they were rare in the Future, where war was everything. So they had made fools of themselves, rushing in and out of stores, salons, tobacconists, going up to their room to get wonderfully ill.

And now here was this stranger doing likewise, doing a thing that only a man from the Future would do who had been starved for liquors and cigarettes for many years.

Susan and William sat and ordered a drink.

The stranger was examining their clothes, their hair, their jewelry—the way they walked and sat.

"Sit easily," said William under his breath. "Look as if you've worn this clothing style all your life."

"We should never have tried to escape."

"My God!" said William, "he's coming over. Let me do the talking."

The stranger bowed before them. There was the faintest tap of heels knocking together. Susan stiffened. That military sound!—unmistakable as that certain ugly rap on your door at midnight.

"Mr. Roger Kristen," said the stranger, "you did not pull up your pant legs when you sat down."

William froze. He looked at his hands lying on either leg, innocently. Susan's heart was beating swiftly.

"You've got the wrong person," said William quickly. "My name's not Krisler."

"Kris*ten*," corrected the stranger.

"I'm William Travis," said William. "And I don't see what my pant legs have to do with you!"

"Sorry." The stranger pulled up a chair. "Let us say I thought I knew you because you did *not* pull your trousers up. *Everyone* does. If they don't, the trousers bag quickly. I am a long way from home, Mr.—Travis, and in need of company. My name is Simms."

"Mr. Simms, we appreciate your loneliness, but we're tired. We're leaving for Acapulco tomorrow."

"A charming spot. I was just there, looking for some friends of mine. They are somewhere. I shall find them yet. Oh, is the lady a bit sick?"

"Good night, Mr. Simms."

They started out the door, William holding Susan's arm firmly. They did not look back when Mr. Simms called, "Oh, just one other thing." He paused and then slowly spoke the words:

"2155 A.D."

Susan shut her eyes and felt the earth falter under her. She kept going, into the fiery plaza, seeing nothing.

* * *

They locked the door of their hotel room. And then she was crying and they were standing in the dark, and the room tilted under them. Far away firecrackers exploded, and there was laughter in the plaza.

"What a damned, loud nerve," said William. "Him sitting there, looking us up and down like animals, smoking his damn cigarettes, drinking his drinks. I should have killed him then!" His voice was nearly hysterical. "He even had the nerve to use his real name to us. The Chief of the Searchers. And the thing about my pant legs. My God, I should have pulled them up when I sat. It's an automatic gesture of this day and age. When I didn't do it, it set me off from the others; it made *him* think, Here's a man who never wore pants, a man used to breech uniforms, and Future styles. I could kill myself for giving us away!"

"No, no, it was my walk—these high heels—that did it. Our haircuts—so new, so fresh. Everything about us odd and uneasy."

He turned on the light. "He's still testing us. He's not positive of us—not completely. We can't run out on him, then. We can't make him certain. We'll go to Acapulco leisurely."

"Maybe he *is* sure of us, but is just playing."

"I wouldn't put it past him. He's got all the time in the world. He can dally here if he wants, and bring us back to the Future sixty seconds after we left it. He might keep us wondering for days, laughing at us."

Susan sat on the bed, wiping the tears from her face, smelling the old smell of charcoal and incense.

"They won't make a scene, will they?"

"They won't dare. They'll have to get us alone to put us in that Time Machine and send us back."

"There's a solution then," she said. "We'll never be alone; we'll always be in crowds. We'll make a million friends, visit markets, sleep in the Official Palaces in each town, pay the Chief of Police to guard us until we find a way to kill Simms and escape, disguise ourselves in new clothes, perhaps as Mexicans."

Footsteps sounded outside their locked door.

They turned out the light and undressed in silence. The footsteps went away. A door closed.

Susan stood by the window looking down at the plaza in the darkness. "So that building there is a church?"

"Yes."

"I've often wondered what a church looked like. It's been so long since anyone saw one. Can we visit it tomorrow?"

"Of course. Come to bed."

They lay in the dark room.

Half an hour later their phone rang. She lifted the receiver.

"Hello?"

"The rabbits may hide in the forest," said the voice, "but a fox can always find them."

She replaced the receiver and lay back straight and cold in the bed.

Outside, in the year 1938, a man played three tunes upon a guitar, one following another.

During the night she put her hand out and almost touched the year 2155. She felt her fingers slide over cool spaces of time, as over a corrugated surface, and she heard the insistent thump of marching feet, a million bands playing a million military tunes, and she saw the fifty thousand rows of disease cultures in their aseptic glass tubes, her hand reaching out to them at her work in that huge factory in the Future; the tubes of leprosy, bubonic, typhoid, tuberculosis, and then the great explosion. She saw her hand burned to a wrinkled plum, felt it recoil from a concussion so immense that the world was lifted and let fall and all the buildings broke and people hemorrhaged and lay silent. Great volcanoes, machines, winds, avalanches slid down to silence and she awoke, sobbing, in the bed, in Mexico, many years away. . . .

In the early morning, drugged with the single hour's sleep they had finally been able to obtain, they awoke to the sound of loud automobiles in the street. Susan peered down from the iron balcony at a small crowd of eight people only now emerging, chattering, yelling, from trucks and cars with red lettering on them. A crowd of Mexicans had followed the trucks.

"*Qué pase?*" Susan called to a little boy.

The boy replied.

Susan turned back to her husband. "An American motion-picture company, here on location."

"Sounds interesting." William was in the shower. "Let's watch them. I don't think we'd better leave today. We'll try to lull Simms. Watch the films being made. They say the primitive film making was something. Get our minds off ourselves."

Ourselves, thought Susan. For a moment, in the bright sun, she had forgotten that somewhere in the hotel, waiting, was a man smoking a thousand cigarettes, it seemed. She saw the eight loud happy Americans below and wanted to call to them: "Save me, hide me, help me! Color my hair, my eyes; clothe me in strange clothes. I need your help. I'm from the year 2155!"

But the words stayed in her throat. The functionaries of Travel in Time, Inc., were not foolish. In your brain, before you left on your trip, they placed a psychological block. You could tell no one your true time or birthplace, nor could you reveal any of the Future to those in the Past. The Past and the Future must be protected from each other. Only with this psychological block were people allowed to travel unguarded through the ages. The Future must be protected from any change brought about by her people traveling in the Past. Even if she wanted to with all her heart, she could not tell any of those happy people below in the plaza who she was, or what her predicament had become.

"What about breakfast?" said William.

Breakfast was being served in the immense dining room. Ham and eggs for everyone. The place was full of tourists. The film people entered, all eight of them—six men and two women, giggling, shoving chairs about. And Susan sat near them, feeling the warmth and protection they offered, even when Mr. Simms came down the lobby stairs, smoking his Turkish cigarette with great intensity. He nodded at them from a distance, and Susan nodded back, smiling, because he couldn't do anything to them here, in front of eight film people and twenty other tourists.

"Those actors," said William. "Perhaps I could hire two of them, say it was a joke, dress them in our clothes, have them drive off in our car when Simms is in such a spot where he can't see their faces. If two people pretending to be us could lure him off for a few hours, we might make it to Mexico City. It'd take him years to find us there!"

"Hey!"

A fat man, with liquor on his breath, leaned on their table.

"American tourists!" he cried. "I'm so sick of seeing Mexicans, I could kiss you!" He shook their hands. "Come on, eat with us. Misery loves company. I'm Misery, this is Miss Gloom, and Mr. and Mrs. Do-We-Hate-Mexico! We all hate it. But we're here for some preliminary shots for a damn film. The rest of the crew arrives tomorrow. My name's Joe Melton. I'm a director. And if this ain't a hell of a country! Funerals in the streets, people dying. Come on, move over. Join the party; cheer us up!"

Susan and William were both laughing.

"Am I funny?" Mr. Melton asked the immediate world.

"Wonderful!" Susan moved over.

Mr. Simms was glaring across the dining room at them. She made a face at him.

Mr. Simms advanced among the tables.

"Mr. and Mrs. Travis," he called. "I thought we were breakfasting together, alone."

"Sorry," said William.

"Sit down, pal," said Mr. Melton. "Any friend of theirs is a pal of mine."

Mr. Simms sat. The film people talked loudly, and while they talked, Mr. Simms said quietly, "I hope you slept well."

"Did you?"

"I'm not used to spring mattresses," replied Mr. Simms wryly. "But there are compensations. I stayed up half the night trying new cigarettes and foods. Odd, fascinating. A whole new spectrum of sensation, these ancient vices."

"We don't know what you're talking about," said Susan.

"Always the play acting." Simms laughed. "It's no use. Nor is this stratagem of crowds. I'll get you alone soon enough. I'm immensely patient."

"Say," Mr. Melton broke in, his face flushed, "is this guy giving you any trouble?"

"It's all right."

"Say the word and I'll give him the bum's rush."

Melton turned back to yell at his associates. In the laughter, Mr. Simms went on: "Let us come to the point. It took me a month of tracing you through towns and cities to find you, and all of yesterday to be sure of you. If you come with me quietly, I might be able to get you off with no punishment, if you agree to go back to work on the hydrogen-plus bomb."

"Science this guy talks at breakfast!" observed Mr. Melton, half listening.

Simms went on, imperturbably. "Think it over. You can't escape. If you kill me, others will follow you."

"We don't know what you're talking about."

"Stop it!" cried Simms irritably. "Use your intelligence! You know we can't let you get away with this escape. Other people in the year 2155 might get the same idea and do what you've done. We need people."

"To fight your wars," said William at last.

"Bill!"

"It's all right, Susan. We'll talk on his terms now. We can't escape."

"Excellent," said Simms. "Really, you've both been incredibly romantic, running away from your responsibilities."

"Running away from horror."

"Nonsense. Only a war."

"What are you guys talking about?" asked Mr. Melton.

Susan wanted to tell him. But you could only speak in

generalities. The psychological block in your mind allowed that. Generalities, such as Simms and William were now discussing.

"Only *the* war," said William. "Half the world dead of leprosy bombs!"

"Nevertheless," Simms pointed out, "the inhabitants of the Future resent you two hiding on a tropical isle, as it were, while they drop off the cliff into hell. Death loves death, not life. Dying people love to know that others die with them. It is a comfort to learn you are not alone in the kiln, in the grave. I am the guardian of their collective resentment against you two."

"Look at the guardian of resentments!" said Mr. Melton to his companions.

"The longer you keep me waiting, the harder it will go for you. We need you on the bomb project, Mr. Travis. Return now—no torture. Later, we'll force you to work, and after you've finished the bomb, we'll try a number of complicated new devices on you, sir."

"I've a proposition," said William. "I'll come back with you if my wife stays here alive, safe, away from that war."

Mr. Simms considered it. "All right. Meet me in the plaza in ten minutes. Pick me up in your car. Drive me to a deserted country spot. I'll have the Travel Machine pick us up there."

"Bill!" Susan held his arm tightly.

"Don't argue." He looked over at her. "It's settled." To Simms: "One thing. Last night you could have gotten in our room and kidnaped us. Why didn't you?"

"Shall we say that I was enjoying myself?" replied Mr. Simms languidly, sucking his new cigar. "I hate giving up this wonderful atmosphere, this sun, this vacation. I regret leaving behind the wine and the cigarettes. Oh, how I regret it. The plaza then, in ten minutes. Your wife will be protected and may stay here as long as she wishes. Say your good-bys."

Mr. Simms arose and walked out.

"There goes Mr. Big Talk!" yelled Mr. Melton at the departing gentleman. He turned and looked at Susan.

"Hey. Someone's crying. Breakfast's no time for people to cry. Now *is* it?"

At nine-fifteen Susan stood on the balcony of their room, gazing down at the plaza. Mr. Simms was seated there, his neat legs crossed, on a delicate bronze bench. Biting the tip from a cigar, he lit it tenderly.

Susan heard the throb of a motor, and far up the street, out of a garage and down the cobbled hill, slowly, came William in his car.

The car picked up speed. Thirty, now forty, now fifty miles an hour. Chickens scattered before it.

Mr. Simms took off his white panama hat and mopped his pink forehead, put his hat back on, and then saw the car.

It was rushing sixty miles an hour, straight on for the plaza.

"William!" screamed Susan.

The car hit the low plaza curb, thundering; it jumped up, sped across the tiles toward the green bench where Mr. Simms now dropped his cigar, shrieked, flailed his hands, and was hit by the car. His body flew up and up in the air, and down and down, crazily, into the street.

On the far side of the plaza, one front wheel broken, the car stopped. People were running.

Susan went in and closed the balcony doors.

They came down the Official Palace steps together, arm in arm, their faces pale, at twelve noon.

"*Adiós, señor*," said the mayor behind them. "*Señora.*"

They stood in the plaza where the crowd was pointing at the blood.

"Will they want to see you again?" asked Susan.

"No, we went over and over it. It was an accident. I lost control of the car. I wept for them. God knows I had to get my relief out somewhere. I *felt* like weeping. I hated to kill him. I've never wanted to do anything like that in my life."

"They won't prosecute you?"

"They talked about it, but no. I talked faster. They believe me. It was an accident. It's over."

"Where will we go? Mexico City? Uruapan?"

"The car's in the repair shop. It'll be ready at four this afternoon. Then we'll get the hell out."

"Will we be followed? Was Simms working alone?"

"I don't know. We'll have a little head start on them, I think."

The film people were coming out of the hotel as they approached. Mr. Melton hurried up, scowling. "Hey, I heard what happened. Too bad. Everything okay now? Want to get your minds off it? We're doing some preliminary shots up the street. You want to watch, you're welcome. Come on, do you good."

They went.

They stood on the cobbled street while the film camera was being set up. Susan looked at the road leading down and away, and the highway going to Acapulco and the sea, past pyramids and ruins and little adobe towns with yellow walls, blue walls, purple walls and flaming bougainvillaea, and she thought, We shall take the roads, travel in clusters and crowds, in markets, in lobbies, bribe police to sleep near, keep double locks, but always the crowds, never alone again, always afraid the next person who passes may be another Simms. Never knowing if we've tricked and lost the Searchers. And always up ahead, in the Future, they'll wait for us to be brought back, waiting with their bombs to burn us and disease to rot us, and their police to tell us to roll over, turn around, jump through the hoop! And so we'll keep running through the forest, and we'll never ever stop or sleep well again in our lives.

A crowd gathered to watch the film being made. And Susan watched the crowd and the streets.

"Seen anyone suspicious?"

"No. What time is it?"

"Three o'clock. The car should be almost ready."

The test film was finished at three forty-five. They all

walked down to the hotel, talking. William paused at the garage. "The car'll be ready at six," he said, coming out, worried.

"But no later than that?"

"It'll be ready, don't worry."

In the hotel lobby they looked around for other men traveling alone, men who resembled Mr. Simms, men with new haircuts and too much cigarette smoke and cologne smell about them, but the lobby was empty. Going up the stairs, Mr. Melton said, "Well, it's been a long hard day. Who'd like to put a header on it? You folks? Martini? Beer?"

"Maybe one."

The whole crowd pushed into Mr. Melton's room and the drinking began.

"Watch the time," said William.

Time, thought Susan. If only they had time. All she wanted was to sit in the plaza all of a long bright day in October, with not a worry or a thought, with the sun on her face and arms, her eyes closed, smiling at the warmth, and never move. Just sleep in the Mexican sun, and sleep warmly and easily and slowly and happily for many, many days. . . .

Mr. Melton opened the champagne.

"To a very beautiful lady, lovely enough for films," he said, toasting Susan. "I might even give you a test."

She laughed.

"I mean it," said Melton. "You're very nice. I could make you a movie star."

"And take me to Hollywood?" cried Susan.

"Get the hell out of Mexico, sure!"

Susan glanced at William and he lifted an eyebrow and nodded. It would be a change of scene, clothing, locale, name, perhaps; and they would be traveling with eight other people, a good shield against any interference from the Future.

"It sounds wonderful," said Susan.

She was feeling the champagne now. The afternoon was

slipping by; the party was whirling about her. She felt safe and good and alive and truly happy for the first time in many years.

"What kind of film would my wife be good for?" asked William, refilling his glass.

Melton appraised Susan. The party stopped laughing and listened.

"Well, I'd like to do a story of suspense," said Melton. "A story of a man and wife, like yourselves."

"Go on."

"Sort of a war story, maybe," said the director, examining the color of his drink against the sunlight.

Susan and William waited.

"A story about a man and wife who live in a little house on a little street in the year 2155, maybe," said Melton. "This is ad lib, understand. But this man and wife are faced with a terrible war, super-plus hydrogen bombs, censorship, death in that year, and—here's the gimmick— they escape into the Past, followed by a man who they think is evil, but who is only trying to show them what their duty is."

William dropped his glass to the floor.

Mr. Melton continued: "And this couple take refuge with a group of film people whom they learn to trust. Safety in numbers, they say to themselves."

Susan felt herself slip down into a chair. Everyone was watching the director. He took a little sip of wine. "Ah, that's a fine wine. Well, this man and woman, it seems, don't realize how important they are to the Future. The man, especially, is the keystone to a new bomb metal. So the Searchers, let's call them, spare no trouble or expense to find, capture, and take home the man and wife, once they get them totally alone, in a hotel room, where no one can see. Strategy. The Searchers work alone, or in groups of eight. One trick or another will do it. Don't you think it would make a wonderful film, Susan? Don't you, Bill?" He finished his drink.

Susan sat with her eyes straight ahead of her.

"Have a drink?" said Mr. Melton.

William's gun was out and fired three times, and one of the men fell, and the others ran forward. Susan screamed. A hand was clamped to her mouth. Now the gun was on the floor and William was struggling, held.

Mr. Melton said, "Please," standing there where he had stood, blood showing on his fingers. "Let's not make matters worse."

Someone pounded on the hall door.

"Let me in!"

"The manager," said Mr. Melton dryly. He jerked his head. "Everyone, let's move!"

"Let me in! I'll call the police!"

Susan and William looked at each other quickly, and then at the door.

"The manager wishes to come in," said Mr. Melton. "Quick!"

A camera was carried forward. From it shot a blue light which encompassed the room instantly. It widened out and the people of the party vanished, one by one.

"Quickly!"

Outside the window, in the instant before she vanished, Susan saw the green land and the purple and yellow and blue and crimson walls and the cobbles flowing down like a river, a man upon a burro riding into the warm hills, a boy drinking Orange Crush, she could feel the sweet liquid in her throat, a man standing under a cool plaza tree with a guitar, she could feel her hand upon the strings, and, far away, the sea, the blue and tender sea, she could feel it roll her over and take her in.

And then she was gone. Her husband was gone.

The door burst wide open. The manager and his staff rushed in.

The room was empty.

"But they were just here! I saw them come in, and now —gone!" cried the manager. "The windows are covered with iron grating. They couldn't get out that way!"

In the late afternoon the priest was summoned and they

opened the room again and aired it out, and had him
sprinkle holy water through each corner and give it his
blessing.

"What shall we do with these?" asked the charwoman.

She pointed to the closet, where there were 67 bottles of
chartreuse, cognac, *crème de cacao*, absinthe, vermouth,
tequila, 106 cartons of Turkish cigarettes, and 198 yellow
boxes of fifty-cent pure Havana-filler cigars. . . .

Skeleton

It was past time for him to see the doctor
again. Mr. Harris turned palely in at the stairwell, and on
his way up the flight saw Dr. Burleigh's name gilded over
a pointing arrow. Would Dr. Burleigh sigh when he
walked in? After all, this would make the tenth trip so far
this year. But Burleigh shouldn't complain; he was paid
for the examinations!

The nurse looked Mr. Harris over and smiled, a bit
amusedly, as she tiptoed to the glazed glass door, opened
it, and put her head in. Harris thought he heard her say,
"Guess who's here, Doctor." And didn't the doctor's voice
reply, faintly, "Oh, my God, *again?*" Harris swallowed uneasily.

When Harris walked in, Dr. Burleigh snorted. "Aches in
your bones again! Ah!!" He scowled and adjusted his
glasses. "My dear Harris, you've been curried with the
finest-toothed combs and bacteria-brushes known to science. You're just nervous. Let's see your fingers. Too many
cigarettes. Let's smell your breath. Too much protein. Let's
see your eyes. Not enough sleep. My response? Go to bed,
stop the protein, no smoking. Ten dollars, please."

Harris stood sulking.

The doctor glanced up from his papers. "*You* still here? You're a hypochondriac! That's *eleven* dollars, now."

"But why should my bones ache?" asked Harris.

Dr. Burleigh spoke as to a child. "You ever had a sore muscle, and kept irritating it, fussing with it, rubbing it? It gets worse, the more you bother it. Then you leave it alone and the pain vanishes. You realize you caused most of the soreness yourself. Well, son, that's what's with you. Leave yourself alone. Take a dose of salts. Get out of here and take that trip to Phoenix you've stewed about for months. Do you good to travel!"

Five minutes later, Mr. Harris riffled through a classified phone directory at the corner druggist's. A fine lot of sympathy one got from blind fools like Burleigh! He passed his finger down a list of BONE SPECIALISTS, found one named M. Munigant. Munigant lacked an M.D. or any other academic lettering behind his name, but his office was conveniently near. Three blocks down, one block over. . . .

M. Munigant, like his office, was small and dark. Like his office, he smelled of iodoform, iodine, and other odd things. He was a good listener, though, and listened with eager shiny moves of his eyes, and when he talked to Harris, his accent was such that he softly whistled each word; undoubtedly because of imperfect dentures.

Harris told all.

M. Munigant nodded. He had seen cases like this before. The bones of the body. Man was not aware of his bones. Ah, yes, the bones. The skeleton. Most difficult. Something concerning an imbalance, an unsympathetic coordination between soul, flesh, and skeleton. Very complicated, softly whistled M. Munigant. Harris listened, fascinated. Now, *here* was a doctor who understood his illness! Psychological, said M. Munigant. He moved swiftly, delicately to a dingy wall and slashed down half a dozen X-rays to haunt the room with their look of things found floating in an ancient tide. Here, here! The skeleton surprised! Here luminous portraits of the long, the short, the large, the small bones. Mr. Harris must be aware of his position, his problem! M. Munigant's hand tapped, rattled, whispered, scratched at faint nebulae of flesh in which hung ghosts of cranium, spinal cord, pelvis, lime, calcium, marrow, here, there, this, that, these, those, and others! Look!

Harris shuddered. The X-rays and the paintings blew in a green and phosphorescent wind from a land peopled by the monsters of Dali and Fuseli.

M. Munigant whistled quietly. Did Mr. Harris wish his bones—treated?

"That depends," said Harris.

Well, M. Munigant could not help Harris unless Harris was in the proper mood. Psychologically, one had to *need* help, or the doctor was useless. But (shrugging) M. Munigant would "try."

Harris lay on a table with his mouth open. The lights were switched off, the shades drawn. M. Munigant approached his patient.

Something touched Harris's tongue.

He felt his jawbones forced out. They creaked and made faint cracking noises. One of those skeleton charts on the dim wall seemed to quiver and jump. A violent shudder seized Harris. Involuntarily, his mouth snapped shut.

M. Munigant shouted. His nose had almost been bitten off! No use, no use! Now was not the time! M. Munigant whispered the shades up, dreadfully disappointed. When Mr. Harris felt he could cooperate psychologically, when Mr. Harris really *needed* help and trusted M. Munigant to help him, then maybe something could be done. M. Munigant held out his little hand. In the meantime, the fee was only two dollars. Mr. Harris must begin to think. Here was a sketch for Mr. Harris to take home and study. It would acquaint him with his body. He must be tremblingly aware of himself. He must be on guard. Skeletons were strange, unwieldy things. M. Munigant's eyes glittered. Good day to Mr. Harris. Oh, and would he care for a breadstick? M. Munigant proffered a jar of long hard salty breadsticks to Harris, taking one himself, saying that chewing breadsticks kept him in—ah—practice. Good day, good day, to Mr. Harris! Mr. Harris went home.

The next day, Sunday, Mr. Harris discovered innumerable fresh aches and pains in his body. He spent the morning, his eyes fixed, staring with new interest at the small, anatomically perfect painting of a skeleton M. Munigant had given him.

His wife, Clarisse, startled him at dinner when she cracked her exquisitely thin knuckles, one by one, until he clapped his hands to his ears and cried, "Stop!"

The rest of the afternoon he quarantined himself in his room. Clarisse played bridge in the parlor laughing and chatting with three other ladies while Harris, hidden away, fingered and weighed the limbs of his body with growing curiosity. After an hour he suddenly rose and called:

"Clarisse!"

She had a way of dancing into any room, her body doing all sorts of soft, agreeable things to keep her feet from ever quite touching the nap of a rug. She excused herself from her friends and came to see him now, brightly. She found him re-seated in a far corner and she saw that he was staring at the anatomical sketch. "Are you still brooding, sweet?" she asked. "Please don't." She sat upon his knees.

Her beauty could not distract him now in his absorption. He juggled her lightness, he touched her kneecap, suspiciously. It seemed to move under her pale, glowing skin. "Is it supposed to do that?" he asked, sucking in his breath.

"Is what supposed to do what?" she laughed. "You mean my kneecap?"

"Is it supposed to run around on top of your knee that way?"

She experimented. "So it *does*," she marveled.

"I'm glad yours slithers, too," he sighed. "I was beginning to worry."

"About what?"

He patted his ribs. "My ribs don't go all the way down,

they stop *here*. And I found some confounded ones that dangle in mid-air!"

Beneath the curve of her small breasts, Clarisse clasped her hands.

"Of course, silly, everybody's ribs stop at a given point. And those funny short ones are floating ribs."

"I hope they don't float around too much." The joke was most uneasy. Now, above all, he wished to be alone. Further discoveries, newer and stranger archaeological diggings, lay within reach of his trembling hands, and he did not wish to be laughed at.

"Thanks for coming in, dear," he said.

"Any time." She rubbed her small nose softly against his.

"Wait! Here, now . . ." He put his finger to touch his nose and hers. "Did you realize? The nose-bone grows down only *this* far. From there on a lot of gristly tissue fills out the rest!"

She wrinkled hers. "Of course, darling!" And she danced from the room.

Now, sitting alone, he felt the perspiration rise from the pools and hollows of his face, to flow in a thin tide down his cheeks. He licked his lips and shut his eyes. Now . . . now . . . next on the agenda, what . . . ? The spinal cord, yes. Here. Slowly, he examined it, in the same way he operated the many push-buttons in his office, thrusting them to summon secretaries, messengers. But now, in these pushings of his spinal column, fears and terrors answered, rushed from a million doors in his mind to confront and shake him! His spine felt horribly—unfamiliar. Like the brittle shards of a fish, freshly eaten, its bones left strewn on a cold china platter. He seized the little rounded knobbins. "Lord! Lord!"

His teeth began to chatter. God Almighty! he thought, why haven't I realized it all these years? All these years I've gone around with a—SKELETON—inside me! How is it we take ourselves for granted? How is it we never question our bodies and our being?

A skeleton. One of those jointed, snowy, hard things,

one of those foul, dry, brittle, gouge-eyed, skull-faced, shake-fingered, rattling things that sway from neck-chains in abandoned webbed closets, one of those things found on the desert all long and scattered like dice!

He stood upright, because he could not bear to remain seated. Inside me now—he grasped his stomach, his head—inside my head is a—skull. One of those curved carapaces which holds my brain like an electrical jelly, one of those cracked shells with the holes in front like two holes shot through it by a double-barreled shotgun! With its grottoes and caverns of bone, its revetments and placements for my flesh, my smelling, my seeing, my hearing, my thinking! A skull, encompassing my brain, allowing it exit through its brittle windows to see the outside world!

He wanted to dash into the bridge party, upset it, a fox in a chickenyard, the cards fluttering all around like chicken feathers burst upward in clouds! He stopped himself only with a violent, trembling effort. Now, now, man, control yourself. This is a revelation, take it for what it's worth, understand it, savor it. BUT A SKELETON! screamed his subconscious. I won't stand for it. It's vulgar, it's terrible, it's frightening. Skeletons are horrors; they clink and tinkle and rattle in old castles, hung from oaken beams, making long, indolently rustling pendulums on the wind. . . .

"Darling, will you come meet the ladies?" His wife's clear, sweet voice called from far away.

Mr. Harris stood. His SKELETON held him up! This thing inside, this invader, this horror, was supporting his arms, legs, and head! It was like feeling someone just behind you who shouldn't be there. With every step, he realized how dependent he was on this other Thing.

"Darling, I'll be with you in a moment," he called weakly. To himself he said, Come on, brace up! You've got to go back to work tomorrow. Friday you must make that trip to Phoenix. It's a long drive. Hundreds of miles. Must be in shape for that trip or you won't get Mr. Creldon to invest in your ceramics business. Chin up, now!

A moment later he stood among the ladies, being introduced to Mrs. Withers, Mrs. Abblematt, and Miss Kirthy, all of whom had skeletons inside them, but took it very calmly, because nature had carefully clothed the bare nudity of clavicle, tibia, and femur with breasts, thighs, calves, with coiffure and eyebrow satanic, with bee-stung lips and—LORD! shouted Mr. Harris inwardly—when they talk or eat, part of their skeleton shows—their *teeth!* I never thought of that. "Excuse me," he gasped, and ran from the room only in time to drop his lunch among the petunias over the garden balustrade.

That night, seated on the bed as his wife undressed, he pared his toenails and fingernails scrupulously. These parts, too, were where his skeleton was shoving, indignantly growing out. He must have muttered part of this theory, because next thing he knew his wife, in negligee, was on the bed, her arms about his neck, yawning, "Oh, my darling, fingernails are *not* bone, they're only hardened epidermis!"

He threw the scissors down. "Are you certain? I hope so. I'd feel better." He looked at the curve of her body, marveling. "I hope all people are made the same way."

"If you aren't the darndest hypochondriac!" She held him at arm's length. "Come on. What's wrong? Tell Mama."

"Something inside me," he said. "Something—I ate."

The next morning and all afternoon at his downtown office, Mr. Harris sorted out the sizes, shapes, and constructions of various bones in his body with displeasure. At ten A.M. he asked to feel Mr. Smith's elbow one moment. Mr. Smith obliged, but scowled suspiciously. And after lunch Mr. Harris asked to touch Miss Laurel's shoulder blade and she immediately pushed herself back against him, purring like a kitten and shutting her eyes.

"Miss Laurel!" he snapped. "Stop that!"

Alone, he pondered his neuroses. The war was just over, the pressure of his work, the uncertainty of the future probably had much to do with his mental outlook. He wanted to leave the office, get into business for himself. He had more than a little talent for ceramics and sculpture. As soon as possible he'd head for Arizona, borrow that money from Mr. Creldon, build a kiln and set up shop. It was a worry. What a case he was. But luckily he had contacted M. Munigant, who seemed eager to understand and help him. He wor'.d fight it out with himself, not go back to either Munigant or Dr. Burleigh unless he was forced to. The alien feeling would pass. He sat staring into space.

The alien feeling did not pass. It grew.

On Tuesday and Wednesday it bothered him terrifically that his epidermis, hair and other appendages were of a high disorder, while this integumented skeleton within was a slick clean structure of efficient organization. Sometimes, in certain lights with his lips drawn morosely down, weighted with melancholy, he imagined he saw his skull grinning at him behind the flesh.

Let go! he cried. Let go of me! My lungs! Stop!

He gasped convulsively, as if his ribs were crushing the breath from him.

My brain—stop squeezing it!

And terrifying headaches burnt his brain to a blind cinder.

My insides, let them be, for God's sake! Stay away from my heart!

His heart cringed from the fanning motion of ribs like pale spiders crouched and fiddling with their prey.

Drenched with sweat, he lay upon the bed one night while Clarisse was out attending a Red Cross meeting. He tried to gather his wits but only grew more aware of the conflict between his dirty exterior and this beautiful cool clean calciumed thing inside.

His complexion: wasn't it oily and lined with worry?

Observe the flawless, snow-white perfection of the skull.

His nose: wasn't it too large?

Then observe the tiny bones of the skull's nose before that monstrous nasal cartilage begins forming the lopsided proboscis.

His body: wasn't it plump?

Well, consider the skeleton; slender, svelte, economical of line and contour. Exquisitely carved oriental ivory! Perfect, thin as a white praying mantis!

His eyes: weren't they protuberant, ordinary, numb-looking?

Be so kind as to note the eye-sockets of the skull; so deep and rounded, somber, quiet pools, all-knowing, eternal. Gaze deep and you never touch the bottom of their dark understanding. All irony, all life, all everything is there in the cupped darkness.

Compare. Compare. Compare.

He raged for hours. And the skeleton, ever the frail and solemn philosopher, hung quietly inside, saying not a word, suspended like a delicate insect within a chrysalis, waiting and waiting.

Harris sat slowly up.

"Wait a minute. Hold on!" he exclaimed. "You're helpless, too. I've got you, too. I can make you do anything I want! You can't prevent it! I say move your carpales, metacarpals, and phalanges and—sswtt—up they go, as I wave to someone!" He laughed "I order the fibula and femur to locomote and *Hunn* two three four, *Hunn* two three four—we walk around the block. There!"

Harris grinned.

"It's a fifty-fifty fight. Even-Stephen. And we'll fight it out, we two! After all, I'm the part that *thinks!* Yes, by God! yes. Even if I didn't have you, I could still think!"

Instantly, a tiger's jaw snapped shut, chewing his brain in half. Harris screamed. The bones of his skull grabbed hold and gave him nightmares. Then slowly, while he shrieked, nuzzled and ate the nightmares one by one, until the last one was gone and the light went out. . . .

At the end of the week he postponed the Phoenix trip because of his health. Weighing himself on a penny scale he saw the slow gliding red arrow point to: 165.

He groaned. Why, I've weighed 175 for years. I can't have lost ten pounds! He examined his cheeks in the fly-dotted mirror. Cold, primitive fear rushed over him in odd little shivers. You, you! I know what you're about, *you!*

He shook his fist at his bony face, particularly addressing his remarks to his superior maxillary, his inferior maxillary, to his cranium and to his cervical vertebrae.

"You damn thing, you! Think you can starve me, make me lose weight, eh? Peel the flesh off, leave nothing but skin on bone. Trying to ditch me, so you can be supreme, ah? No, no!"

He fled into a cafeteria.

Turkey, dressing, creamed potatoes, four vegetables, three desserts, he could eat none of it, he was sick to his stomach. He forced himself. His teeth began to ache. Bad teeth, is it? he thought angrily. I'll eat in spite of every tooth clanging and banging and rattling so they fall in my gravy.

His head blazed, his breath jerked in and out of a constricted chest, his teeth raged with pain, but he knew one small victory. He was about to drink milk when he stopped and poured it into a vase of nasturtiums. No calcium for you, my boy, no calcium for you. Never again shall I eat foods with calcium or other bone-fortifying minerals. I'll eat for one of us, not both, my lad.

"One hundred and fifty pounds," he said the following week to his wife. "Do you *see* how I've changed?"

"For the better," said Clarisse. "You were always a little plump for your height, darling." She stroked his chin. "I like your face. It's so much nicer; the lines of it are so firm and strong now."

"They're not *my* lines, they're his, damn him! You mean to say you like him better than you like me?"

"Him? Who's '*him*'?"

In the parlor mirror, beyond Clarisse, his skull smiled back at him behind his fleshy grimace of hatred and despair.

Fuming, he popped malt tablets into his mouth. This was one way of gaining weight when you couldn't keep other foods down. Clarisse noticed the malt pellets.

"But, darling, really, you don't have to regain the weight for me," she said.

Oh, shut up! he felt like saying.

She made him lie with his head in her lap. "Darling," she said, "I've watched you lately. You're so—badly off. You don't say anything, but you look—hunted. You toss in bed at night. Maybe you should go to a psychiatrist. But I think I can tell you everything he would say. I've put it all together from hints you've let escape you. I can tell you that you and your skeleton are one and the same, 'one nation, indivisible, with liberty and justice for all.' United you stand, divided you fall. If you two fellows can't get along like an old married couple in the future, go back and see Dr. Burleigh. But, first, relax. You're in a vicious circle; the more you worry, the more your bones stick out, the more you worry. After all, who picked this fight—you or that anonymous entity you claim is lurking around behind your alimentary canal?"

He closed his eyes. "I did. I guess I did. Go on, Clarisse, keep talking."

"You rest now," she said softly. "Rest and forget."

Mr. Harris felt buoyed up for half a day, then he began to sag. It was all very well to blame his imagination, but this particular skeleton, by God, was fighting back.

Harris set out for M. Munigant's office late in the day. Walking for half an hour until he found the address, he caught sight of the name "M. Munigant" initialed in ancient, flaking gold on a glass plate outside the building. Then, his bones seemed to explode from their moorings, blasted and erupted with pain. Blinded, he staggered away. When he opened his eyes again he had rounded a corner. M. Munigant's office was out of sight.

The pains ceased.

M. Munigant was the man to help him. If the sight of his name could cause so titanic a reaction of course M. Munigant *must* be just the man.

But, not today. Each time he tried to return to that

office, the terrible pains took hold. Perspiring, he had to give up and swayed into a cocktail bar.

Moving across the dim lounge, he wondered briefly if a lot of blame couldn't be put on M. Munigant's shoulders. After all, it was Munigant who'd first drawn specific attention to his skeleton, and let the psychological impact of it slam home! Could M. Munigant be using him for some nefarious purpose? But what purpose? Silly to suspect him. Just a little doctor. Trying to be helpful. Munigant and his jar of breadsticks. Ridiculous. M. Munigant was okay, okay . . .

There was a sight within the cocktail lounge to give him hope. A large, fat man, round as a butterball, stood drinking consecutive beers at the bar. Now *there* was a successful man. Harris repressed a desire to go up, clap the fat man's shoulder, and inquire as to how he'd gone about impounding his bones. Yes, the fat man's skeleton was luxuriously closeted. There were pillows of fat here, resilient bulges of it there, with several round chandeliers of fat under his chin. The poor skeleton was lost; it could never fight clear of that blubber. It might have tried once —but not now. Overwhelmed, not a bony echo of the fat man's supporter remained.

Not without envy, Harris approached the fat man as one might cut across the bow of an ocean liner. Harris ordered a drink, drank it, and then dared to address the fat man:

"Glands?"

"You talking to me?" asked the fat man.

"Or is there a special diet?" wondered Harris. "I beg your pardon, but, as you see, I'm down. Can't seem to put on any weight. I'd like a stomach like that one of yours. Did you grow it because you were afraid of something?"

"You," announced the fat man, "are drunk. But—I like drunkards." He ordered more drinks. "Listen close, I'll tell you. Layer by layer," said the fat man, "twenty years, man and boy, I built this." He held his vast stomach like a globe of the world, teaching his audience its gastronomical geography. "It was no overnight circus. The tent was not raised before dawn on the wonders installed within. I have cultivated my inner organs as if they were thoroughbred dogs, cats, and other animals. My stomach is a fat pink Persian tom slumbering, rousing at intervals to purr, mew, growl, and cry for chocolate titbits. I feed it well, it will 'most sit up for me. And, my dear fellow, my intestines are the rarest pure-bred Indian anacondas you ever viewed in the sleekest, coiled, fine and ruddy health. Keep 'em in prime, I do, all my pets. For fear of something? Perhaps."

This called for another drink for everyone.

"Gain weight?" The fat man savored the words on his tongue. "Here's what you do: get yourself a quarreling bird of a wife, a baker's dozen of relatives who can flush a covey of troubles out from behind the veriest molehill. Add to these a sprinkling of business associates whose prime motivation is snatching your last lonely quid, and you are well on your way to getting fat. How so? In no time you'll begin subconsciously building fat betwixt yourself and them. A buffer epidermal state, a cellular wall. You'll soon find that eating is the only fun on earth. But one needs to be bothered by outside sources. Too many people in this world haven't enough to worry about, then they begin picking on themselves, and they lose weight. Meet all of the vile, terrible people you can possibly meet, and pretty soon you'll be adding the good old fat!"

And with that advice, the fat man launched himself out into the dark tide of night, swaying mightily and wheezing.

"That's exactly what Dr. Burleigh told me, slightly changed," said Harris thoughtfully. "Perhaps that trip to Phoenix, now, at this time——"

The trip from Los Angeles to Phoenix was a sweltering one, crossing, as it did, the Mojave desert on a broiling yellow day. Traffic was thin and inconstant, and for long stretches there would not be a car on the road for miles ahead or behind. Harris twitched his fingers on the steering wheel. Whether or not Creldon, in Phoenix, lent him the money he needed to start his business, it was still a good thing to get away, to put distance behind.

The car moved in the hot sluice of desert wind. The one Mr. H. sat inside the other Mr. H. Perhaps both perspired. Perhaps both were miserable.

On a curve, the inside Mr. H. suddenly constricted the outer flesh, causing him to jerk forward on the hot steering wheel.

The car plunged off the road into boiling sand and turned half over.

Night came, a wind rose, the roof was lonely and silent. The few cars that passed went swiftly on their way, their view obstructed. Mr. Harris lay unconscious, until very late he heard a wind rising out of the desert, felt the sting of little sand needles on his cheeks, and opened his eyes.

Morning found him gritty-eyed and wandering in thoughtless senseless circles, having, in his delirium, got away from the road. At noon he sprawled in the poor shade of a bush. The sun struck him with a keen sword edge, cutting through to his—bones. A vulture circled.

Harris's parched lips cracked open. "So that's it?" he whispered, red-eyed, bristle-cheeked. "One way or another you'll walk me, starve me, thirst me, kill me." He swallowed dry burrs of dust. "Sun cook off my flesh so you can peek out. Vultures lunch off me, and there you'll lie, grinning. Grinning with victory. Like a bleached xylophone strewn and played by vultures with an ear for odd music. You'd like that. Freedom."

He walked on through a landscape that shivered and bubbled in the direct pour of sunlight; stumbling, falling flat, lying to feed himself little mouths of fire. The air was blue alcohol flame, and vultures roasted and steamed and glittered as they flew in glides and circles. Phoenix. The road. Car. Water. Safety.

"Hey!"

Someone called from way off in the blue alcohol flame.

Mr. Harris propped himself up.

"Hey!"

The call was repeated. A crunching of footsteps, quick.

With a cry of unbelievable relief, Harris rose, only to collapse again into the arms of someone in a uniform with a badge.

The car tediously hauled, repaired, Phoenix reached, Harris found himself in such an unholy state of mind that the business transaction was a numb pantomime. Even when he got the loan and held the money in his hand, it meant nothing. This Thing within him like a hard white sword in a scabbard tainted his business, his eating, colored his love for Clarisse, made it unsafe to trust an automobile; all in all this Thing had to be put in its place. The desert incident had brushed too close. Too near the bone, one might say with an ironic twist of one's mouth. Harris heard himself thanking Mr. Creldon, dimly, for the money. Then he turned his car and motored back across the long miles, this time cutting across to San Diego, so he would miss that desert stretch between El Centro and Beaumont. He drove north along the coast. He didn't trust that desert. But—careful! Salt waves boomed, hissing on the beach outside Laguna. Sand, fish and crustacea would cleanse his bones as swiftly as vultures. Slow down on the curves over the surf.

Damn, he was sick!

Where to turn? Clarisse? Burleigh? Munigant? Bone specialist. Munigant. Well?

"Darling!" Clarisse kissed him. He winced at the solidness of the teeth and jaw behind the passionate exchange.

"Darling," he said, slowly, wiping his lips with his wrist, trembling.

"You look thinner; oh, darling, the business deal——?"

"It went through. I guess. Yes, it did."

She kissed him again. They ate a slow, falsely cheerful dinner, with Clarisse laughing and encouraging him. He studied the phone; several times he picked it up indecisively, then laid it down.

His wife walked in, putting on her coat and hat. "Well, sorry, but I have to leave." She pinched him on the cheek.

"Come on now, cheer up! I'll be back from Red Cross in three hours. You lie around and snooze. I simply *have* to go."

When Clarisse was gone, Harris dialed the phone, nervously.

"M. Munigant?"

The explosions and the sickness in his body after he set the phone down were unbelievable. His bones were racked with every kind of pain, cold and hot, he had ever thought of or experienced in wildest nightmare. He swallowed all the aspirin he could find, in an effort to stave off the assault; but when the doorbell finally rang an hour later, he could not move; he lay weak and exhausted, panting, tears streaming down his cheeks.

"Come in! Come in, for God's sake!"

M. Munigant came in. Thank God the door was unlocked.

Oh, but Mr. Harris looked terrible. M. Munigant stood in the center of the living room, small and dark. Harris nodded. The pains rushed through him, hitting him with large iron hammers and hooks. M. Munigant's eyes glittered as he saw Harris's protuberant bones. Ah, he saw that Mr. Harris was now psychologically prepared for aid. Was it not so? Harris nodded again, feebly, sobbing. M. Munigant still whistled when he talked; something about his tongue and the whistling. No matter. Through his shimmering eyes Harris seemed to see M. Munigant shrink, get smaller. Imagination, of course. Harris sobbed out his story of the Phoenix trip. M. Munigant sympathized. This skeleton was a—a traitor! They would fix him for once and for all!

"M. Munigant," sighed Harris, faintly, "I—I never noticed before. Your tongue. Round, tube-like. Hollow? My eyes. Delirious. What do I do?"

M. Munigant whistled softly, appreciatively, coming closer. If Mr. Harris would relax in his chair, and open his mouth? The lights were switched off. M. Munigant peered into Harris's dropped jaw. Wider, please? It had been so hard, that first visit, to help Harris, with both body and bone in revolt. Now, he had cooperation from the flesh of the man, anyway, even if the skeleton protested. In the darkness, M. Munigant's voice got small, small, tiny, tiny. The whistling became high and shrill. Now. Relax, Mr. Harris. NOW!

Harris felt his jaw pressed violently in all directions, his tongue depressed as with a spoon, his throat clogged. He gasped for breath. Whistle. He couldn't breathe! Something squirmed, corkscrewed his cheeks out, bursting his jaws. Like a hot-water douche, something squirted into his sinuses, his ears clanged! "Ahhhh!" shrieked Harris, gagging. His head, its carapaces riven, shattered, hung loose. Agony shot fire through his lungs.

Harris could breathe again, momentarily. His watery eyes sprang wide. He shouted. His ribs, like sticks picked up and bundled, were loosened in him. Pain! He fell to the floor, wheezing out his hot breath.

Lights flickered in his senseless eyeballs, he felt his limbs swiftly cast loose and free. Through streaming eyes he saw the parlor.

The room was empty.

"M. Munigant? In God's name, where are you, M. Munigant? Come help me!"

M. Munigant was gone.

"Help!"

Then he heard it.

Deep down in the subterranean fissures of his body, the minute, unbelievable noises; little smackings and twistings and little dry chippings and grindings and nuzzling sounds —like a tiny hungry mouse down in the red-blooded dimness, gnawing ever so earnestly and expertly at what might have been, but was not, a submerged timber . . . !

Clarisse, walking along the sidewalk, held her head high and marched straight toward her house on Saint James Place. She was thinking of the Red Cross as she turned the corner and almost ran into this little dark man who smelled of iodine.

Clarisse would have ignored him if it were not for the fact that as she passed, he took something long, white and oddly familiar from his coat and proceeded to chew on it, as on a peppermint stick. Its end devoured, his extraordinary tongue darted within the white confection, sucking out the filling, making contented noises. He was still crunching his goody as she proceeded up the sidewalk to her house, turned the doorknob and walked in.

"Darling?" she called, smiling around. "Darling, where are you?" She shut the door, walked down the hall and into the living room. "Darling . . ."

She stared at the floor for twenty seconds, trying to understand.

She screamed.

Outside in the sycamore darkness, the little man pierced a long white stick with intermittent holes; then, softly, sighing, his lips puckered, played a little sad tune upon the improvised instrument to accompany the shrill and awful singing of Clarisse's voice as she stood in the living room.

Many times as a little girl Clarisse had run on the beach sands, stepped on a jellyfish and screamed. It was not so bad, finding an intact, gelatin-skinned jellyfish in one's living room. One could step back from it.

It was when the jellyfish *called you by name* . . .

Dandelion Wine

Illumination

Crossing the lawn that morning, Douglas Spaulding broke a spider web with his face. A single invisible line on the air touched his brow and snapped without a sound.

So, with the subtlest of incidents, he knew that this day was going to be different. It would be different also, because, as his father explained, driving Douglas and his ten-year-old brother Tom out of town toward the country, there were some days compounded completely of odor, nothing but the world blowing in one nostril and out the other. And some days, he went on, were days of hearing every trump and trill of the universe. Some days were good for tasting and some for touching. And some days were good for all the senses at once. This day now, he nodded, smelled as if a great and nameless orchard had grown up overnight beyond the hills to fill the entire visible land with its warm freshness. The air felt like rain, but there were no clouds. Momentarily, a stranger might laugh off in the woods, but there was silence . . .

Douglas watched the traveling land. He smelled no orchards and sensed no rain, for without apple trees or clouds he knew neither could exist. And as for that stranger laughing deep in the woods . . . ?

Yet the fact remained—Douglas shivered—this, without reason, was a special day.

The car stopped at the very center of the quiet forest.

"All right, boys, behave."

They had been jostling elbows.

"Yes, sir."

They climbed out, carrying the blue tin pails away from the lonely dirt road into the smell of fallen rain.

"Look for bees," said Father. "Bees hang around grapes like boys around kitchens. Doug?"

Douglas looked up suddenly.

"You're off a million miles," said Father. "Look alive. Walk with us."

"Yes, sir."

And they walked through the forest, Father very tall, Douglas moving in his shadow, and Tom very small, trotting in his brother's shade. They came to a little rise and looked ahead. Here, here, did they see? Father pointed. Here was where the big summer-quiet winds lived and passed in the green depths, like ghost whales, unseen.

Douglas looked quickly, saw nothing, and felt put upon by his father who, like Grandpa, lived on riddles. But . . . But, still . . . Douglas paused and listened.

Yes, something's going to happen, he thought, I know it!

"Here's maidenhair fern." Dad walked, the tin pail belling in his fist. "Feel this?" He scuffed the earth. "A million years of good rich leafmold laid down. Think of the autumns that got by to make this."

"Boy, I walk like an Indian," said Tom. "Not a sound."

Douglas felt but did not feel the deep loam, listening, watchful. We're surrounded! he thought. It'll happen! What? He stopped. Come out, wherever you are, whatever you are! he cried silently.

Tom and Dad strolled on the hushed earth ahead.

"Finest lace there is," said Dad quietly.

And he was gesturing up through the trees above to show them how it was woven across the sky or how the sky was woven into the trees, he wasn't sure which. But there it was, he smiled, and the weaving went on, green and blue, if you watched and saw the forest shift its humming loom. Dad stood comfortably saying this and that, the words easy in his mouth. He made it easier by laughing at his own declarations just so often. He liked to listen to the silence, he said, if silence could be listened to, for, he went on, in that silence you could hear wildflower pollen sifting down the bee-fried air, by God, the bee-fried air! Listen! the waterfall of bird-song beyond those trees!

Now, thought Douglas, here it comes! Running! I don't see it! Running! Almost on me!

"Fox grapes!" said Father. "We're in luck, look here!"

Don't! Douglas gasped.

But Tom and Dad bent down to shove their hands deep in rattling bush. The spell was shattered. The terrible prowler, the magnificent runner, the leaper, the shaker of souls, vanished.

Douglas, lost and empty, fell to his knees. He saw his fingers sink through green shadow and come forth stained with such color that it seemed he had somehow cut the forest and delved his hand in the open wound.

"Lunch time, boys!"

With buckets half burdened with fox grapes and wild strawberries, followed by bees which were, no more, no less, said Father, the world humming under its breath, they sat on a green-mossed log chewing sandwiches and trying to listen to the forest the same way Father did. Douglas felt Dad watching him, quietly amused. Dad started to say something that had crossed his mind, but instead tried another bite of sandwich and mused over it.

"Sandwich outdoors isn't a sandwich any more. Tastes different than indoors, notice? Got more spice. Tastes like mint and pinesap. Does wonders for the appetite."

Douglas's tongue hesitated on the texture of bread and deviled ham. No . . . no . . . it was just a sandwich.

Tom chewed and nodded. "Know just what you mean, Dad!"

It almost happened, thought Douglas. Whatever it was it was Big, my gosh, it was Big! Something scared it off. Where is it now? Back of that bush! No, behind me! No, here . . . almost *here* . . . He kneaded his stomach secretly.

If I wait, it'll come back. It won't hurt; somehow I know it's not here to hurt me. What then? What? What?

"You know how many baseball games we played this year, last year, year before?" said Tom, apropos of nothing.

Douglas watched Tom's quickly moving lips.

"Wrote it down! One thousand five hundred sixty-eight games! How many times I brushed my teeth in ten years? Six thousand! Washed my hands: fifteen thousand. Slept: four thousand some-odd times, not counting naps. Ate six hundred peaches, eight hundred apples. Pears: two hundred. I'm not hot for pears. Name a thing, I got the statistics! Runs to the billion millions, things I done, add 'em up, in ten years."

Now, thought Douglas, it's coming close again. Why? Tom talking? But why Tom? Tom chatting along, mouth crammed with sandwich, Dad there, alert as a mountain cat on the log, and Tom letting the words rise like quick soda bubbles in his mouth:

"Books I read: four hundred. Matinees I seen: forty Buck Joneses, thirty Jack Hoxies, forty-five Tom Mixes, thirty-nine Hoot Gibsons, one hundred and ninety-two single and separate Felix-the-Cat cartoons, ten Douglas Fairbankses, eight repeats on Lon Chaney in *The Phantom of the Opera*, four Milton Sillses, and one Adolph Menjou thing about love where I spent ninety hours in the theater toilet waiting for the mush to be over so I could see *The Cat and the Canary* or *The Bat*, where everybody held onto everybody else and screamed for two hours without letting go. During that time I figure four hundred lollipops, three hundred Tootsie Rolls, seven hundred ice-cream cones . . ."

Tom rolled quietly along his way for another five minutes and then Dad said, "How many berries you picked so far, Tom?"

"Two hundred fifty-six on the nose!" said Tom instantly.

Dad laughed and lunch was over and they moved again into the shadows to find fox grapes and the tiny wild strawberries, bent down, all three of them, hands coming and going, the pails getting heavy, and Douglas holding his breath, thinking, Yes, yes, it's near again! Breathing on my neck, almost! Don't look! Work. Just pick, fill up the pail. If you look you'll scare it off. Don't lose it this time! But how, how do you bring it around here where you can see it, stare it right in the eye? How? How?

"Got a snowflake in a matchbox," said Tom, smiling at the wine-glove on his hand.

Shut up! Douglas wanted to yell. But no, the yell would scare the echoes, and run the Thing away!

And, wait . . . the more Tom talked, the closer the great Thing came, it wasn't scared of Tom, Tom drew it with his breath, Tom was part of it!

"Last February," said Tom, and chuckled. "Held a matchbox up in a snowstorm, let one old snowflake fall in, shut it up, ran inside the house, stashed it in the icebox!"

Close, very close. Douglas stared at Tom's flickering lips. He wanted to jump around, for he felt a vast tidal wave lift up behind the forest. In an instant it would smash down, crush them forever . . .

"Yes, sir," mused Tom, picking grapes, "I'm the only guy in all Illinois who's got a snowflake in summer. Precious as diamonds, by gosh. Tomorrow I'll open it. Doug, you can look, too . . ."

Any other day Douglas might have snorted, struck out, denied it all. But now, with the great Thing rushing near, falling down in the clear air above <u>him</u>, he could only nod, eyes shut.

Tom, puzzled, stopped picking berries and turned to stare over at his brother.

Douglas, hunched over, was an ideal target. Tom leaped, yelling, landed. They fell, thrashed, and rolled.

No! Douglas squeezed his mind shut. No! But suddenly
. . . Yes, it's all right! Yes! The tangle, the contact of
bodies, the falling tumble had not scared off the tidal sea
that crashed now, flooding and washing them along the
shore of grass deep through the forest. Knuckles struck his
mouth. He tasted rusty warm blood, grabbed Tom hard,
held him tight, and so in silence they lay, hearts churning,
nostrils hissing. And at last, slowly, afraid he would find
nothing, Douglas opened one eye.

And everything, absolutely everything, was there.

The world, like a great iris of an even more gigantic
eye, which has also just opened and stretched out to en-
compass everything, stared back at him.

And he knew what it was that had leaped upon him to
stay and would not run away now.

I'm alive, he thought.

His fingers trembled, bright with blood, like the bits of a
strange flag now found and before unseen, and him wondering what country and what allegiance he owed to it.
Holding Tom, but not knowing him there, he touched his
free hand to that blood as if it could be peeled away, held
up, turned over. Then he let go of Tom and lay on his
back with his hand up in the sky and he was a head from
which his eyes peered like sentinels through the portcullis
of a strange castle out along a bridge, his arm, to those
fingers where the bright pennant of blood quivered in the
light.

"You all right, Doug?" asked Tom.

His voice was at the bottom of a green moss well somewhere underwater, secret, removed.

The grass whispered under his body. He put his arm
down, feeling the sheath of fuzz on it, and, far away,
below, his toes creaking in his shoes. The wind sighed over
his shelled ears. The world slipped bright over the glassy
round of his eyeballs like images sparked in a crystal
sphere. Flowers were sun and fiery spots of sky strewn
through the woodland. Birds flickered like skipped stones
across the vast inverted pond of heaven. His breath raked
over his teeth, going in ice, coming out fire. Insects

shocked the air with electric clearness. Ten thousand indi-
vidual hairs grew a millionth of an inch on his head. He
heard the twin hearts beating in each ear, the third heart
beating in his throat, the two hearts throbbing his wrists,
the real heart pounding his chest. The million pores on his
body opened.

I'm *really* alive! he thought. I never knew it before, or
if I did I don't remember!

He yelled it loud but silent, a dozen times! Think of it,
think of it! Twelve years old and only now! Now dis-
covering this rare timepiece, this clock gold-bright and
guaranteed to run threescore and ten, left under a tree and
found while wrestling.

"Doug, you okay?"

Douglas yelled, grabbed Tom, and rolled.

"Doug, you're crazy!"

"Crazy!"

They spilled downhill, the sun in their mouths, in their
eyes like shattered lemon glass, gasping like trout thrown
out on a bank, laughing till they cried.

"Doug, you're not mad?"

"No, no, no, no, no!"

Douglas, eyes shut, saw spotted leopards pad in the
dark.

"Tom!" Then quieter. "Tom . . . does everyone in the
world . . . know he's alive?"

"Sure. Heck, yes!"

The leopards trotted soundlessly off through darker
lands where eyeballs could not turn to follow.

"I hope they do," whispered Douglas. "Oh, I sure hope
they know."

Douglas opened his eyes. Dad was standing high above
him there in the green-leafed sky, laughing, hands on
hips. Their eyes met. Douglas quickened. Dad knows, he
thought. It was all planned. He brought us here on purpose, so this could happen to me! He's in on it, he knows it
all. And now he knows that I know.

A hand came down and seized him through the air.
Swayed on his feet with Tom and Dad, still bruised and

rumpled, puzzled and awed, Douglas held his strange-boned elbows tenderly and licked the fine cut lip with satisfaction. Then he looked at Dad and Tom.

"I'll carry all the pails," he said. "This once, let me haul everything."

They handed over the pails with quizzical smiles.

He stood swaying slightly, the forest collected, full-weighted and heavy with syrup, clenched hard in his down-slung hands. I want to feel all there is to feel, he thought. Let me feel tired, now, let me feel tired. I mustn't forget, I'm alive, I know I'm alive, I mustn't forget it tonight or tomorrow or the day after that.

The bees followed and the smell of fox grapes and yellow summer followed as he walked heavy-laden and half drunk, his fingers wondrously callused, arms numb, feet stumbling so his father caught his shoulder.

"No," mumbled Douglas, "I'm all right. I'm fine . . ."

It took half an hour for the sense of the grass, the roots, the stones, the bark of the mossy log, to fade from where they had patterned his arms and legs and back. While he pondered this, let it slip, slide, dissolve away, his brother and his quiet father followed behind, allowing him to pathfind the forest alone out toward that incredible highway which would take them back to the town. . . .

Dandelion Wine

The town, then, later in the day. And yet another harvest.

Grandfather stood on the wide front porch like a captain surveying the vast unmotioned calms of a season dead ahead. He questioned the wind and the untouchable sky and the lawn on which stood Douglas and Tom to question only him.

"Grandpa, are they ready? Now?"

Grandfather pinched his chin. "Five hundred, a thousand, two thousand easy. Yes, yes, a good supply. Pick 'em easy, pick 'em all. A dime for every sack delivered to the press!"

"Hey!"

The boys bent, smiling. They picked the golden flowers. The flowers that flooded the world, dripped off lawns onto brick streets, tapped softly at crystal cellar windows and agitated themselves so that on all sides lay the dazzle and glitter of molten sun.

"Every year," said Grandfather. "They run amuck; I let them. Pride of lions in the yard. Stare, and they burn a hole in your retina. A common flower, a weed that no one sees, yes. But for us, a noble thing, the dandelion."

So, plucked carefully, in sacks, the dandelions were carried below. The cellar dark glowed with their arrival. The wine press stood open, cold. A rush of flowers warmed it. The press, replaced, its screw rotated, twirled by Grandfather, squeezed gently on the crop.

"There . . . so . . ."

The golden tide, the essence of this fine fair month ran, then gushed from the spout below, to be crocked, skimmed of ferment, and bottled in clean ketchup shakers, then ranked in sparkling rows in cellar gloom.

Dandelion wine.

The words were summer on the tongue. The wine was summer caught and stoppered. And now that Douglas knew, really knew he was alive, and moved turning through the world to touch and see it all, it was only right and proper that some of his new knowledge, some of this special vintage day should be sealed away for opening on a January day with snow falling fast and the sun unseen for weeks or months and perhaps some of the miracle by then forgotten and in need of renewal. Since this was going to be a summer of unguessed wonders, he wanted it all salvaged and labeled so that any time he wished, he might tiptoe down in this dank twilight and reach up his finger tips.

And there, row upon row, with the soft gleam of flowers opened at morning, with the light of this June sun glowing through a faint skin of dust, would stand the dandelion wine. Peer through it at the wintry day—the snow melted to grass, the trees were reinhabited with bird, leaf, and blossoms like a continent of butterflies breathing on the wind. And peering through, color sky from iron to blue.

Hold summer in your hand, pour summer in a glass, a tiny glass of course, the smallest tingling sip for children; change the season in your veins by raising glass to lip and tilting summer in.

"Ready, now, the rain barrel!"

Nothing else in the world would do but the pure waters which had been summoned from the lakes far away and the sweet fields of grassy dew on early morning, lifted to the open sky, carried in laundered clusters, nine hundred miles brushed with wind, electrified with high voltage, and condensed upon cool air. This water, falling, raining, gathered yet more of the heavens in its crystals. Taking something of the east wind and the west wind and the north wind and the south, the water made rain and the rain, within this hour of rituals, would be well on its way to wine.

Douglas ran with the dipper. He plunged it deep in the rain barrel. "Here we go!"

The water was silk in the cup; clear, faintly blue silk. It softened the lip and the throat and the heart, if drunk. This water must be carried in dipper and bucket to the cellar, there to be leavened in freshets, in mountain streams, upon the dandelion harvest.

Even Grandma, when snow was whirling fast, dizzying the world, blinding windows, stealing breath from gasping mouths, even Grandma, one day in February, would vanish to the cellar.

Above, in the vast house, there would be coughings, sneezings, wheezings, and groans, childish fevers, throats raw as butcher's meat, noses like bottled cherries, the stealthy microbe everywhere.

Then, rising from the cellar like a June goddess, Grandma would come, something hidden but obvious under her knitted shawl. This, carried to every miserable room upstairs-and-down, would be dispensed with aroma and clarity into neat glasses, to be swigged neatly. The medicines of another time, the balm of sun and idle August afternoons, the faintly heard sounds of ice wagons passing on brick avenues, the rush of silver skyrockets and the fountaining of lawn mowers moving through ant countries, all these, all these in a glass.

Yes, even Grandma, drawn to the cellar of winter for a June adventure, might stand alone and quietly, in secret conclave with her own soul and spirit, as did Grandfather and Father and Uncle Bert, or some of the boarders, communing with a last touch of a calendar long departed, with the picnics and the warm rains and the smell of fields of wheat and new popcorn and bending hay. Even Grandma, repeating and repeating the fine and golden words, even as they were said now in this moment when the flowers were dropped into the press, as they would be repeated every winter for all the white winters in time. Saying them over and over on the lips, like a smile, like a sudden patch of sunlight in the dark.

Dandelion wine. Dandelion wine. Dandelion wine.

Statues

The facts about John Huff, aged twelve, are simple and soon stated. He could pathfind more trails than any Choctaw or Cherokee since time began, could leap from the sky like a chimpanzee from a vine, could live underwater two minutes and slide fifty yards downstream from where you last saw him. The baseballs you pitched him he hit in the apple trees, knocking down harvests. He could jump six-foot orchard walls, swing up branches faster and come down, fat with peaches, quicker than anyone else in the gang. He ran laughing. He sat easy. He was not a bully. He was kind. His hair was dark and curly and his teeth were white as cream. He remembered the words to all the cowboy songs and would teach you if you asked. He knew the names of all the wild flowers and when the moon would rise and set and when the tides came in or out. He was, in fact, the only god living in the whole of Green Town, Illinois, during the twentieth century that Douglas Spaulding knew of.

And right now he and Douglas were hiking out beyond town on another warm and marble-round day, the sky blue blown-glass reaching high, the creeks bright with mirror waters fanning over white stones. It was a day as perfect as the flame of a candle.

Douglas walked through it thinking it would go on this way forever. The perfection, the roundness, the grass smell traveled on out ahead as far and fast as the speed of light. The sound of a good friend whistling like an oriole, pegging the softball, as you horse-danced, key-jingled the dusty paths, all of it was complete, everything could be touched; things stayed near, things were at hand and would remain.

It was such a fine day and then suddenly a cloud crossed the sky, covered the sun, and did not move again.

John Huff had been speaking quietly for several minutes. Now Douglas stopped on the path and looked over at him.

"John, say that again."

"You heard me the first time, Doug."

"Did you say you were—going away?"

"Got my train ticket here in my pocket. Whoo-whoo, clang! Shush-shush-shush-shush. Whooooooooo . . ."

His voice faded.

John took the yellow and green train ticket solemnly from his pocket and they both looked at it.

"Tonight!" said Douglas. "My gosh! Tonight we were going to play Red Light, Green Light and Statues! How come, all of a sudden? You been here in Green Town all my life. You just don't pick up and leave!"

"It's my father," said John. "He's got a job in Milwaukee. We weren't sure until today . . ."

"My gosh, here it is with the Baptist picnic next week and the big carnival Labor Day and Halloween—can't your dad wait till then?"

John shook his head.

"Good grief!" said Douglas. "Let me sit down!"

They sat under an old oak tree on the side of the hill looking back at town, and the sun made large trembling shadows around them; it was cool as a cave in under the tree. Out beyond, in sunlight, the town was painted with heat, the windows all gaping. Douglas wanted to run back in there where the town, by its very weight, its houses, their bulk, might enclose and prevent John's ever getting up and running off.

"But we're friends," Douglas said helplessly.

"We always will be," said John.

"You'll come back to visit every *week* or so, won't you?"

"Dad says only once or twice a year. It's eighty miles."

"Eighty miles ain't far!" shouted Douglas.

"No, it's not far at all," said John.

"My grandma's got a phone. I'll call you. Or maybe we'll all visit up your way, too. That'd be great!"

John said nothing for a long while.

"Well," said Douglas, "let's talk about something."

"What?"

"My gosh, if you're going away, we got a million things to talk about! All the things we would've talked about next month, the month after! Praying mantises, zeppelins, acrobats, sword swallowers! Go on like you was back there, grasshoppers spitting tobacco!"

"Funny thing is I don't feel like talking about grasshoppers."

"You always did!"

"Sure." John looked steadily at the town. "But I guess this just ain't the time."

"John, what's wrong? You look funny . . ."

John had closed his eyes and screwed up his face. "Doug, the Terle house, upstairs, you know?"

"Sure."

"The colored windowpanes on the little round windows, have they *always* been there?"

"Sure."

"You *positive?*"

"Darned old windows been there since before we were born. Why?"

"I never saw them before today," said John. "On the way walking through town I looked up and there they were. Doug, what was I *doing* all these years I didn't see them?"

"You had other things to do."

"Did I?" John turned and looked in a kind of panic at Douglas. "Gosh, Doug, why should those darn windows scare me? I mean, that's nothing to be scared of, is it? It's just . . ." He floundered. "It's just, if I didn't see those windows until today, what *else* did I miss? And what about all the things I *did* see here in town? Will I be able to remember them when I go away?"

"Anything you want to remember, you remember. I went to camp two summers ago. Up *there* I remembered."

"No, you didn't! You told me. You woke nights and couldn't remember your mother's face."

"*No!*"

"Some nights it happens to me in my own house; scares heck out of me. I got to go in my folks' room and look at their faces while they sleep, to be sure! And I go back to my room and lose it again. Gosh, Doug, oh gosh!" He held on to his knees tight. "Promise me just one thing, Doug. Promise you'll remember me, promise you'll remember my face and everything. Will you promise?"

"Easy as pie. Got a motion-picture machine in my head. Lying in bed nights I can just turn on a light in my head and out it comes on the wall, clear as heck, and there you'll be, yelling and waving at me."

"Shut your eyes, Doug. Now, tell me, what color eyes I got? Don't peek. What color eyes I got?"

Douglas began to sweat. His eyelids twitched nervously. "Aw heck, John, that's not fair."

"Tell me!"

"Brown!"

John turned away. "No, sir."

"What you mean, no?"

"You're not even close!" John closed his eyes.

"Turn around here," said Douglas. "Open up, let me see."

"It's no use," said John. "You forgot already. Just the way I said."

"Turn around here!" Douglas grabbed him by the hair and turned him slowly.

"Okay, Doug."

John opened his eyes.

"Green." Douglas, dismayed, let his hand drop. "Your eyes are green . . . Well, that's close to brown. Almost hazel!"

"Doug, don't lie to me."

"All right," said Doug quietly. "I won't."

They sat there listening to the other boys running up the hill, shrieking and yelling at them.

They raced along the railroad tracks, opened their lunch in brown-paper sacks, and sniffed deeply of the wax-wrapped deviled-ham sandwiches and green-sea pickles and colored peppermints. They ran and ran again and Douglas bent to scorch his ear on the hot steel rails, hearing trains so far away they were unseen voyagings in other lands, sending Morse-code messages to him here under the killing sun. Douglas stood up, stunned.

"John!"

For John was running, and this was terrible. Because if you ran, time ran. You yelled and screamed and raced and rolled and tumbled and all of a sudden the sun was gone and the whistle was blowing and you were on your long way home to supper. When you weren't looking, the sun got around behind you! The only way to keep things slow was to watch everything and do nothing! You could stretch a day to three days, sure, just by watching!

"John!"

There was no way to get him to help now, save by a trick.

"John, ditch, ditch the others!"

Yelling, Douglas and John sprinted off, kiting the wind

downhill, letting gravity work for them, over meadows, around barns until at last the sound of the pursuers faded.

John and Douglas climbed into a haystack which was like a great bonfire crisping under them.

"Let's not do anything," said John.

"Just what I was going to say," said Douglas.

They sat quietly, getting their breath.

There was a small sound like an insect in the hay.

They both heard it, but they didn't look at the sound. When Douglas moved his wrist the sound ticked in another part of the haystack. When he brought his arm around on his lap the sound ticked in his lap. He let his eyes fall in a brief flicker. The watch said three o'clock.

Douglas moved his right hand stealthily to the ticking, pulled out the watch stem. He set the hands back.

Now they had all the time they would ever need to look long and close at the world, feel the sun move like a fiery wind over the sky.

But at last John must have felt the bodiless weight of their shadows shift and lean, and he spoke.

"Doug, what time is it?"

"Two-thirty."

John looked at the sky.

Don't! thought Douglas.

"Looks more like three-thirty, four," said John. "Boy Scout. You learn them things."

Douglas sighed and slowly turned the watch ahead.

John watched him do this, silently. Douglas looked up. John punched him, not hard at all, in the arm.

With a swift stroke, a plunge, a train came and went so quickly the boys all leaped aside, yelling, shaking their fists after it, Douglas and John with them. The train roared down the track, two hundred people in it, gone. The dust followed it a little way toward the south, then settled in the golden silence among the blue rails.

The boys were walking home.

"I'm going to Cincinnati when I'm seventeen and be a railroad fireman," said Charlie Woodman.

"I got an uncle in New York," said Jim. "I'll go there and be a printer."

Doug did not ask the others. Already the trains were chanting and he saw their faces drifting off on back observation platforms, or pressed to windows. One by one they slid away. And then the empty track and the summer sky and himself on another train run in another direction.

Douglas felt the earth move under his feet and saw their shadows move off the grass and color the air.

He swallowed hard, then gave a screaming yell, pulled back his fist, shot the indoor ball whistling in the sky. "Last one home's a rhino's behind!"

They pounded down the tracks, laughing, flailing the air. There went John Huff, not touching the ground at all. And here came Douglas, touching it all the time.

It was seven o'clock, supper over, and the boys gathering one by one from the sound of their house doors slammed and their parents crying to them not to slam the doors. Douglas and Tom and Charlie and John stood among half a dozen others and it was time for hide-and-seek and Statues.

"Just one game," said John. "Then I got to go home. The train leaves at nine. Who's going to be 'it'?"

"Me," said Douglas.

"That's the first time I ever heard of anybody volunteering to be 'it,' " said Tom.

Douglas looked at John for a long moment. "Start running," he said.

The boys scattered, yelling. John backed away, then turned and began to lope. Douglas counted slowly. He let them run far, spread out, separate, each to his own small world. When they had got their momentum up and were almost out of sight he took a deep breath.

"Statues!"

Everyone froze.

Very quietly Douglas moved across the lawn to where John Huff stood like an iron deer in the twilight.

Far away, the other boys stood hands up, faces grimaced, eyes bright as stuffed squirrels.

But here was John, alone and motionless, and no one rushing or making a great outcry to spoil this moment.

Douglas walked around the statue one way, walked around the statue the other way. The statue did not move. It did not speak. It looked at the horizon, its mouth half smiling.

It was like that time years ago in Chicago when they had visited a big place where the carved marble figures were, and his walking around among them in the silence. So here was John Huff with grass stains on his knees and the seat of his pants, and cuts on his fingers and scabs on his elbows. Here was John Huff with the quiet tennis shoes, his feet sheathed in silence. There was the mouth that had chewed many an apricot pie come summer, and said many a quiet thing or two about life and the lay of the land. And there were the eyes, not blind like statues' eyes, but filled with molten green-gold. And there the dark hair blowing now north now south or any direction in the little breeze there was. And there the hands with all the town on them, dirt from roads and bark-slivers from trees, the fingers that smelled of hemp and vine and green apple, old coins or pickle-green frogs. There were the ears with the sunlight shining through them like bright warm peach wax and here, invisible, his spearmint-breath upon the air.

"John, now," said Douglas, "don't you move so much as an eyelash. I absolutely command you to stay here and not move at all for the next three hours!"

"Doug . . ."

John's lips moved.

"Freeze!" said Douglas.

John went back to looking at the sky, but he was not smiling now.

"I got to go," he whispered.

"Not a muscle, it's the game!"

"I just got to get home now," said John.

Now the statue moved, took its hands down out of the air and turned its head to look at Douglas. They stood looking at each other. The other kids were putting their arms down, too.

"We'll play one more round," said John, "except this time, I'm 'it.' Run!"

The boys ran.

"Freeze!"

The boys froze, Douglas with them.

"Not a muscle!" shouted John. "Not a hair!"

He came and stood by Douglas.

"Boy, this is the only way to do it," he said.

Douglas looked off at the twilight sky.

"Frozen statues, every single one of you, the next three minutes!" said John.

Douglas felt John walking around him even as he had walked around John a moment ago. He felt John sock him on the arm once, not too hard. "So long," he said.

Then there was a rushing sound and he knew without looking that there was nobody behind him now.

Far away, a train whistle sounded.

Douglas stood that way for a full minute, waiting for the sound of the running to fade, but it did not stop. He's still running away, but he doesn't sound any further off, thought Douglas. Why doesn't he stop running?

And then he realized it was only the sound of his heart in his body.

Stop! He jerked his hand to his chest. Stop running! I don't *like* that sound!

And then he felt himself walking across the lawns among all the other statues now, and whether they, too, were coming to life he did not know. They did not seem to be moving at all. For that matter he himself was only moving from the knees down. The rest of him was cold stone, and very heavy.

Going up the front porch of his house, he turned suddenly to look at the lawns behind him.

The lawns were empty.

A series of rifle shots. Screen doors banged one after the other, a sunset volley, along the street.

Statues are best, he thought. They're the only things

you can keep on your lawn. Don't ever let them move. Once you do, you can't do a thing with them.

Suddenly his fist shot out like a piston from his side and it shook itself hard at the lawns and the street and the gathering dusk. His face was choked with blood, his eyes were blazing.

"John!" he cried. "You, John! John, you're my enemy, you hear? You're no friend of mine! Don't come back now, ever! Get away, you! Enemy, you hear? That's what you are! It's all off between us, you're dirt, that's all, dirt! John, you hear me, John!"

As if a wick had been turned a little lower in a great clear lamp beyond the town, the sky darkened still more. He stood on the porch, his mouth gasping and working. His fist still thrust straight out at that house across the street and down the way. He looked at the fist and it dissolved, the world dissolved beyond it.

Going upstairs, in the dark, where he could only feel his face but see nothing of himself, not even his fists, he told himself over and over, I'm mad, I'm angry, I hate him, I'm mad, I'm angry, I hate him!

Ten minutes later, slowly he reached the top of the stairs, in the dark . . .

Green Wine for Dreaming

Faintly, the voice chanted under the fiery green trees at noon.

". . . nine, ten, eleven, twelve . . ."

Douglas moved slowly across the lawn. "Tom, what you counting?"

". . . thirteen, fourteen, shut up, sixteen, seventeen, cicadas, eighteen, nineteen . . . !"

"Cicadas?"

"Oh hell!" Tom unsqueezed his eyes. "Hell, hell, hell!"

"Better not let people hear you swearing."

"Hell, hell, hell is a place!" Tom cried. "Now I got to

start all over. I was counting the times the cicadas buzz every fifteen seconds." He held up his two-dollar watch. "You time it, then add thirty-nine and you get the temperature at that very moment." He looked at the watch, one eye shut, tilted his head and whispered again, "One, two, three . . . !"

Douglas turned his head slowly, listening. Somewhere in the burning bone-colored sky a great copper wire was strummed and shaken. Again and again the piercing metallic vibrations, like charges of raw electricity, fell in paralyzing shocks from the stunned trees.

"Seven!" counted Tom. "Eight."

Douglas walked slowly up the porch steps. Painfully he peered into the hall. He stayed there a moment, then slowly he stepped back out on the porch and called weakly to Tom. "It's exactly eighty-seven degrees Farenheit."

"—twenty-seven, twenty-eight—"

"Hey, Tom, you hear me?"

"I hear you—thirty, thirty-one! Get away! Two, three, thirty-four!"

"You can stop counting now, right inside on that old thermometer it's eighty-seven and going up, without the help of no katydids."

"Cicadas! Thirty-nine, forty! Not katydids! Forty-two!"

"Eighty-seven degrees, I thought you'd like to know."

"Forty-five, that's inside, not outside! Forty-nine, fifty, fifty-one! Fifty-two, fifty-three! Fifty-three plus thirty-nine is—ninety-two degrees!"

"Who says?"

"I say! Not eighty-seven degrees Fahrenheit! But ninety-two degrees Spaulding!"

"You and who else?"

Tom jumped up and stood red-faced, staring at the sun. "Me and the cicadas, that's who! Me and the cicadas! You're outnumbered! Ninety-two, ninety-two, ninety-two degrees Spaulding, by gosh!"

They both stood looking at the merciless unclouded sky like a camera that has broken and stares, shutter wide, at a motionless and stricken town dying in a fiery sweat.

Douglas shut his eyes and saw two idiot suns dancing
on the reverse side of the pinkly translucent lids.

"One . . . two . . . three . . ."

Douglas felt his lips move.

". . . four . . . five . . . six   ."

This time the cicadas sang even faster.

From noontime to sundown, from midnight to sunrise,
one man, one horse, and one wagon were known to all
twenty-six thousand three hundred forty-nine inhabitants
of Green Town, Illinois.

In the middle of the day, for no reason quickly appar-
ent, children would stop still and say:

"Here comes Mr. Jonas!"

"Here comes Ned!"

"Here comes the wagon!"

Older folks might peer north or south, east or west and
see no sign of the man named Jonas, the horse named
Ned, or the wagon which was a Conestoga of the kind that
bucked the prairie tides to beach on the wilderness.

But then if you borrowed the ear of a dog and tuned it
high and stretched it taut you could hear, miles and miles
across the town, a singing like a rabbi in the lost lands, a
Moslem in a tower. Always, Mr. Jonas's voice went clear
before him so people had a half an hour, an hour, to
prepare for his arrival. And by the time his wagon appeared, the curbs were lined by children, as for a parade.

So here came the wagon and on its high board seat
under a persimmon-colored umbrella, the reins like a
stream of water in his gentle hands, was Mr. Jonas,
singing.

"Junk! Junk!
No, sir, not Junk!
Junk! Junk!
No, ma'am, not Junk!

Bricabracs, brickbats!
Knitting needles, knick-knacks!
Kickshaws! Curios!
Camisoles! Cameos!
But . . . Junk!
Junk!
No, sir, not . . . Junk!"

As anyone could tell who had heard the songs Mr. Jonas made up as he passed, he was no ordinary junkman. To all appearances, yes, the way he dressed in tatters of moss-corduroy and the felt cap on his head, covered with old presidential campaign buttons going back before Manila Bay. But he was unusual in this way: not only did he tread the sunlight, but often you could see him and his horse swimming along the moonlit streets, circling and recircling by night the islands, the blocks where all the people lived he had known all of his life. And in that wagon he carried things he had picked up here and there and carried for a day or a week or a year until someone wanted and needed them. Then all they had to say was, "I want that clock," or "How about the mattress?" And Jonas would hand it over, take no money, and drive away, considering the words for another tune.

So it happened that often he was the only man alive in all Green Town at three in the morning and often people with headaches, seeing him amble by with his moon-shimmered horse, would run out to see if by any chance he had aspirin, which he did. More than once he had delivered babies at four in the morning and only then had people noticed how incredibly clean his hands and fingernails were—the hands of a rich man who had another life somewhere they could not guess. Sometimes he would drive people to work downtown, or sometimes, when men could not sleep, go up on their porch and bring cigars and sit with them and smoke and talk until dawn.

Whoever he was or whatever he was and no matter how different and crazy he seemed, he was not crazy. As he himself had often explained gently, he had tired of business in Chicago many years before and looked around for a way to spend the rest of his life. Couldn't stand churches, though he appreciated their ideas, and having a tendency toward preaching and decanting knowledge, he bought the horse and wagon and set out to spend the rest of his life seeing to it that one part of town had a chance to pick over what the other part of town had cast off. He looked upon himself as a kind of process, like osmosis, that made various cultures within the city limits available one to another. He could not stand waste, for he knew that one man's junk is another man's luxury.

So adults, and especially children, clambered up to peer over into the vast treasure hoard in the back of the wagon.

"Now, remember," said Mr. Jonas, "you can have what you want if you really want it. The test is, ask yourself, Do I want it with all my heart? Could I live through the day without it? If you figure to be dead by sundown, grab the darned thing and run. I'll be happy to let you have whatever it is."

And the children searched the vast heaps of parchments and brocades and bolts of wallpaper and marble ash trays and vests and roller skates and great fat overstuffed chairs and end tables and crystal chandeliers. For a while you just heard whispering and rattling and tinkling. Mr. Jonas watched, comfortably puffing on his pipe, and the children knew he watched. Sometimes their hands reached out for a game of checkers or a string of beads or an old chair, and just as they touched it they looked up and there were Mr. Jonas's eyes gently questioning them. And they pulled their hands away and looked further on. Until at last each of them put his hand on a single item and left it there. Their faces came up and this time their faces were so bright Mr. Jonas had to laugh. He put up his hand as if to fend off the brightness of their faces from his eyes. He covered his eyes a moment. When he did this, the children yelled their thanks, grabbed their roller skates or clay tiles or bumbershoots and, dropping off, ran.

And the children came back in a moment with something of their own in their hands, a doll or a game they had grown tired of, something the fun had gone out of, like flavor from gum, and now it was time for it to pass on to some other part of town where, seen for the first time, it would be revivified and would revivify others. These tokens of exchange were shyly dropped over the rim of the wagon down into unseen riches and then the wagon was trundling on, flickering light on its great spindling sunflower wheels and Mr. Jonas singing again . . .

> *"Junk! Junk!*
> *No, sir, not Junk!*
> *No, ma'am, not Junk!"*

until he was out of sight and only the dogs, in the shadow pools under trees, heard the rabbi in the wilderness, and twitched their tails . . .

". . . junk . . ."

Fading.

". . . junk . . ."

A whisper.

". . . *junk* . . ." Gone.

And the dogs asleep.

The sidewalks were haunted by dust ghosts all night as the furnace wind summoned them up, swung them about, and gentled them down in a warm spice on the lawns. Trees, shaken by the footsteps of late-night strollers, sifted avalanches of dust. From midnight on, it seemed a volcano beyond the town was showering red-hot ashes every-where, crusting slumberless night watchmen and irritable dogs. Each house was a yellow attic smoldering with spontaneous combustion at three in the morning.

Dawn, then, was a time where things changed element for element. Air ran like hot spring waters nowhere, with no sound. The lake was a quantity of steam very still and deep over valleys of fish and sand held baking under its serene vapors. Tar was poured licorice in the streets, red bricks were brass and gold, roof tops were paved with bronze. The high tension wires were lightning held forever, blazing, a threat above the unslept houses.

The cicadas sang louder and yet louder.

The sun did not rise, it overflowed.

In his room, his face a bubbled mass of perspiration, Douglas melted on his bed.

"Wow," said Tom, entering. "Come on, Doug. We'll drown in the river all day."

Douglas breathed out. Douglas breathed in. Sweat trickled down his neck.

"Doug, you awake?"

The slightest nod of the head.

"You don't feel good, huh? Boy, this house'll burn down today." He put his hand on Douglas's brow. It was like touching a blazing stove lid. He pulled his fingers away, startled. He turned and went downstairs.

"Mom," he said, "Doug's really sick."

His mother, taking eggs out of the icebox, stopped, let a quick look of concern cross her face, put the eggs back, and followed Tom upstairs.

Douglas had not moved so much as a finger.

The cicadas were screaming now.

At noon, running as if the sun were after him to smash him to the ground, the doctor pulled up on the front porch, gasping, his eyes weary already, and gave his bag to Tom.

At one o'clock the doctor came out of the house, shaking his head. Tom and his mother stood behind the screen door, as the doctor talked in a low voice, saying over and over again he didn't know, he didn't know. He put his Panama hat on his head, gazed at the sunlight blistering and shriveling the trees overhead, hesitated like a man plunging into the outer rim of hell, and ran again for his car. The exhaust of the car left a great pall of blue smoke in the pulsing air for five minutes after he was gone.

Tom took the ice pick in the kitchen and chipped a pound of ice into prisms, which he carried upstairs. Mother was sitting on the bed and the only sound in the room was Douglas breathing in steam and breathing out fire. They put the ice in handkerchiefs on his face and along his body. They drew the shades and made the room like a cave. They sat there until two o'clock, bringing up more ice. Then they touched Douglas's brow again and it was like a lamp that had burned all night. After touching him you looked at your fingers to make sure they weren't seared to the bone.

Mother opened her mouth to say something, but the cicadas were so loud now they shook dust down from the ceiling.

Inside redness, inside blindness, Douglas lay listening to the dim piston of his heart and the muddy ebb and flow of the blood in his arms and legs.

His lips were heavy and would not move. His thoughts were heavy and barely ticked, like seed pellets falling in an hourglass slow one by falling one. Tick.

Around a bright steel corner of rail a trolley swung, throwing a crumbling wave of sizzling sparks, its clamorous bell knocking ten thousand times until it blended with the cicadas. Mr. Tridden waved. The trolley stormed around a corner like a cannonade and dissolved. Mr. Tridden!

Tick. A pellet fell. *Tick.*

"Chug-a-chug-ding! Woo-woooo!"

On the roof top a boy locomoted, pulling an invisible whistle string, then froze into a statue. "John! John Huff, you! Hate you, John! John, we're pals! Don't hate you, no."

John fell down the elm-tree corridor like someone falling down an endless summer well, dwindling away.

Tick. John Huff. Tick. Sand pellet dropping. Tick. John . . .

Douglas moved his head flat over, crashing on the white white terribly white pillow.

The ladies in the Green Machine sailed by in a sound of

black seal barking, lifting hands as white as doves. They sank into the lawn's deep waters, their gloves still waving to him as the grass closed over . . .

Miss Fern! Miss Roberta!

Tick . . . Tick . . .

And quickly then from a window across the way Colonel Freeleigh leaned out with the face of a clock, and buffalo dust sprang up in the street. Colonel Freeleigh spanged and rattled, his jaw fell open, a mainspring shot out and dangled on the air instead of his tongue. He collapsed like a puppet on the sill, one arm still waving . . .

Mr. Auffmann rode by in something that was bright and something like the trolley and the green electric runabout; and it trailed glorious clouds and it put out your eyes like the sun. "Mr. Auffmann, did you invent it?" he cried. "Did you finally build the Happiness Machine?"

But then he saw there was no bottom to the machine. Mr. Auffmann ran along on the ground, carrying the whole incredible frame from his shoulders.

"Happiness, Doug, here goes happiness!" And he went the way of the trolley, John Huff, and the dove-fingered ladies.

Above on the roof a tapping sound. Tap-rap-bang. Pause. Tap-rap-bang. Nail and hammer. Hammer and nail. A bird choir. And an old woman singing in a frail but hearty voice.

"Yes, we'll gather at the river . . . river . . . river . . .
Yes, we'll gather at the river . . .
That flows by the throne of God . . ."

"Grandma! Great-grandma!"

Tap, softly, tap. Tap, softly, tap.

". . . river . . . river . . ."

And now it was only the birds picking up their tiny feet and putting them down again on the roof. Rattle-rattle. Scratch. Peep. Peep. Soft. Soft.

". . . river . . ."

Douglas took one breath and let it all out at once, wailing.

He did not hear his mother run into the room.

A fly, like the burning ash of a cigarette, fell upon his senseless hand, sizzled, and flew away.

Four o'clock in the afternoon. Flies dead on the pavement. Dogs wet mops in their kennels. Shadows herded under trees. Downtown stores shut up and locked. The lake shore empty. The lake full of thousands of people up to their necks in the warm but soothing water.

Four-fifteen. Along the brick streets of town the junk wagon moved, with Mr. Jonas singing on it.

Tom, driven out of the house by the scorched look on Douglas's face, walked slowly down to the curb as the wagon stopped.

"Hi, Mr. Jonas."

"Hello, Tom."

Tom and Mr. Jonas were alone on the street with all that beautiful junk in the wagon to look at and neither of them looking at it. Mr. Jonas didn't say anything right away. He lit his pipe and puffed it, nodding his head as if he knew before he asked, that something was wrong.

"Tom?" he said.

"It's my brother," said Tom. "It's Doug."

Mr. Jonas looked up at the house.

"He's sick," said Tom. "He's dying!"

"Oh, now, that can't be so," said Mr. Jonas, scowling around at the very real world where nothing that vaguely looked like death could be found on this quiet day.

"He's dying," said Tom. "And the doctor doesn't know what's wrong. The heat, he said, nothing but the heat. Can that be, Mr. Jonas? Can the heat kill people, even in a dark room?"

"Well," said Mr. Jonas and stopped.

For Tom was crying now.

"I always thought I hated him . . . that's what I thought . . . we fight half the time . . . I guess I did hate him . . . sometimes . . . but now . . . now. Oh, Mr. Jonas, if only . . ."

"If only what, boy?"

"If only you had something in this wagon would help. Something I could pick and take upstairs and make him okay."

Tom cried again.

Mr. Jonas took out his red bandanna handkerchief and handed it to Tom. Tom wiped his nose and eyes with the handkerchief.

"It's been a tough summer," Tom said. "Lots of things have happened to Doug."

"Tell me about them," said the junkman.

"Well," said Tom, gasping for breath, not quite done crying yet, "he lost his best aggie for one, a real beaut. And on top of that somebody stole his catcher's mitt, it cost a dollar ninety-five. Then there was the bad trade he made of his fossil stones and shell collection with Charlie Woodman for a Tarzan clay statue you got by saving up macaroni box tops. Dropped the Tarzan statue on the sidewalk second day he had it."

"That's a shame," said the junkman and really saw all the pieces on the cement.

"Then he didn't get the book of magic tricks he wanted for his birthday, got a pair of pants and a shirt instead. That's enough to ruin the summer right there."

"Parents sometimes forget how it is," said Mr. Jonas.

"Sure," Tom continued in a low voice, "then Doug's genuine set of Tower-of-London manacles left out all night and rusted. And worst of all, I grew one inch taller, catching up with him almost."

"Is that all?" asked the junkman quietly.

"I could think of ten dozen other things, all as bad or worse. Some summers you get a run of luck like that. It's been silverfish getting in his comics collections or mildew in his new tennis shoes ever since Doug got out of school."

"I remember years like that," said the junkman.

He looked off at the sky and there were all the years.

"So there you are, Mr. Jonas. That's it. That's why he's dying . . ."

Tom stopped and looked away.

"Let me think," said Mr. Jonas.

"Can you help, Mr. Jonas? *Can* you?"

Mr. Jonas looked deep in the big old wagon and shook his head. Now, in the sunlight, his face looked tired and he was beginning to perspire. Then he peered into the mounds of vases and peeling lamp shades and marble nymphs and satyrs made of greening copper. He sighed. He turned and picked up the reins and gave them a gentle shake. "Tom," he said, looking at the horse's back, "I'll see you later. I got to plan. I got to look around and come again after supper. Even then, who knows? Until then . . ." He reached down and picked up a little set of Japanese wind-crystals. "Hang these in his upstairs window. They make a nice cool music!"

Tom stood with the wind-crystals in his hands as the wagon rolled away. He held them up and there was no wind, they did not move. They could not make a sound.

Seven o'clock. The town resembled a vast hearth over which the shudderings of heat moved again and again from the west. Charcoal-colored shadows quivered outward from every house, every tree. A red-haired man moved along below. Tom, seeing him illumined by the dying but ferocious sun, saw a torch proudly carrying itself, saw a fiery fox, saw the devil marching in his own country.

At seven-thirty Mrs. Spaulding came out of the back door of the house to empty some watermelon rinds into the garbage pail and saw Mr. Jonas standing there.

"How is the boy?" said Mr. Jonas.

Mrs. Spaulding stood there for a moment, a response trembling on her lips.

"May I see him, please?" said Mr. Jonas.

Still she could say nothing.

"I know the boy well," he said. "Seen him most every day of his life since he was out and around. I've something for him in the wagon."

"He's not——" She was going to say "conscious," but

she said, "awake. He's not awake, Mr. Jonas. The doctor said he's not to be disturbed. Oh, we don't know *what's* wrong!"

"Even if he's not 'awake,'" said Mr. Jonas, "I'd like to talk to him. Sometimes the things you hear in your sleep are more important, you listen better, it gets through."

"I'm sorry, Mr. Jonas, I just can't take the chance." Mrs. Spaulding caught hold of the screen-door handle and held fast to it. "Thanks. Thank you, anyway, for coming by."

"Yes, ma'am," said Mr. Jonas.

He did not move. He stood looking up at the window above. Mrs. Spaulding went in the house and shut the screen door.

Upstairs, on his bed, Douglas breathed.

It was a sound like a sharp knife going in and out, in and out, of a sheath.

At eight o'clock the doctor came and went again, shaking his head, his coat off, his tie untied, looking as if he had lost thirty pounds that day. At nine o'clock Tom and Mother and Father carried a cot outside and brought Douglas down to sleep in the yard under the apple tree where, if there might be a wind, it would find him sooner than in the terrible rooms above. Then they went back and forth until eleven o'clock, when they set the alarm clock to wake them at three and chip more ice to refill the packs.

The house was dark and still at last, and they slept.

At twelve thirty-five, Douglas's eyes flinched.

The moon had begun to rise.

And far away a voice began to sing.

It was a high sad voice rising and falling. It was a clear voice and it was in tune. You could not make out the words.

The moon came over the edge of the lake and looked upon Green Town, Illinois, and saw it all and showed it all, every house, every tree, every prehistoric-remembering dog twitching in his simple dreams.

And it seemed that the higher the moon the nearer and louder and clearer the voice that was singing.

And Douglas turned in his fever and sighed.

Perhaps it was an hour before the moon spilled all its light upon the world, perhaps less. But the voice was nearer now and a sound like the beating of a heart which was really the motion of a horse's hoofs on the brick streets muffled by the hot thick foliage of the trees.

And there was another sound like a door slowly opening or closing, squeaking, squealing softly from time to time. The sound of a wagon.

And down the street in the light of the risen moon came the horse pulling the wagon and the wagon riding the lean body of Mr. Jonas easy and casual on the high seat. He wore his hat as if he were still out under the summer sun and he moved his hands on occasion to ripple the reins like a flow of water on the air above the horse's back. Very slowly the wagon moved down the street with Mr. Jonas singing, and in his sleep Douglas seemed for a moment to stop breathing and listen.

"Air, air . . . who will buy this air . . . Air like water and air like ice . . . buy it once and you'll buy it twice . . . here's the April air . . . here's an autumn breeze . . . here's papaya wind from the Antilles . . . Air, air, sweet pickled air . . . fair . . . rare . . . from everywhere . . . bottled and capped and scented with thyme, all that you want of air for a dime!"

At the end of this the wagon was at the curb. And someone stood in the yard, treading his shadow, carrying two beetle-green bottles which glittered like cats' eyes. Mr. Jonas looked at the cot there and called the boy's name once, twice, three times, softly. Mr. Jonas swayed in indecision, looked at the bottles he carried, made his decision, and moved forward stealthily to sit on the grass and look at this boy crushed down by the great weight of summer.

"Doug," he said, "you just lie quiet. You don't have to say anything or open your eyes. You don't even have to pretend to listen. But inside there, I know you hear me, and it's old Jonas, your friend. Your friend," he repeated and nodded.

He reached up and picked an apple off the tree, turned it round, took a bite, chewed, and continued.

"Some people turn sad awfully young," he said. "No special reason, it seems, but they seem almost to be born that way. They bruise easier, tire faster, cry quicker, remember longer and, as I say, get sadder younger than anyone else in the world. I know, for I'm one of them."

He took another bite of the apple and chewed it.

"Well, now, where are we?" he asked.

"A hot night, not a breath stirring, in August," he answered himself. "Killing hot. And a long summer it's been and too much happening, eh? Too much. And it's getting on toward one o'clock and no sign of a wind or rain. And in a moment now I'm going to get up and go. But when I go, and remember this clearly, I will leave these two bottles here upon your bed. And when I've gone I want you to wait a little while and then slowly open your eyes and sit up and reach over and drink the contents of these bottles. Not with your mouth, no. Drink with your nose. Tilt the bottles, uncork them, and let what is in them go right down into your head. Read the labels first, of course. But here, let me read them for you."

He lifted one bottle into the light.

"'GREEN DUSK FOR DREAMING BRAND PURE NORTHERN AIR,'" he read. "'Derived from the atmosphere of the white Arctic in the spring of 1900, and mixed with the wind from the upper Hudson Valley in the month of April, 1910, and containing particles of dust seen shining in the sunset of one day in the meadows around Grinnell, Iowa, when a cool air rose to be captured from a lake and a little creek and a natural spring.'

"Now the small print," he said. He squinted. "'Also containing molecules of vapor from menthol, lime, papaya and watermelon and all other water-smelling, cool-savored fruits and trees like camphor and herbs like wintergreen and the breath of a rising wind from the Des Plaines River itself. Guaranteed most refreshing and cool. To be taken on summer nights when the heat passes ninety.'"

He picked up the other bottle.

"This one the same, save I've collected a wind from the Aran Isles and one from off Dublin Bay with salt on it and a strip of flannel fog from the coast of Iceland."

He put the two bottles on the bed.

"One last direction." He stood by the cot and leaned over and spoke quietly. "When you're drinking these, remember: It was bottled by a friend. The S. J. Jonas Bottling Company, Green Town, Illinois—August, 1928. A vintage year, boy . . . a vintage year."

A moment later there was the sound of reins slapping the back of the horse in the moonlight, and the rumble of the wagon down the street and away.

After a moment Douglas's eyes twitched and, very slowly, opened.

"Mother!" whispered Tom. "Dad! Doug, it's Doug! He's going to be well. I just went down to check and—come on!"

Tom ran out of the house. His parents followed.

Douglas was asleep as they approached. Tom motioned to his parents, smiling wildly. They bent over the cot.

A single exhalation, a pause, a single exhalation, a pause, as the three bent there.

Douglas's mouth was slightly open and from his lips and from the thin vents of his nostrils, gently there rose a scent of cool night and cool water and cool white snow and cool green moss, and cool moonlight on silver pebbles lying at the bottom of a quiet river and cool clear water at the bottom of a small white stone well.

It was like holding their heads down for a brief moment to the pulse of an apple-scented fountain flowing cool up into the air and washing their faces.

They could not move for a long time.

Kaleidoscope

The first concussion cut the rocket up the side with a giant can opener. The men were thrown into space like a dozen wriggling silverfish. They were scattered into a dark sea; and the ship, in a million pieces, went on, a meteor swarm seeking a lost sun.

"Barkley, Barkley, where are you?"

The sound of voices calling like lost children on a cold night.

"Woode, Woode!"

"Captain!"

"Hollis, Hollis, this is Stone."

"Stone, this is Hollis. Where are you?"

"I don't know. How can I? Which way is up? I'm falling. Good God, I'm falling."

They fell. They fell as pebbles fall down wells. They were scattered as jackstones are scattered from a gigantic throw. And now instead of men there were only voices—all kinds of voices, disembodied and impassioned, in varying degrees of terror and resignation.

"We're going away from each other."

This was true. Hollis, swinging head over heels, knew

this was true. He knew it with a vague acceptance. They were parting to go their separate ways, and nothing could bring them back. They were wearing their sealed-tight space suits with the glass tubes over their pale faces, but they hadn't had time to lock on their force units. With them they could be small lifeboats in space, saving themselves, saving others, collecting together, finding each other until they were an island of men with some plan. But without the force units snapped to their shoulders they were meteors, senseless, each going to a separate and irrevocable fate.

A period of perhaps ten minutes elapsed while the first terror died and a metallic calm took its place. Space began to weave its strange voices in and out, on a great dark loom, crossing, recrossing, making a final pattern.

"Stone to Hollis. How long can we talk by phone?"

"It depends on how fast you're going your way and I'm going mine."

"An hour, I make it."

"That should do it," said Hollis, abstracted and quiet.

"What happened?" said Hollis a minute later.

"The rocket blew up, that's all. Rockets do blow up."

"Which way are you going?"

"It looks like I'll hit the moon."

"It's Earth for me. Back to old Mother Earth at ten thousand miles per hour. I'll burn like a match." Hollis thought of it with a queer abstraction of mind. He seemed to be removed from his body, watching it fall down and down through space, as objective as he had been in regard to the first falling snowflakes of a winter season long gone.

The others were silent, thinking of the destiny that had brought them to this, falling, falling, and nothing they could do to change it. Even the captain was quiet, for there was no command or plan he knew that could put things back together again.

"Oh, it's a long way down. Oh, it's a long way down, a long, long, long way down," said a voice. "I don't want to die, I don't want to die, it's a long way down."

"Who's that?"

"I don't know."

"Stimson, I think. Stimson, is that you?"

"It's a long, long way and I don't like it. Oh, God, I don't like it."

"Stimson, this is Hollis. Stimson, you hear me?"

A pause while they fell separate from one another.

"Stimson?"

"Yes." He replied at last.

"Stimson, take it easy; we're all in the same fix."

"I don't want to be here. I want to be somewhere else."

"There's a chance we'll be found."

"I must be, I must be," said Stimson. "I don't believe this; I don't believe any of this is happening."

"It's a bad dream," said someone.

"Shut up!" said Hollis.

"Come and make me," said the voice. It was Applegate. He laughed easily, with a similar objectivity. "Come and shut me up."

Hollis for the first time felt the impossibility of his position. A great anger filled him, for he wanted more than anything at this moment to be able to do something to Applegate. He had wanted for many years to do something and now it was too late. Applegate was only a telephonic voice.

Falling, falling, falling . . .

Now, as if they had discovered the horror, two of the men began to scream. In a nightmare Hollis saw one of them float by, very near, screaming and screaming.

"Stop it!" The man was almost at his fingertips, screaming insanely. He would never stop. He would go on screaming for a million miles, as long as he was in radio range, disturbing all of them, making it impossible for them to talk to one another.

Hollis reached out. It was best this way. He made the extra effort and touched the man. He grasped the man's ankle and pulled himself up along the body until he reached the head. The man screamed and clawed frantically, like a drowning swimmer. The screaming filled the universe.

One way or the other, thought Hollis. The moon or Earth or meteors will kill him, so why not now?

He smashed the man's glass mask with his iron fist. The screaming stopped. He pushed off from the body and let it spin away on its own course, falling.

Falling, falling down space Hollis and the rest of them went in the long, endless dropping and whirling of silence.

"Hollis, you still there?"

Hollis did not speak, but felt the rush of heat in his face.

"This is Applegate again."

"All right, Applegate."

"Let's talk. We haven't anything else to do."

The captain cut in. "That's enough of that. We've got to figure a way out of this."

"Captain, why don't you shut up?" said Applegate.

"What!"

"You heard me, Captain. Don't pull your rank on me, you're ten thousand miles away by now, and let's not kid ourselves. As Stimson puts it, it's a long way down."

"See here, Applegate!"

"Can it. This is a mutiny of one. I haven't a damn thing to lose. Your ship was a bad ship and you were a bad captain and I hope you break when you hit the moon."

"I'm ordering you to stop!"

"Go on, order me again." Applegate smiled across ten thousand miles. The captain was silent. Applegate continued, "Where were we, Hollis? Oh yes, I remember. I hate you too. But you know that. You've known it for a long time."

Hollis clenched his fists, helplessly.

"I want to tell you something," said Applegate. "Make you happy. I was the one who blackballed you with the Rocket Company five years ago."

A meteor flashed by. Hollis looked down and his left hand was gone. Blood spurted. Suddenly there was no air in his suit. He had enough air in his lungs to move his

right hand over and twist a knob at his left elbow,
tightening the joint and sealing the leak. It had happened
so quickly that he was not surprised. Nothing surprised
him any more. The air in the suit came back to normal in
an instant now that the leak was sealed. And the blood
that had flowed so swiftly was pressured as he fastened the
knob yet tighter, until it made a tourniquet.

All of this took place in a terrible silence on his part.
And the other men chatted. That one man, Lespere, went
on and on with his talk about his wife on Mars, his wife on
Venus, his wife on Jupiter, his money, his wondrous times,
his drunkenness, his gambling, his happiness. On and on,
while they all fell. Lespere reminisced on the past, happy,
while he fell to his death.

It was so very odd. Space, thousands of miles of space,
and these voices vibrating in the center of it. No one
visible at all, and only the radio waves quivering and
trying to quicken other men into emotion.

"Are you angry, Hollis?"

"No." And he was not. The abstraction had returned
and he was a thing of dull concrete, forever falling nowhere.

"You wanted to get to the top all your life, Hollis. You
always wondered what happened. I put the black mark on
you just before I was tossed out myself."

"That isn't important," said Hollis. And it was not. It
was gone. When life is over it is like a flicker of bright
film, an instant on the screen, all of its prejudices and
passions condensed and illumined for an instant on space,
and before you could cry out, "There was a happy day,
there a bad one, there an evil face, there a good one," the
film burned to a cinder, the screen went dark.

From this outer edge of his life, looking back, there was
only one remorse, and that was only that he wished to go
on living. Did all dying people feel this way, as if they had
never lived? Did life seem that short, indeed, over and
done before you took a breath? Did it seem this abrupt

and impossible to everyone, or only to himself, here, now, with a few hours left to him for thought and deliberation?

One of the other men, Lespere, was talking. "Well, I had me a good time: I had a wife on Mars, Venus, and Jupiter. Each of them had money and treated me swell. I got drunk and once I gambled away twenty thousand dollars."

But you're here now, thought Hollis. I didn't have any of those things. When I was living I was jealous of you, Lespere; when I had another day ahead of me I envied you your women and your good times. Women frightened me and I went into space, always wanting them and jealous of you for having them, and money, and as much happiness as you could have in your own wild way. But now, falling here, with everything over, I'm not jealous of you any more, because it's over for you as it is for me, and right now it's like it never was. Hollis craned his face forward and shouted into the telephone.

"It's all over, Lespere!"

Silence.

"It's just as if it never was, Lespere!"

"Who's that?" Lespere's faltering voice.

"This is Hollis."

He was being mean. He felt the meanness, the senseless meanness of dying. Applegate had hurt him; now he wanted to hurt another. Applegate and space had both wounded him.

"You're out here, Lespere. It's all over. It's just as if it had never happened, isn't it?"

"No."

"When anything's over, it's just like it never happened. Where's your life any better than mine, now? Now is what counts. Is it any better? Is it?"

"Yes, it's better!"

"How!"

"Because I got my thoughts, I remember!" cried Lespere, far away, indignant, holding his memories to his chest with both hands.

And he was right. With a feeling of cold water rushing through his head and body, Hollis knew he was right. There were differences between memories and dreams. He had only dreams of things he had wanted to do, while Lespere had memories of things done and accomplished. And this knowledge began to pull Hollis apart, with a slow, quivering precision.

"What good does it do you?" he cried to Lespere. "Now? When a thing's over it's not good any more. You're no better off than me."

"I'm resting easy," said Lespere. "I've had my turn. I'm not getting mean at the end, like you."

"Mean?" Hollis turned the word on his tongue. He had never been mean, as long as he could remember, in his life. He had never dared to be mean. He must have saved it all of these years for such a time as this. "Mean." He rolled the word into the back of his mind. He felt tears start into his eyes and roll down his face. Someone must have heard his gasping voice.

"Take it easy, Hollis."

It was, of course, ridiculous. Only a minute before he had been giving advice to others, to Stimson; he had felt a braveness which he had thought to be the genuine thing, and now he knew that it had been nothing but shock and the objectivity possible in shock. Now he was trying to pack a lifetime of suppressed emotion into an interval of minutes.

"I know how you feel, Hollis," said Lespere, now twenty thousand miles away, his voice fading. "I don't take it personally."

But aren't we equal? he wondered. Lespere and I? Here, now? If a thing's over, it's done, and what good is it? You die anyway. But he knew he was rationalizing, for it was like trying to tell the difference between a live man and a corpse. There was a spark in one, and not in the other—an aura, a mysterious element.

So it was with Lespere and himself; Lespere had lived a good full life, and it made him a different man now, and he, Hollis, had been as good as dead for many years. They came to death by separate paths and, in all likelihood, if there were kinds of death, their kinds would be as different as night from day. The quality of death, like that of life, must be of an infinite variety, and if one has already died once, then what was there to look for in dying for good and all, as he was now?

It was a second later that he discovered his right foot was cut sheer away. It almost made him laugh. The air was gone from his suit again. He bent quickly, and there was blood, and the meteor had taken flesh and suit away to the ankle. Oh, death in space was most humorous. It cut you away, piece by piece, like a black and invisible butcher. He tightened the valve at the knee, his head whirling into pain, fighting to remain aware, and with the valve tightened, the blood retained, the air kept, he straightened up and went on falling, falling, for that was all there was left to do.

"Hollis?"

Hollis nodded sleepily, tired of waiting for death.

"This is Applegate again," said the voice.

"Yes."

"I've had time to think. I listened to you. This isn't good. It makes us bad. This is a bad way to die. It brings all the bile out. You listening, Hollis?"

"Yes."

"I lied. A minute ago. I lied. I didn't blackball you. I don't know why I said that. Guess I wanted to hurt you. You seemed the one to hurt. We've always fought. Guess I'm getting old fast and repenting fast. I guess listening to you be mean made me ashamed. Whatever the reason, I want you to know I was an idiot too. There's not an ounce of truth in what I said. To hell with you."

Hollis felt his heart begin to work again. It seemed as if it hadn't worked for five minutes, but now all of his limbs began to take color and warmth. The shock was over, and the successive shocks of anger and terror and loneliness were passing. He felt like a man emerging from a cold shower in the morning, ready for breakfast and a new day.

"Thanks, Applegate."

"Don't mention it. Up your nose, you bastard."

"Hey," said Stone.

"What?" Hollis called across space; for Stone, of all of them, was a good friend.

"I've got myself into a meteor swarm, some little asteroids."

"Meteors?"

"I think it's the Myrmidone cluster that goes out past Mars and in toward Earth once every five years. I'm right in the middle. It's like a big kaleidoscope. You get all kinds of colors and shapes and sizes. God, it's beautiful, all that metal."

Silence.

"I'm going with them," said Stone. "They're taking me off with them. I'll be damned." He laughed.

Hollis looked to see, but saw nothing. There were only the great diamonds and sapphires and emerald mists and velvet inks of space, with God's voice mingling among the crystal fires. There was a kind of wonder and imagination in the thought of Stone going off in the meteor swarm, out past Mars for years and coming in toward Earth every five years, passing in and out of the planet's ken for the next million centuries, Stone and the Myrmidone cluster eternal and unending, shifting and shaping like the kaleidoscope colors when you were a child and held the long tube to the sun and gave it a twirl.

"So long, Hollis." Stone's voice, very faint now. "So long."

"Good luck," shouted Hollis across thirty thousand miles.

"Don't be funny," said Stone, and was gone.

The stars closed in.

Now all the voices were fading, each on his own trajectory, some to Mars, others into farthest space. And Hollis himself . . . He looked down. He, of all the others, was going back to Earth alone.

"So long."

"Take it easy."

"So long, Hollis." That was Applegate.

The many good-bys. The short farewells. And now the great loose brain was disintegrating. The components of the brain which had worked so beautifully and efficiently in the skull case of the rocket ship firing through space were dying one by one; the meaning of their life together was falling apart. And as a body dies when the brain ceases functioning, so the spirit of the ship and their long time together and what they meant to one another was dying. Applegate was now no more than a finger blown from the parent body, no longer to be despised and worked against. The brain was exploded, and the sense-less, useless fragments of it were far scattered. The voices faded and now all of space was silent. Hollis was alone, falling.

They were all alone. Their voices had died like echoes of the words of God spoken and vibrating in the starred deep. There went the captain to the moon; there Stone with the meteor swarm; there Stimson; there Applegate toward Pluto; there Smith and Turner and Underwood and all the rest, the shards of the kaleidoscope that had formed a thinking pattern for so long, hurled apart.

And I? thought Hollis. What can I do? Is there anything I can do now to make up for a terrible and empty life? If only I could do one good thing to make up for the mean-ness I collected all these years and didn't even know was in me! But there's no one here but myself, and how can you do good all alone? You can't. Tomorrow night I'll hit Earth's atmosphere.

I'll burn, he thought, and be scattered in ashes all over the continental lands. I'll be put to use. Just a little bit, but ashes are ashes and they'll add to the land.

He fell swiftly, like a bullet, like a pebble, like an iron weight, objective, objective all of the time now, not sad or happy or anything, but only wishing he could do a good thing now that everything was gone, a good thing for just himself to know about.

When I hit the atmosphere, I'll burn like a meteor.

"I wonder," he said, "if anyone'll see me?"

 •   •   •

The small boy on the country road looked up and screamed. "Look, Mom, look! A falling star!"

The blazing white star fell down the sky of dusk in Illinois.

"Make a wish," said his mother. "Make a wish."

Sun and Shadow

The camera clicked like an insect. It was blue and metallic, like a great fat beetle held in the man's precious and tenderly exploiting hands. It winked in the flashing sunlight.

"Hsst, Ricardo, come away!"

"You down there!" cried Ricardo out the window.

"Ricardo, stop!"

He turned to his wife. "Don't tell me to stop, tell them to stop. Go down and tell them, or are you afraid?"

"They aren't hurting anything," said his wife patiently.

He shook her off and leaned out the window and looked down into the alley. "You there!" he cried.

The man with the black camera in the alley glanced up, then went on focusing his machine at the lady in the salt-white beach pants, the white bra, and the green checkered scarf. She leaned against the cracked plaster of the building. Behind her a dark boy smiled, his hand to his mouth.

"Tomás!" yelled Ricardo. He turned to his wife. "Oh, Jesus the Blessed, Tomás is in the street, my own son laughing there." Ricardo started out the door.

"Don't do anything!" said his wife.

"I'll cut off their heads!" said Ricardo, and was gone.

In the street the lazy woman was lounging now against the peeling blue paint of a banister. Ricardo emerged in time to see her doing this. "That's my banister!" he said.

The cameraman hurried up. "No, no, we're taking pictures. Everything's all right. We'll be moving on."

"Everything's not all right," said Ricardo, his brown eyes flashing. He waved a wrinkled hand. "She's on my house."

"We're taking fashion pictures," smiled the photographer.

"*Now* what am I to do?" said Ricardo to the blue sky. "Go mad with this news? Dance around like an epileptic saint?"

"If it's money, well, here's a five-peso bill," smiled the photographer.

Ricardo pushed the hand away. "I *work* for my money. You don't understand. Please go."

The photographer was bewildered. "Wait . . ."

"Tomás, get in the house!"

"But, Papa . . ."

"Gahh!" bellowed Ricardo.

The boy vanished.

"This has *never* happened before," said the photographer.

"It is long past time! What are we? Cowards?" Ricardo asked the world.

A crowd was gathering. They murmured and smiled and nudged each other's elbows. The photographer with irritable good will snapped his camera shut, said over his shoulder to the model, "All right, we'll use that other street. I saw a nice cracked wall there and some nice deep shadows. If we hurry . . ."

The girl, who had stood during this exchange nervously twisting her scarf, now seized her make-up kit and darted by Ricardo, but not before he touched at her arm. "Do not misunderstand," he said quickly. She stopped, blinked at him. He went on. "It is not you I am mad at. Or you." He addressed the photographer.

"Then why——" said the photographer.

Ricardo waved his hand. "You are employed; I am employed. We are all people employed. We must understand each other. But when you come to my house with your camera that looks like the complex eye of a black horsefly, then the understanding is over. I will not have my alley used because of its pretty shadows, or my sky used because of its sun, or my house used because there is an interesting crack in the wall, here! You *see!* Ah, how beautiful! Lean here! Stand there! Sit here! Crouch there! Hold it! Oh, I *heard* you. Do you think I am stupid? I have books up in my room. You see that window? Maria!"

His wife's head popped out. "Show them my books!" he cried.

She fussed and muttered, but a moment later she held out one, then two, then half a dozen books, eyes shut, head turned away, as if they were old fish.

"And two dozen more like them upstairs!" cried Ricardo. "You're not talking to some cow in the forest, you're talking to a man!"

"Look," said the photographer, packing his plates swiftly. "We're going. Thanks for nothing."

"Before you go, you must see what I am getting at," said Ricardo. "I am not a mean man. But I *can* be a very angry man. Do I look like a cardboard cutout?"

"Nobody said anybody looked like anything." The photographer hefted his case and started off.

"There is a photographer two blocks over," said Ricardo, pacing him. "They have cutouts. You stand in front of them. It says 'GRAND HOTEL.' They take a picture of you and it looks like you are in the Grand Hotel. Do you see what I mean? My alley is my alley, my life is my life, my son is my son. My son is not cardboard! I saw you putting my son against the wall, so, and thus, in the background. What do you call it—for the correct air? To make the whole attractive, and the lovely lady in front of him?"

"It's getting late," said the photographer, sweating. The model trotted along on the other side of him.

"We are poor people," said Ricardo. "Our doors peel paint, our walls are chipped and cracked, our gutters fume in the street, the alleys are all cobbles. But it fills me with a terrible rage when I see you make over these things as if I had *planned* it this way, as if I had years ago induced the wall to crack. Did you think I knew you were coming and aged the paint? Or that I knew you were coming and put my boy in his dirtiest clothes? We are *not* a studio! We are people and must be given attention as people. Have I made it clear?"

"With abundant detail," said the photographer, not looking at him, hurrying.

"Now that you know my wishes and my reasoning, you will do the friendly thing and go home?"

"You are a hilarious man," said the photographer. "Hey!" They had joined a group of five other models and a second photographer at the base of a vast stone stairway which in layers, like a bridal cake, led up to the white town square. "How you doing, Joe?"

"We got some beautiful shots near the Church of the Virgin, some statuary without any noses, lovely stuff," said Joe. "What's the commotion?"

"Pancho here got in an uproar. Seems we leaned against his house and knocked it down."

"My name is Ricardo. My house is completely intact."

"We'll shoot it *here*, dear," said the first photographer. "Stand by the archway of that store. There's a nice antique wall going up there." He peered into the mysteries of his camera.

"So!" A dreadful quiet came upon Ricardo. He watched them prepare. When they were ready to take the picture he hurried forward, calling to a man in a doorway. "Jorge! What are you *doing?*"

"I'm standing here," said the man.

"Well," said Ricardo, "isn't that *your* archway? Are you going to let them *use* it?"

"I'm not bothered," said Jorge.

Ricardo shook his arm. "They're treating your property like a movie actor's place. Aren't you insulted?"

"I haven't thought about it." Jorge picked his nose.

"Jesus upon earth, man, *think!*"

"I can't see any harm," said Jorge.

"Am I the *only* one in the world with a tongue in my mouth?" said Ricardo to his empty hands. "And taste on my tongue? Is this a town of backdrops and picture sets? Won't *anyone* do something about this except me?"

The crowd had followed them down the street, gathering others to it as it came; now it was of a fair size and more were coming, drawn by Ricardo's bullish shouts. He stomped his feet. He made fists. He spat. The cameraman and the models watched him nervously. "Do you want a *quaint* man in the background?" he said wildly to the cameraman. "I'll pose back here. Do you want me near this wall, my hat *so*, my feet *so*, the light so and thus on my sandals which I made myself? Do you want me to rip this hole in my shirt a bit larger, eh, like *this? So!* Is my face smeared with enough perspiration? Is my hair long enough, kind sir?"

"Stand there if you want," said the photographer.

"I won't look in the camera," Ricardo assured him.

The photographer smiled and lifted his machine. "Over to your left one step, dear." The model moved. "Now turn your right leg. That's fine. Fine, fine. *Hold* it!"

The model froze, chin tilted up.

Ricardo dropped his pants.

"Oh, my God!" said the photographer.

Some of the models squealed. The crowd laughed and pummeled each other a bit. Ricardo quietly raised his pants and leaned against the wall.

"Was that quaint enough?" he said.

"Oh, my God!" muttered the photographer.

"Let's go down to the docks," said his assistant.

"I think *I'll* go there too," Ricardo smiled.

"Good God, what can we do with the idiot?" whispered the photographer.

"Buy him off!"

"I *tried* that!"

"You didn't go high enough."

"Listen, you run get a policeman. I'll put a stop to this."
The assistant ran. Everyone stood around smoking cigarettes nervously, eying Ricardo. A dog came by and briefly
made water against the wall.

"Look at that!" cried Ricardo. "What art! What a pattern! Quick, before the sun dries it!"

The cameraman turned his back and looked out to sea.

The assistant came rushing along the street. Behind him,
a native policeman strolled quietly. The assistant had to
stop and run back to urge the policeman to hurry. The
policeman assured him with a gesture, at a distance, that
the day was not yet over and in time they would arrive at
the scene of whatever disaster lay ahead.

The policeman took up a position behind the two cam-
eramen. "What seems to be the trouble?"

"That man up there. We want him removed."

"That man up there seems only to be leaning against a
wall," said the officer.

"No, no, it's not the leaning, he—— Oh hell," said the
cameraman. "The only way to explain is to show you. Take
your pose, dear."

The girl posed. Ricardo posed, smiling casually.

"Hold it!"

The girl froze.

Ricardo dropped his pants.

Click went the camera.

"Ah," said the policeman.

"Got the evidence right in this old camera if you need
it!" said the cameraman.

"Ah," said the policeman, not moving, hand to chin.
"So." He surveyed the scene like an amateur photographer
himself. He saw the model with the flushed, nervous marble face, the cobbles, the wall, and Ricardo. Ricardo
magnificently smoking a cigarette there in the noon sunlight under the blue sky, his pants where a man's pants
rarely are.

"Well, officer?" said the cameraman, waiting.

"Just what," said the policeman, taking off his cap and wiping his dark brow, "do you want me to do?"

"Arrest that man! Indecent exposure!"

"Ah," said the policeman.

"Well?" said the cameraman.

The crowd murmured. All the nice lady models were looking out at the sea gulls and the ocean.

"That man up there against the wall," said the officer, "I know him. His name is Ricardo Reyes."

"Hello, Esteban!" called Ricardo.

The officer called back at him, "Hello, Ricardo."

They waved at each other.

"He's not doing anything I can see," said the officer.

"What do you mean?" asked the cameraman. "He's as naked as a rock. It's immoral!"

"That man is doing nothing immoral. He's just standing there," said the policeman. "Now if he were *doing* something with his hands or body, something terrible to view, I would act upon the instant. However, since he is simply leaning against the wall, not moving a single limb or muscle, there *is* nothing wrong."

"He's naked, *naked!*" screamed the cameraman.

"I don't understand." The officer blinked.

"You just don't go around naked, that's all!"

"There are naked people and naked people," said the officer. "Good and bad. Sober and with drink in them. I judge this one to be a man with no drink in him, a good man by reputation; naked, yes, but doing nothing with this nakedness in any way to offend the community."

"What *are* you, his *brother?* What are you, his confederate?" said the cameraman. It seemed that at any moment he might snap and bite and bark and woof and race around in circles under the blazing sun. "Where's the justice? What's going *on* here? Come on, girls, we'll go somewhere else!"

"France," said Ricardo.

"What!" The photographer whirled.

"I said France, or Spain," suggested Ricardo. "Or Sweden. I have seen some nice pictures of walls in Sweden. But not many cracks in them. Forgive my suggestion."

"We'll get pictures in spite of you!" The cameraman shook his camera, his fist.

"I will be there," said Ricardo. "Tomorrow, the next day, at the bullfights, at the market, anywhere, everywhere you go I go, quietly, with grace. With dignity, to perform my necessary task."

Looking at him, they knew it was true.

"Who are you—who in hell do you think you are?" cried the photographer.

"I have been waiting for you to ask me," said Ricardo. "Consider me. Go home and think of me. As long as there is one man like me in a town of ten thousand, the world will go on. Without me, all would be chaos."

"Good night, nurse," said the photographer, and the entire swarm of ladies, hatboxes, cameras, and make-up kits retreated down the street toward the docks. "Time out for lunch, dears. We'll figure something later!"

Ricardo watched them go, quietly. He had not moved from his position. The crowd still looked upon him and smiled.

Now, Ricardo thought, I will walk up the street to my house, which has paint peeling from the door where I have brushed it a thousand times in passing, and I shall walk over the stones I have worn down in forty-six years of walking, and I shall run my hand over the crack in the wall of my own house, which is the crack made by the earthquake in 1930. I remember well the night, us all in bed, Tomás as yet unborn, and Maria and I much in love, and thinking it was our love which moved the house, warm and great in the night; but it was the earth trembling, and in the morning, that crack in the wall. And I shall climb the steps to the lacework-grille balcony of my father's house, which grillwork he made with his own hands, and I shall eat the food my wife serves me on the balcony, with the books near at hand. And my son Tomás, whom I created out of whole cloth, yes, bed sheets, let us admit it, with my good wife. And we shall sit eating and talking, not photographs, not backdrops, not paintings, not stage furniture, any of us. But actors, all of us, very fine actors indeed.

As if to second this last thought, a sound startled his ear. He was in the midst of solemnly, with great dignity and grace, lifting his pants to belt them around his waist, when he heard this lovely sound. It was like the winging of soft doves in the air. It was applause.

The small crowd, looking up at him, enacting the final scene of the play before the intermission for lunch, saw with what beauty and gentlemanly decorum he was elevating his trousers. The applause broke like a brief wave upon the shore of the nearby sea.

Ricardo gestured and smiled to them all.

On his way home up the hill he shook hands with the dog that had watered the wall.

The Illustrated Man

"Hey, the Illustrated Man!"

A calliope screamed, and Mr. William Philippus Phelps stood, arms folded, high on the summer-night platform, a crowd unto himself.

He was an entire civilization. In the Main Country, his chest, the Vasties lived—nipple-eyed dragons swirling over his fleshpot, his almost feminine breasts. His navel was the mouth of a slit-eyed monster—an obscene, in-sucked mouth, toothless as a witch. And there were secret caves where Darklings lurked, his armpits, adrip with slow subterranean liquors, where the Darklings, eyes jealously ablaze, peered out through rank creeper and hanging vine.

Mr. William Philippus Phelps leered down from his freak platform with a thousand peacock eyes. Across the sawdust meadow he saw his wife, Lisabeth, far away, ripping tickets in half, staring at the silver belt buckles of passing men.

Mr. William Philippus Phelps' hands were tattooed roses. At the sight of his wife's interest, the roses shriveled, as with the passing of sunlight.

A year before, when he had led Lisabeth to the marriage bureau to watch her work her name in ink, slowly, on the form, his skin had been pure and white and clean. He glanced down at himself in sudden horror. Now he was like a great painted canvas, shaken in the night wind! How had it happened? Where had it all begun?

It had started with the arguments, and then the flesh, and then the pictures. They had fought deep into the summer nights, she like a brass trumpet forever blaring at him. And he had gone out to eat five thousand steaming hot dogs, ten million hamburgers, and a forest of green onions, and to drink vast red seas of orange juice. Peppermint candy formed his brontosaur bones, the hamburgers shaped his balloon flesh, and strawberry pop pumped in and out of his heart valves sickeningly, until he weighed three hundred pounds.

"William Philippus Phelps," Lisabeth said to him in the eleventh month of their marriage, "you're dumb and fat."

That was the day the carnival boss handed him the blue envelope. "Sorry, Phelps. You're no good to me with all that gut on you."

"Wasn't I always your best tent man, boss?"

"Once. Not any more. Now you sit, you don't get the work out."

"Let me be your Fat Man."

"I *got* a Fat Man. Dime a dozen." The boss eyed him up and down. "Tell you what, though. We ain't had a Tattooed Man since Gallery Smith died last year. . . ."

That had been a month ago. Four short weeks. From someone, he had learned of a tattoo artist far out in the rolling Wisconsin country, an old woman, they said, who knew her trade. If he took the dirt road and turned right at the river and then left . . .

He had walked out across a yellow meadow, which was crisp from the sun. Red flowers blew and bent in the wind as he walked, and he came to the old shack, which looked as if it had stood in a million rains.

Inside the door was a silent, bare room, and in the center of the bare room sat an ancient woman.

Her eyes were stitched with red resin-thread. Her nose

was sealed with black wax-twine. Her ears were sewn, too, as if a darning-needle dragonfly had stitched all her senses shut. She sat, not moving, in the vacant room. Dust lay in a yellow flour all about, unfootprinted in many weeks; if she had moved it would have shown, but she had not moved. Her hands touched each other like thin, rusted instruments. Her feet were naked and obscene as rain rubbers, and near them sat vials of tattoo milk—red, lightning-blue, brown, cat-yellow. She was a thing sewn tight into whispers and silence.

Only her mouth moved, unsewn: "Come in. Sit down. I'm lonely here."

He did not obey.

"You came for the pictures," she said in a high voice. "I have a picture to show you first."

She tapped a blind finger to her thrust-out palm. "See!" she cried.

It was a tattoo-portrait of William Philippus Phelps.

"Me!" he said.

Her cry stopped him at the door. "Don't run."

He held to the edges of the door, his back to her. "That's me, that's me on your hand!"

"It's been there fifty years." She stroked it like a cat, over and over.

He turned. "It's an *old* tattoo." He drew slowly nearer. He edged forward and bent to blink at it. He put out a trembling finger to brush the picture. "Old. That's impossible! You don't know *me*. I don't know *you*. Your eyes, all sewed shut."

"I've been waiting for you," she said. "And many people." She displayed her arms and legs, like the spindles of an antique chair. "I have pictures on me of people who have already come here to see me. And there are other pictures of other people who are coming to see me in the next one hundred years. And you, you have come."

"How do you know it's me? You can't see!"

"You *feel* like the lions, the elephants, and the tigers to me. Unbutton your shirt. You need me. Don't be afraid. My needles are as clean as a doctor's fingers. When I'm

finished with illustrating you, I'll wait for someone else to
walk along out here and find me. And someday, a hundred
summers from now, perhaps, I'll just go lie down in the
forest under some white mushrooms, and in the spring you
won't find anything but a small blue cornflower. . . ."

He began to unbutton his sleeves.

"I know the Deep Past and the Clear Present and the
even Deeper Future," she whispered, eyes knotted into
blindness, face lifted to this unseen man. "It is on my flesh.
I will paint it on yours, too. You will be the only *real*
Illustrated Man in the universe. I'll give you special pictures you will never forget. Pictures of the Future on your
skin."

She pricked him with a needle.

He ran back to the carnival that night in a drunken
terror and elation. Oh, how quickly the old dust-witch had
stitched him with color and design. At the end of a long
afternoon of being bitten by a silver snake, his body was
alive with portraiture. He looked as if he had dropped and
been crushed between the steel rollers of a print press,
and come out like an incredible rotogravure. He was
clothed in a garment of trolls and scarlet dinosaurs.

"Look!" he cried to Lisabeth. She glanced up from her
cosmetic table as he tore his shirt away. He stood in the
naked bulb-light of their car-trailer, expanding his impossible chest. Here, the Tremblies, half-maiden, half-goat,
leaping when his biceps flexed. Here, the Country of Lost
Souls, his chins. In so many accordion pleats of fat, numer-
ous small scorpions, beetles, and mice were crushed, held,
hid, darting into view, vanishing, as he raised or lowered
his chins.

"My God," said Lisabeth. "My husband's a freak."

She ran from the trailer and he was left alone to pose
before the mirror. Why had he done it? To have a job, yes,
but, most of all, to cover the fat that had larded itself
impossibly over his bones. To hide the fat under a layer of
color and fantasy, to hide it from his wife, but most of all
from himself.

He thought of the old woman's last words. She had needled him two *special* tattoos, one on his chest, another for his back, which she would not let him see. She covered each with cloth and adhesive.

"You are not to look at these two," she had said.

"Why?"

"Later, you may look. The Future is in these pictures. You can't look now or it may spoil them. They are not quite finished. I put ink on your flesh and the sweat of you forms the rest of the picture, the Future—your sweat and your thought." Her empty mouth grinned. "Next Saturday night, you may advertise! The Big Unveiling! Come see the Illustrated Man unveil his picture! You can make money in that way. You can charge admission to the Unveiling, like to an art gallery. Tell them you have a picture that even *you* never have seen, that *nobody* has seen yet. The most unusual picture ever painted. Almost alive. And it tells the Future. Roll the drums and blow the trumpets. And you can stand there and unveil at the Big Unveiling."

"That's a good idea," he said.

"But only unveil the picture on your chest," she said. "That is first. You must save the picture on your back, under the adhesive, for the following week. Understand?"

"How much do I owe you?"

"Nothing," she said. "If you walk with these pictures on you, I will be repaid with my own satisfaction. I will sit here for the next two weeks and think how clever my pictures are, for I make them fit each man himself and what is inside him. Now, walk out of this house and never come back. Good-by."

"Hey! The Big Unveiling!"

The red signs blew in the night wind: NO ORDINARY TATTOOED MAN! THIS ONE IS "ILLUSTRATED"! GREATER THAN MICHELANGELO! TONIGHT! ADMISSION 10 CENTS!

Now the hour had come. Saturday night, the crowd stirring their animal feet in the hot sawdust.

"In one minute—" the carny boss pointed his cardboard megaphone—"in the tent immediately to my rear, we will unveil the Mysterious Portrait upon the Illustrated Man's chest! Next Saturday night, the same hour, same location, we'll unveil the Picture upon the Illustrated Man's *back!* Bring your friends!"

There was a stuttering roll of drums.

Mr. William Philippus Phelps jumped back and vanished; the crowd poured into the tent, and, once inside, found him re-established upon another platform, the band brassing out a jig-time melody.

He looked for his wife and saw her, lost in the crowd, like a stranger, come to watch a freakish thing, a look of contemptuous curiosity upon her face. For, after all, he was her husband, and this was a thing she didn't know about him herself. It gave him a feeling of great height and warmness and light to find himself the center of the jangling universe, the carnival world, for one night. Even the other freaks—the Skeleton, the Seal Boy, the Yoga, the Magician, and the Balloon—were scattered through the crowd.

"Ladies and gentlemen, the great moment!"

A trumpet flourish, a hum of drumsticks on tight cowhide.

Mr. William Philippus Phelps let his cape fall. Dinosaurs, trolls, and half-women-half-snakes writhed on his skin in the stark light.

Ah, murmured the crowd, for surely there had never been a tattooed man like this! The beast eyes seemed to take red fire and blue fire, blinking and twisting. The roses on his fingers seemed to expel a sweet pink bouquet. The tyrannosaurus-rex reared up along his leg, and the sound of the brass trumpet in the hot tent heavens was a prehistoric cry from the red monster throat. Mr. William Philippus Phelps was a museum jolted to life. Fish swam in seas of electric-blue ink. Fountains sparkled under yellow suns. Ancient buildings stood in meadows of harvest wheat. Rockets burned across spaces of muscle and flesh. The slightest inhalation of his breath threatened to make chaos of the entire printed universe. He seemed afire, the creatures flinching from the flame, drawing back from the great heat of his pride, as he expanded under the audience's rapt contemplation.

The carny boss laid his fingers to the adhesive. The audience rushed forward, silent in the oven vastness of the night tent.

"You ain't seen nothing yet!" cried the carny boss.

The adhesive ripped free.

There was an instant in which nothing happened. An instant in which the Illustrated Man thought that the Unveiling was a terrible and irrevocable failure.

But then the audience gave a low moan.

The carny boss drew back, his eyes fixed.

Far out at the edge of the crowd, a woman, after a moment, began to cry, began to sob, and did not stop.

Slowly, the Illustrated Man looked down at his naked chest and stomach.

The thing that he saw made the roses on his hands discolor and die. All of his creatures seemed to wither, turn inward, shrivel with the arctic coldness that pumped from his heart outward to freeze and destroy them. He stood trembling. His hands floated up to touch that incredible picture, which lived, moved and shivered with life. It was like gazing into a small room, seeing a thing of someone else's life so intimate, so impossible that one could not believe and one could not long stand to watch without turning away.

It was a picture of his wife, Lisabeth, and himself.

And he was killing her.

Before the eyes of a thousand people in a dark tent in the center of a black-forested Wisconsin land, he was killing his wife.

His great flowered hands were upon her throat, and her face was turning dark and he killed her and he killed her and did not ever in the next minute stop killing her. It was real. While the crowd watched, she died, and he turned very sick. He was about to fall straight down into the crowd. The tent whirled like a monster bat wing, flapping grotesquely. The last thing he heard was a woman, sobbing, far out on the shore of the silent crowd.

And the crying woman was Lisabeth, his wife.

In the night, his bed was moist with perspiration. The carnival sounds had melted away, and his wife, in her own bed, was quiet now, too. He fumbled with his chest. The adhesive was smooth. They had made him put it back.

He had fainted. When he revived, the carny boss had yelled at him, "Why didn't you *say* what that picture was like?"

"I didn't know, I didn't," said the Illustrated Man.

"Good God!" said the boss. "Scare hell outa everyone. Scared hell outa Lizzie, scared hell outa me. Christ, where'd you *get* that damn tattoo?" He shuddered. "Apologize to Lizzie, now."

His wife stood over him.

"I'm sorry, Lisabeth," he said, weakly, his eyes closed. "I didn't know."

"You did it on purpose," she said. "To scare me."

"I'm sorry."

"Either it goes or I go," she said.

"Lisabeth."

"You heard me. That picture comes off or I quit this show."

"Yeah, Phil," said the boss. "That's how it is."

"Did you lose money? Did the crowd demand refunds?"

"It ain't the money, Phil. For that matter, once the word got around, hundreds of people wanted in. But I'm runnin' a clean show. That tattoo comes off! Was this your idea of a practical joke, Phil?"

He turned in the warm bed. No, not a joke. Not a joke at all. He had been as terrified as anyone. Not a joke. That little old dust-witch, what had she *done* to him and how had she done it? Had she put the picture there? No; she had said that the picture was unfinished, and that he himself, with his thoughts and perspiration, would finish it. Well, he had done the job all right.

But what, if anything, was the significance? He didn't want to kill anyone. He didn't want to kill Lisabeth. Why should such a silly picture burn here on his flesh in the dark?

He crawled his fingers softly, cautiously down to touch the quivering place where the hidden portrait lay. He pressed tight, and the temperature of that spot was enormous. He could almost feel that little evil picture killing and killing and killing all through the night.

I don't wish to kill her, he thought, insistently, looking over at her bed. And then, five minutes later, he whispered aloud: "Or *do* I?"

"What?" she cried, awake.

"Nothing," he said, after a pause, "Go to sleep."

The man bent forward, a buzzing instrument in his hand. "This costs five bucks an inch. Costs more to peel tattoos off than put 'em on. Okay, jerk the adhesive."

The Illustrated Man obeyed.

The skin man sat back. "Christ! No wonder you want that off! That's ghastly. *I* don't even want to look at it." He flicked his machine. "Ready? This won't hurt."

The carny boss stood in the tent flap, watching. After five minutes, the skin man changed the instrument head, cursing. Ten minutes later he scraped his chair back and scratched his head. Half an hour passed and he got up, told Mr. William Philippus Phelps to dress, and packed his kit.

"Wait a minute," said the carny boss. "You ain't done the job."

"And I ain't going to," said the skin man.

"I'm paying good money. What's wrong?"

"Nothing, except that damn picture just won't come off. Damn thing must go right down to the bone."

"You're crazy."

"Mister, I'm in business thirty years and never seen a tattoo like this. An inch deep, if it's anything."

"But I've got to get it off!" cried the Illustrated Man.

The skin man shook his head. "Only one way to get rid of that."

"How?"

"Take a knife and cut off your chest. You won't live long, but the picture'll be gone."

"Come back here!"
But the skin man walked away.

They could hear the big Sunday-night crowd, waiting.
"That's a big crowd," said the Illustrated Man.
"But they ain't going to see what they came to see," said the carny boss. "You ain't going out there, except with the adhesive. Hold still now, I'm curious about this *other* picture, on your back. We might be able to give 'em an Unveiling on this one instead."
"She said it wouldn't be ready for a week or so. The old woman said it would take time to set, make a pattern."
There was a soft ripping as the carny boss pulled aside a flap of white tape on the Illustrated Man's spine.
"What do you see?" gasped Mr. Phelps, bent over.
The carny boss replaced the tape. "Buster, as a Tattooed Man, you're a washout, ain't you? Why'd you let that old dame fix you up this way?"
"I didn't know who she was."
"She sure cheated you on this one. No design to it. Nothing. No picture at all."
"It'll come clear. You wait and see."
The boss laughed. "Okay. Come on. We'll show the crowd part of you, anyway."
They walked out into an explosion of brassy music.

He stood monstrous in the middle of the night, putting out his hands like a blind man to balance himself in a world now tilted, now rushing, now threatening to spin him over and down into the mirror before which he raised his hands. Upon the flat, dimly lighted table top were peroxides, acids, silver razors, and squares of sandpaper. He took each of them in turn. He soaked the vicious tattoo upon his chest, he scraped at it. He worked steadily for an hour.
He was aware, suddenly, that someone stood in the trailer door behind him. It was three in the morning. There was a faint odor of beer. She had come home from

town. He heard her slow breathing. He did not turn. "Lisabeth?" he said.

"You'd better get rid of it," she said, watching his hands move the sandpaper. She stepped into the trailer.

"I didn't want the picture this way," he said.

"You did," she said. "You planned it."

"I didn't."

"I know you," she said. "Oh, I know you hate me. Well, that's nothing. I hate you, I've hated you a long time now. Good God, when you started putting on the fat, you think anyone could love you then? I could teach you some things about hate. Why don't you ask me?"

"Leave me alone," he said.

"In front of that crowd, making a spectacle out of me!"

"I didn't know what was under the tape."

She walked around the table, hands fitted to her hips, talking to the beds, the walls, the table, talking it all out of her. And he thought: *Or did I know? Who made this picture, me or the witch? Who formed it? How? Do I really want her dead? No! And yet. . . .* He watched his wife draw nearer, nearer, he saw the ropy strings of her throat vibrate to her shouting. This and this and *this* was wrong with him! That and that and *that* was unspeakable about him! He was a liar, a schemer, a fat, lazy, ugly man, a child. Did he think he could compete with the carny boss or the tentpeggers? Did he think he was sylphine and graceful, did he think he was a framed El Greco? DaVinci, huh! Michelangelo, my eye! She brayed. She showed her teeth. "Well, you can't scare me into staying with someone I don't want touching me with their slobby paws!" she finished, triumphantly.

"Lisabeth," he said.

"Don't Lisabeth me!" she shrieked. "I know your plan. You had that picture put on to scare me. You thought I wouldn't *dare* leave you. Well!"

"Next Saturday night, the Second Unveiling," he said. "You'll be proud of me."

"Proud! You're silly and pitiful. God, you're like a whale. You ever see a beached whale? I saw one when I was a kid. There it was, and they came and shot it. Some lifeguards shot it. Jesus, a whale!"

"Lisabeth."

"I'm leaving, that's all, and getting a divorce."

"Don't."

"And I'm marrying a man, not a fat woman—that's what you are, so much fat on you there ain't no sex!"

"You can't leave me," he said.

"Just watch!"

"I love you," he said.

"Oh," she said. "Go look at your pictures."

He reached out.

"Keep your hands off," she said.

"Lisabeth."

"Don't come near. You turn my stomach."

"Lisabeth."

All the eyes of his body seemed to fire, all the snakes to move, all the monsters to seethe, all the mouths to widen and rage. He moved toward her—not like a man, but a crowd.

He felt the great blooded reservoir of orangeade pump through him now, the sluice of cola and rich lemon pop pulse in sickening sweet anger through his wrists, his legs, his heart. All of it, the oceans of mustard and relish and all the million drinks he had drowned himself in in the last year were aboil; his face was the color of a steamed beef. And the pink roses of his hands became those hungry, carnivorous flowers kept long years in tepid jungle and now let free to find their way on the night air before him.

He gathered her to him, like a great beast gathering in a struggling animal. It was a frantic gesture of love, quickening and demanding, which, as she struggled, hardened to another thing. She beat and clawed at the picture on his chest.

"You've got to love me, Lisabeth."

"Let go!" she screamed. She beat at the picture that burned under her fists. She slashed at it with her fingernails.

"Oh, Lisabeth," he said, his hands moving up her arms.

"I'll scream," she said, seeing his eyes.

"Lisabeth." The hands moved up to her shoulders, to her neck. "Don't go away."

"Help!" she screamed. The blood ran from the picture on his chest.

He put his fingers about her neck and squeezed.

She was a calliope cut in mid-shriek.

Outside, the grass rustled. There was the sound of running feet.

Mr. William Philippus Phelps opened the trailer door and stepped out.

They were waiting for him. Skeleton, Midget, Balloon, Yoga, Electra, Popeye, Seal Boy. The freaks, waiting in the middle of the night, in the dry grass.

He walked toward them. He moved with a feeling that he must get away; these people would understand nothing, they were not thinking people. And because he did not flee, because he only walked, balanced, stunned, between the tents, slowly, the freaks moved to let him pass. They watched him, because their watching guaranteed that he would not escape. He walked out across the black meadow, moths fluttering in his face. He walked steadily as long as he was visible, not knowing where he was going. They watched him go, and then they turned and all of them shuffled to the silent car-trailer together and pushed the door slowly wide. . . .

The Illustrated Man walked steadily in the dry meadows beyond the town.

"He went that way!" a faint voice cried. Flashlights bobbled over the hills. There were dim shapes, running.

Mr. William Philippus Phelps waved to them. He was tired. He wanted only to be found now. He was tired of running away. He waved again.

"There he is!" The flashlights changed direction. "Come on! We'll get the bastard!"

When it was time, the Illustrated Man ran again. He was careful to run slowly. He deliberately fell down twice.

Looking back, he saw the tent stakes they held in their hands.

He ran toward a far crossroads lantern, where all the summer night seemed to gather; merry-go-rounds of fireflies whirling, crickets moving their song toward that light, everything rushing, as if by some midnight attraction, toward that one high-hung lantern—the Illustrated Man first, the others close at his heels.

As he reached the light and passed a few yards under and beyond it, he did not need to look back. On the road ahead, in silhouette, he saw the upraised tent stakes sweep violently up, up, and then *down!*

A minute passed.

In the country ravines, the crickets sang. The freaks stood over the sprawled Illustrated Man, holding their tent stakes loosely.

Finally they rolled him over on his stomach. Blood ran from his mouth.

They ripped the adhesive from his back. They stared down for a long moment at the freshly revealed picture. Someone whispered. Someone else swore, softly. The Thin Man pushed back and walked away and was sick. Another and another of the freaks stared, their mouths trembling, and moved away, leaving the Illustrated Man on the deserted road, the blood running from his mouth.

In the dim light, the unveiled Illustration was easily seen.

It showed a crowd of freaks bending over a dying fat man on a dark and lonely road, looking at a tattoo on his back which illustrated a crowd of freaks bending over a dying fat man on a . . .

The Fog Horn

Out there in the cold water, far from land, we waited every night for the coming of the fog, and it came, and we oiled the brass machinery and lit the fog light up in the stone tower. Feeling like two birds in the gray sky, McDunn and I sent the light touching out, red, then white, then red again, to eye the lonely ships. And if they did not see our light, then there was always our Voice, the great deep cry of our Fog Horn shuddering through the rags of mist to startle the gulls away like decks of scattered cards and make the waves turn high and foam.

"It's a lonely life, but you're used to it now, aren't you?" asked McDunn.

"Yes," I said. "You're a good talker, thank the Lord."

"Well, it's your turn on land tomorrow," he said, smiling, "to dance the ladies and drink gin."

"What do you think, McDunn, when I leave you out here alone?"

"On the mysteries of the sea." McDunn lit his pipe. It was a quarter past seven of a cold November evening, the heat on, the light switching its tail in two hundred directions, the Fog Horn bumbling in the high throat of the tower. There wasn't a town for a hundred miles down the coast, just a road which came lonely through dead country to the sea, with few cars on it, a stretch of two miles of cold water out to our rock, and rare few ships.

"The mysteries of the sea," said McDunn thoughtfully. "You know, the ocean's the biggest damned snowflake ever? It rolls and swells a thousand shapes and colors, no two alike. Strange. One night, years ago, I was here alone, when all of the fish of the sea surfaced out there. Something made them swim in and lie in the bay, sort of trembling and staring up at the tower light going red, white, red, white, across them so I could see their funny eyes. I turned cold. They were like a big peacock's tail, moving out there until midnight. Then, without so much as a sound, they slipped away, the million of them was gone. I kind of think maybe, in some sort of way, they came all those miles to worship. Strange. But think how the tower must look to them, standing seventy feet above the water, the God-light flashing out from it, and the tower declaring itself with a monster voice. They never came back, those fish, but don't you think for a while they thought they were in the Presence?"

I shivered. I looked out at the long gray lawn of the sea stretching away into nothing and nowhere.

"Oh, the sea's full." McDunn puffed his pipe nervously, blinking. He had been nervous all day and hadn't said why. "For all our engines and so-called submarines, it'll be ten thousand centuries before we set foot on the real bottom of the sunken lands, in the fairy kingdoms there, and know *real* terror. Think of it, it's still the year 300,000 before Christ down under there. While we've paraded around with trumpets, lopping off each other's countries and heads, they have been living beneath the sea twelve miles deep and cold in a time as old as the beard of a comet."

"Yes, it's an old world."

"Come on. I got something special I been saving up to tell you."

We ascended the eighty steps, talking and taking our time. At the top, McDunn switched off the room lights so there'd be no reflection in the plate glass. The great eye of the light was humming, turning easily in its oiled socket. The Fog Horn was blowing steadily, once every fifteen seconds.

"Sounds like an animal, don't it?" McDunn nodded to himself. "A big lonely animal crying in the night. Sitting here on the edge of ten billion years calling out to the Deeps, I'm here, I'm here, I'm here. And the Deeps do answer, yes, they do. You been here now for three months, Johnny, so I better prepare you. About this time of year," he said, studying the murk and fog, "something comes to visit the lighthouse."

"The swarms of fish like you said?"

"No, this is something else. I've put off telling you because you might think I'm daft. But tonight's the latest I can put it off, for if my calendar's marked right from last year, tonight's the night it comes. I won't go into detail, you'll have to see it yourself. Just sit down there. If you want, tomorrow you can pack your duffel and take the motorboat in to land and get your car parked there at the dinghy pier on the cape and drive on back to some little inland town and keep your lights burning nights, I won't question or blame you. It's happened three years now, and this is the only time anyone's been here with me to verify it. You wait and watch."

Half an hour passed with only a few whispers between us. When we grew tired waiting, McDunn began describing some of his ideas to me. He had some theories about the Fog Horn itself.

"One day many years ago a man walked along and stood in the sound of the ocean on a cold sunless shore and said, 'We need a voice to call across the water, to warn ships; I'll make one. I'll make a voice like all of time and all of the fog that ever was; I'll make a voice that is like an empty bed beside you all night long, and like an empty house when you open the door, and like trees in autumn with no leaves. A sound like the birds flying south, crying, and a sound like November wind and the sea on the hard, cold shore. I'll make a sound that's so alone that no one can miss it, that whoever hears it will weep in their souls, and hearths will seem warmer, and being inside will seem better to all who hear it in the distant towns. I'll make me a sound and an apparatus and they'll call it a Fog Horn and whoever hears it will know the sadness of eternity and the briefness of life.' "

The Fog Horn blew.

"I made up that story," said McDunn quietly, "to try to explain why this thing keeps coming back to the lighthouse every year. The Fog Horn calls it, I think, and it comes. . . ."

"But——" I said.

"Sssst!" said McDunn. "There!" He nodded out to the Deeps.

Something was swimming toward the lighthouse tower.

It was a cold night, as I have said; the high tower was cold, the light coming and going, and the Fog Horn calling and calling through the raveling mist. You couldn't see far and you couldn't see plain, but there was the deep sea moving on its way about the night earth, flat and quiet, the color of gray mud, and here were the two of us alone in the high tower, and there, far out at first, was a ripple, followed by a wave, a rising, a bubble, a bit of froth. And then, from the surface of the cold sea came a head, a large head, dark-colored, with immense eyes, and then a neck. And then—not a body—but more neck and more! The head rose a full forty feet above the water on a slender and beautiful dark neck. Only then did the body, like a little island of black coral and shells and crayfish, drip up from the subterranean. There was a flicker of tail. In all, from head to tip of tail, I estimated the monster at ninety or a hundred feet.

I don't know what I said. I said something.

"Steady, boy, steady," whispered McDunn.

"It's impossible!" I said.

"No, Johnny, *we're* impossible. *It's* like it always was ten million years ago. *It* hasn't changed. It's *us* and the land that've changed, become impossible. *Us!*"

It swam slowly and with a great dark majesty out in the icy waters, far away. The fog came and went about it, momentarily erasing its shape. One of the monster eyes caught and held and flashed back our immense light, red, white, red, white, like a disk held high and sending a message in primeval code. It was as silent as the fog through which it swam.

"It's a dinosaur of some sort!" I crouched down, holding to the stair rail.

"Yes, one of the tribe."

"But they died out!"

"No, only hid away in the Deeps. Deep, deep down in the deepest Deeps. Isn't *that* a word now, Johnny, a real word, it says so much: the Deeps. There's all the coldness and darkness and deepness in a word like that."

"What'll we do?"

"Do? We got our job, we can't leave. Besides, we're safer here than in any boat trying to get to land. That thing's as big as a destroyer and almost as swift."

"But here, why does it come *here?*"

The next moment I had my answer.

The Fog Horn blew.

And the monster answered.

A cry came across a million years of water and mist. A cry so anguished and alone that it shuddered in my head and my body. The monster cried out at the tower. The Fog Horn blew. The monster roared again. The Fog Horn blew. The monster opened its great toothed mouth and the sound that came from it was the sound of the Fog Horn itself. Lonely and vast and far away. The sound of isolation, a viewless sea, a cold night, apartness. That was the sound.

"Now," whispered McDunn, "do you know why it comes here?"

I nodded.

"All year long, Johnny, that poor monster there lying far out, a thousand miles at sea, and twenty miles deep maybe, biding its time, perhaps it's a million years old, this one creature. Think of it, waiting a million years; could *you* wait that long? Maybe it's the last of its kind. I sort of think that's true. Anyway, here come men on land and build this lighthouse, five years ago. And set up their Fog Horn and sound it and sound it out toward the place where you bury yourself in sleep and sea memories of a world where there were thousands like yourself, but now you're alone, all alone in a world not made for you, a world where you have to hide.

"But the sound of the Fog Horn comes and goes, comes and goes, and you stir from the muddy bottom of the Deeps, and your eyes open like the lenses of two-foot cameras and you move, slow, slow, for you have the ocean sea on your shoulders, heavy. But that Fog Horn comes through a thousand miles of water, faint and familiar, and the furnace in your belly stokes up, and you begin to rise, slow, slow. You feed yourself on great slakes of cod and minnow, on rivers of jellyfish, and you rise slow through the autumn months, through September when the fogs started, through October with more fog and the horn still calling you on, and then, late in November, after pressurizing yourself day by day, a few feet higher every hour, you are near the surface and still alive. You've got to go slow; if you surfaced all at once you'd explode. So it takes you all of three months to surface, and then a number of days to swim through the cold waters to the lighthouse. And there you are, out there, in the night, Johnny, the biggest damn monster in creation. And here's the lighthouse calling to you, with a long neck like your neck sticking way up out of the water, and a body like your body, and, most important of all, a voice like your voice. Do you understand now, Johnny, do you understand?"

The Fog Horn blew.

The monster answered.

I saw it all, I knew it all—the million years of waiting alone, for someone to come back who never came back. The million years of isolation at the bottom of the sea, the insanity of time there, while the skies cleared of reptile-birds, the swamps dried on the continental lands, the sloths and saber-tooths had their day and sank in tar pits, and men ran like white ants upon the hills.

The Fog Horn blew.

"Last year," said McDunn, "that creature swam round and round, round and round, all night. Not coming too near, puzzled, I'd say. Afraid, maybe. And a bit angry after coming all this way. But the next day, unexpectedly, the fog lifted, the sun came out fresh, the sky was as blue as a painting. And the monster swam off away from the heat and the silence and didn't come back. I suppose it's been brooding on it for a year now, thinking it over from every which way."

The monster was only a hundred yards off now, it and the Fog Horn crying at each other. As the lights hit them, the monster's eyes were fire and ice, fire and ice.

"That's life for you," said McDunn. "Someone always waiting for someone who never comes home. Always someone loving some thing more than that thing loves them. And after a while you want to destroy whatever that thing is, so it can't hurt you no more."

The monster was rushing at the lighthouse.

The Fog Horn blew.

"Let's see what happens," said McDunn.

He switched the Fog Horn off.

The ensuing minute of silence was so intense that we could hear our hearts pounding in the glassed area of the tower, could hear the slow greased turn of the light.

The monster stopped and froze. Its great lantern eyes blinked. Its mouth gaped. It gave a sort of rumble, like a volcano. It twitched its head this way and that, as if to seek the sounds now dwindled off into the fog. It peered at the lighthouse. It rumbled again. Then its eyes caught fire. It reared up, threshed the water, and rushed at the tower, its eyes filled with angry torment.

"McDunn!" I cried. "Switch on the horn!"

McDunn fumbled with the switch. But even as he flicked it on, the monster was rearing up. I had a glimpse of its gigantic paws, fishskin glittering in webs between the finger-like projections, clawing at the tower. The huge eye on the right side of its anguished head glittered before me like a caldron into which I might drop, screaming. The tower shook. The Fog Horn cried; the monster cried. It seized the tower and gnashed at the glass, which shattered in upon us.

McDunn seized my arm. "Downstairs!"

The tower rocked, trembled, and started to give. The Fog Horn and the monster roared. We stumbled and half fell down the stairs. "Quick!"

We reached the bottom as the tower buckled down toward us. We ducked under the stairs into the small stone cellar. There were a thousand concussions as the rocks rained down; the Fog Horn stopped abruptly. The monster crashed upon the tower. The tower fell. We knelt together, McDunn and I, holding tight, while our world exploded.

Then it was over, and there was nothing but darkness and the wash of the sea on the raw stones.

That and the other sound.

"Listen," said McDunn quietly. "Listen."

We waited a moment. And then I began to hear it. First a great vacuumed sucking of air, and then the lament, the bewilderment, the loneliness of the great monster, folded over and upon us, above us, so that the sickening reek of its body filled the air, a stone's thickness away from our cellar. The monster gasped and cried. The tower was gone. The light was gone. The thing that had called to it across a million years was gone. And the monster was opening its mouth and sending out great sounds. The sounds of a Fog Horn, again and again. And ships far at sea, not finding the light, not seeing anything, but passing and hearing late that night, must've thought: There it is, the lonely sound, the Lonesome Bay horn. All's well. We've rounded the cape.

And so it went for the rest of that night.

● ● ●

The sun was hot and yellow the next afternoon when the rescuers came out to dig us from our stoned-under cellar.

"It fell apart, is all," said Mr. McDunn gravely. "We had a few bad knocks from the waves and it just crumbled." He pinched my arm.

There was nothing to see. The ocean was calm, the sky blue. The only thing was a great algaic stink from the green matter that covered the fallen tower stones and the shore rocks. Flies buzzed about. The ocean washed empty on the shore.

The next year they built a new lighthouse, but by that time I had a job in the little town and a wife and a good small warm house that glowed yellow on autumn nights, the doors locked, the chimney puffing smoke. As for McDunn, he was master of the new lighthouse, built to his own specifications, out of steel-reinforced concrete. "Just in case," he said.

The new lighthouse was ready in November. I drove down alone one evening late and parked my car and looked across the gray waters and listened to the new horn sounding, once, twice, three, four times a minute far out there, by itself.

The monster?

It never came back.

"It's gone away," said McDunn. "It's gone back to the Deeps. It's learned you can't love anything too much in this world. It's gone into the deepest Deeps to wait another million years. Ah, the poor thing! Waiting out there, and waiting out there, while man comes and goes on this pitiful little planet. Waiting and waiting."

I sat in my car, listening. I couldn't see the lighthouse or the light standing out in Lonesome Bay. I could only hear the Horn, the Horn, the Horn. It sounded like the monster calling.

I sat there wishing there was something I could say.

The Dwarf

Aimee watched the sky, quietly.

Tonight was one of those motionless hot summer nights. The concrete pier empty, the strung red, white, yellow bulbs burning like insects in the air above the wooden emptiness. The managers of the various carnival pitches stood, like melting wax dummies, eyes staring blindly, not talking, all down the line.

Two customers had passed through an hour before. Those two lonely people were now in the roller coaster, screaming murderously as it plummeted down the blazing night, around one emptiness after another.

Aimee moved slowly across the strand, a few worn wooden hoopla rings sticking to her wet hands. She stopped behind the ticket booth that fronted the MIRROR MAZE. She saw herself grossly misrepresented in three rippled mirrors outside the Maze. A thousand tired replicas of herself dissolved in the corridor beyond, hot images among so much clear coolness.

She stepped inside the ticket booth and stood looking a long while at Ralph Banghart's thin neck. He clenched an unlit cigar between his long uneven yellow teeth as he laid out a battered game of solitaire on the ticket shelf.

When the roller coaster wailed and fell in its terrible avalanche again, she was reminded to speak.

"What kind of people go up in roller coasters?"

Ralph Banghart worked his cigar a full thirty seconds. "People wanna die. That rollie coaster's the handiest thing to dying there is." He sat listening to the faint sound of rifle shots from the shooting gallery. "This whole damn carny business's crazy. For instance, that dwarf. You seen him? Every night, pays his dime, runs in the Mirror Maze all the way back through to Screwy Louie's Room. You should see this little runt head back there. My God!"

"Oh, yes," said Aimee, remembering. "I always wonder what it's like to be a dwarf. I always feel sorry when I see him."

"I could play him like an accordion."

"Don't say that!"

"My Lord." Ralph patted her thigh with a free hand. "The way you carry on about guys you never even met." He shook his head and chuckled. "Him and his secret. Only he don't know I know, see? Boy howdy!"

"It's a hot night." She twitched the large wooden hoops nervously on her damp fingers.

"Don't change the subject. He'll be here, rain or shine."

Aimee shifted her weight.

Ralph seized her elbow. "Hey! You ain't mad? You wanna see that dwarf, don't you? Sh!" Ralph turned. "Here he comes now!"

The Dwarf's hand, hairy and dark, appeared all by itself reaching up into the booth window with a silver dime. An invisible person called, "One!" in a high, child's voice.

Involuntarily, Aimee bent forward.

The Dwarf looked up at her, resembling nothing more than a dark-eyed, dark-haired, ugly man who has been locked in a winepress, squeezed and wadded down and down, fold on fold, agony on agony, until a bleached, outraged mass is left, the face bloated shapelessly, a face you know must stare wide-eyed and awake at two and three and four o'clock in the morning, lying flat in bed, only the body asleep.

Ralph tore a yellow ticket in half. "One!"

The Dwarf, as if frightened by an approaching storm, pulled his black coat-lapels tightly about his throat and waddled swiftly. A moment later, ten thousand lost and wandering dwarfs wriggled between the mirror flats, like frantic dark beetles, and vanished.

"Quick!"

Ralph squeezed Aimee along a dark passage behind the mirrors. She felt him pat her all the way back through the tunnel to a thin partition with a peekhole.

"This is rich," he chuckled. "Go on—look."

Aimee hesitated, then put her face to the partition.

"You *see* him?" Ralph whispered.

Aimee felt her heart beating. A full minute passed.

There stood the Dwarf in the middle of the small blue room. His eyes were shut. He wasn't ready to open them yet. Now, now he opened his eyelids and looked at a large mirror set before him. And what he saw in the mirror made him smile. He winked, he pirouetted, he stood sidewise, he waved, he bowed, he did a little clumsy dance.

And the mirror repeated each motion with long, thin arms, with a tall, tall body, with a huge wink and an enormous repetition of the dance, ending in a gigantic bow!

"Every night the same thing," whispered Ralph in Aimee's ear. "Ain't that rich?"

Aimee turned her head and looked at Ralph steadily out of her motionless face, for a long time, and she said nothing. Then, as if she could not help herself, she moved her head slowly and very slowly back to stare once more through the opening. She held her breath. She felt her eyes begin to water.

Ralph nudged her, whispering.

"Hey, what's the little gink doin' *now?*"

They were drinking coffee and not looking at each other in the ticket booth half an hour later, when the Dwarf came out of the mirrors. He took his hat off and started to approach the booth, when he saw Aimee and hurried away.

"He wanted something," said Aimee.

"Yeah." Ralph squashed out his cigarette, idly. "I know what, too. But he hasn't got the nerve to ask. One night in this squeaky little voice he says, 'I bet those mirrors are expensive.' Well, I played dumb. I said yeah they were. He sort of looked at me, waiting, and when I didn't say any more, he went home, but next night he said, 'I bet those mirrors cost fifty, a hundred bucks.' I bet they do, I said. I laid me out a hand of solitaire."

"Ralph," she said.

He glanced up. "Why you look at me that way?"

"Ralph," she said, "why don't you sell him one of your extra ones?"

"Look, Aimee, do I tell you how to run your hoop circus?"

"How much do those mirrors cost?"

"I can get 'em secondhand for thirty-five bucks."

"Why don't you tell him where he can buy one, then?"

"Aimee, you're not smart." He laid his hand on her knee. She moved her knee away. "Even if I told him where to go, you think he'd buy one? Not on your life. And why? He's self-conscious. Why, if he even knew I knew he was flirtin' around in front of that mirror in Screwy Louie's Room, he'd never come back. He plays like he's goin' through the Maze to get lost, like everybody else. Pretends like he don't care about that special room. Always waits for business to turn bad, late nights, so he has that room to himself. What he does for entertainment on nights when business is good, God knows. No, sir, he wouldn't dare go buy a mirror anywhere. He ain't got no friends, and even if he did he couldn't ask them to buy him a thing like that. Pride, by God, pride. Only reason he even mentioned it to me is I'm practically the only guy he knows. Besides, look at him—he ain't got enough to buy a mirror like those. He might be savin' up, but where in hell in the world today can a dwarf work? Dime a dozen, drug on the market, outside of circuses."

"I feel awful. I feel sad." Aimee sat staring at the empty boardwalk. "Where does he live?"

"Flytrap down on the waterfront. The Ganghes Arms. Why?"

"I'm madly in love with him, if you must know."

He grinned around his cigar. "Aimee," he said. "You and your very funny jokes."

A warm night, a hot morning, and a blazing noon. The sea was a sheet of burning tinsel and glass.

Aimee came walking, in the locked-up carnival alleys out over the warm sea, keeping in the shade, half a dozen sun-bleached magazines under her arm. She opened a flaking door and called into hot darkness. "Ralph?" She picked her way through the black hall behind the mirrors, her heels tacking the wooden floor. "Ralph?"

Someone stirred sluggishly on the canvas cot. "Aimee?"

He sat up and screwed a dim light bulb into the dressing table socket. He squinted at her, half blinded. "Hey, you look like the cat swallowed a canary."

"Ralph, I came about the midget!"

"Dwarf, Aimee honey, dwarf. A midget is in the cells, born that way. A dwarf is in the glands. . . ."

"Ralph! I just found out the most wonderful thing about him!"

"Honest to God," he said to his hands, holding them out as witnesses to his disbelief. "This woman! Who in hell gives two cents for some ugly little——"

"Ralph!" She held out the magazines, her eyes shining. "He's a writer! Think of that!"

"It's a pretty hot day for thinking." He lay back and examined her, smiling faintly.

"I just happened to pass the Ganghes Arms, and saw Mr. Greeley, the manager. He says the typewriter runs all night in Mr. Big's room!"

"Is *that* his name?" Ralph began to roar with laughter.

"Writes just enough pulp detective stories to live. I found one of his stories in the secondhand magazine place, and, Ralph, guess what?"

"I'm tired, Aimee."

"This little guy's got a soul as big as all outdoors; he's got *everything* in his head!"

"Why ain't he writin' for the big magazines, then, I ask you?"

"Because maybe he's afraid—maybe he doesn't know he can do it. That happens. People don't believe in themselves. But if he only tried, I bet he could sell stories anywhere in the world."

"Why ain't he rich, I wonder?"

"Maybe because ideas come slow because he's down in the dumps. Who wouldn't be? So small that way? I bet it's hard to think of anything except being so small and living in a one-room cheap apartment."

"Hell!" snorted Ralph. "You talk like Florence Nightingale's grandma."

She held up the magazine. "I'll read you part of his crime story. It's got all the guns and tough people, but it's told by a dwarf. I bet the editors never guessed the author knew what he was writing about. Oh, please don't sit there like that, Ralph! Listen."

And she began to read aloud.

"I am a dwarf and I am a murderer. The two things cannot be separated. One is the cause of the other.

"The man I murdered used to stop me on the street when I was twenty-one, pick me up in his arms, kiss my brow, croon wildly to me, sing Rock-a-bye Baby, haul me into meat markets, toss me on the scales and cry, 'Watch it. Don't weigh your thumb, there, butcher!'

"Do you *see* how our lives moved toward murder? This fool, this persecutor of my flesh and soul!

"As for my childhood: my parents were small people, not quite dwarfs, not quite. My father's inheritance kept us in a doll's house, an amazing thing like a white-scrolled wedding cake—little rooms, little chairs, miniature paintings, cameos, ambers with insects caught inside, everything tiny, tiny, tiny! The world of Giants far away, an ugly rumor beyond the garden wall. Poor mama, papa! They meant only the best for me. They kept me, like a porcelain vase, small and treasured, to themselves, in our ant world, our beehive rooms, our microscopic library, our land of beetle-sized doors and moth windows. Only now do I see the magnificent size of my parents' psychosis! They must have dreamed they would live forever, keeping me like a butterfly under glass. But first father died, and then fire ate up the little house, the wasp's nest, and every postage-stamp mirror and saltcellar closet within. Mama, too, gone! And myself alone, watching the fallen embers, tossed out into a world of Monsters and Titans, caught in a landslide of reality, rushed, rolled, and smashed to the bottom of the cliff!

"It took me a year to adjust. A job with a sideshow was unthinkable. There seemed no place for me in the world. And then, a month ago, the Persecutor came into my life, clapped a bonnet on my unsuspecting head, and cried to friends, 'I want you to meet the little woman!' "

Aimee stopped reading. Her eyes were unsteady and the magazine shook as she handed it to Ralph. "You finish it. The rest is a murder story. It's all right. But don't you see? That little man. That little man."

Ralph tossed the magazine aside and lit a cigarette lazily. "I like Westerns better."

"Ralph, you got to read it. He needs someone to tell him how good he is and keep him writing."

Ralph looked at her, his head to one side. "And guess who's going to do it? Well, well, ain't we just the Saviour's right hand?"

"I won't listen!"

"Use your head, damn it! You go busting in on him he'll think you're handing him pity. He'll chase you screamin' outa his room."

She sat down, thinking about it slowly, trying to turn it over and see it from every side. "I don't know. Maybe you're right. Oh, it's not just pity, Ralph, honest. But maybe it'd look like it to him. I've got to be awful careful."

He shook her shoulder back and forth, pinching softly, with his fingers. "Hell, hell, lay off him, is all I ask; you'll get nothing but trouble for your dough. God, Aimee, I never *seen* you so hepped on anything. Look, you and me, let's make it a day, take a lunch, get us some gas, and just drive on down the coast as far as we can drive; swim, have supper, see a good show in some little town—to hell with the carnival, how about it? A damn nice day and no worries. I been savin' a coupla bucks."

"It's because I know he's different," she said, looking off into darkness. "It's because he's something we can never be—you and me and all the rest of us here on the pier. It's so funny, so funny. Life fixed him so he's good for nothing but carny shows, yet there he is on the land. And life made us so we wouldn't have to work in the carny shows, but here we are, anyway, way out here at sea on the pier. Sometimes it seems a million miles to shore. How come, Ralph, that we got the bodies, but he's got the brains and can think things we'll never even guess?"

"You haven't even been listening to me!" said Ralph.

She sat with him standing over her, his voice far away. Her eyes were half shut and her hands were in her lap, twitching.

"I don't like that shrewd look you're getting on," he said, finally.

She opened her purse slowly and took out a small roll of bills and started counting. "Thirty-five, forty dollars. There. I'm going to phone Billie Fine and have him send out one of those tall-type mirrors to Mr. Bigelow at the Ganghes Arms. Yes, I am!"

"What!"

"Think how wonderful for him, Ralph, having one in his own room any time he wants it. Can I use your phone?"

"Go ahead, *be* nutty."

Ralph turned quickly and walked off down the tunnel. A door slammed.

Aimee waited, then after a while put her hands to the phone and began to dial, with painful slowness. She paused between numbers, holding her breath, shutting her eyes, thinking how it might seem to be small in the world, and then one day someone sends a special mirror by. A mirror for your room where you can hide away with the big reflection of yourself, shining, and write stories and stories, never going out into the world unless you had to. How might it be then, alone, with the wonderful illusion all in one piece in the room. Would it make you happy or sad, would it help your writing or hurt it? She shook her head back and forth, back and forth. At least this way there would be no one to look down at you. Night after night, perhaps rising secretly at three in the cold morning, you could wink and dance around and smile and wave at yourself, so tall, so tall, so very fine and tall in the bright looking glass.

A telephone voice said, "Billie Fine's."

"Oh, *Billie!*" she cried.

Night came in over the pier. The ocean lay dark and loud under the planks. Ralph sat cold and waxen in his glass coffin, laying out the cards, his eyes fixed, his mouth stiff. At his elbow, a growing pyramid of burnt cigarette butts grew larger. When Aimee walked along under the hot red and blue bulbs, smiling, waving, he did not stop setting the cards down slow and very slow. "Hi, Ralph!" she said.

"How's the love affair?" he asked, drinking from a dirty glass of iced water. "How's Charlie Boyer, or is it Cary Grant?"

"I just went and bought me a new hat," she said, smiling. "Gosh, I feel *good!* You know why? Billie Fine's sending a mirror out tomorrow! Can't you just see the nice little guy's face?"

"I'm not so hot at imagining."

"Oh, Lord, you'd think I was going to marry him or something."

"Why not? Carry him around in a suitcase. People say,

Where's your husband? all you do is open your bag, yell,
Here he is! Like a silver cornet. Take him outa his case
any old hour, play a tune, stash him away. Keep a little
sandbox for him on the back porch."

"I was feeling so good," she said.

"Benevolent is the word." Ralph did not look at her, his
mouth tight. "Ben-ev-o-*lent*. I suppose this all comes from
me watching him through that knothole, getting my kicks?
That why you sent the mirror? People like you run around
with tambourines, taking the joy out of my life."

"Remind me not to come to your place for drinks any
more. I'd rather go with no people at all than mean
people."

Ralph exhaled a deep breath. "Aimee, Aimee. Don't you
know you can't help that guy? He's bats. And this crazy
thing of yours is like saying, Go ahead, *be* batty, I'll help
you, pal."

"Once in a lifetime anyway, it's nice to make a mistake
if you think it'll do somebody some good," she said.

"God deliver me from do-gooders, Aimee."

"Shut up, shut up!" she cried, and then said nothing
more.

He let the silence lie awhile, and then got up, putting
his finger-printed glass aside. "Mind the booth for me?"

"Sure. Why?"

She saw ten thousand cold white images of him stalking
down the glassy corridors, between mirrors, his mouth
straight and his fingers working themselves.

She sat in the booth for a full minute and then suddenly
shivered. A small clock ticked in the booth and she turned
the deck of cards over, one by one, waiting. She heard a
hammer pounding and knocking and pounding again, far
away inside the Maze; a silence, more waiting, and then
ten thousand images folding and refolding and dissolving,
Ralph striding, looking out at ten thousand images of her
in the booth. She heard his quiet laughter as he came
down the ramp.

"Well, what's put you in such a good mood?" she asked,
suspiciously.

"Aimee," he said, carelessly, "we shouldn't quarrel. You say tomorrow Billie Fine's sending that mirror out to Mr. Big's?"

"You're not going to try anything funny?"

"Me?" He moved her out of the booth and took over the cards, humming, his eyes bright. "Not me, oh no, not me." He did not look at her, but started quickly to slap out the cards. She stood behind him. Her right eye began to twitch a little. She folded and unfolded her arms. A minute ticked by. The only sound was the ocean under the night pier, Ralph breathing in the heat, the soft ruffle of the cards. The sky over the pier was hot and thick with clouds. Out at sea, faint glows of lightning were beginning to show.

"Ralph," she said at last.

"Relax, Aimee," he said.

"About that trip you wanted to take down the coast——"

"Tomorrow," he said. "Maybe next month. Maybe next year. Old Ralph Banghart's a patient guy. I'm not worried, Aimee. Look." He held up a hand. "I'm calm."

She waited for a roll of thunder at sea to fade away.

"I just don't want you mad, is all. I just don't want anything bad to happen, promise me."

The wind, now warm, now cool, blew along the pier. There was a smell of rain in the wind. The clock ticked. Aimee began to perspire heavily, watching the cards move and move. Distantly, you could hear targets being hit and the sound of the pistols at the shooting gallery.

And then, there he was.

Waddling along the lonely concourse, under the insect bulbs, his face twisted and dark, every movement an effort. From a long way down the pier he came, with Aimee watching. She wanted to say to him, This is your last night, the last time you'll have to embarrass yourself by coming here, the last time you'll have to put up with being watched by Ralph, even in secret. She wished she could cry out and laugh and say it right in front of Ralph. But she said nothing.

"Hello, hello!" shouted Ralph. "It's free, on the house, tonight! Special for old customers!"

The Dwarf looked up, startled, his little black eyes darting and swimming in confusion. His mouth formed the word thanks and he turned, one hand to his neck, pulling his tiny lapels tight up about his convulsing throat, the other hand clenching the silver dime secretly. Looking back, he gave a little nod, and then scores of dozens of compressed and tortured faces, burnt a strange dark color by the lights, wandered in the glass corridors.

"Ralph," Aimee took his elbow. "What's going on?"

He grinned. "I'm being benevolent, Aimee, benevolent."

"Ralph," she said.

"Sh," he said. "*Listen.*"

They waited in the booth in the long warm silence.

Then, a long way off, muffled, there was a scream.

"Ralph!" said Aimee.

"Listen, listen!" he said.

There was another scream, and another and still another, and a threshing and a pounding and a breaking, a rushing around and through the Maze. There, there, wildly colliding and ricocheting, from mirror to mirror, shrieking hysterically and sobbing, tears on his face, mouth gasped open, came Mr. Bigelow. He fell out in the blazing night air, glanced about wildly, wailed, and ran off down the pier.

"Ralph, what happened?"

Ralph sat laughing and slapping at his thighs.

She slapped his face. "What'd you *do?*"

He didn't quite stop laughing. "Come on. I'll show you!"

And then she was in the Maze, rushed from white-hot mirror to mirror, seeing her lipstick all red fire a thousand times repeated on down a burning silver cavern where strange hysterical women much like herself followed a quick-moving, smiling man. "Come on!" he cried. And they broke free into a dust-smelling tiny room.

"Ralph!" she said.

They both stood on the threshold of the little room

where the Dwarf had come every night for a year. They both stood where the Dwarf had stood each night before opening his eyes to see the miraculous image in front of him.

Aimee shuffled slowly, one hand out, into the dim room.

The mirror had been changed.

This new mirror made even normal people small, small, small; it made even tall people little and dark and twisted smaller as you moved forward.

And Aimee stood before it thinking and thinking that if it made big people small, standing here, God, what would it do to a dwarf, a tiny dwarf, a dark dwarf, a startled and lonely dwarf?

She turned and almost fell. Ralph stood looking at her. "Ralph," she said. "God, why did you do it?"

"Aimee, come back!"

She ran out through the mirrors, crying. Staring with blurred eyes, it was hard to find the way, but she found it. She stood blinking at the empty pier, started to run one way, then another, then still another, then stopped. Ralph came up behind her, talking, but it was like a voice heard behind a wall late at night, remote and foreign.

"Don't talk to me," she said.

Someone came running up the pier. It was Mr. Kelly from the shooting gallery. "Hey, any you see a little guy just now? Little stiff swiped a pistol from my place, loaded, run off before I'd get a hand on him! You help me find him?"

And Kelly was gone, sprinting, turning his head to search between all the canvas sheds, on away under the hot blue and red and yellow strung bulbs.

Aimee rocked back and forth and took a step.

"Aimee, where you going?"

She looked at Ralph as if they had just turned a corner, strangers passing, and bumped into each other. "I guess," she said, "I'm going to help search."

"You won't be able to do nothing."

"I got to try, anyway. Oh God, Ralph, this is all my fault! I shouldn't have phoned Billie Fine! I shouldn't've ordered a mirror and got you so mad you did this! It's *me* should've gone to Mr. Big, not a crazy thing like I bought! I'm going to find him if it's the last thing I ever do in my life."

Swinging about slowly, her cheeks wet, she saw the quivery mirrors that stood in front of the Maze. Ralph's reflection was in one of them. She could not take her eyes away from the image; it held her in a cool and trembling fascination, with her mouth open.

"Aimee, what's wrong? What're you——"

He sensed where she was looking and twisted about to see what was going on. His eyes widened.

He scowled at the blazing mirror.

A horrid, ugly little man, two feet high, with a pale, squashed face under an ancient straw hat, scowled back at him. Ralph stood there glaring at himself, his hands at his sides.

Aimee walked slowly and then began to walk fast and then began to run. She ran down the empty pier and the wind blew warm and it blew large drops of hot rain out of the sky on her all the time she was running.

Fever Dream

They put him between fresh, clean, laundered sheets and there was always a newly squeezed glass of thick orange juice on the table under the dim pink lamp. All Charles had to do was call and Mom or Dad would stick their heads into his room to see how sick he was. The acoustics of the room were fine; you could hear the toilet gargling its porcelain throat of mornings, you could hear rain tap the roof or sly mice run in the secret walls or the canary singing in its cage downstairs. If you were very alert, sickness wasn't too bad.

He was thirteen, Charles was. It was mid-September, with the land beginning to burn with autumn. He lay in the bed for three days before the terror overcame him.

His hand began to change. His right hand. He looked at it and it was hot and sweating there on the counterpane alone. It fluttered, it moved a bit. Then it lay there, changing color.

That afternoon the doctor came again and tapped his thin chest like a little drum. "How are you?" asked the doctor, smiling. "I know, don't tell me: 'My *cold* is fine, Doctor, but *I* feel awful!' Ha!" He laughed at his own oft-repeated joke.

Charles lay there and for him that terrible and ancient jest was becoming a reality. The joke fixed itself in his mind. His mind touched and drew away from it in a pale terror. The doctor did not know how cruel he was with his jokes! "Doctor," whispered Charles, lying flat and colorless. "My *hand*, it doesn't *belong* to me any more. This morning it *changed* into something else. I want you to change it back, Doctor, Doctor!"

The doctor showed his teeth and patted his hand. "It looks fine to me, son. You just had a little fever dream."

"But it changed, Doctor, oh, Doctor," cried Charles, pitifully holding up his pale wild hand. "It *did!*"

The doctor winked. "I'll give you a pink pill for that." He popped a tablet onto Charles' tongue. "Swallow!"

"Will it make my hand change back and become *me* again?"

"Yes, yes."

The house was silent when the doctor drove off down the road in his car under the quiet, blue September sky. A clock ticked far below in the kitchen world. Charles lay looking at his hand.

It did not change back. It was still something else.

The wind blew outside. Leaves fell against the cool window.

At four o'clock his other hand changed. It seemed almost to become a fever. It pulsed and shifted, cell by cell. It beat like a warm heart. The fingernails turned blue and then red. It took about an hour for it to change and when it was finished, it looked just like any ordinary hand. But it was not ordinary. It no longer was him any more. He lay in a fascinated horror and then fell into an exhausted sleep.

Mother brought the soup up at six. He wouldn't touch it. "I haven't any hands," he said, eyes shut.

"Your hands are perfectly good," said Mother.

"No," he wailed. "My hands are gone. I feel like I have stumps. Oh, Mama, Mama, hold me, hold me, I'm scared!"

She had to feed him herself.

"Mama," he said, "get the doctor, please, again. I'm so sick."

"The doctor'll be here tonight at eight," she said, and went out.

At seven, with night dark and close around the house, Charles was sitting up in bed when he felt the thing happening to first one leg and then the other. "Mama! Come quick!" he screamed.

But when Mama came the thing was no longer happening.

When she went downstairs, he simply lay without fighting as his legs beat and beat, grew warm, red-hot, and the room filled with the warmth of his feverish change. The glow crept up from his toes to his ankles and then to his knees.

"May I come in?" The doctor smiled in the doorway.

"Doctor!" cried Charles. "Hurry, take off my blankets!"

The doctor lifted the blankets tolerantly. "There you are. Whole and healthy. Sweating, though. A little fever. I told you not to move around, bad boy."

He pinched the moist pink cheek. "Did the pills help? Did your hand change back?"

"No, no, now it's my other hand and my legs!"

"Well, well, I'll have to give you three more pills, one for each limb, eh, my little peach?" laughed the doctor.

"Will they help me? Please, please. What've I *got?*"

"A mild case of scarlet fever, complicated by a slight cold."

"Is it a germ that lives and has more little germs in me?"

"Yes."

"Are you *sure* it's scarlet fever? You haven't taken any tests!"

"I guess I know a certain fever when I see one," said the doctor, checking the boy's pulse with cool authority.

Charles lay there, not speaking until the doctor was

crisply packing his black kit. Then in the silent room, the boy's voice made a small, weak pattern, his eyes alight with remembrance. "I read a book once. About petrified trees, wood turning to stone. About how trees fell and rotted and minerals got in and built up and they look just like trees, but they're not, they're stone." He stopped. In the quiet warm room his breathing sounded.

"Well?" asked the doctor.

"I've been thinking," said Charles after a time. "Do germs ever get big? I mean, in biology class they told us about one-celled animals, amoebas and things, and how millions of years ago they got together until there was a bunch and they made the first body. And more and more cells got together and got bigger and then finally maybe there was a fish and finally here *we* are, and all we are is a bunch of cells that decided to get together, to help each other out. Isn't that right?" Charles wet his feverish lips.

"What's all this about?" The doctor bent over him.

"I've got to tell you this. Doctor, oh, I've got to!" he cried. "What would happen, oh just pretend, please pretend, that just like in the old days, a lot of microbes got together and wanted to make a bunch, and reproduced and made *more*——"

His white hands were on his chest now, crawling toward his throat.

"And they decided to *take over* a person!" cried Charles.

"Take over a person?"

"Yes, *become* a person. *Me*, my hands, my feet! What if a disease somehow knew how to kill a person and yet live after him?"

He screamed.

The hands were on his neck.

The doctor moved forward, shouting.

At nine o'clock the doctor was escorted out to his car by the mother and father, who handed him his bag. They conversed in the cool night wind for a few minutes. "Just be sure his hands are kept strapped to his legs," said the doctor. "I don't want him hurting himself."

"Will he be all right, Doctor?" The mother held to his arm a moment.

He patted her shoulder. "Haven't I been your family physician for thirty years? It's the fever. He imagines things."

"But those bruises on his throat, he almost choked himself."

"Just you keep him strapped; he'll be all right in the morning."

The car moved off down the dark September road.

At three in the morning, Charles was still awake in his small black room. The bed was damp under his head and his back. He was very warm. Now he no longer had any arms or legs, and his body was beginning to change. He did not move on the bed, but looked at the vast blank ceiling space with insane concentration. For a while he had screamed and thrashed, but now he was weak and hoarse from it, and his mother had gotten up a number of times to soothe his brow with a wet towel. Now he was silent, his hands strapped to his legs.

He felt the walls of his body change, the organs shift, the lungs catch fire like burning bellows of pink alcohol. The room was lighted up as with the flickerings of a hearth.

Now he had no body. It was all gone. It was under him, but it was filled with a vast pulse of some burning, lethargic drug. It was as if a guillotine had neatly lopped off his head, and his head lay shining on a midnight pillow while the body, below, still alive, belonged to somebody else. The disease had eaten his body and from the eating had reproduced itself in feverish duplicate.

There were the little hand hairs and the fingernails and the scars and the toenails and the tiny mole on his right hip, all done again in perfect fashion.

I am dead, he thought. I've been killed, and yet I live. My body is dead, it is all disease and nobody will know. I will walk around and it will not be me, it will be something else. It will be something all bad, all evil, so big and so evil it's hard to understand or think about. Something that will buy shoes and drink water and get married some day maybe and do more evil in the world than has ever been done.

Now the warmth was stealing up his neck, into his cheeks, like a hot wine. His lips burned, his eyelids, like leaves, caught fire. His nostrils breathed out blue flame, faintly, faintly.

This will be all, he thought. It'll take my head and my brain and fix each eye and every tooth and all the marks in my brain, and every hair and every wrinkle in my ears, and there'll be nothing left of me.

He felt his brain fill with a boiling mercury. He felt his left eye clench in upon itself and, like a snail, withdraw, shift. He was blind in his left eye. It no longer belonged to him. It was enemy territory. His tongue was gone, cut out. His left cheek was numbed, lost. His left ear stopped hearing. It belonged to someone else now. This thing that was being born, this mineral thing replacing the wooden log, this disease replacing healthy animal cell.

He tried to scream and he was able to scream loud and high and sharply in the room, just as his brain flooded down, his right eye and right ear were cut out, he was blind and deaf, all fire, all terror, all panic, all death.

His scream stopped before his mother ran through the door to his side.

It was a good, clear morning, with a brisk wind that helped carry the doctor up the path before the house. In the window above, the boy stood, fully dressed. He did not wave when the doctor waved and called, "What's this? Up? My God!"

The doctor almost ran upstairs. He came gasping into the bedroom.

"What are you doing out of bed?" he demanded of the boy. He tapped his thin chest, took his pulse and temperature. "Absolutely amazing! Normal. Normal, by God!"

"I shall never be sick again in my life," declared the boy, quietly, standing there, looking out the wide window. "Never."

"I hope not. Why, you're looking fine, Charles."

"Doctor?"

"Yes, Charles?"

"Can I go to school *now?*" asked Charles.

"Tomorrow will be time enough. You sound positively eager."

"I am. I like school. All the kids. I want to play with them and wrestle with them, and spit on them and play with the girls' pigtails and shake the teacher's hand, and rub my hands on all the cloaks in the cloakroom, and I want to grow up and travel and shake hands with people all over the world, and be married and have lots of children, and go to libraries and handle books and—*all* of that I want to!" said the boy, looking off into the September morning. "What's the name you called me?"

"What?" The doctor puzzled. "I called you nothing but Charles."

"It's better than no name at all, I guess." The boy shrugged.

"I'm glad you want to go back to school," said the doctor.

"I really anticipate it," smiled the boy. "Thank you for your help, Doctor. Shake hands."

"Glad to."

They shook hands gravely, and the clear wind blew through the open window. They shook hands for almost a minute, the boy smiling up at the old man and thanking him.

Then, laughing, the boy raced the doctor downstairs and out to his car. His mother and father followed for the happy farewell.

"Fit as a fiddle!" said the doctor. "Incredible!"

"And strong," said the father. "He got out of his straps himself during the night. Didn't you, Charles?"

"Did I?" said the boy.

"You did! How?"

"Oh," the boy said, "that was a long time ago."

"A long time ago!"

They all laughed, and while they were laughing, the

quiet boy moved his bare foot on the sidewalk and merely touched, brushed against a number of red ants that were scurrying about on the sidewalk. Secretly, his eyes shining, while his parents chatted with the old man, he saw the ants hesitate, quiver, and lie still on the cement. He sensed they were cold now.

"Good-by!"

The doctor drove away, waving.

The boy walked ahead of his parents. As he walked he looked away toward the town and began to hum "School Days" under his breath.

"It's good to have him well again," said the father.

"Listen to him. He's so looking forward to school!"

The boy turned quietly. He gave each of his parents a crushing hug. He kissed them both several times.

Then without a word he bounded up the steps into the house.

In the parlor, before the others entered, he quickly opened the bird cage, thrust his hand in, and petted the yellow canary, once.

Then he shut the cage door, stood back, and waited.

The Wonderful Ice Cream Suit

It was summer twilight in the city, and out front of the quiet-clicking pool hall three young Mexican-American men breathed the warm air and looked around at the world. Sometimes they talked and sometimes they said nothing at all but watched the cars glide by like black panthers on the hot asphalt or saw trolleys loom up like thunderstorms, scatter lightning, and rumble away into silence.

"Hey," sighed Martínez at last. He was the youngest, the most sweetly sad of the three. "It's a swell night, huh? Swell."

As he observed the world it moved very close and then drifted away and then came close again. People, brushing by, were suddenly across the street. Buildings five miles away suddenly leaned over him. But most of the time everything—people, cars, and buildings—stayed way out on the edge of the world and could not be touched. On this quiet warm summer evening Martínez's face was cold.

"Nights like this you wish . . . lots of things."

"Wishing," said the second man, Villanazul, a man who shouted books out loud in his room but spoke only in whispers on the street. "Wishing is the useless pastime of the unemployed."

"Unemployed?" cried Vamenos, the unshaven. "Listen to him! We got no jobs, no money!"

"So," said Martínez, "we got no friends."

"True." Villanazul gazed off toward the green plaza where the palm trees swayed in the soft night wind. "Do you know what I wish? I wish to go into that plaza and speak among the businessmen who gather there nights to talk big talk. But dressed as I am, poor as I am, who would listen? So, Martínez, we have each other. The friendship of the poor is real friendship. We——"

But now a handsome young Mexican with a fine thin mustache strolled by. And on each of his careless arms hung a laughing woman.

"*Madre mía!*" Martínez slapped his own brow. "How does that one rate *two* friends?"

"It's his nice new white summer suit." Vamenos chewed a black thumbnail. "He looks sharp."

Martínez leaned out to watch the three people moving away, and then at the tenement across the street, in one fourth-floor window of which, far above, a beautiful girl leaned out, her dark hair faintly stirred by the wind. She had been there forever, which was to say for six weeks. He had nodded, he had raised a hand, he had smiled, he had blinked rapidly, he had even bowed to her, on the street, in the hall when visiting friends, in the park, downtown. Even now, he put his hand up from his waist and moved his fingers. But all the lovely girl did was let the summer wind stir her dark hair. He did not exist. He was nothing.

"*Madre mía!*" He looked away and down the street where the man walked his two friends around a corner. "Oh, if I just had one suit, one! I wouldn't need money if I *looked* okay."

"I hesitate to suggest," said Villanazul, "that you see Gómez. But he's been talking some crazy talk for a month now about clothes. I keep on saying I'll be in on it to make him go away. That Gómez."

"Friend," said a quiet voice.

"Gómez!" Everyone turned to stare.

Smiling strangely, Gómez pulled forth an endless thin yellow ribbon which fluttered and swirled on the summer air.

"Gómez," said Martínez, "what you doing with that tape measure?"

Gómez beamed. "Measuring people's skeletons."

"Skeletons!"

"Hold on." Gómez squinted at Martínez. "*Caramba!* Where you *been* all my life! Let's try *you!*"

Martínez saw his arm seized and taped, his leg measured, his chest encircled.

"Hold still!" cried Gómez. "Arm—perfect. Leg—chest— *perfecto!* Now quick, the height! There! Yes! Five foot five. You're in! Shake!" Pumping Martínez's hand, he stopped suddenly. "Wait. You got . . . ten bucks?"

"I have!" Vamenos waved some grimy bills. "Gómez, measure me!"

"All I got left in the world is nine dollars and ninety-two cents." Martínez searched his pockets. "That's enough for a new suit? Why?"

"Why? Because you got the right skeleton, that's why!"

"Señor Gómez, I don't hardly know you——"

"Know me? You're going to live with me! Come on!"

Gómez vanished into the poolroom. Martínez, escorted by the polite Villanazul, pushed by an eager Vamenos, found himself inside.

"Domínguez!" said Gómez.

Domínguez, at a wall telephone, winked at them. A woman's voice squeaked on the receiver.

"Manulo!" said Gómez.

Manulo, a wine bottle tilted bubbling to his mouth, turned.

Gómez pointed at Martínez.

"At last we found our fifth volunteer!"

Domínguez said, "I got a date, don't bother me——"

and stopped. The receiver slipped from his fingers. His little black telephone book full of fine names and numbers went quickly back into his pocket. "Gómez, you——?"

"Yes, yes! Your money, now! *Ándale!*"

The woman's voice sizzled on the dangling phone.

Domínguez glanced at it uneasily.

Manulo considered the empty wine bottle in his hand and the liquor-store sign across the street.

Then very reluctantly both men laid ten dollars each on the green velvet pool table.

Villanazul, amazed, did likewise, as did Gómez, nudging Martínez. Martínez counted out his wrinkled bills and change. Gómez flourished the money like a royal flush.

"Fifty bucks! The suit costs sixty! All we need is ten bucks!"

"Wait," said Martínez. "Gómez, are we talking about *one* suit? *Uno?*"

"*Uno!*" Gómez raised a finger. "One wonderful white ice cream summer suit! White, white as the August moon!"

"But who will own this one suit?"

"Me!" said Manulo.

"Me!" said Domínguez.

"Me!" said Villanazul.

"Me!" cried Gómez. "*And* you, Martínez. Men, let's show him. Line up!"

Villanazul, Manulo, Domínguez, and Gómez rushed to plant their backs against the poolroom wall.

"Martínez, you too, the other end, line up! Now, Vamenos, lay that billiard cue across our heads!"

"Sure, Gómez, sure!"

Martínez, in line, felt the cue tap his head and leaned out to see what was happening. "Ah!" he gasped.

The cue lay flat on all their heads, with no rise or fall, as Vamenos slid it along, grinning.

"We're all the same height!" said Martínez.

"The same!" Everyone laughed.

Gómez ran down the line, rustling the yellow tape measure here and there on the men so they laughed even more wildly.

"Sure!" he said. "It took a month, four weeks, mind you, to find four guys the same size and shape as me, a month of running around measuring. Sometimes I found guys with five-foot-five skeletons, sure, but all the meat on their bones was too much or not enough. Sometimes their bones were too long in the legs or too short in the arms. Boy, all the bones! I tell you! But now, five of us, same shoulders, chests, waists, arms, and as for weight? Men!"

Manulo, Domínguez, Villanazul, Gómez, and at last Martínez stepped onto the scales which flipped ink-stamped cards at them as Vamenos, still smiling wildly, fed pennies. Heart pounding, Martínez read the cards.

"One hundred thirty-five pounds . . . one thirty-six . . . one thirty-three . . . one thirty-four . . . one thirty-seven . . . a miracle!"

"No," said Villanazul simply, "Gómez."

They all smiled upon that genius who now circled them with his arms.

"Are we not fine?" he wondered. "All the same size, all the same dream—the suit. So each of us will look beautiful at least one night each week, eh?"

"I haven't looked beautiful in years," said Martínez. "The girls run away."

"They will run no more, they will freeze," said Gómez, "when they see you in the cool white summer ice cream suit."

"Gómez," said Villanazul, "just let me ask one thing."

"Of course, *compadre.*"

"When we get this nice new white ice cream summer suit, some night you're not going to put it on and walk down to the Greyhound bus in it and go live in El Paso for a year in it, are you?"

"Villanazul, Villanazul, how can you say that?"

"My eye sees and my tongue moves," said Villanazul. "How about the *Everybody Wins!* Punchboard Lotteries you ran and you kept running when nobody won? How about the United Chili Con Carne and Frijole Company you were going to organize and all that ever happened was the rent ran out on a two-by-four office?"

"The errors of a child now grown," said Gómez. "Enough! In this hot weather someone may buy the special suit that is made just for us that stands waiting in the window of SHUMWAY'S SUNSHINE SUITS! We have fifty dollars. Now we need just one more skeleton!"

Martínez saw the men peer around the pool hall. He looked where they looked. He felt his eyes hurry past Vamenos, then come reluctantly back to examine his dirty shirt, his huge nicotined fingers.

"Me!" Vamenos burst out at last. "My skeleton, measure it, it's great! Sure, my hands are big, and my arms, from digging ditches! But——"

Just then Martínez heard passing on the sidewalk outside that same terrible man with his two girls, all laughing together.

He saw anguish move like the shadow of a summer cloud on the faces of the other men in this poolroom.

Slowly Vamenos stepped onto the scales and dropped his penny. Eyes closed, he breathed a prayer.

"*Madre mía*, please . . ."

The machinery whirred; the card fell out. Vamenos opened his eyes.

"Look! One thirty-five pounds! Another miracle!"

The men stared at his right hand and the card, at his left hand and a soiled ten-dollar bill.

Gómez swayed. Sweating, he licked his lips. Then his hand shot out, seized the money.

"The clothing store! The suit! *Vamos!*"

Yelling, everyone ran from the poolroom.

The woman's voice was still squeaking on the abandoned telephone. Martínez, left behind, reached out and hung the voice up. In the silence he shook his head. "*Santos*, what a dream! Six men," he said, "one suit. What will come of this? Madness? Debauchery? Murder? But I go with God. Gómez, wait for me!"

Martínez was young. He ran fast.

Mr. Shumway, of SHUMWAY'S SUNSHINE SUITS, paused while adjusting a tie rack, aware of some subtle atmospheric change outside his establishment.

"Leo," he whispered to his assistant. "Look . . ."

Outside, one man, Gómez, strolled by, looking in. Two men, Manulo and Domínguez, hurried by, staring in. Three men, Villanazul, Martínez, and Vamenos, jostling shoulders, did the same.

"Leo." Mr. Shumway swallowed. "Call the police!"

Suddenly six men filled the doorway.

Martínez, crushed among them, his stomach slightly upset, his face feeling feverish, smiled so wildly at Leo that Leo let go the telephone.

"Hey," breathed Martínez, eyes wide. "There's a great suit over there!"

"No." Manulo touched a lapel. "*This* one!"

"There is only one suit in all the world!" said Gómez coldly. "Mr. Shumway, the ice-cream white, size thirty-four, was in your window just an hour ago! It's gone! You didn't——"

"Sell it?" Mr. Shumway exhaled. "No, no. In the dressing room. It's still on the dummy."

Martínez did not know if he moved and moved the crowd or if the crowd moved and moved him. Suddenly they were all in motion. Mr. Shumway, running, tried to keep ahead of them.

"This way, gents. Now which of you . . ?"

"All for one, one for all!" Martínez heard himself say, and laughed. "We'll all try it on!"

"All?" Mr. Shumway clutched at the booth curtain as if his shop were a steamship that had suddenly tilted in a great swell. He stared.

That's it, thought Martínez, look at our smiles. Now, look at the skeletons behind our smiles! Measure here, there, up, down, yes, do you *see?*

Mr. Shumway saw. He nodded. He shrugged.

"All!" He jerked the curtain. "There! Buy it, and I'll throw in the dummy free!"

Martínez peered quietly into the booth, his motion drawing the others to peer too.

The suit was there.

And it was white.

Martínez could not breathe. He did not want to. He did not need to. He was afraid his breath would melt the suit. It was enough, just looking.

But at last he took a great trembling breath and exhaled, whispering, "*Ay. Ay, caramba!*"

"It puts out my eyes," murmured Gómez.

"Mr. Shumway," Martínez heard Leo hissing. "Ain't it dangerous precedent, to sell it? I mean, what if everybody bought *one* suit for *six* people?"

"Leo," said Mr. Shumway, "you ever hear one single fifty-nine-dollar suit make so many people happy at the same time before?"

"Angels' wings," murmured Martínez. "The wings of white angels."

Martínez felt Mr. Shumway peering over his shoulder into the booth. The pale glow filled his eyes.

"You know something, Leo?" he said in awe. "That's a *suit!*"

Gómez, shouting, whistling, ran up to the third-floor landing and turned to wave to the others, who staggered, laughed, stopped, and had to sit down on the steps below.

"Tonight!" cried Gómez. "Tonight you move in with me, eh? Save rent as well as clothes, eh? Sure! Martínez, you got the suit?"

"Have I?" Martínez lifted the white gift-wrapped box high. "From us to us! *Ay-hah!*"

"Vamenos, you got the dummy?"

"Here!"

Vamenos, chewing an old cigar, scattering sparks, slipped. The dummy, falling, toppled, turned over twice, and banged down the stairs.

"Vamenos! Dumb! Clumsy!"

They seized the dummy from him. Stricken, Vamenos looked about as if he'd lost something.

Manulo snapped his fingers. "Hey, Vamenos, we got to celebrate! Go borrow some wine!"

Vamenos plunged downstairs in a whirl of sparks.

The others moved into the room with the suit, leaving Martínez in the hall to study Gómez's face.

"Gómez, you look sick."

"I am," said Gómez. "For what have I done?" He nodded to the shadows in the room working about the dummy. "I pick Domínguez, a devil with the women. All right. I pick Manulo, who drinks, yes, but who sings as sweet as a girl, eh? Okay. Villanazul reads books. You, you wash behind your ears. But then what do I do? Can I wait? No! I got to buy that suit! So the last guy I pick is a clumsy slob who has the right to wear *my* suit——" He stopped, confused. "Who gets to wear *our* suit one night a week, fall down in it, or not come in out of the rain in it! Why, why, why did I do it!"

"Gómez," whispered Villanazul from the room. "The suit is ready. Come see if it looks as good using *your* light bulb."

Gómez and Martínez entered.

And there on the dummy in the center of the room was the phosphorescent, the miraculously white-fired ghost with the incredible lapels, the precise stitching, the neat buttonholes. Standing with the white illumination of the suit upon his cheeks, Martínez suddenly felt he was in church. White! White! It was white as the whitest vanilla ice cream, as the bottled milk in tenement halls at dawn. White as a winter cloud all alone in the moonlit sky late at night. Seeing it here in the warm summer-night room made their breath almost show on the air. Shutting his eyes, he could see it printed on his lids. He knew what color his dreams would be this night.

"White . . ." murmured Villanazul. "White as the snow on that mountain near our town in Mexico, which is called the Sleeping Woman."

"Say that again," said Gómez.

Villanazul, proud yet humble, was glad to repeat his tribute.

". . . white as the snow on the mountain called——"

"I'm back!"

Shocked, the men whirled to see Vamenos in the door, wine bottles in each hand.

"A party! Here! Now tell us, who wears the suit first tonight? Me?"

"It's too late!" said Gómez.

"Late! It's only nine-fifteen!"

"Late?" said everyone, bristling. "Late?"

Gómez edged away from these men who glared from him to the suit to the open window.

Outside and below it was, after all, thought Martínez, a fine Saturday night in a summer month and through the calm warm darkness the women drifted like flowers on a quiet stream. The men made a mournful sound.

"Gómez, a suggestion." Villanazul licked his pencil and drew a chart on a pad. "You wear the suit from nine-thirty to ten, Manulo till ten-thirty, Domínguez till eleven, myself till eleven-thirty, Martínez till midnight, and——"

"Why me *last*?" demanded Vamenos, scowling.

Martínez thought quickly and smiled. "After midnight is the *best* time, friend."

"Hey," said Vamenos, "that's right. I never thought of that. Okay."

Gómez sighed. "All right. A half hour each. But from now on, remember, we each wear the suit just one night a week. Sundays we draw straws for who wears the suit the extra night."

"Me!" laughed Vamenos. "I'm lucky!"

Gómez held onto Martínez, tight.

"Gómez," urged Martínez, "you first. Dress."

Gómez could not tear his eyes from that disreputable Vamenos. At last, impulsively, he yanked his shirt off over his head. "Ay-yeah!" he howled. "*Ay-yeee!*"

Whisper rustle . . . the clean shirt.

"Ah . . . !"

How clean the new clothes feel, thought Martínez, holding the coat ready. How clean they sound, how clean they smell!

Whisper . . . the pants . . . the tie, rustle . . . the suspenders. Whisper . . . now Martínez let loose the coat, which fell in place on flexing shoulders.

"*Ole!*"

Gómez turned like a matador in his wondrous suit-of-lights.

"*Ole*, Gómez, *ole!*"

Gómez bowed and went out the door.

Martínez fixed his eyes to his watch. At ten sharp he heard someone wandering about in the hall as if he had forgotten where to go. Martínez pulled the door open and looked out.

Gómez was there, heading for nowhere.

He looks sick, thought Martínez. No, stunned, shook up, surprised, many things.

"Gómez! This is the place!"

Gómez turned around and found his way through the door.

"Oh, friends, friends," he said. "Friends, what an experience! This suit! This suit!"

"Tell us, Gómez!" said Martínez.

"I can't, how can I say it?" He gazed at the heavens, arms spread, palms up.

"*Tell* us, Gómez!"

"I have no words, no words. You must see, yourself! Yes, you must see——" And here he lapsed into silence, shaking his head until at last he remembered they all stood watching him. "Who's next? Manulo?"

Manulo, stripped to his shorts, leapt forward.

"Ready!"

All laughed, shouted, whistled.

Manulo, ready, went out the door. He was gone twenty-nine minutes and thirty seconds. He came back holding to doorknobs, touching the wall, feeling his own elbows, putting the flat of his hand to his face.

"Oh, let me tell you," he said. "*Compadres*, I went to the bar, eh, to have a drink? But no, I did not go in the bar, do you hear? I did not drink. For as I walked I began to laugh and sing. Why, why? I listened to myself and asked this. Because. The suit made me feel better than wine ever did. The suit made me drunk, drunk! So I went to the *Guadalajara Refriteria* instead and played the guitar and sang four songs, very high! The suit, ah, the suit!"

Domínguez, next to be dressed, moved out through the world, came back from the world.

The black telephone book! thought Martínez. He had it in his hands when he left! Now, he returns, hands empty! What? What?

"On the street," said Domínguez, seeing it all again, eyes wide, "on the street I walked, a woman cried, 'Domínguez, is that *you?*' Another said, 'Domínguez? No, Quetzalcoatl, the Great White God come from the East,' do you hear? And suddenly I didn't want to go with six women or eight, no. One, I thought. One! And to this one, who knows *what* I would say? 'Be mine!' Or 'Marry me!' *Caramba!* This suit is dangerous! But I did not care! I live, I live! Gómez, did it happen this way with you?"

Gómez, still dazed by the events of the evening, shook his head. "No, no talk. It's too much. Later. Villanazul . . . ?"

Villanazul moved shyly forward.

Villanazul went shyly out.

Villanazul came shyly home.

"Picture it," he said, not looking at them, looking at the floor, talking to the floor. "The Green Plaza, a group of elderly businessmen gathered under the stars and they are talking, nodding, talking. Now one of them whispers. All turn to stare. They move aside, they make a channel through which a white-hot light burns its way as through ice. At the center of the great light is this person. I take a deep breath. My stomach is jelly. My voice is very small, but it grows louder. And what do I say? I say, 'Friends. Do you know Carlyle's *Sartor Resartus?* In that book we find *his* Philosophy of Suits. . . .' "

And at last it was time for Martínez to let the suit float him out to haunt the darkness.

Four times he walked around the block. Four times he paused beneath the tenement porches, looking up at the window where the light was lit; a shadow moved, the beautiful girl was there, not there, away and gone, and on

the fifth time there she was on the porch above, driven out
by the summer heat, taking the cooler air. She glanced
down. She made a gesture.

At first he thought she was waving to him. He felt like a
white explosion that had riveted her attention. But she was
not waving. Her hand gestured and the next moment a
pair of dark-framed glasses sat upon her nose. She gazed
at him.

Ah, ah, he thought, so that's it. So! Even the blind may
see this suit! He smiled up at her. He did not have to
wave. And at last she smiled back. She did not have to
wave either. Then, because he did not know what else to
do and he could not get rid of this smile that fastened
itself to his cheeks, he hurried, almost ran, around the
corner, feeling her stare after him. When he looked back
she had taken off her glasses and gazed now with the look
of the nearsighted at what, at most, must be a moving
blob of light in the great darkness here. Then for good
measure he went around the block again, through a city so
suddenly beautiful he wanted to yell, then laugh, then yell
again.

Returning, he drifted, oblivious, eyes half closed, and
seeing him in the door, the others saw not Martínez but
themselves come home. In that moment, they sensed that
something had happened to them all.

"You're late!" cried Vamenos, but stopped. The spell
could not be broken.

"Somebody tell me," said Martínez. "Who am I?"

He moved in a slow circle through the room.

Yes, he thought, yes, it's the suit, yes, it had to do with
the suit and them all together in that store on this fine
Saturday night and then here, laughing and feeling more
drunk without drinking as Manulo said himself, as the
night ran and each slipped on the pants and held,
toppling, to the others, and, balanced, let the feeling get
bigger and warmer and finer as each man departed and the
next took his place in the suit until now here stood
Martínez all splendid and white as one who gives orders
and the world grows quiet and moves aside.

"Martínez, we borrowed three mirrors while you were
gone. Look!"

The mirrors, set up as in the store, angled to reflect
three Martínezes and the echoes and memories of those
who had occupied this suit with him and known the bright
world inside this thread and cloth. Now, in the shimmering
mirror, Martínez saw the enormity of this thing they were
living together and his eyes grew wet. The others blinked.
Martínez touched the mirrors. They shifted. He saw a
thousand, a million white-armored Martínezes march off
into eternity, reflected, re-reflected, forever, indomitable,
and unending.

He held the white coat out on the air. In a trance, the
others did not at first recognize the dirty hand that
reached to take the coat. Then:

"Vamenos!"

"Pig!"

"You didn't wash!" cried Gómez. "Or even shave, while
you waited! *Compadres,* the bath!"

"The bath!" said everyone.

"No!" Vamenos flailed. "The night air! I'm dead!"

They hustled him yelling out and down the hall.

Now here stood Vamenos, unbelievable in white suit,
beard shaved, hair combed, nails scrubbed.

His friends scowled darkly at him.

For was it not true, thought Martínez, that when Vamenos passed by, avalanches itched on mountaintops? If
he walked under windows, people spat, dumped garbage,
or worse. Tonight now, this night, he would stroll beneath
ten thousand wide-opened windows, near balconies, past
alleys. Suddenly the world absolutely sizzled with flies.
And here was Vamenos, a fresh-frosted cake.

"You sure look keen in that suit, Vamenos," said Manulo
sadly.

"Thanks." Vamenos twitched, trying to make his skeleton comfortable where all their skeletons had so recently
been. In a small voice Vamenos said, "Can I go now?"

"Villanazul!" said Gómez. "Copy down these rules."

Villanazul licked his pencil.

"First," said Gómez, "don't fall down in that suit, Vamenos!"

"I won't."

"Don't lean against buildings in that suit."

"No buildings."

"Don't walk under trees with birds in them in that suit. Don't smoke. Don't drink——"

"Please," said Vamenos, "can I *sit down* in this suit?"

"When in doubt, take the pants off, fold them over a chair."

"Wish me luck," said Vamenos.

"Go with God, Vamenos."

He went out. He shut the door.

There was a ripping sound.

"Vamenos!" cried Martínez.

He whipped the door open.

Vamenos stood with two halves of a handkerchief torn in his hands, laughing.

"Rrrip! Look at your faces! Rrrip!" He tore the cloth again. "Oh, oh, your faces, your faces! Ha!"

Roaring, Vamenos slammed the door, leaving them stunned and alone.

Gómez put both hands on top of his head and turned away. "Stone me. Kill me. I have sold our souls to a demon!"

Villanazul dug in his pockets, took out a silver coin, and studied it for a long while.

"Here is my last fifty cents. Who else will help me buy back Vamenos' share of the suit?"

"It's no use." Manulo showed them ten cents. "We got only enough to buy the lapels and the buttonholes."

Gómez, at the open window, suddenly leaned out and yelled. "Vamenos! No!"

Below on the street, Vamenos, shocked, blew out a match and threw away an old cigar butt he had found somewhere. He made a strange gesture to all the men in the window above, then waved airily and sauntered on. Somehow, the five men could not move away from the window. They were crushed together there.

"I bet he eats a hamburger in that suit," mused Villanazul. "I'm thinking of the mustard."

"Don't!" cried Gómez. "No, no!"

Manulo went out and shut the door.

"I need a drink, bad."

"Manulo, there's wine here, that bottle on the floor——"

Manulo went out and shut the door.

A moment later Villanazul stretched with great exaggeration and strolled about the room.

"I think I'll walk down to the plaza, friends."

He was not gone a minute when Domínguez, waving his black book at the others, winked and turned the doorknob.

"Domínguez," said Gómez.

"Yes?"

"If you see Vamenos, by accident," said Gómez. "warn him away from Mickey Murrillo's Red Rooster Café. They got fights not only on TV but out front of the TV too."

"He wouldn't go into Murrillo's," said Domínguez. "That suit means too much to Vamenos. He wouldn't do anything to hurt it."

"He'd shoot his mother first," said Martínez.

"Sure he would."

Martínez and Gómez, alone, listened to Domínguez's footsteps hurry away down the stairs. They circled the undressed window dummy.

For a long while, biting his lips, Gómez stood at the window, looking out. He touched his shirt pocket twice, pulled his hand away, and then at last pulled something from the pocket. Without looking at it, he handed it to Martínez.

"Martínez, take this."

"What is it?"

Martínez looked at the piece of folded pink paper with print on it, with names and numbers. His eyes widened.

"A ticket on the bus to El Paso three weeks from now!"
Gómez nodded. He couldn't look at Martínez. He
stared out into the summer night.

"Turn it in. Get the money," he said. "Buy us a nice
white panama hat and a pale blue tie to go with the white
ice cream suit, Martínez. Do that."

"Gómez——"

"Shut up. Boy, is it hot in here! I need air."

"Gómez. I am touched. Gómez——"

But the door stood open. Gómez was gone.

Mickey Murrillo's Red Rooster Café and Cocktail
Lounge was squashed between two big brick buildings
and, being narrow, had to be deep. Outside, serpents of
red and sulphur-green neon fizzed and snapped. Inside,
dim shapes loomed and swam away to lose themselves in a
swarming night sea.

Martínez, on tiptoe, peeked through a flaked place on
the red-painted front window.

He felt a presence on his left, heard breathing on his
right. He glanced in both directions.

"Manulo! Villanazul!"

"I decided I wasn't thirsty," said Manulo. "So I took a
walk."

"I was just on my way to the plaza," said Villanazul,
"and decided to go the long way around."

As if by agreement, the three men shut up now and
turned together to peer on tiptoe through various flaked
spots on the window.

A moment later, all three felt a new very warm presence
behind them and heard still faster breathing.

"Is our white suit in there?" asked Gómez's voice.

"Gómez!" said everybody, surprised. "Hi!"

"Yes!" cried Domínguez, having just arrived to find his
own peephole. "There's the suit! And, praise God, Vamenos
is still *in* it!"

"I can't see!" Gómez squinted, shielding his eyes.
"What's he *doing*?"

Martínez peered. Yes! There, way back in the shad-

dows, was a big chunk of snow and the idiot smile of
Vamenos winking above it, wreathed in smoke.

"He's smoking!" said Martínez.

"He's drinking!" said Domínguez.

"He's eating a taco!" reported Villanazul.

"A *juicy* taco," added Manulo.

"No," said Gómez. "No, no, no. . . ."

"Ruby Escuadrillo's with him!"

"Let me see that!" Gómez pushed Martínez aside.

Yes, there was Ruby! Two hundred pounds of glittering
sequins and tight black satin on the hoof, her scarlet
fingernails clutching Vamenos' shoulder. Her cowlike face,
floured with powder, greasy with lipstick, hung over him!

"That hippo!" said Domínguez. "She's crushing the
shoulder pads. Look, she's going to sit on his lap!"

"No, no, not with all that powder and lipstick!" said
Gómez. "Manulo, inside! Grab that drink! Villanazul, the
cigar, the taco! Domínguez, date Ruby Escuadrillo, get
her away. *Ándale, men!*"

The three vanished, leaving Gómez and Martínez to
stare, gasping, through the peephole.

"Manulo, he's got the drink, he's *drinking* it!"

"*Ay!* There's Villanazul, he's got the cigar, he's eating
the taco!"

"Hey, Domínguez, he's got Ruby! What a *brave* one!"

A shadow bulked through Murrillo's front door, traveling fast.

"Gómez!" Martínez clutched Gómez's arm. "That was
Ruby Escuadrillo's boy friend, Toro Ruíz. If he finds her
with Vamenos, the ice cream suit will be covered with
blood, *covered* with blood——"

"Don't make me nervous," said Gómez. "Quickly!"

Both ran. Inside they reached Vamenos just as Toro
Ruíz grabbed about two feet of the lapels of that wonderful ice cream suit.

"Let go of Vamenos!" said Martínez.

"Let go that *suit!*" corrected Gómez.

Toro Ruíz, tap-dancing Vamenos, leered at these in-
truders.

Villanazul stepped up shyly.

Villanazul smiled. "Don't hit him. Hit me."

Toro Ruíz hit Villanazul smack on the nose.

Villanazul, holding his nose, tears stinging his eyes, wandered off.

Gómez grabbed one of Toro Ruíz's arms, Martínez the other.

"Drop him, let go, *cabrón, coyote, vaca!*"

Toro Ruíz twisted the ice cream suit material until all six men screamed in mortal agony. Grunting, sweating, Toro Ruíz dislodged as many as climbed on. He was winding up to hit Vamenos when Villanazul wandered back, eyes streaming.

"Don't hit him. Hit me!"

As Toro Ruíz hit Villanazul on the nose, a chair crashed on Toro's head.

"*Ai!*" said Gómez.

Toro Ruíz swayed, blinking, debating whether to fall. He began to drag Vamenos with him.

"Let go!" cried Gómez. "Let go!"

One by one, with great care, Toro Ruíz's banana-like fingers let loose of the suit. A moment later he was ruins at their feet.

"*Compadres,* this way!"

They ran Vamenos outside and set him down where he freed himself of their hands with injured dignity.

"Okay, okay. My time ain't up. I still got two minutes and, let's see—ten seconds."

"What!" said everybody.

"Vamenos," said Gómez, "you let a Guadalajara cow climb on you, you pick fights, you smoke, you drink, you eat tacos, and *now* you have the nerve to say your time ain't up?"

"I got two minutes and one second left!"

"Hey, Vamenos, you sure look sharp!" Distantly, a woman's voice called from across the street.

Vamenos smiled and buttoned the coat.

"It's Ramona Álvarez! Ramona, wait!" Vamenos stepped off the curb.

"Vamenos," pleaded Gómez. "What can you do in one minute and"—he checked his watch—"forty seconds!"

"Watch! Hey, Ramona!"

Vamenos loped.

"Vamenos, look out!"

Vamenos, surprised, whirled, saw a car, heard the shriek of brakes.

"No," said all five men on the sidewalk.

Martínez heard the impact and flinched. His head moved up. It looks like white laundry, he thought, flying through the air. His head came down.

Now he heard himself and each of the men make a different sound. Some swallowed too much air. Some let it out. Some choked. Some groaned. Some cried aloud for justice. Some covered their faces. Martínez felt his own fists pounding his heart in agony. He could not move his feet.

"I don't want to live," said Gómez quietly. "Kill me, someone."

Then, shuffling, Martínez looked down and told his feet to walk, stagger, follow one after the other. He collided with other men. Now they were trying to run. They ran at last and somehow crossed a street like a deep river through which they could only wade, to look down at Vamenos.

"Vamenos!" said Martínez: "You're alive!"

Strewn on his back, mouth open, eyes squeezed tight, tight, Vamenos motioned his head back and forth, back and forth, moaning.

"Tell me, tell me, oh, tell me, tell me."

"Tell you what, Vamenos?"

Vamenos clenched his fists, ground his teeth.

"The suit, what have I done to the suit, the suit, the suit!"

The men crouched lower.

"Vamenos, it's . . . why, it's *okay!*"

"You lie!" said Vamenos. "It's torn, it must be, it must be, it's torn, all around, *underneath?*"

"No." Martínez knelt and touched here and there. "Vamenos, all around, underneath even, it's okay!"

Vamenos opened his eyes to let the tears run free at last. "A miracle," he sobbed. "Praise the saints!" He quieted at last. "The car?"

"Hit and run." Gómez suddenly remembered and glared at the empty street. "It's good he didn't stop. We'd have——"

Everyone listened.

Distantly a siren wailed.

"Someone phoned for an ambulance."

"Quick!" said Vamenos, eyes rolling. "Set me up! Take off our coat!"

"Vamenos——"

"Shut up, idiots!" cried Vamenos. "The coat, that's it! Now, the pants, the pants, quick, quick, *peónes!* Those doctors! You seen movies? They rip the pants with razors to get them off! They don't *care!* They're maniacs! Ah, God, quick, quick!"

The siren screamed.

The men, panicking, all handled Vamenos at once.

"Right leg, *easy,* hurry, cows! Good! Left leg, now, left, you hear, there, easy, *easy!* Ow, God! Quick! Martínez, your pants, take them off!"

"What?" Martínez froze.

The siren shrieked.

"Fool!" wailed Vamenos. "All is lost! Your pants! Give me!"

Martínez jerked at his belt buckle.

"Close in, make a circle!"

Dark pants, light pants flourished on the air.

"Quick, here come the maniacs with the razors! Right leg on, left leg, *there!*"

"The zipper, cows, zip my zipper!" babbled Vamenos.

The siren died.

"*Madre mía,* yes, just in time! They arrive." Vamenos lay back down and shut his eyes. "*Gracias.*"

Martínez turned, nonchalantly buckling on the white pants as the interns brushed past.

"Broken leg," said one intern as they moved Vamenos onto a stretcher.

"*Compadres,*" said Vamenos, "don't be mad with me."

Gómez snorted. "Who's mad?"

In the ambulance, head tilted back, looking out at them upside down, Vamenos faltered.

"*Compadres,* when . . . when I come from the hospital . . . am I still in the bunch? You won't kick me out? Look, I'll give up smoking, keep away from Murrillo's, swear off women——"

"Vamenos," said Martínez gently, "don't promise nothing."

Vamenos, upside down, eyes brimming wet, saw Martínez there, all white now against the stars.

"Oh, Martínez, you sure look great in that suit. *Compadres,* don't he look *beautiful?*"

Villanazul climbed in beside Vamenos. The door slammed. The four remaining men watched the ambulance drive away.

Then, surrounded by his friends, inside the white suit, Martínez was carefully escorted back to the curb.

In the tenement, Martínez got out the cleaning fluid and the others stood around, telling him how to clean the suit and, later, how not to have the iron too hot and how to work the lapels and the crease and all. When the suit was cleaned and pressed so it looked like a fresh gardenia just opened, they fitted it to the dummy.

"Two o'clock," murmured Villanazul. "I hope Vamenos sleeps well. When I left him at the hospital, he looked good."

Manulo cleared his throat. "Nobody else is going out with that suit tonight, huh?"

The others glared at him.

Manulo flushed. "I mean . . . it's late. We're tired. Maybe no one will use the suit for forty-eight hours, huh? Give it a rest. Sure. Well. Where do we sleep?"

The night being still hot and the room unbearable, they carried the suit on its dummy out and down the hall. They brought with them also some pillows and blankets. They climbed the stairs toward the roof of the tenement. There, thought Martínez, is the cooler wind, and sleep.

On the way, they passed a dozen doors that stood open, people still perspiring and awake, playing cards, drinking pop, fanning themselves with movie magazines.

I wonder, thought Martínez. I wonder if—— Yes!

On the fourth floor, a certain door stood open.

The beautiful girl looked up as the men passed. She wore glasses and when she saw Martínez she snatched them off and hid them under her book.

The others went on, not knowing they had lost Martínez, who seemed stuck fast in the open door.

For a long moment he could say nothing. Then he said: "José Martínez."

And she said:

"Celia Obregón."

And then both said nothing.

He heard the men moving up on the tenement roof. He moved to follow.

She said quickly, "I saw you tonight!"

He came back.

"The suit," he said.

"The suit," she said, and paused. "But not the suit."

"Eh?" he said.

She lifted the book to show the glasses lying in her lap. She touched the glasses.

"I do not see well. You would think I would wear my glasses, but no. I walk around for years now, hiding them, seeing nothing. But tonight, even without the glasses, I see. A great whiteness passes below in the dark. So white! And I put on my glasses quickly!"

"The suit, as I said," said Martínez.

"The suit for a little moment, yes, but there is another whiteness above the suit."

"Another?"

"Your teeth! Oh, such white teeth, and so many!"

Martínez put his hand over his mouth.

"So happy, Mr. Martínez," she said. "I have not often seen such a happy face and such a smile."

"Ah," he said, not able to look at her, his face flushing now.

"So, you see," she said quietly, "the suit caught my eye, yes, the whiteness filled the night below. But the teeth were much whiter. Now, I have forgotten the suit."

Martínez flushed again. She, too, was overcome with what she had said. She put her glasses on her nose, and then took them off, nervously, and hid them again. She looked at her hands and at the door above his head.

"May I——" he said, at last.

"May you——"

"May I call for you," he asked, "when next the suit is mine to wear?"

"Why must you wait for the suit?" she said.

"I thought——"

"You do not need the suit," she said.

"But——"

"If it were just the suit," she said, "anyone would be fine in it. But no, I watched. I saw many men in that suit, all different, this night. So again I say, you do not need to wait for the suit."

"*Madre mía, madre mía!*" he cried happily. And then, quieter, "I will need the suit for a little while. A month, six months, a year. I am uncertain. I am fearful of many things. I am young."

"That is as it should be," she said.

"Good night, Miss——"

"Celia Obregón."

"Celia Obregón," he said, and was gone from the door.

The others were waiting on the roof of the tenement. Coming up through the trapdoor, Martínez saw they had placed the dummy and the suit in the center of the roof and put their blankets and pillows in a circle around it. Now they were lying down. Now a cooler night wind was blowing here, up in the sky.

Martínez stood alone by the white suit, smoothing the lapels, talking half to himself.

"Ay, *caramba*, what a night! Seems ten years since seven o'clock, when it all started and I had no friends.

Two in the morning, I got all *kinds* of friends. . . ." He paused and thought, Celia Obregón, Celia Obregón. ". . . all kinds of friends," he went on. "I got a room, I got clothes. You tell *me*. You know what?" He looked around at the men lying on the rooftop, surrounding the dummy and himself. "It's funny. When I wear this suit, I know I will win at pool, like Gómez. A woman will look at me like Domínguez. I will be able to sing like Manulo, sweetly. I will talk fine politics like Villanazul. I'm strong as Vamenos. So? So, tonight, I am more than Martínez. I am Gómez, Manulo, Domínguez, Villanazul, Vamenos. I am everyone. Ay . . . ay . . ." He stood a moment longer by this suit which could save all the ways they sat or stood or walked. This suit which could move fast and nervous like Gómez or slow and thoughtfully like Villanazul or drift like Domínguez, who never touched ground, who always found a wind to take him somewhere. This suit which belonged to them but which also owned them all. This suit that was—what? A parade.

"Martínez," said Gómez. "You going to sleep?"

"Sure. I'm just thinking."

"What?"

"If we ever get rich," said Martínez softly, "it'll be kind of sad. Then we'll all have suits. And there won't be no more nights like tonight. It'll break up the old gang. It'll never be the same after that."

The men lay thinking of what had just been said.

Gómez nodded gently.

"Yeah . . . it'll never be the same . . . after that."

Martínez lay down on his blanket. In darkness, with the others, he faced the middle of the roof and the dummy, which was the center of their lives.

And their eyes were bright, shining, and good to see in the dark as the neon lights from nearby buildings flicked on, flicked off, flicked on, flicked off, revealing and then vanishing, revealing and then vanishing, their wonderful white vanilla ice cream summer suit.

There Will Come Soft Rains

In the living room the voice-clock sang, *Tick-tock, seven o'clock, time to get up, time to get up, seven o'clock!* as if it were afraid that nobody would. The morning house lay empty. The clock ticked on, repeating and repeating its sounds into the emptiness. *Seven-nine, breakfast time, seven-nine!*

In the kitchen the breakfast stove gave a hissing sigh and ejected from its warm interior eight pieces of perfectly browned toast, eight eggs sunnyside up, sixteen slices of bacon, two coffees, and two cool glasses of milk.

"Today is August 4, 2026," said a second voice from the kitchen ceiling, "in the city of Allendale, California." It repeated the date three times for memory's sake. "Today is Mr. Featherstone's birthday. Today is the anniversary of Tilita's marriage. Insurance is payable, as are the water, gas, and light bills."

Somewhere in the walls, relays clicked, memory tapes glided under electric eyes.

Eight-one, tick-tock, eight-one o'clock, off to school, off to work, run, run, eight-one! But no doors slammed, no carpets took the soft tread of rubber heels. It was raining outside. The weather box on the front door sang quietly: "Rain, rain, go away; rubbers, raincoats for today . . ." And the rain tapped on the empty house, echoing.

Outside, the garage chimed and lifted its door to reveal the waiting car. After a long wait the door swung down again.

At eight-thirty the eggs were shriveled and the toast was like stone. An aluminum wedge scraped them into the sink, where hot water whirled them down a metal throat which digested and flushed them away to the distant sea. The dirty dishes were dropped into a hot washer and emerged twinkling dry.

Nine-fifteen, sang the clock, *time to clean.*

Out of warrens in the wall, tiny robot mice darted. The rooms were acrawl with the small cleaning animals, all rubber and metal. They thudded against chairs, whirling their mustached runners, kneading the rug nap, sucking gently at hidden dust.

Then, like mysterious invaders, they popped into their burrows. Their pink electric eyes faded. The house was clean.

Ten o'clock. The sun came out from behind the rain. The house stood alone in a city of rubble and ashes. This was the one house left standing. At night the ruined city gave off a radioactive glow which could be seen for miles.

Ten-fifteen. The garden sprinklers whirled up in golden founts, filling the soft morning air with scatterings of brightness. The water pelted windowpanes, running down the charred west side where the house had been burned evenly free of its white paint. The entire west face of the house was black, save for five places. Here the silhouette in paint of a man mowing a lawn. Here, as in a photograph, a woman bent to pick flowers. Still farther over, their images burned on wood in one titanic instant, a small boy, hands flung into the air; higher up, the image of a thrown ball, and opposite him a girl, hands raised to catch a ball which never came down.

The five spots of paint—the man, the woman, the children, the ball—remained. The rest was a thin charcoaled layer.

The gentle sprinkler rain filled the garden with falling light.

Until this day, how well the house had kept its peace. How carefully it had inquired, "Who goes there? What's the password?" and, getting no answer from lonely foxes and whining cats, it had shut up its windows and drawn shades in an old-maidenly preoccupation with self-protection which bordered on a mechanical paranoia.

It quivered at each sound, the house did. If a sparrow brushed a window, the shade snapped up. The bird, startled, flew off! No, not even a bird must touch the house!

The house was an altar with ten thousand attendants, big, small, servicing, attending, in choirs. But the gods had gone away, and the ritual of the religion continued senselessly, uselessly.

Twelve noon.

A dog whined, shivering, on the front porch.

The front door recognized the dog voice and opened. The dog, once huge and fleshy, but now gone to bone and covered with sores, moved in and through the house, tracking mud. Behind it whirred angry mice, angry at having to pick up mud, angry at inconvenience.

For not a leaf fragment blew under the door but what the wall panels flipped open and the copper scrap rats flashed swiftly out. The offending dust, hair, or paper, seized in miniature steel jaws, was raced back to the burrows. There, down tubes which fed into the cellar, it was dropped into the sighing vent of an incinerator which sat like evil Baal in a dark corner.

The dog ran upstairs, hysterically yelping to each door, at last realizing, as the house realized, that only silence was here.

It sniffed the air and scratched the kitchen door. Behind

the door, the stove was making pancakes which filled the house with a rich baked odor and the scent of maple syrup.

The dog frothed at the mouth, lying at the door, sniffing, its eyes turned to fire. It ran wildly in circles, biting at its tail, spun in a frenzy, and died. It lay in the parlor for an hour.

Two o'clock, sang a voice.

Delicately sensing decay at last, the regiments of mice hummed out as softly as blown gray leaves in an electrical wind.

Two-fifteen.

The dog was gone.

In the cellar, the incinerator glowed suddenly and a whirl of sparks leaped up the chimney.

Two thirty-five.

Bridge tables sprouted from patio walls. Playing cards fluttered onto pads in a shower of pips. Martinis manifested on an oaken bench with egg-salad sandwiches. Music played.

But the tables were silent and the cards untouched.

At four o'clock the tables folded like great butterflies back through the paneled walls.

Four-thirty.

The nursery walls glowed.

Animals took shape: yellow giraffes, blue lions, pink antelopes, lilac panthers cavorting in crystal substance. The walls were glass. They looked out upon color and fantasy. Hidden films clocked through well-oiled sprockets, and the walls lived. The nursery floor was woven to resemble a crisp cereal meadow. Over this ran aluminum roaches and iron crickets, and in the hot still air butterflies of delicate red tissue wavered among the sharp aroma of animal spoors! There was the sound like a great matted yellow hive of bees within a dark bellows, the lazy bumble of a purring lion. And there was the patter of okapi feet and the murmur of a fresh jungle rain, like other hoofs, falling upon the summer-starched grass. Now the walls dissolved into distances of parched weed, mile on mile, and warm endless sky. The animals drew away into thorn brakes and water holes.

It was the children's hour.

Five o'clock. The bath filled with clear hot water.

Six, seven, eight o'clock. The dinner dishes manipulated like magic tricks, and in the study a *click*. In the metal stand opposite the hearth where a fire now blazed up warmly, a cigar popped out, half an inch of soft gray ash on it, smoking, waiting.

Nine o'clock. The beds warmed their hidden circuits, for nights were cool here.

Nine-five. A voice spoke from the study ceiling:

"Mrs. McClellan, which poem would you like this evening?"

The house was silent.

The voice said at last, "Since you express no preference, I shall select a poem at random." Quiet music rose to back the voice. "Sara Teasdale. As I recall, your favorite. . . .

"There will come soft rains and the smell of the ground,
And swallows circling with their shimmering sound;

And frogs in the pools singing at night,
And wild plum trees in tremulous white;

Robins will wear their feathery fire,
Whistling their whims on a low fence-wire;

And not one will know of the war, not one
Will care at last when it is done.

Not one would mind, neither bird nor tree,
If mankind perished utterly;

And Spring herself, when she woke at dawn
Would scarcely know that we were gone."

The fire burned on the stone hearth and the cigar fell away into a mound of quiet ash on its tray. The empty chairs faced each other between the silent walls, and the music played.

At ten o'clock the house began to die.

The wind blew. A falling tree bough crashed through the kitchen window. Cleaning solvent, bottled, shattered over the stove. The room was ablaze in an instant!

"Fire!" screamed a voice. The house lights flashed, water pumps shot water from the ceilings. But the solvent spread on the linoleum, licking, eating, under the kitchen door, while the voices took it up in chorus: "Fire, fire, fire!"

The house tried to save itself. Doors sprang tightly shut, but the windows were broken by the heat and the wind blew and sucked upon the fire.

The house gave ground as the fire in ten billion angry sparks moved with flaming ease from room to room and then up the stairs. While scurrying water rats squeaked from the walls, pistoled their water, and ran for more. And the wall sprays let down showers of mechanical rain.

But too late. Somewhere, sighing, a pump shrugged to a stop. The quenching rain ceased. The reserve water supply which had filled baths and washed dishes for many quiet days was gone.

The fire crackled up the stairs. It fed upon Picassos and Matisses in the upper halls, like delicacies, baking off the oily flesh, tenderly crisping the canvases into black shavings.

Now the fire lay in beds, stood in windows, changed the colors of drapes!

And then, reinforcements.

From attic trapdoors, blind robot faces peered down with faucet mouths gushing green chemical.

The fire backed off, as even an elephant must at the sight of a dead snake. Now there were twenty snakes whipping over the floor, killing the fire with a clear cold venom of green froth.

But the fire was clever. It had sent flame outside the house, up through the attic to the pumps there. An explosion! The attic brain which directed the pumps was shattered into bronze shrapnel on the beams.

The fire rushed back into every closet and felt of the clothes hung there.

The house shuddered, oak bone on bone, its bared skeleton cringing from the heat, its wire, its nerves revealed as if a surgeon had torn the skin off to let the red veins and capillaries quiver in the scalded air. Help, help! Fire! Run, run! Heat snapped mirrors like the first brittle winter ice. And the voices wailed Fire, fire, run, run, like a tragic nursery rhyme, a dozen voices, high, low, like children dying in a forest, alone, alone. And the voices fading as the wires popped their sheathings like hot chestnuts. One, two, three, four, five voices died.

In the nursery the jungle burned. Blue lions roared, purple giraffes bounded off. The panthers ran in circles, changing color, and ten million animals, running before the fire, vanished off toward a distant steaming river. . . .

Ten more voices died. In the last instant under the fire avalanche, other choruses, oblivious, could be heard announcing the time, playing music, cutting the lawn by remote-control mower, or setting an umbrella frantically out and in the slamming and opening front door, a thousand things happening, like a clock shop when each clock strikes the hour insanely before or after the other, a scene of maniac confusion, yet unity; singing, screaming, a few last cleaning mice darting bravely out to carry the horrid ashes away! And one voice, with sublime disregard for the situation, read poetry aloud in the fiery study, until all the film spools burned, until all the wires withered and the circuits cracked.

The fire burst the house and let it slam flat down, puffing out skirts of spark and smoke.

In the kitchen, an instant before the rain of fire and timber, the stove could be seen making breakfasts at a psychopathic rate, ten dozen eggs, six loaves of toast, twenty dozen bacon strips, which, eaten by fire, started the stove working again, hysterically hissing!

The crash. The attic smashing into kitchen and parlor. The parlor into cellar, cellar into sub-cellar. Deep freeze, armchair, film tapes, circuits, beds, and all like skeletons thrown in a cluttered mound deep under.

Smoke and silence. A great quantity of smoke.

Dawn showed faintly in the east. Among the ruins, one wall stood alone. Within the wall, a last voice said, over and over again and again, even as the sun rose to shine upon the heaped rubble and steam:

"Today is August 5, 2026, today is August 5, 2026, today is . . ."

About the Author

RAY BRADBURY has published some 25 books—novels, stories, plays, and poems—since his first story appeared in *Rob Wagner's Script* when he was twenty years old.

In 1964, Mr. Bradbury created his own Pandemonium Theater to produce his plays *The Wonderful Ice Cream Suit, The World of Ray Bradbury,* and *Falling Upward,* a comedy about his year in Ireland working for John Huston on the screenplay of *Moby Dick.* In 1964-65 he also created the basic scenario for a Journey through United States History, which occupied the entire top floor of the United States Pavilion at the New York World's Fair. He created the metaphors around which Spaceship Earth was constructed for EPCOT, at Disney World, Florida.

Mr. Bradbury is working with Jimmy Webb, composing lyrics for a musical version of his *Dandelion Wine*; and his opera, *Fahrenheit 451,* premiered in the fall of 1988. He plans to start soon on the concept of a 21st century city to be built near Tokyo.

Most recently, Mr. Bradbury published *The Toynbee Convector,* his first collection of stories since the publication in 1980 of *The Stories of Ray Bradbury.*